Take Me to the Willow

A Novel

Shelly Brimley

This is a work of fiction. All of the characters and events portrayed in this novel are either products of the author's imagination or are used fictitiously.

Cover Design by KPGS Design
ISBN 978-0-9970816-0-2 (pbk)

Bales Cove Publishing

For my angel parents who introduced me to love and showed me what it was all about, and who continue to fill the world with goodness.

And to Brian, you will forever be my fave.

Take Me to the Willow

February 23, 1905

I don't rightly agree with all them psychology folk, talkin' about how a man is the way he is on account of what happened to him when he was a young'un. I had lots of ugliness all around me, but you don't find me fixin' to blame Mama and Daddy for my poor judgment. I won't even point a finger at Uncle Albert who put his sinful hands on me and Jessie when we weren't but five and six years old; couldn't rightly tell anyone about it anyhow. I imagine Daddy would have put a bullet clean through that old devil if he ever knew. I reckon some things are just better left unsaid, seein' as how Uncle Albert is Mama's only kin.

I always wanted to know more about where I come from. Sometimes I try to get it out of Mama and Daddy, but neither of them takes kindly to me askin' lots of questions. I tried talkin' to Grandma Wright once, but she was real old and not quite right in the head, so who knows if what she told me was true. After she passed and we were goin' through her things, I found a bunch of old letters she and Grandpa wrote to each other when they were younger. The letters were interestin' enough, but it was mostly lovey-dovey stuff couples write to each other; didn't do me any good. Jessie took to readin' those letters more than I did, but she's a girl, and that's what you'd expect.

I was real surprised when Mama gave me some of her old diaries and told me it'd be fine to read them if I wanted; never even knew she had them. She said it was a might surprisin' that a young man of eighteen would have any interest in her diaries, but was pleased all the same that I did. It took me dang near two weeks to get through those books. They were filled with private information, story after story of Mama's life. There were a few places where some pages were missin'. I imagine she was keepin' those to herself; don't everything need to be shared. After everyone was in bed at night, I found myself readin' page after page until the heaviness of my eyelids made the decision for me to call it quits. Daddy scolded me a few different times for leavin' the lamp burnin' all night. I just found it so interestin' to read about things I never would have known about otherwise. So that's why I'm writin' in this here journal—so my kin will have somethin' to know me by. And they should know about my folks and Jessie too.

February 26, 1905

I'd be lyin' if I said I didn't miss the whole lot of them—Jessie, Mama and Daddy. It doesn't help any that this place wreaks of stale urine and old men's cologne. Don't rightly know who was stuck in here before me, but I'm guessin' it was someone brought in to sober up after a long night of heavy boozin'.

I didn't realize how lonely a cell could be, even with a cellmate. Sheriff Coleman brought Leroy Simmons in night before last after he found him out back of Tom Martin's shed. Seems Leroy was talked into cuttin' down some of Tom's apricot trees for fun by some of them city boys. Leroy is dumb as rocks. He doesn't know any better, never did. And while he's a good foot taller than me now, no amount of growin' is gonna brighten the lamp in that boy's head. He's as dim as they come, poor soul. Them other boys know better too, out there takin' advantage of Leroy. You'd think the sheriff would lock them up for their hand in things, knowin' what he knows about Leroy. I believe it would do them some good, buncha cowards. But it's not likely to happen when two of them hooligans are the mayor's sons. It just so happens that the good sheriff and Mayor Harper were seen leavin' the tavern east of town together, not two nights ago, both of them three sheets to the wind. Ain't that somethin'? So it looks like me and Leroy are gonna pass the time together until Sherriff Coleman says we can leave.

I've only been in this cell for three days, but it feels like a might lot longer than that. I know what I did wasn't considered proper by most folks down here in the South, but I don't regret doin' it. And I'd do it again, if I had the chance. Charlie never did anything wrong. He's just colored. Not much he can do about that, and even if he could, I suppose he wouldn't want to anyhow. I didn't feel it right that Charlie be ignored when all he came to do was buy feed and tools like the rest of us. So when Eli Carver said he don't take no "colored" money, I thought it best to point out that he must be blind as a bat since Charlie's dollar and my dollar are both the same shade of green. And when I held the two right in front of Mr. Carver's face and politely asked him to show me the difference, he later told Sheriff Coleman I was threatenin' and causin' a disturbance. When I heard that, it just made my blood boil, and I decided Eli Carver needed to be taught a lesson. I went back to that store, although Charlie tried to get me to leave it be, but the next thing I knew, I was holdin' Eli a foot off the ground against the door to his very own supply store. If Sheriff Coleman hadn't been right there, I might have been able to argue my side, but there's no point arguin' against proof and common sense. Besides that, Sherriff Coleman is known for his feelin's about colored people, so I knew I was beat before I started. I suppose I just didn't care.

Can't ever figure why people around here get so fired up about all this stuff anyhow. I mean, I know all about the history behind why folks are so hateful when it comes to coloreds, but at this point, I think they do it more out of habit than anything else. If they'd just stop and think about it a minute, they'd realize it makes no sense at all, not to mention it's an awful waste of energy. Me and Charlie have been friends since we were born, practically. His daddy works for my daddy, not as a slave, mind you, but as a well- paid hand. Lawrence and Charlie are like family to us, and I believe they feel the same. Daddy and Lawrence have known each other since before me and Charlie were even alive. Mama and Adelaide, Lawrence's wife, were real close friends. Lawrence needed work at the time, and it was dang near impossible for colored folks to find decent wages. Daddy needed an honest hand who could work as hard as he did. And that's how we came to know the Dixons.

Charlie was born two years before me in 1885. His Mama had some problems deliverin' him, and Lawrence couldn't find a doctor who would help. So Mama and Daddy went, but they didn't know what to do. The baby finally came out, but Adelaide just kept on bleedin'. She died while holdin' Charlie for the first time. Mama said she's never seen so much blood. Ever since then, it's just been Lawrence and Charlie. They live in a little place a couple miles down the road from us. We like to have them close by on account of them bein' harassed sometimes. The Klan hasn't been around these parts for some time, but there are still a few who would join right up if they had the chance. They're the ones who make things hard for colored folks around here. Most people where we live seem decent enough... that is to say that they don't go out of their way to make trouble, but then you have people like Sherriff Coleman and Eli Carver.

I remember one time when Lawrence and Daddy were sittin' on the front porch after a hard day's work, and some men from town rode by just hollerin' and cursin' somethin' awful, callin' Lawrence a dirty jigaboo and sayin' that Daddy deserved what he got for bein' an ape lover. Had to have been eight or ten men on horseback. A few of them threw rocks and such; bloodied Lawrence real bad. Daddy took one to the side of the head, and

Doc Wilson had to put in ten stitches. Sherriff didn't do anything even though we could identify at least half the men. The next Sunday, those same bounders sat on the pew in front of us, singin' from the hymnal and actin' all Christian-like. Doesn't make any sense to me how you can beat a man on Thursday for doin' nothin, then sit in church and worship the good Lord on Sunday. If them people are heaven bound, then I'm fixin' to find me a different final destination.

February 27, 1905

The time is draggin' on and on, but Leroy doesn't seem to mind much. Since he doesn't fancy talkin', I reckon we played about a hundred hands of cards already. It's a wonder how that boy can play a winnin' hand dang near every time, but he can't put two words together to save his life.

February 28, 1905

When Mama and Daddy showed up, I wasn't quite sure how to act. I knew they weren't pleased, but they didn't seem too angry, either. I watched as Daddy and Sheriff Coleman were talkin'. Daddy looked real serious, but Sheriff Coleman didn't seem to care very much. They spoke for a good long while before Daddy came over to me and Mama.

"Ain't no two ways about it, Daddy. What Eli Carver did to Charlie wasn't ri—"

His eyes burrowed right through me as he held up one unforgivin' finger, makin' me choke on the word before I could finish sayin' it.

"You're in here a good week, boy," Daddy whispered gruffly. "Can't do nothin' about that now. So you keep quiet and do your time."

He had that real stern look on his face... the one he gets when he's downright put out about somethin', but his voice wasn't as harsh as I had expected, so I figured he was probably more upset with Sheriff Coleman than he was with me.

"Your mama brought you some cornbread and beans, and that'll have to do," said Daddy, losin' a bit of the chill he came in with.

We both knew that a pesky quarrel like the one me and Mr. Carver had will get a fella a night in a cell. The week I was servin' was no rightful sentence; it was a message, clear as day.

"Hey there, Leroy," Mama said through the bars. Leroy looked up, grinnin' from ear to ear. "Where's your Pa, son?"

Leroy took to rockin' back and forth, just gigglin' and clappin' his hands like a poor fool. Everybody knew Joe Simmons wasn't gonna do anything about the predicament his boy was in. Leroy has always been a handful, but things have just gone downhill since Emma Simmons passed two summers ago. A boy like Leroy needs his Mama about him, since other folks don't look out for him the way she would. It's a cryin' shame, if you ask me.

Mama looked at Sheriff Coleman, her eyes growin' real narrow.

"You ought to be ashamed of yourself, Sheriff, keeping this boy locked up," she scolded.

You know that man didn't even look up at Mama. Just mumbled, "uh huh," and kept on readin' his newspaper. Daddy acted real composed, but the look of fire he kept hidden under the brim of his hat as he and Mama left the jail could have set the place ablaze. It takes a whole lot to get under Daddy's skin, but disrespectin' Mama is the one thing that can set him off somethin' fierce. Daddy doesn't involve himself in mischief, but if he did, that sheriff would be at the top of the list of men deservin' of a good whoopin'.

After they were gone, I just sat on that lumpy old mattress and stared, for who knows how long, at a brown stain on the floor I'd hoped was coffee, wrestlin' inside myself. I'm no violent man, but I can't seem to tolerate nonsense and ugliness. Thinkin' back on it, I suppose the best thing for me to do was leave Eli Carver to his ignorant ways and find a new place to buy feed. At least that's what my head is tellin' me now. Problem is my head ain't the one doin' the talkin' most of the time. It's not me I'm worried for. Charlie doesn't need any more trouble, and it seems he finds most of his with me—not to mention Daddy havin' two times the amount a work this week since I'm not there to do my chores. Daddy says you've got to pick your fights real careful, because there are only some things truly worth fightin' for, and the rest don't matter all that much. Besides that, tryin' to knock some sense into a man like Eli Carver is like arguin' with a fence post, and you might end up havin' better luck with the fence post! So while I've got half a mind to finish what I started with Mr. Carver when I get out of here, I won't. I'll do like Daddy says and get my time done.

March 2, 1905

Daddy grew up hard. I suspect that's why he drives us the way he does. His daddy did the same to him but even worse. Grandpa Wright was as good a man as there was, but he wasn't about to put up with nonsense of any kind. There was always a good deal of hard work to be done and no time for much else. I read in one of Mama's diaries that Grandpa Wright had a few coloreds workin' the ranch with him. I suppose they were considered slaves. That's just how things were around here at that time. I was surprised to learn about it, seein' as how I was brought up different. Daddy never took to slavery. He said it wasn't natural for men to own other men. Couldn't figure how a man's skin made that any different. He took hell from other southern folk for his opinion, but he paid them no mind.

When I grew old enough to notice, I suppose I wondered why Daddy saw things the way he did, but it all made sense to me after readin' Mama's diaries. She said that there was this one time that Grandpa was movin' sheep across state lines. There was a shortcut he liked to use, even though it was a might dangerous on account of the forty foot drop-off he had to herd those animals around. Anyhow, the story reads that Grandpa got himself into terrible trouble one night when he tried to bring in some strays that had gone near that cliff. Grandpa's horse lost his footin' when he caught some loose dirt, and the two of them barreled down all forty feet. The horse was dead when they reached the bottom, and Grandpa was trapped underneath it, darn near death himself. Normally men don't herd alone, but Grandpa had sent the other three hands ahead with the herd and said he'd catch up when he got the strays. I guess he laid in that ditch, bleedin' and unable to move for more than a night and a half. His head was pinned to one side which left him lyin' there, starin' at a jagged tip of bone that had made its way through the skin of his right arm.

The folks that found him there were colored – a man, his wife, and their boy – Mama said. Do you know that they spent the next several hours doin' what needed to be done to get Grandpa out of there. They were miles away from help, so the man and his son rigged up what rope they had with them to their wagon, climbed down in, tied Grandpa up best they could, and pulled him out. Townsfolk said that the dirt was stained red until the season's first rain, from where they dragged his broken body up the mountainside. Anyhow, the family that found him, got him to town and made sure he was in good hands before leavin' him.

That was the last day Grandpa ever owned a slave, and he started payin' his colored hands the same as the white men. I guess when I really sit and think about it, I'm glad that happened to Grandpa Wright. I'm glad because it was enough to make him change his ways, and him changin' his ways meant my daddy knew better, and knowin' better meant he got to be with Mama. She wouldn't have considered for two seconds marryin' a man that looked down on coloreds, or anyone else for that matter. There isn't an inch of that woman's soul that could put up with the smallest amount of meanness.

Daddy got real lucky when it came to fallin' in love with Mama. There's no tellin' how he got a woman like her to love him back. Don't think, in all my life, I ever heard him tell her either. But she knows he loves her. She doesn't care much about words, which is good, because Daddy doesn't use many, and the ones he does use aren't the likes of those that would soften a lady. Mama is more interested in someone decent. Lucky for her, that's just what Daddy is-decent to the core. He's hard as nails, mind you, but as good as good can be. She used to tell Jessie what kind of husband to look for once she was all grown up. She'd say, "words don't get the cows milked and the mules hitched to plow. And they don't bring a man home at night to the bed where he ought to be."

Jessie would nod and say, "yes ma'am," but I knew she was sweet on that lazy, good-for-nothin' Jacob Harris. I told her that she'd gone back on her raisin' to even think about a boy like him in that way. Jacob's granddaddy has made life miserable for my family for as long as I can remember and before that too. That scoundrel is as ornery as the day is long and would like nothin' better than to take our land and all that's attached to it. And even knowin' that, Jessie still gets all red cheeked and bashful when Jacob rides past, like she's got no sense at all. I'm not even sure what the Harrises do in that house of theirs which, by the way, is big enough to fit two houses just like ours inside their front room. Jacob is probably waited on hand and foot, and it would drive Daddy to drink to have him as a son-in-law. All the work that ever gets done around there is done by folks hired to do it.

Workin' the ranch is what I know. My hands have been dirty since I was old enough to hold a garden hoe, and even a good scrubbin' from Mama's homemade oil and brine soap doesn't get rid of the dirt I got buried in my fingernails. I remember sittin' in front of Daddy on his favorite brown mare when I was barely big enough to see over its head. We'd ride to the top of Sad Man's Ridge to get us a good look at the valley below and see where our sheep were. He started teachin' me right off the bat, first how to ride and then how to herd. Daddy has worked this land all his life. His daddy before him settled here in 1859. Grandpa Wright had three girls and only one son, so naturally Daddy took over the sheep ranchin' business after Grandpa passed. Daddy's sisters never had much interest in it anyhow, and we haven't seen much of them since then. They all seemed happy to get married and be free of sheepin'.

Now while sheepin' is our business, it was Mama's idea to start up with chickens. She watched real careful while Daddy worked himself to the bone every day. I think she wanted to find some way of helpin' out. The neighbors just west of us raised chickens and made a mighty fine business out of it, what with sellin' the birds when they were mature enough to eat, not to mention the eggs that they produced. Mama was never able to sell the birds or their eggs, but she became a master at tradin' services. There was one time she traded half a dozen chickens for a winter's worth of firewood; kept me and Daddy from havin' to wood hunt that summer. Then there was another time she traded eggs with Mr. Martin for some of his fresh honey from the hives he kept on his property. As much as I've learned from Daddy about workin' hard and carin' for a family, I've learned just as much about those things from Mama. She's always been a woman who sees what needs to be done, and gets it done.

Now I remember that Mama had to talk Daddy into the idea of chickens at first, but once she did, that Spring he ordered two hundred baby chicks. Lots a folks thought that keepin' a few roosters in with the layin' flock got those chickens to lay more eggs. Some of the roosters got to be darn near two times bigger than the chickens. We learned real quick that roosters ain't the sort that can get along together. They took to fightin' and carryin' on. One of them took an awful dislikin' to me, and he harassed me like he would another rooster. That dumb bird would chase me around, flappin' them razor sharp wings, like he was possessed. There's no explainin' why it was he hated me like he did; never really did nothin' to deserve it... except maybe the time I wanted to see how well a rooster could fly, and dropped that rascal off the roof of the barn when I was twelve. After months of bein' bothered somethin' terrible by that rooster, Mama finally took my side and marched him to the choppin' block. She might have sided with the bird if she'd known I threw him off the roof, so I just kept that to myself. I got about as much satisfaction as a boy could get, watchin' that rooster brownin' in the roastin' pan; was almost better than gettin' a brand new set of shiny glass marbles. I ate a little slower than usual at supper that night, enjoyin' every bite of that mean old bird. And I feel alright in sayin' that he had it comin'.

Mama married Daddy when she was Jessie's age. Grandpa Doyle didn't care much for him. I used to think it was on account of Daddy bein' so much older than Mama, what with her just barely seventeen at the time they started courtin'. But now that I'm grown, it's real clear to see it was about money—or the fact that Daddy didn't have any, that is.

Grandpa Doyle was a good man, I suppose, but didn't seem to know much about anything except pills and potions. He was what you call a "pharmacist"; don't rightly know how he came to be one, other than he followed a man in a white coat around a local drug store for a time. He wasn't the kind of man to get his hands dirty; wouldn't know what to do with some cedar logs and a shovel if his life depended on it. His money came from his daddy, who got his money from his daddy ... and so on and so forth.

Mama's great-great-grandpa was some kinda big shot back in Ireland. That's where her people come from. But they've been here in Arkansas a good long time now. Mama has an old cedar box at the foot of hers and Daddy's bed with all her fancy things in it. She put them away after they got married; ain't much use for such things out here ... never heard her complain about it though. She knew what she was gettin' with Daddy, and I don't think she'd mind me sayin' that she prefers a man with calluses on his hands to some fancy-pants doctor or lawyer with lots of money. Mama learned the hard way that money doesn't mean happiness. Her mama had lots of it, and was downright miserable—not to mention unpleasant all the time, to boot—from what I've read in Mama's diaries; ended up hangin' herself from a chandelier with a fine silk scarf when mama was only twelve years old. I never knew Grandma Doyle, of course, but I can't say it sounds like I was missin' much.

March 6, 1905

Me and Jessie are the only kids our folks have. Mama had twin baby girls a few years after Jessie came along, but those babies didn't live more than a single day. They're buried out back by the crick that separates our land from the Harris orchard. Jessie asked Mama why they never put up tiny headstones to remember the babies by. Mama squirmed a bit at the question and then swallowed real hard before tellin' Jessie that she remembers them just fine. Then Mama acted like she'd caught a piece of dirt in her eye and excused herself to go inside. Almost right after it happened—the babies dyin', that is—Mama sort of disappeared. I mean, she was still there, but her eyes were glassed over, and she stopped smilin' all together.

A few weeks went by, and Mama was sadder than I ever knew she could be. I was real young too, but won't ever forget what I saw; she'd gone outside to beat the rugs, and ended up down on her knees in the dirt with her face in her hands, just sobbin' and shakin'; stayed there a good long while too, 'til Daddy came back from the barn and saw her there. He didn't say a word, just knelt down in the dirt next to Mama and held her real tight. That night was the first time in all my life I ever remember Daddy fixin' supper. Then one night of that turned into two, two into three, and so on. After a while though, Mama stopped sleepin' so much and got back to her chores. Lots of years went by before she stopped cryin' about it. But whenever Mama goes missin' for too long, you can find her sittin' out back underneath the sycamore and cottonwood trees by that crick where her babies are buried.

I imagine the whole thing hurt Daddy real bad too, but men don't seem to feel it the way women folk do. Mama knew those babies different on account of them bein' inside her all that time. They were strangers to Daddy, so he didn't mourn them same as Mama did. I reckon it was too much heartache for her to have any more children after that. Besides, Doc Wilson said that Mama almost died havin' me; said I was the biggest baby he'd ever seen, what with me bein' twelve pounds when I came out. He weighed me on the same scale they used to weigh corn flour and sugar and such because that's all he had. Doc said that Mama suffered bad for almost three days before I was born. He finally had to use some kind of instruments to get it done. I still have a scar under my left eye from where Doc grabbed on and pulled me out. Then Mama had Jessie a year later, and Doc said they were lucky to get her without havin' all the trouble they had with me; might have been a mistake to try for more after Jessie. Their luck had just plain run out. I know they wanted more babies, but we get along just fine, the four of us.

March 15, 1905

It's been more than two weeks since I got home, and Mama and Daddy haven't said anything to me about bein' in jail for what I did to Eli Carver. Part of me wants to mention it so I can get it over with, but I can't bring myself to do it. Instead, I just keep waitin' with a knot in my stomach. Every time one of them walks in the room, my heart starts beatin' harder, but they just go about their business and leave me to mine.

I'm not sure if they've got nothin' to say on the matter or if they're just concentratin' on Jessie and her flirtatious ways with respect to Jacob Harris. The day after I got home, I heard Mama and Daddy talkin' real quiet in their bedroom about Jessie; appears she was found out back of the school house with Jacob a good hour after school was let out. There wasn't much goin' on, except some hand holdin' and ridiculous amounts of grinnin', I imagine. Ms. May Price, Jessie's teacher, separated the two lovebirds and sent Jessie directly home with a note for Mama and Daddy explainin' why she was late. After he finished readin' the note, Daddy scowled and stared at the floor for a minute or two before he looked up at Jessie.

"Daddy!," Jessie started, "we were just—"

Mama shot Jessie a look that told her to shut her mouth, and lucky for her, she did.

"Go on and get your chores done before supper," Mama urged. "We'll talk more about this later tonight."

"Alright Mama," Jessie said as she pushed by me to get outside.

I'm not sure what about all this makes Daddy so upset. It could be any number of things. Maybe it's that his only daughter is out there carryin' on without a care in the world for whoever is watchin'. Or it could be that Jessie doesn't seem to pay any mind to knowin' that Charles Harris spends a good amount of his time makin' life difficult for Daddy.

The Harris family has been growin' pecan trees since Charles settled that land in 1861. It was a hard time to settle, what with the fightin' goin' on. People in these parts talk about the civil war like it's still happenin' today, but I suppose that's because a lot a folks are still dealin' with the trouble it caused them. It's public information that Charles had his orchards almost wiped out from the fightin', and he had to start again from nothin'. When you've got to start from scratch like that, it takes a good six to ten years for pecan trees to mature enough to make it worth havin' them, and Charles Harris couldn't produce a decent crop for all that time. He spent a fair number of years raisin' turkeys while he waited for his trees to grow. Had to have some kind of income, and turkeys were about the best he could do at the time.

My understandin' is that Charles Harris and Grandpa Wright started out as good friends. They came to Arkansas about the same time and were growin' their crops and their families together. But after Mr. Harris lost his trees and started replantin', he wanted some of Grandpa's land so he could space the trees out further than they were before. Each of them had nearly eleven acres and Grandpa was usin' his for corn, cotton, and, of course, sheep. The story goes that Grandpa gave Mr. Harris two full acres out of the goodness of his heart, and Mr. Harris promised to give Grandpa a fair share of the production at harvest to help make up the difference. While they waited for the trees to grow, they were thick as thieves.

Then about seven years into it, the trees started producin'. It wasn't much at first, but it was enough to get by. Grandpa didn't say anything on account of knowin' Mr. Harris needed a season or two to get back on his feet. A couple more years passed, and Mr.

Harris was doin' real well. He was able to get rid of them turkeys and had a fine pecan crop each October. Finally, about four Harvests had gone by, and Grandpa went to Mr. Harris to talk about their arrangement. Would you believe that Charles Harris acted like Grandpa was talkin' crazy? Said he never made no such agreement and that Grandpa was bein' greedy. Of all the low-down, dirty things to say!-especially after Grandpa parted with two full acres in the name of friendship. Friendship! I use that word real loose when talkin' about Charles Harris. He wouldn't know what friendship meant if it was a rattler that bit him on his backside.

I remember askin' Grandma about it when I was younger. I heard the stories around town all my life and wanted to know the truth of it from someone who knew exactly what the truth was. Unfortunately for me, Grandma was a Christian woman, and all she had to say about the matter was, "now Willie, every dog has a few fleas". I was only nine or ten at the time and had no idea what in the devil that meant; couldn't figure out what dogs and fleas had to do with Grandpa and Mr. Harris. When I think on it now, it makes more sense. It took me all these years to finally get the story out of one of Mama's diaries, and part of me wishes I hadn't read it at all; makes me so mad.

Grandpa Wright was a man who believed in four things: God, family, hard work, and forgiveness. He was a lot like Daddy; did what needed to be done and minded his business while doin' it. He wasn't warm, but he had his principles, and there wasn't a soul alive that could make him go back on them, especially a dog (as Grandma put it) like Charles Harris.

So Grandpa let it go. I imagine they all could have lived in peace if it wasn't for Mr. Harris comin' back for more a year or so later. Turns out he wanted to plant more pecan trees since the ones he had were producin' so well. Problem is, you gotta space them trees forty feet apart and he just ran out of land. That thief went back to Grandpa, askin' for more land-this time with a signed contract statin' that Grandpa would get ten percent of the money from the pecans sold on his land. I don't know what's more insultin'—that he acted like he never did Grandpa any wrong in the first place, or that he took him for a fool that would sign that piece of paper. Why would a man agree to ten percent of what's already one hundred percent his? That cheat could make a pastor cuss!

When Grandpa passed, Charles Harris came to the funeral and acted all cordial, expressin' his sympathies. Grandma didn't want a thing from that man, least of all his sympathies! But Grandma, bein' the kind of woman she was, thanked him kindly and kept her real feelings private. Grandpa's body was barely in the ground before Mr. Harris came to Grandma with that same filthy contract, askin' her to sign. Lucky for Grandma, Daddy was grown at that point and knew better. I'm sure it was a thorn in Mr. Harris's side to have Daddy there helpin' Grandma. She passed a few years after Grandpa; went plum crazy first, so it was a blessin' to see her go. Now the land belongs to Daddy, and I'm certain Charles Harris is gonna keep on tryin' to get it until the day he keels over. I bet he doesn't even care about the trees or the money at this point; he's just doin' it to be nasty and is too proud to let it go. Daddy says this is Wright land and will be until there are no more Wright's alive to claim it. If I was a bettin' man, my money would be on Daddy.

March 17, 1905

Springtime is about as nice as it could be here in Arkansas. While the blue and yellow flowers that grow wild along the hillside by our house are Mama's favorites, I can't say I care too much about flowers in general. They're nice to look at, I suppose, but what I like the most is the smell of spring grass and freshly plowed crops after a rainstorm. Wantin' it to be that time of year always hits me in March, and when I get that feelin, I know it's just a month or so away.

About a mile and a half out, our property backs up against the forest. In springtime, it's green and thick and makes a perfect place for young'uns to build their tree forts. In September and October, the leaves start to change from green to bright red and orange, and when the early mornin' light hits those leaves just right, you'd swear the forest is on fire. Me, Jessie, and Charlie spent so much time as kids playin' in those woods that our horses wore out the ground, creatin' a permanent trail between the forest and our house. And then there's the old willow tree that towers over our property. When we were small, we'd take runnin' leaps at her feathery branches, holdin' on for dear life to see who could swing the farthest. Charlie and I hate to admit it even still, but Jessie beat us more than she didn't. While we haven't played the game for some years now, the shade of that tree makes a mighty fine place to take an afternoon nap, if you can sneak one in when Daddy's not lookin', that is. Those are the memories that make me want to stay in Arkansas so that when my kids come along, they'll have what I had.

April 3, 1905

I never knew any other house than the one I'm livin' in now. I reckon it's as good as any other. When Daddy's folks were lookin' for a place to settle, this is where they ended up. It's plenty big but we've never been able to get the smell out of that back room. It's especially bad in the summer time. Grandpa Wright said that the folks who owned the property before him were German and that they were pig farmers. When they were just startin' out, before they got enough land to put up some fences, they used that back room as a pig pen. Can you imagine? Now I like a good pork chop for dinner or some bacon on Sunday mornin's, but I've got no interest in sharin' a house with them filthy creatures. If that's how they do things in Germany, I reckon I'm glad I live in Arkansas.

May 22, 1905

I find myself in a state of terrible distraction lately. Hannah Brown may be the prettiest and nicest-smellin' girl in all of Arkansas. Her Daddy, Jeremiah, is the new pastor. They've been here five weeks already come Sunday. Mama and Daddy wondered why I was showin' such interest in goin' to church every week with them. I mean, me and Jessie always go to church (not like we have a say in the matter) but we're never too excited about goin'. Henry Thomas was the pastor before Jeremiah Brown, and his sermons were about as excitin' as watchin' a slug race a snail. He was nice enough, but boy he could sure put you to sleep in a hurry. Jessie and I used to call him "Preacher Man Thomas" behind his back, but Mama said that wasn't proper, seein' as how we're Presbyterian. She knew we were just playin' around but told us to give him the respect he deserved and call him "Pastor" like everyone else.

I tried to make it seem like the reason I suddenly wanted to go to church so bad was because I found Pastor Brown more interestin' than Pastor Thomas, but Mama caught me starin' at Hannah while everyone was singin' "Abide With Me." On the ride home, Mama was pokin' fun at me and said I looked like a big-mouth bass holdin' a hymnal. I was supposed to be singin', but I was lookin' at Hannah instead and didn't know the words by heart, so I just moved my mouth like I was singin'; thought I got away with it too, but Mama told me otherwise. Daddy didn't say a word while Mama was teasin' me; just sat next to her, chucklin'. It sure gave Jessie somethin' to harass me with. I might normally be put out about the teasin', but Mama doesn't have one single ugly intention in her whole body, so I just shrugged my shoulders and laughed along with them. No point in takin' offense when only fun was intended. Now if I could work up the nerve to talk to Hannah...

July 26, 1905

I made a darn fool of myself today. Charlie said it wasn't that bad, but I can't rightly expect him to tell me straight. It's painful to tell the folks you care about the truth sometimes.

Hannah was standin' outside the post office, waitin' for her Daddy like she does every Wednesday. She had on a yellow dress, you know the kind with lace and what not hangin' off the front of it. She looked like a ray of sunshine, out there fannin' herself from the July heat. She wears the kind of clothes Mama has tucked away in her cedar chest. Hannah's family came here from New York and it seems they come from high society. Most of them people think they're too good for the rest of us, but every now and again you come across some that don't stick their noses in the air when you're around.

Mama is one of the good ones, and I suspect the Browns are too. The only thing from her upbringin' that Mama brought with her when she married Daddy was her proper talkin'. She never uses words like "ain't" the way he does. It's hard sometimes to abide by her teachin' since I spend so much time with Daddy. I still say a few things that make Mama crazy, but I always make sure to try extra hard when I'm around her. I suppose I'm grateful to Mama for the trainin', mostly because the Browns talk like she does. I guess it makes me feel like we have somethin' in common. If I ever get the chance to talk to Hannah, I'll have to concentrate real hard on the teachin' I got from Mama.

Pastor Brown is real friendly and happy all the time; can't imagine where he gets all that energy from, but he's a pleasant fella to be around. Mrs. Brown is a handsome woman, for an older lady, that is. She carries herself in a real dignified way; don't know much about her personality since she keeps pretty quiet, but there has

never been a time when she hasn't smiled and nodded when she's
seen me. I'm still tryin' to make heads or tails about the other
daughters. I haven't really talked to any of them, and every time I
see them, they just cover their mouths and giggle; can't figure what
it is I'm doin' that's so dang funny all the time. The Browns have
five girls and not one single boy! I don't know much about livin'
with girls, but if you took Jessie and put four more just like her in
the same house, you might find me sleepin' in the barn with the
horses.

I'm tryin' to figure if it's me or Charlie to blame for ruinin' my
chances with Hannah. He's the one who convinced me to go and
talk to her. Oh, I know it's not Charlie's fault; I'm just lookin' for a
way to not feel so bad. Blamin' Charlie doesn't really accomplish
that. After all, he did give me a decent pep talk beforehand and it
was my decision to go talk to her.

"Will, you been wantin' to talk to Hannah Brown for three
months now," said Charlie. "Now's as good a time as any."

"I know, I know, Charlie. But what if she doesn't want to talk to
me, or what if I choke on my own tongue?"

Charlie shook his head and laughed right out loud.

"How you gonna marry her if you can't even talk to her?"

I knew he was right. And I knew the first time I laid eyes on
Miss Hannah Brown that she was gonna be my wife someday. So I
mustered up the only courage I could find, held my head up
straight, and headed in her direction with a daisy Charlie picked
from the flower display in front of Eli Carver's store. There was a
touch of sweet justice, stealin' one of his flowers.

Hannah was standin' at the far end of the wood porch that
wrapped around the post office. There was only about twenty feet
or so between us, but it felt like I was walkin' from Arkansas to
Texas. As I got closer, she looked up from her Harper's Monthly
and started to smile in my direction. I felt nothin' I ever felt before
– like I had a bunch a butterflies beatin' against the inside of my

stomach. I felt hot too, hotter than what was normal for July. I remembered what Charlie said about havin' to talk to her before I could marry her, so I told myself to settle down and just say hello.

"Mornin', Miss Brown," I said as I tipped my hat.

"Good morning, Mr. Wright," Hannah said.

"I... I thought you might like to have a flower," I said.

"Oh my, how lovely. Well aren't you sweet!"

She put her head down and smiled, then looked up at me with those green eyes of hers. In that moment I wished I'd played poker so I'd know what kind of face to make. I was fairly certain the one I was makin' wasn't the right one.

I took a step closer to hand her the daisy, and wouldn't you know that my boot caught a rusty nail stickin' out of the wood plank under my foot. I tried to stop myself from trippin' but couldn't manage, and I fell right into her! By the time I reached her, I had so much momentum goin' that I dang near plowed her through the post office wall! I'm only prayin' my hands didn't land on anything improper; can't say for certain since it all happened so fast; smashed the daisy in the process too. She acted real polite and said she was just fine, but I know she could see I wanted to die of embarrassment and was doin' her part to make me feel better. I handed her the crumpled up flower and left quick as I could.

When I got around the corner to where Charlie was waitin', I didn't even stop when I saw him. I just kept on walkin'. I would have started runnin' if I didn't think Hannah could see me.

"Will, it wasn't as bad as you think," Charlie said as he ran to catch up with me.

I didn't say a word.

"It'll go better next time," he said.

I know he was just tryin' to help, but I couldn't imagine there bein' a next time since I was plannin' on movin' far away, or at least hidin' under a rock.

"Let's go, Will!" called Daddy from the front porch.

I laid in bed tryin' to figure a way out of goin' to church. I just couldn't see Hannah again after what happened. Daddy wouldn't understand that. He'd call it nonsense and make me go anyhow.

"Go on without me!" I called out to him.

"What's wrong with that boy today? Is he sick?" I heard him ask Mama.

"I don't know," she said, soundin' irritated. "He knows how I hate to be late to church."

I watched from my window as Mama hurried down from the buggy, pattin' Daddy's knee on the way, and came back in the house.

"Will, are you alright?" she said as she opened the door to my room.

"I'm fine, Mama," I said. "I'm just not goin' today is all."

"What do you mean you're not going?"

"Just what I said," I snapped.

Mama startled a bit. I regretted it as soon as I said it, but I didn't feel like discussin' what happened, and there wasn't time even if I did want to talk about it.

"What's the matter, son?" Mama asked. "Are you sick?"

"I've already told you I'm just fine. Now you're gonna be late, so just leave me be and go."

Mama's face looked hurt, but she left it alone.

"We're invited to have some shortbread and coffee with Lawrence and Charlie after the service is over. Shall I bring you some?" she asked.

"I'll have shortbread another time," I said.

I could hear Daddy outside gettin' impatient and cursin' under his breath.

"Alright then," said Mama. "We'll be home after six. There are some biscuits and honey in the cupboard if you get hungry."

I watched them ride away, and part of me wished I'd gone with them. Another part of me wished I hadn't talked to Mama the way I did. But the biggest part of me was relieved to have one more day that I didn't have to face Hannah.

July 31, 1905

This mornin' started out pleasant enough but turned sour within minutes of seein' Daddy. He wasn't at the table for breakfast, and Mama told me he wanted me to meet him at the West pasture to help bring back some sheep that got separated from the flock durin' the rainstorm last night. As soon as I got to where he was, Daddy squared off his horse against mine and laid into me.

"You know the one thing I don't abide, Will, is sassin' your Mama," he started.

It looked like he had more to say so I cut him off before he could.

"I'm eighteen years old!" I said, tryin' to sound tougher than I felt. "I'm old enough to decide if I want to go to church or not!"

I held my breath while I waited for Daddy's reaction, and even though I wanted to look away, I didn't. I felt my face get hot and my heart started poundin'. Why did Mama have to say anything to him about it anyhow?

He looked at the ground, and all I could see of his face under his hat was his clenched jaw. I tried to keep my nerve. After a minute or so, he looked up.

"You goin' or not goin' to church is not my concern," Daddy said real firm. "But you hear me on this, son. You won't ever backtalk your Mama the way you did yesterday. And if I hear about it again, I'll take you out back behind the shed and remind you that I won't have it."

Daddy stared at me hard and I couldn't hold his gaze. I put my head down and nodded.

We spent the next hour or so in silence while we tried to get those dumb sheep back with the others. I was spittin' mad, and Daddy knew it; don't think he cared one lick. I rode my horse a little slower than usual and was real lazy when it came time to drive the sheep. Daddy could tell I wasn't workin' hard out of spite.

"You ain't no use to me like this," Daddy barked. "Get on home."

"I'll stay and help you finish," I said, tryin' to make it sound like I'd been workin' hard the whole time.

"Did you hear what I said, boy?" Daddy shouted as he spun around on his horse and took a few quick steps toward me.

My horse backed up as his came closer. I think I'd pushed Daddy about as far as he had patience for, and as mad as I was, I still wasn't brave enough to see what would happen if I kept on; so I gave my horse a kick harder than he deserved and rode on home.

When I got home, Jessie and Mama were makin' a chicken pie for tonight's supper. They were laughin' with each other and havin' a nice time. I stormed through the kitchen and grabbed the firewood pail by the back door.

"That was fast," Mama said. "Did you find all the missing sheep already?"

"Daddy's still lookin'," I mumbled.

"Why aren't you with him?" Mama asked.

"He doesn't need my help after all," I said as I headed out the door, lettin' the screen slam shut behind me.

I headed over to the big stump by the barn and started choppin' the wood Mama asked me to get to yesterday. I chopped real hard for a good long while, and by the time I was finished, I was drenched in my own sweat. I sat on the stump to rest a spell, when Jessie came outside to collect some eggs from the hen house.

"Why are you so ornery lately?" she asked.

I kinda wanted to yell at her too for askin' me that, but truth is, I was too dang tired from all that wood choppin', and didn't have the energy to create one more enemy.

"I don't know," I said.

"You keep on hurtin' Mama's feelin's," Jessie said.

I rested my elbows on my knees and sighed long and hard, watchin' the sweat drip from my head, makin' marks in the dirt underneath me.

"I'm not really mad at Mama and Daddy. I suppose I'm just feelin' like an idiot over Hannah and takin' it out on them."

"Why do you think Mama's makin' chicken pie?" Jessie said. "'Cause it's your favorite, and she's tryin' to make you feel better. I told her she should make you turnip pie with pickle sauce since all you deserve is somethin' bitter and sour like the way you've been treatin' everybody around here."

Jessie finished collectin' the eggs and headed back inside. I sat there feelin' the sun beat down on me and knew I'd done wrong. I needed some time to get myself straight, so I made my way out to the crick behind the house and jumped in, clothes and all. I floated there on my back, watchin' the leaves from the old maple swayin' back and forth above me in the breeze, lettin' in bits of sunshine on my face. I'd made a mess of things with Hannah and was bettin' my chances with her were as scarce as a hen's teeth. But Jessie was right about me not deservin' chicken pie. I'd like to say that I wouldn't even eat any as a way to punish myself for bein' so awful, but if you'd ever had Mama's chicken pie, you wouldn't hold it against me for not goin' through with that. So I'll apologize to Mama, eat some of that delicious pie, and forget about Hannah Brown all together.

After layin' in the warm grass long enough to dry my clothes and calm my temper, I went on back to the house. Mama was out back hangin' clothes on the line. Just seein' her there made me feel even worse than I already felt. Mama is the last person I should be takin' my woes out on. And as forgivin' as she is, it would suit me better not to give her such reason for it.

Mama was shakin' out the extra water from the blanket she took off Jessie's bed before hangin' it. She has this quiet whistle that she always does, so quiet it's almost like there's no sound comin' from it, just pushin' air around. She takes to whistlin' when she's happy or when she's workin'; don't know why, but I just love the sound of that whistle. I walked over and stood in front of her. I reached over and picked up the other side of the blanket to help her. We didn't say anything to each other, just stood there shakin' water off the blanket together. Then we hung it up, and Mama pinned the ends so the wind couldn't blow it down. As she pinned the last corner, I reached up and took her hands.

"I'm real sorry, Mama," I said.

Mama smiled. "There's my boy. I've been wondering where you were," she teased. Then she put her arms around me and hugged me tight the way she always did, only this time, I hugged her just a might tighter than she hugged me.

"Now we better get these chores finished up before your Pa comes home," she said as she pulled away. "I'm guessing it's going to take more than chicken pie to make him happy today!"

"Yes ma'am," I said. "I reckon you're right about that."

After all the grief I caused Mama, I realized that she never asked me why I did it. I hadn't told her about Hannah, and she must be thinkin' that I've changed my mind about bein' a Christian since I keep avoidin' church. I imagine she's been prayin' for my soul. What she doesn't know is that my soul is fine, it's my pride that needs prayin' for.

Daddy came home late this afternoon and I knew I had to make it right with him too. I opened the gate to the corral so he could drive those sheep in, then I made my way over to where he was tyin' up his mare.

"I apologized to Mama," I said.

I suddenly felt kinda nervous and choked on my own spit as I said it, which made me swallow real hard and cut my words off before I could finish sayin' them.

"I wanted to say sorry to you too, Daddy."

He kept undoin' the saddle straps and never looked up at me once.

"Then it's settled," he said.

"Yes sir," I said as I helped him take the saddle off the horse's back.

Daddy was checkin' the horse's shoes and I started brushin' him down.

"Mama's makin' chicken pie for supper," I said after a few minutes.

Daddy didn't say a thing, but if I had to swear to it, I'd say the corners of his mouth curled up a bit when I mentioned Mama's chicken pie.

August 6, 1905

I begged Mama not to make me go to church today.

"I just don't understand you, Will," Mama said. "For weeks you've been chomping at the bit to get to church, and the past couple Sundays you can't bear the thought of going?"

I thought about tellin' her I was feelin' sick, but I knew if I did that she'd get out the castor oil.

"I'm too embarrassed to go, Mama."

Mama stopped scrubbin' the pan she used for breakfast that mornin', and after wipin' her hands on the towel next to the sink, she came over to sit down next to me at the table. Mama was the one person I could always talk to. She had a real soft way about her and listened like she really cared about what you had to say.

"What on earth are you embarrassed about?" she said.

I took a deep breath.

"I practically killed Hannah Brown on Wednesday before last, and it might just be best for me to stop goin' to church... or switch religions and go somewhere else," I said.

Mama stared at me for a good minute. She put her hand over her mouth, and I might be wrong, but it looked like she was tryin' not to smile. I told her the story about runnin' Hannah into the wall of the post office.

"I'm so mad at Rex Smith for not fixin' them old wood planks, I could spit!" I said.

"Those planks," Mama corrected.

I put my head in my hands and sighed.

"*Those* planks," I said.

"Oh, son. I know it feels like the most awful thing now, but Hannah seems like a girl who's got her head on straight," Mama said. "I'd be surprised if a thing like that would change her mind about liking you."

"Likin' me? You think she likes me?" I asked.

"Well, all I know is that when you're not looking at her in church, she's looking at you," said Mama.

"Did I ruin my chances?"

"Let's head on to church and find out."

I rested my head on the table and sat for a minute, thinkin' about what Mama said. She kissed me on the back of my head and got back to scrubin' that pan. I guess I'd hate to give up too soon if I still have a chance, and I'm gonna have to see her again to know for sure. Even a blind hog finds an acorn now and then.

When we got to church, I sent Jessie in before me to see if she could see Hannah. She came outside a few minutes later and motioned for me to come in. I felt ridiculous havin' Jessie spy for me, but the last thing I needed was to bump into Hannah before I was prepared to see her. I walked inside and headed straight for the back row. The choir was practicin' up in front, and there was

Hannah, singin' her beautiful heart out. I had to remind myself not to stare. I've been real nervous about that ever since Mama pointed it out to me. I mean, can you imagine the impression I'm leavin' on this girl... plowin' her down in the street and starin' at her in church? I'll consider myself lucky if she'll say two words to me after all that.

She had a sister on either side of her, and I saw one of them elbow her in the ribs while lookin' over at me. Hannah just kept on singin' while her sisters took to gigglin'. I couldn't tell if that was a good sign or a bad sign. I had already decided that I didn't want her to know I was there, but once I knew she'd seen me, I suppose I was hopin' for... oh I don't know what I was hopin' for. My stomach was all tangled up in knots and I was regrettin' the fact that I let Mama talk me into comin'.

The sermon was on hellfire and damnation. As nice as Pastor Brown is Monday through Saturday, come Sunday he could scare the evil out of the devil himself! I always come home from church on Sunday evenin's wantin' to take a hot bath with a rough sponge. I sat through that whole sermon without lookin' at Hannah once. I felt real proud of myself until I realized that if I wasn't lookin' at her, how was I to know if she was lookin' at me? The whole thing was just exasperatin'!

As if that wasn't enough to deal with, there was Maryanne Stephenson in the front row of the choir, makin' googly eyes at me! I hate it when she does that. A lot of fellas around here fancy Maryanne, but there is just somethin' about that girl that makes me awful uncomfortable. She's pretty enough, I suppose, but you gotta wonder about a girl who feels right at home flirtin' with a different fella every time the wind shifts. We were the same age in school, and Ms. Price was constantly tellin' Maryanne to keep her hands to herself and stop talkin' durin' class. That girl would lean over to me a hundred times a day and whisper some kind of nonsense, each time touchin' my hand or my leg.

There were a few times she got us both in trouble, and I finally marched right up to Ms. Price one day after school and told her just what was goin' on. The next day she had moved Maryanne's desk to the front of the class. When Maryanne walked in the room, she was fit to be tied! She sat there all mornin' with her arms folded real tight and an ugly scowl painted on her face. There was no one in arm's reach for her to touch! You'd think that would have sent the message that I wasn't interested, but here she was, two years later, still flirtin' with me, and in church too!

When Pastor Brown had finished his sermon, the choir stood up to sing Amazin' Grace. I found myself scannin' the choir members but was tryin' to be casual about it. Would you believe that just as I got to Hannah, she glanced over at me and smiled! Other people might not call what she did a smile, but that's alright since it wasn't meant for them anyhow. That one little smile made my stomach do what it does when you're about to jump off of that rickety bridge over Mill's pond.

After church was over, everyone was standin' around talkin and exchangin' pleasantries. I waited until the pastor was sort of on his own so I could say to him what it was I had to say without the whole congregation knowin' my business. I had to take a few deep breaths and get my nerves calm before goin' over to him. I politely pushed my way through the crowd of women who always stand huddled together in the center isle like a herd of old heifers, just smilin' and noddin' to each other with their best Sunday bonnets on. Just before I reached Pastor Brown, I wiped the sweat off my hand onto my trousers and held it out to shake his.

"That was a fine sermon," I said as formal as I knew how.

"Well that's kind of you to say, Mr. Wright," said the pastor.

"I suppose it makes a man want to change his ways," I said. "Uh... not that my ways need changin'...," I stuttered. "I just meant... that your words can inspire the best of us to do better.

Oh... and when I say the best of us, I'm not meanin' to imply that I'm the best..."

Pastor Brown started laughin' that full bellied laugh he does, which I was grateful for, because as dumb as I was feelin', heaven only knows how long I would have rambled on like that.

"I think I understand you, son, and I'll kindly take the compliment," he said.

I stood there wantin' to say somethin', but nothin' would come out.

"Alright then," he said as he smiled and started to turn away. "Enjoy your Sunday now."

"Pastor Brown!" I said, much louder than I had intended.

"Yes, Mr. Wright," he said, lookin' startled.

"Well sir, it's just that... I was hopin' to have your permission to come by your house this evenin' and sit on the porch with Hannah for a spell."

His eyes widened a bit, and he turned to face me head on. He put both hands on my shoulders, and I was preparin' myself for what he would say, not knowin' if it was good or bad.

"As far as I'm concerned, you may sit on my porch any time you like," he said. "But if your sole purpose for doing so is to be with Hannah, then I believe you'll need to ask for her permission. I've learned better than to speak for one of my daughters."

He gave me a big friendly smile, and I couldn't help but smile back.

"Then I'll see how she feels on the matter," I said. "Thank you, sir!"

Just then Mrs. Martin tapped him on the shoulder, and he turned to talk with her.

I looked around tryin' to find Hannah; seems she had disappeared. I looked inside and out until Mama finally waved at me from the buggy and called that it was time to leave. I started walkin' toward the buggy, feelin' real disappointed, when I heard the voice of an angel call my name.

"Mr. Wright!" said Hannah as she squeezed her way through the group of people standin' on the front steps laughin' and talkin'.

I turned around in a hurry and saw her comin' toward me. Stay calm, Will!, I said to myself. Don't be an idiot!

"Mr. Wright, my Pa said that you were looking for me."

"Miss Brown, you look lovely today," I said.

I hadn't planned on sayin' it but couldn't get the words back once I did; so they just floated there in the air for a minute while I tried to figure out what to say next.

"Why, thank you," she said.

She stood there lookin' at me. Then she raised her eyebrows and started to smile.

"Is that why you were looking for me? To tell me that I look lovely?" she asked.

"No," I said. "But now that you're here, I thought it best to mention it."

She smiled and said, "May I ask what the original reason was that you were looking for me?"

"I was wonderin' if I might come over tonight and sit on your porch and talk with you for a while. Your daddy gave his blessin' but said it was up to you."

She looked surprised.

"Pa gave his blessing, did he?" she said.

"Well, he said I could sit on the porch whenever I want, but you'd have to answer for yourself about sittin' there with me. Truth is, Miss Brown, as nice an invitation as that is, I have no interest in sittin' on your porch without you," I said.

"Alright then, Mr. Wright—"

"Will," I interrupted. "If it suits you, please call me Will."

"Alright then, Will," she said, now smilin' a full-fledged, white-toothed, beautiful red-lipped smile. "We're having Bible study with the Thompsons at five, so I'll expect you around six?"

I tipped my hat and tried to keep from lookin' as excited as I was feelin'.

"And if it suits you, please call me Hannah," she said as she turned and walked back to the church buildin'.

Hannah... that name rang in my mind like a sweet song playin' over and over again. Yes, I believe that suits me just fine, I thought to myself.

As I walked toward the buggy, Mama, Daddy, and Jessie were all smilin' somethin' awful. It was quite a scene, and I was prayin' that Hannah had gone back in the church already. I climbed in and sat next to Jessie.

"I'll thank you kindly to get a hold of yourselves and not embarrass me," I whispered.

"Turns out that coming to church was just what you needed after all," Mama said as she leaned forward and winked at me.

"Amen," I said.

Mama scowled at me for bein' irreverent, but I knew she wasn't too upset about it.

"I reckon sometimes we're moved to go to church by somethin' other than the good word," Daddy said as he laughed to himself.

While we rode home, I felt the warm breeze on my face, and hard as I tried, I couldn't remember a time when I was happier than I was in that moment.

I arrived at six like I promised, and Mrs. Brown brought us some sweet tea and corn muffins. The pastor came outside for a minute to shake my hand and give me a proper welcome. Then the two of them politely excused themselves and let me and Hannah alone to talk. At first there wasn't much to say. We exchanged pleasantries and talked about the nice evenin' breeze. I learned real quick that you can only do so much of that before you run out of things to comment on. And we did. Thank heaven for Hannah bein' a might better at conversation than I am. Otherwise, I'm fairly certain there would have been a whole lot of awkward smilin', and the night would have ended quicker than I'd hoped.

"Tell me about yourself," she said.

Since we had just been talkin' about the weather, her request caught me off guard. I thought about it for a minute and realized I wasn't sure what she was gettin' at.

"Um, what about me?" I asked.

"Like what are your interests, for example?"

"Interests?" I said.

"Yes. What kinds of things do you like to do?" she laughed.

"Well, I enjoy swimmin' in the crick on a hot day. And I like racin' Charlie to the crooked fencepost just before you get to town. Even though he usually beats me by a good four or five seconds, I still like the run. I'm fixin' to beat him one of these days."

She smiled real polite, but I couldn't tell if I was borin' her to tears or not. I was just answerin' her question is all, but Daddy says I have a tendency to ramble on.

"Did you ever see the Statue of Liberty," I asked.

"Just once," she said. "It was after my Pa told us we were moving, and on our way here we passed her. She's really something to see."

"I bet you saw lots of interestin' things in New York," I said. "I've never been outside of Arkansas."

She didn't respond at first, just sat there like she was ponderin' something important.

"New York is an interesting place," she said. "But I've found that it's more about the people that makes a place feel like home.

We were in New York my whole life before coming here, and I feel more at home in Arkansas than I ever did in New York."

"You do?" I asked real surprised.

"Everyone has been so friendly since we got here. And the church is full every Sunday to hear my Pa give his sermons. Back home we were lucky to have twenty people show up each week."

"What were the rest of the people doin' on a Sunday if they weren't goin' to church?" I asked.

Hannah laughed out loud and then looked away. She doesn't seem shy until she laughs. I like that about her.

"That's what I love about this place," she said. "You people can't imagine doing anything other than attending church on Sunday. This is just the kind of place my Pa has needed for a long time."

"If you'd been to one of Henry Thomas's sermons, you'd understand me when I say that we needed your daddy much more than he needed us!"

We both took to laughin'. It probably wasn't right to make fun of Pastor Thomas like that, but what I said was the honest truth.

After that, we settled down and just kinda sat there together a while.

"Is Charlie your only friend, Will?" Hannah asked.

Her face turned red, and she seemed embarrassed by her own question. She jumped in before I could even answer it.

"I'm sorry," she said. "That didn't come out right, and I meant no offense by it."

I smiled and said, "I'm not offended."

"It's just that I've never seen you with any of the other boys from town. You and Charlie seem to spend most of your time together."

"I suppose we do," I said. "It'd be alright if some of them other fellas wanted to be included with me and Charlie, but the awful truth is that they won't have anything to do with me as long as Charlie's around. And even if Charlie wasn't around, I'm guessin' they still wouldn't want to on account of Charlie bein' my best friend."

Hannah frowned and her voice got real quiet. "Is that true?" she said.

"I'm afraid so," I said. "Things are a might different here than they are where you come from, I imagine."

"I guess they are," she said."Didn't you have the Klan up there in New York?" I asked.

"I can't honestly answer that question," she said. "They may have been there, but I didn't know anything about it if they were. Pa tries to keep us protected from the evils of the world. I think he believes that's his job as a father and a pastor."

"I can't rightly fault a man who does what he does in the name of protectin' his family," I said. "I reckon I don't know if I'll be able to stick with the opinion I have on it now until I have a family of my own."

"What about your parents?" Hannah asked. "Don't they want to protect you and Jessie?"

I thought about her question a long time before answerin'. "If what you mean by protectin' us is not havin' colored friends, then no. Now that would just be participatin' in the ugliness itself. And in these parts, I suppose we can't avoid knowin' about the evil things that go on like you can in other places. The Klan doesn't exist because of colored folks, Hannah; it exists because the devil got a hold of the wrong people and turned their hearts to hate."

Hannah held on to her cup, just starin' inside it and lookin' like she might cry.

"I wasn't tryin' to hurt your feelings," I said real concerned.
She shook her head.

"You didn't hurt my feelings," she said. "I guess I just feel kind of closed off to the world sometimes. My pa is a really good man, Will. My mother said that he's seen some awful things, and so he tries to make life for us as pleasant as he can."

"That's respectable," I said.

"At least his intention is," Hannah said. "Is the Klan here in Arkansas?"

"I don't believe the Klan is very strong anywhere right now," I said. "But there are a few men around here that I suspect would like it to be."

"I see," she said.

"Can I ask you a question," I said.

"Of course."

"How does your daddy survive livin' with six women in the same house?" I teased.

"It's pure torture, I'm sure!" she said.

That broke the serious mood enough that we could smile again and just sit together. I wanted to leave her feelin' happy after seein' me.

Hannah looked at me, and I realized I had been starin' again.

"You're beautiful," I said without thinkin'.

She put her head down and tried to keep from grinnin' too wide.

"It's getting late," she said.

"I suppose it is," I said as I looked up at the sky just startin' to turn dark.

"Will you call on me again, Will?" she asked.

"I believe I'd call on you every day if you'd let me," I said. Is the evenin' young enough that I might hold your hand a minute or two?"

This time she couldn't hide the grin. She held out her hand and I put it in mine. It was then that I knew. Two hands that aren't meant to be together don't fit as perfect as mine and Hannah's.

I rode home real slow, not hardly pullin' on the reins at all. I was just soakin' up the world around me and enjoyin' the feelin' of bein' in love. At least I think that's what I was feelin'. If it isn't love, it sure is a good imitation. The Browns' dog walked along side me about a half mile before turnin' back and headin' home. I suppose I was a little jealous of him.

It took me twice as long to get home, and I put old Trotter back in his stall. (We named him that on account of him bein' the laziest horse you ever saw, not willin' to move faster than a slow trot on his best day.) I went inside to wash up before bed. There was still a lamp burnin' in the front room, and Mama was sittin' in the rocker doin' her sewin'. Daddy was asleep next to her on the couch.

"Well, I was going to ask you if you had a nice time, but your face already answered my question," she said real quiet, tryin' not to wake Daddy.

I went over and gave Mama a kiss on her cheek.

"I'll see you in the mornin'," I whispered.

August 7, 1905

Mama was already sweepin' off the front porch this mornin' when I woke up. I changed out of my night clothes and into my trousers. Then I went right outside and gave her a hug.

"Well good morning to you too, son!" she said as she laughed.

All I could say was, "thank you, Mama!"

"Thank me for what?"

"If I didn't know for sure before last night, I'm certain of it this mornin'," I said.

"What are you going on about, Will?" Mama asked as she took up sweepin' again.

"Mama, I'm fixin' to marry that girl."

"So that's what we're talking about!" Mama teased. "Well don't you suppose you should spend some more time with her before deciding something like that? Marriage is an awfully important decision, son."

"Oh Mama, I'm not gonna ask her today!" I said. "What I'm tryin' to tell you is my heart already knows that when the time is right, she'll be the one I ask."

Jessie pushed open the screen door and sat down on the bench underneath the front window.

"Ask who, what?" she said as she took a bite of her apple.

"We're talkin' about askin' Mrs. Jones what she recommends doin' about nosy little sisters!" I said.

Harriet Jones is known around town for bein' a know-it-all. There isn't a thing in the world she doesn't have an opinion on. She'll tell you where's the best place to buy supplies, how much time every day you should spend doin' what, which medicines and remedies to use for which ailments, and so on and so forth. Thing is, nobody ever asks her to impart her words of wisdom, she just takes it upon herself to share them. She claims to hate gossip too but seems to feel different about it when she's the one spreadin' it around. And if someone points out to her that what she's doin' counts as gossip, she says that she's simply sharin' important information as a way to help folks learn from others' mistakes. She's helpin' to bring us all to repentance, you see.

"Well excuse me for tryin' to take part in a conversation happenin' on my very own front porch!" Jessie said. "I didn't realize that what you were talkin' about was such a secret. Hmmm... let me guess, you're talkin' about Hannah Brown."

Mama chuckled and shook her head.

"Believe it or not, big brother, that wasn't too hard to figure out!" said Jessie.

Mama stopped sweepin' and looked back at Jessie.

"Jessie Maye Wright! Are you eating one of my apples?" she scolded. "The very apples I told you were for cobbler tomorrow night?"

Jessie quit chewin' and looked at the apple in her hand.

"Um... I forgot?" she said with her mouth full of apple.

"Forgot, my eye!" said Mama.

"It just looked so delicious, Mama! And it's only one apple," she said.

"Yes, your one apple plus the two your Pa ate last night after supper— oh for heaven sake!"

"Sorry, Mama," Jessie said.

"Well I guess that means that you and your Pa will be eating bread and milk tomorrow while the rest of us have cobbler!" Mama teased. "Now run and catch up with your Pa before he leaves. He's headed into town for feed. Tell him to pick up some more apples."

"Okay," Jessie called as she jumped off the porch and ran over to the barn where Daddy was saddlin' up.

Mama went back inside, and I sat down on the front steps, thinkin' about last night. I start lookin' forward to Sunday evenin' first thing Monday mornin'. I could have sat on Hannah's porch all night long, listenin' to her talk and watchin' as the right side of her mouth turned up just a second before the left side did when she was about to smile. That would have been enough by itself, but of course she had to smell like honeysuckles in the evenin' after it's been rainin' all day. I've had some time to think on it, and I've made up my mind; this ain't no imitation. It's love.

August 24, 1905

Lawrence sent me and Charlie into town for some blades he needed so he could fix the plow. We didn't argue one bit, seein' as how we were happy as a tick on a fat dog to get out of this August heat for a while. He told us to hurry, but I can't say we put too much effort into that. Before headin' out, we stopped at the house to let Mama know we were goin'. It isn't that long of a ride back from town, but Charlie really played it up good for Mama, hopin' she'd feel bad for us.

"Sure is a hot one today!" he said real loud so that Mama could hear him on our way out.

"Hot? Oh I've been feeling a little chilled all morning. I even thought I'd take a rest from tending these flowers and go get my shawl," she teased.

"I might believe you better if your forehead wasn't sweatin', Miss Lilly," Charlie said as he and Mama laughed.

Mama threw a clump of dirt at Charlie and wiped her forehead on her apron.

"Well, I guess we'll be headin' out now," Charlie said. "We'll be pickin' up those blades my daddy needs; there anything else needs pickin' up, Miss Lilly?"

"Now that you mention it, we do need some ginger ale for the chickens," she said, winkin' at Charlie.

That surprised me and Charlie both, and we got a good laugh out of it.

"Our chickens are pretty good about sharing," Mama said, "so if the bottles are partly empty by the time you boys get them back here, I think it'll be alright."

Mama gave us ten cents for the cold ginger ales, but she didn't tell Daddy. He's careful when it comes to money. Mama is too, but Daddy doesn't see the need very often for things that aren't necessary. Daddy wants us to be responsible. Mama wants us to be responsible and happy.

As we headed out, I sighed and shook my head at Charlie who was still laughin'. It's nice to see him get on so well with Mama since his own Mama isn't around anymore. And if you can't have your own about you, mine is about as good as second best gets, I imagine. His aunt Lena, Adelaide's sister, helped take care of Lawrence and Charlie for a while, but her husband moved their family back to Alabama a few years after Adelaide passed. Charlie had some cousins around him those first three years – and a woman who loved him probably about as much as his own mama would have. Daddy said that Lena tried to get Lawrence and Charlie to go with them, but Lawrence wouldn't leave the home he and Adelaide had lived in together. I reckon it felt like the only part of her he had left, except for Charlie.

In between shearin' season and the fall harvest every year, Lawrence takes Charlie to see Lena and the others down in Alabama. I don't think Charlie would mind me mentionin' Anita. She's this real pretty girl that he spends time with when he's down there. I met her once when she came through for a visit on their way to see family in Arizona. He says he likes her the same way I like Hannah. If that's true, I wouldn't be surprised if that's who Charlie ends up with for the long haul. She'd be lucky to have him too. And from what I know of her, he'd be just as lucky.

I like to see Charlie feelin' comfortable enough to joke some, the way he does with Mama. He was real shy growin' up. I'm not sure if it's because he didn't have a Mama at home or if it's because he got treated so bad by a lot of these folks around here and just decided it was better to keep to himself. Either way, it's good to see he's different now. He's got about two inches on me and is about as strong as two bulls put together. There isn't a man in all of Arkansas that could take Charlie if it was just the two of them; but the thing about Charlie is, he's kind hearted. He's big and strong alright, but he takes after his Daddy. They both have a peaceful way about them. You'd think bein' treated the way they have in these parts would make them hateful, but it hasn't.

There's one thing, too, about Lawrence that stands out. I've never heard that man say a single thing that wasn't kind and true. He's quiet like Daddy, but when he does talk, it's because he has somethin' important to say. Charlie listens to his Daddy. You can see how close they are just by bein' in the same room with them for a minute or two. I always wished me and Daddy could be like that, but I suspect that Lawrence and Charlie talk more than me and

Daddy do when it's just the two of them. Daddy is quiet no matter who's around.

Charlie looks up to Lawrence and for good reason. Lawrence makes dang sure to be the right kind of man. I know he'd be decent even if he didn't have Charlie, but I believe he's just a little bit better since he knows he's got his boy watchin' him to learn how to be a man. Mama told Charlie once to just call her Lilly, but Lawrence wouldn't have it. Said it wasn't respectful to call a woman older than you by her first name alone, and said it right in front of Mama too. So Charlie has called her 'Miss Lilly' ever since.

We got to town right around one. The sun was high in the sky and our horses were feelin' the heat at least as much as we were. We tied them up next to the waterin' trough and made our way toward Tom Martin's drug store. Everybody knows that Carver's has the coldest ginger ale, but we weren't about to give that man a single cent. So we went to Martin's and decided ahead of time to enjoy the ginger ale we got, no matter what its condition. Lucky for us, it wasn't too bad. It would have been nice if it had the beads of sweat runnin' down the bottle on account of it bein' so cold, like it does at Carvers, but at least it had a little chill to it. On our way out the door, Mr. Martin told us to enjoy our drinks outside the shop on the new oak chairs that he finished makin' just yesterday.

"Let me know how they sit, boys, would ya?" Mr. Martin said.

A lot of shop owners wouldn't have Charlie sittin' on their chairs if he was the last payin' customer on earth. But Tom Martin wasn't like that. He figured one person was just the same as the next, and until a man gave him a reason to do otherwise, Tom would treat him as good as any other fella. Growin' up, I always thought Tom was just an old bachelor, but a few years back there was a rumor goin' around that Tom fell in love with a colored woman and they had a half-breed baby together. Her parents were so angry about the whole thing that they came and took her and the baby back to Virginia with them; don't know if he ever tried to, but I reckon Tom hasn't seen her or his boy since that happened. He lost some longtime customers over it, but he seems to be doin' alright now.

While we were sittin' outside, drinkin' our sodas, I saw two female figures walkin' toward us. I'd hoped it was Hannah, and for a split second, I thought it might be, but then I saw that it was only Jessie. I squinted to see who was with her, and low and behold it was Maryanne! Why in the world was Jessie in town with Maryanne Stephenson?

"Hey Will. Hey Charlie," Jessie said as she got closer.

"Jessie, what are you doin' here?" I asked.

"Me and Maryanne are shoppin' for fabric so we can get a start on our dresses for the fall harvest celebration," she said, just as happy as could be.

"Well how do you like that?" Maryanne pouted. "I don't even get a proper hello, Will?"

"Hello Maryanne," I mumbled under my breath.

"And who is your handsome friend?" she asked, makin' Charlie feel real uncomfortable.

"This is Charlie, Maryanne," I said, feelin' awfully annoyed. "He's grown up with us our whole lives, and you know it."

"Oh, is this that same Charlie?" she said like she was surprised it was him. Then she held her hand out like she was the Queen or somethin' and was expectin' him to kiss it.

Charlie wasn't quite sure what to do, so he held onto the tips of Maryanne's fingers and shook her hand best he could.

"Real nice to see you again," Charlie said politely.

"Well aren't you just the cutest thing?" Maryanne said as she pulled her hand back and held it up to her cheek.

I stepped in between Charlie and Maryanne and motioned for Jessie to come with us.

"We'd best be on our way," I said. "Mama is expectin' us back anytime now. Come on home with us Jessie."

Jessie stomped her foot on the ground and stiffened both arms so they were straight at her sides, just like she used to do when she was little.

"I'm not goin' home with you, Will!" she sassed. "I already told you that me and Maryanne have some shoppin' to do. Mama gave me permission this mornin'."

Maryanne started gigglin' somethin' terrible, which just made everybody even more uncomfortable.

"Now don't you worry yourself about Jessie here," Maryanne said as she put her hand on my shoulder. "I'll make sure she gets home safe and sound."

"There's no need for you to get her home if I'm already here to do it," I said as nice as I could in the moment.

Maryanne threw her head back and laughed like I'd gone and said somethin' funny, which I hadn't.

"Oh Will Wright, you're too much," she said.

Jessie looked at me defiantly. "Maryanne has been invited over for supper tonight," she said, "and her daddy is gonna bring us home in his car when we're done in town."

Maryanne Stephenson – comin' to my house for supper? Well of all the awful things that could happen, this was at the top of the list! And to think her daddy would be drivin' her there in his car. Mr. Stephenson is one of the few men in our town who even has a car of his own and he makes that fact known to as many people as he can. You'll find him in conversation sayin' things like, "I'll be seein' ya'll at church on Sunday. I suppose I'll drive my car and save the horses!" or "Careful not to kick up dirt when you're ridin' by. Cleanin' this little beauty is more work than you'd think." He could drive a sober man to drink with all that talk. If you want to share somethin excitin' with me, I'll be happy to congratulate you once. But then I'll need to move on from there.

"Well it sounds like you've got it all worked out then," I said to Jessie.

"Yes, I do!" she snapped, now standin' there with her arms folded tight.

I knew Jessie was just tryin' to look older than she is in front of Maryanne. I didn't want to embarrass her, so I let it be, but she and I both knew that I'd be talkin' to her later about spendin' time with the likes of Maryanne Stephenson.

"Well then, it looks like we have a dinner date tonight, Will," Maryanne said.

It was all I could do to be polite, but I just couldn't get myself to respond to that, so I tipped my hat instead.

"You girls have fun," I said.

Maryanne and Jessie strolled off arm in arm toward the fabric store.

"What was that look you gave me?" Charlie asked as we started back to get our horses.

"What look?" I said.

"When Jessie mentioned bein' brought home by Mr. Stephenson, you gave me a look," Charlie said.

"If you want to know what Roger Stephenson is like," I said, "just imagine an older, male version of Maryanne."

Charlie shook his head back and forth and started to laugh.

"I'm afraid it's as bad as what you're picturin' in your mind," I said.

"It's too bad I can't make it for supper tonight," Charlie said as he untied his mare and climbed up on her back.

"Why not?" I asked.

"I'm sure I'll come up with somethin' by the time we get back to the house," he said.

It was quiet for a minute, and then we both broke out laughin'.

I knew he was kiddin', but I wouldn't blame him even for a second if he held true to that and got out as quick as he could!

We were still workin' in the yard when Roger Stephenson drove up in his fancy car with Maryanne and Jessie in tow. We'd spent all afternoon helpin' Lawrence get that plow right and then went to help Daddy dig out the big rocks in Mama's garden. She'd managed the small ones on her own, but there was a handful of them that were too big for her.

Mama came out on the porch with her apron on and a kitchen towel over her shoulder. She stood there ready to welcome our dinner guests. Daddy looked up at Mama and grinned.

"Sure smells good," he said.

"Ben, would you go find Lawrence and let him know it's just about time for supper?" Mama asked.

"As you wish, dear," Daddy said.

"I saw him go into the barn about ten minutes ago," I said.

Daddy nodded and left in the direction of the barn.

"Why don't you boys put down the shovels for today and go get washed up for supper," said Mama.

"I don't think I'll be stayin', Miss Lilly," said Charlie.

"Nonsense, Charlie. I already spoke to your pa, and he accepted the invitation for both of you."

I tried to hold in my laughter as Charlie punched me in the arm.

Just then Jessie came runnin' up to the house.

"Mama! Look at the fabric I got for my dress! Isn't it just the most beautiful thing you've ever seen?" she said.

"Oh Jessie, it really is!" Mama answered, tryin' to match Jessie's excitement.

Mama was good at that, even if she really wasn't all that interested in whatever it was we were fired up about. It always made us feel like we were the most important thing to her.

"It looks awfully expensive honey," Mama said as she took a closer look at the material.

"Now don't you think about that for another second," Maryanne said, strollin' up behind Jessie. "I just put all the fabric on my ticket."

"Oh...," said Mama. That was such a thoughtful thing to do, Maryanne, but I'm afraid I'm just not comfortable with it. I'm certain this fabric costs more than the allowance we gave Jessie for her dress."

Mama had barely finished her sentence when Mr. Stephenson, who had come up to where we were, piped up. "Ladies, ladies," he said. "What's all the fuss?"

Mama was caught in between tryin' to be polite, tryin' to be welcomin', and finishin' the discussion that had been takin' place about the fabric Jessie let Maryanne buy for her.

"Good afternoon, Mr. Stephenson," Mama said. "We were just talkin' about—"

"Oh I know you're all flustered about the fabric. I told Maryanne you would be. But don't you worry your pretty little head about it," he said without even really lookin' at Mama in the face. "Besides that, the allowance Jessie was given wouldn't cover the fabric she wanted."

I could see the look of frustration on Mama's face turn to irritation. I knew if Daddy had been close enough to hear the way that man was talkin' to Mama, the pleasant dinner party she had planned might turn unpleasant in a hurry.

"Mr. Stephenson," Mama said as she took a deep breath, "I appreciate your intention, I really do, but Jessie's pa and I would like to pay for her fabric."

"Don't be silly!" he said.

"I insist," Mama said sternly.

"Well it's already been taken care of, so I won't hear another word about it," he said in such a way that you'd think he was under the impression he was doin' Mama a favor!

Mama put both hands on her hips and, with fierce determination on her face, said, "Mr. Stephenson, the final word is that I'll be paying for the fabric!"

Mr. Stephenson threw both hands up in the air and started laughin', the same way Maryanne does right after creatin' an awkward situation and makin' everyone feel uncomfortable.

"No need to get yourself worked up, Mrs. Wright!"

Mama smoothed her apron and put a smile on her face. If you didn't know Mama very well, you might think she was just fine. For those of us who do know Mama well, we knew otherwise.

"I'm glad we understand each other," she said cordially. "Now, why don't we head on in the house and get ready for supper."

"Oh good!" Maryanne said. "I'm just famished!"

Maryanne is so dramatic all the time. She makes everything seem like a bigger deal than it really is. I feel tired at just the thought of bein' around her! Well, to be truthful, bein' around her is downright exhausting! I'd rather dig out rocks all night than have supper with her.

"Is it alright to leave my car parked where it is?" Mr. Stephenson asked Mama.

"I don't see why not," Mama said.

Everyone headed inside, and Mama asked Jessie to go fetch Daddy from the barn.

"I can't imagine what is taking him so long," she said.

She never cared before about how long it takes him to come inside for supper. She knows how Daddy feels about leavin' things undone, and so there's no fuss when he doesn't come right away. I'm guessin' she wasn't interested in bein' alone with Mr.

Stephenson, and the sooner supper started, the sooner It'd be over too!

Maryanne and her daddy came inside and Mama showed them to the main room.

"Have a seat and relax while I finish up in the kitchen," Mama said. Charlie and Will can keep you company until supper is ready.

I gritted my teeth, and me and Charlie dragged ourselves over to the sofa that sat across from where Mr. Stephenson and Maryanne were sittin'.

"Well, this is the sweetest little house I do believe I've ever seen, Lillian," said Maryanne.

That girl sure has some nerve, callin' Mama by her first name when she barely knows her better than a stranger on the street!

"Thank you, Maryanne," Mama called from the kitchen. "It's been a good home for us."

Mama always leaves a bowl of soapy water and a towel outside the door for Daddy to clean up with before comin' inside for supper. I could hear him and Lawrence outside usin' it and could hardly wait for them to get inside.

"Do you not have a parlor?" Maryanne asked, battin' her eyes at nothin'.

"Never understood what use there was for a parlor?" Daddy said as he and Lawrence came in the front door, bringin' with them the smell of a hard day's work.

"I suppose we haven't needed one so far," Mama said, kinda scowlin' at Daddy like she was tellin' him to mind his manners. "The main room seems to work just fine for us."

"Of course it does," Maryanne said, holdin' her gloved hand up to her nose as Lawrence walked past. I suppose Maryanne isn't accustomed to the scent of sweat mixed with pig fertilizer.

Jessie had come in a few minutes earlier and sat on the chair next to Maryanne. Daddy sat next to Charlie on the other end of the couch, and Lawrence made his way to the rocker that has become his favorite place to sit. Whenever Lawrence is with us, we all avoid that chair since we know he'll be fixin' to sit there at some point in the evenin'.

"How's the sheep business working out for you, Ben?" asked Mr. Stephenson as he sat back and undid the buttons on his suit.

"It works about as well as a man could hope," Daddy said.

"Glad to hear it," said Mr. Stephenson.

"What do you do for work?" Lawrence asked Mr. Stephenson.

"I'm a banker," he said. "It's complicated work, really. I wouldn't want to bore you with the details you wouldn't understand."

If Roger Stephenson spent more than ten seconds talkin' to Lawrence, he'd realize what a great mind he has. Lawrence didn't have the chance to go to school when he was a young'un, seein' as how he came from a family of slaves. So when he got older, he decided to spend some time learnin'. He asked Mama to teach him how to read, which she did.

I remember bein' eleven or twelve and watchin' them sit at the kitchen table together after supper while Mama had Lawrence read to her. They started out with real easy books at first until Lawrence got the hang of it. I imagine he felt silly readin' those kids books, but he never showed it. I guess he just knew that to get to the harder stuff, he had to start with the easy stuff. Sometimes they would work so late that Lawrence and Charlie would just sleep on the sofas in the main room instead of makin' the trip home, only to have to turn right around in the mornin' and come back. Me and Jessie always liked when that happened because we knew that, that meant we would be havin' Mama's cinnamon cake and sausage for breakfast. It was Charlie's favorite, and Mama liked to make it for him every chance she got.

Mr. Stephenson looked at Lawrence and then over at Charlie.

"And you feed your help after a hard day's work too? Well, that's what I call a decent employer!" he said.

Daddy twitched at that, and he got that look on his face he gets when he's tryin' to keep from sayin' somethin' unfriendly.

"This is my friend, Lawrence Dixon, and his boy, Charlie," Daddy said, already soundin' annoyed, and he'd only been in the room less than five minutes.

"Oh, I see," said Mr. Stephenson. "Well good for you!"

"Supper's ready!" Mama called with a hint of nervousness in her voice. "Everybody come on in to the table here, and let's get started."

Jessie took Maryanne by the hand, and they giggled about somethin' as they made their way over to the table.

"I believe I'll sit next to Will," Maryanne announced. "It will be just like when we were in school together."

Jessie looked hurt.

"That'll be just fine, won't it, son," Mama said without waitin' for my reply. It was more of a statement than a question.

I sighed and moved around to the other side of the table where Maryanne was sittin'. I pulled my chair out and sat as close to the side edge of it away from Maryanne as I could without fallin' off onto the floor.

"Well," said Mr. Stephenson, "if it tastes as good as it smells, we're in for a real treat!"

"That's kind of you," Mama said. "I hope you'll enjoy it."

"Will you say grace for us, Lawrence?" Daddy asked.

Lawrence nodded and held his hands out on either side of him. We always take the hands of the people sittin' next to us when we offer a blessin' on the food. That's Grandma Wright's doin'. She wouldn't eat if the food hadn't been blessed and if the blessin' hadn't been offered while holdin' hands around the table. I suppose there was no need to do things any different with company, so we kept to our ways and invited Maryanne and her daddy to join us.

Mr. Stephenson was sittin' in between Mama and Charlie, and I could see he was reluctant to take Charlie's hand, but as soon as he realized that everyone else was holdin' hands already and Lawrence was waitin' on him, he smiled and grabbed onto Charlie's hand like there'd been no hesitatin' at all.

I don't know if anyone else saw him wipe his hand on his napkin after grace was said, but I did, and it took every bit of control I had in me not to kick him under the table.

"So, Maryanne," Mama said, "Jessie tells me that you have a trip coming up."

"Oh it's just a little thing mother and I like to do together each year," she said.

"And where will you go?" Mama asked.

"We'll take the train to Boston to see mother's family, and from there we'll go on to New York like we always do."

"Do you have family in New York as well?"

"If you count Macy's department store as family!" Mr. Stephenson chimed in.

"Oh Pa, Really!" Maryanne replied, tryin' to sound put out.

"Every time they go to New York, I end up with a new set of expensive china!" laughed Mr. Stephenson. "I've got more plates and cups than I know what to do with!"

We all chuckled out of sheer politeness, but that was all.

"I'm sorry your wife wasn't able to come tonight," Mama said to Mr. Stephenson. "It would have been nice to have her with us."

"Oh, you know Lucy," he responded—like we'd been best of friends with her for years—" it's bridge night, and I don't think I could drag her away from her card group if I tied her to the back of my car!"

Charlie glanced over at me, and we both looked hard at our plates, tryin' not to grin. We had bet each other that there wouldn't be twenty minutes go by without there bein' some mention of that car. Accordin' to Grandpa Doyle's floor clock that stood by the fireplace, it had only been sixteen.

I looked over at Jessie, but she was poutin' somethin' awful. I think her feelin's had been hurt by Maryanne. I was glad she was startin' to see that Maryanne was just spendin' time with her as a means of gettin' close to me. That was no kind of friendship, and the sooner Jessie realized it, the better.

Mr. Stephenson finished chewin' his food and then looked over at Lawrence.

"So, Mr. Dixon... Lawrence is it? Where's the little lady tonight?" he asked.

The room got real quiet. Mama and Daddy looked at each other, and Jessie took a quick drink of water to help her with the piece of pork chop she started chokin' on when Mr. Stephenson asked that question. Lawrence wiped his mouth with his napkin and swallowed the bite of food he'd just taken.

"If you mean my wife, Mr. Stephenson, well, she passed on a while back," Lawrence said softly.

"Oh, I'm terribly sorry to hear that," said Mr. Stephenson. "What was it that took her? Pneumonia? Influenza?"

We all know how Lawrence feels about discussin' Adelaide. He's a fiercely private man, and there are some things that just aren't ever talked about, especially over pork chops and mashed potatoes. Charlie had said that he asked his daddy lots of questions about his Mama when he was younger, but Lawrence wouldn't ever discuss it. Finally, when Charlie was about fifteen or so, Lawrence sat him down and told him he could ask whatever he wanted about her. When they were done talkin', Lawrence told Charlie that it would be the last time they would mention her. If Charlie ever wants to know somethin' he didn't get the answer to before, he asks Mama. Mama said that Adelaide was the love of

Lawrence's life, and there are some pains that go too deep to talk about.

Lawrence looked at Mr. Stephenson square in the eyes. "All due respect, sir, I prefer we don't discuss it," he said.

I'm convinced the only reason he even said that much was because he was a guest at Mama's table and has too much respect for her to ignore the man all together.

"Well I meant no offense," Mr. Stephenson offered lamely. "I was just tryin' to make conversation."

Lawrence didn't respond.

"Make sure to save some room for dessert!" Mama said cheerfully. "I've got a nice berry pie for us tonight!"

"Sounds good, Miss Lilly," Charlie said, tryin' to help the situation some.

"You make your own pies too, Lillian?" Maryanne asked.

Daddy stopped chewin' his food when Maryanne called Mama by her first name. He didn't look up, but his jaw clenched a minute before he took to chewin' again.

"I do make my own pies," Mama responded. "In fact, Jessie helped me with this one this morning."

"Well isn't that wonderful?" Maryanne said.

"Where do you get your pies?" Charlie asked.

Maryanne giggled and shook her finger at Charlie like he was five years old or somethin'.

"I don't bake them myself, if that's what you're implyin'!" she said.

"Well who bakes them?" said Charlie in all seriousness.

Maryanne looked around at everybody like what Charlie said was a joke. Then she realized that he was serious, and she flustered a bit.

"Well, the help, of course," she said. Nobody said anything; just kept on eatin'.

"My hands are very delicate," she continued. "I don't work outside like you all do, so my hands haven't toughened up the same way yours have. Baking would just destroy my skin! I don't have the luxury of calluses to protect it, I'm afraid."

I saw Jessie open up her hand and hold it in her lap so she could get a good look at it. Then she frowned and folded her arms.

"Some women just weren't made for that type of thing," Mr. Stephenson added.

"No, I suppose not," said Mama politely.

I knew that gettin' anything else out of Daddy or Lawrence for the rest of the night was gonna take a miracle. Daddy lost respect for Mr. Stephenson as soon as he referred to Lawrence as 'the help'. I reckon it was Mr. Stephenson automatically thinkin' that Lawrence couldn't have been anything but that, and that it didn't even occur to him that Lawrence and Charlie were dinner guests, same as he was. At this point, Daddy was only doin' his duty for Mama's sake, and she knew it as much as I did. Lawrence would never be impolite, but he saw pretty early on that Roger Stephenson had no interest in genuine conversation with him. It was clear how he saw Lawrence, and there was just no point in spendin' the evenin' tryin' to make him see otherwise.

I was surprised that Daddy lasted as long as he did. He made it through the rest of supper – and even through dessert – before callin' an end to the evenin'.

"I thank you for bringin' Jessie home safe and sound today," Daddy said.

"Well, you're very welcome," said Mr. Stephenson. "And Lillian, thank you for the fine supper."

"It was lovely to have you," Mama said kindly.

"We'll have to see about makin' this a more frequent occurrence," Maryanne said as she wrapped her arm inside Jessie's. "Next time, everyone will have to come to our house for drinks in the parlor and a light lunch."

Nobody said anything at first, and I could see that Mama was tryin' to figure a way to get out of it without seemin' rude or ungrateful for the invitation. Only problem was, Mama had a hard time tellin' untruths. That's why she couldn't just make up excuses same as other people could, and why she'd spoil it if me and Jessie ever wanted to try and play a prank on Daddy and ask her not to tell. So Mama just smiled, and Daddy stepped in at this point—

"Want me to unhitch your mule, or can you manage?"

Mr. Stephenson roared with laughter and slapped Daddy on the back on his way out. It wasn't like Daddy to joke, but I suppose a man does things different than he normally would in desperate times.

"If that was your way of asking to take my car for a drive, then I'll have to hand it to you, Ben!"

Daddy shook Mr. Stephenson's hand and smiled best he could.

"It wasn't," he said, holdin' the front door open.

If Roger Stephenson was able to read other people just the tiniest bit, he'd know he was bein' kicked out... in the most polite way possible, mind you, but kicked out all the same. And that last mention of his car made seven for the whole night, not includin' the first one he made when he asked Mama where he should park.

"Would you be a sweetheart and help me on with my shawl?" Maryanne asked coyly.

She didn't give me much choice in sayin' yes or no. She was standin' less than a foot in front of me with her back to me, holdin' her shawl up in the air over her shoulders and waitin' for me to grab onto it and put in on her back. If she could manage that, you'd think she could pull her hands forward a bit and let the dang thing fall into place.

I want to say that I think I tried to take the shawl and help her on with it, but my hands wouldn't do what my brain was tellin' them to. I just stood there, lookin' at the back of her head. I shouldn't admit that I imagined, for just a tiny second, wrappin' that shawl around Maryanne's stuck-up neck and givin' it a quick squeeze, puttin' us all out of our misery. Mama came up behind me and pinched me awful hard in the ribs, which made me jump some, but I guess it gave me the motivation I needed to take hold of Maryanne's shawl and put it over her shoulders.

After they were gone, we all went inside and sat in the main room. Everyone looked exhausted, especially Mama.

"May I be excused to bed?" Jessie asked.

Mama looked at the clock.

"It's only seven thirty, honey. Are you OK?" Mama said.

"I just don't feel well," said Jessie. "I think I just need a good night's rest."

"Well alright," Mama said. "Leave the lamp burning, and I'll come check on you in a while."

"You don't have to, Mama. I'm just gonna go to sleep."

"If you're sure," Mama said.

"I'm sure," said Jessie. "Goodnight, Lawrence. Goodnight, Charlie."

Jessie gave Mama and Daddy a kiss and headed off to bed.

"I wonder what's ailing her," Mama said.

"She's upset with Maryanne," I said.

"She was beaming when she came home from their shopping trip today," said Mama. "What's happened between now and then?"

"Will happened," said Charlie.

Mama looked over at me.

"What Charlie means is that Maryanne fancies me and is pretendin' to be Jessie's friend so she can spend time around me," I said.

"Well that's just awful!" Mama whispered so that Jessie wouldn't hear we were talkin' about her.

"Jessie needs to break free of that in a hurry," Lawrence said as he positioned the sofa cushion behind his back.

"I have to agree," Daddy said.

"There's only trouble to be found with a person who doesn't feel at all swayed from usin' other folk for her own gain," said Lawrence.

"Maybe I should go check on Jessie," Mama said, sittin' forward in her chair.

I stood up and put my hand on Mama's shoulder. "It might be better if I go," I said.

Mama nodded and sat back. Daddy reached around the side of the chair where he was sittin' and grabbed his guitar. That's always been the best endin' to a long day. Sometimes, if everyone isn't too beat and can muster up some energy, we sing along while Daddy plays. He knows all our favorites. But most of the time, he just plays and we all take to relaxin' in our own ways. Mama usually has some kinda sewin' on-goin', or she brushes Jessie's hair; Lawrence reads, I write in my journal, and Charlie sits by the back door and uses his blade to carve animal figures.

He started doin' that when he was real young, and Lawrence could see pretty quick that his son had a steady hand and an artistic eye. He's carved all kinds of things, but he mostly sticks to animals. Lawrence talked Charlie into tryin' to sell them once, but they both knew that nobody in this town would buy somethin' made by Charlie. So they talked to Tom Martin, who agreed to put them on his shelves, and I swear he sells at least three every month. The original agreement was that Tom would take a portion of whatever sold, but he's never held to that. He just sells them and gives Charlie the money.

Every month, Charlie tries to give Mr. Martin what they agreed on, but Mr. Martin just says that he can't rightly take any money from Charlie when Charlie is the one doin' him the favor by bringin' business into his shop. He says the shelf was empty anyhow before Charlie started sellin' his figures there, so there's no inconvenience. Boy, if the people buyin' those figures knew they come from Charlie, they'd be mad as hornets. It's about as backward as it could be. I'm not sure how Charlie feels on the subject. I reckon he's glad to sell his work, but only for the extra money it brings in to help Lawrence. I imagine there just can't be any satisfaction in knowin' he has to sell it the way he does. And if he didn't think Lawrence needed the money, I'm certain he wouldn't do it anymore.

As Daddy continued to play, I walked back to Jessie's room and knocked on her door.

"I'm alright, Mama," Jessie called.

"It's me," I said. "Are you decent?"

"Yes," said Jessie. "You can come in if you want to."

I went in and sat down at the foot of Jessie's bed. Her eyes were red and puffy, and it made me sad when she tried to pretend like she hadn't been cryin' somethin' terrible.

"Jess, I'm sorry," I said.

As hard as she tried, she couldn't keep it in. I didn't know what to do for her. We weren't really the huggin' kind, not with each other anyway. I suppose she could have used a hug, but I don't think it would have done the good it needed to, comin' from me.

"I'm not mad at you, Will," Jessie said.

"You're not?"

"No. I guess I just feel so stupid!" she said as she wiped her eyes.

"About what?" I asked. "You didn't do anything wrong."

"I thought it was weird at first when Maryanne asked me at church on Sunday if I wanted to go shoppin' with her this week. But she's older than me, and she's really pretty, and I just thought..."

Jessie started cryin' again and buried her face in her hands.

"You thought she wanted to be friends with you," I said.

"I really did," she said between sobs. She told me that she'd always wanted to be my friend and that it would fun to see where I lived. She said she just couldn't believe we'd known each other all these years and never spent time together. Then she told me that she liked my dress. I thought she meant it."

"That doesn't make you stupid," Jessie. "That makes her mean," I said.

I sat and waited for Jessie to calm down a bit.

"And besides," I continued, "she doesn't deserve to be your friend. She may be pretty and have lots of money, but you're ten times the girl she is," Jess. "You would never treat someone the way she treated you. Maryanne Stephenson would be lucky to be your friend, not the other way around."

Jessie wiped her eyes again and took a deep breath.

"Well, even if it's not true," she said, "thanks for sayin' it."

"It is true," I said.

Jessie tried not to smile.

"Now, do you really want to go to bed at seven thirty?" I teased. "It's still light outside, sis."

"Let me get myself together, and I'll be out in a minute. Does it look like I've been cryin'?" she asked.

I figure some lies aren't sins. There are times when it's better to spare someone's feelin's than tell them the awful truth. This was one of those times.

"Nope," I lied. "You look just fine."

I walked back into the main room and joined the others. Daddy kept on with his playin'. A few minutes later, Jessie came out and sat in front of Mama, who put down her sewin' and started braidin' Jessie's hair.

"Change your mind?" Mama said to Jessie.

"I can't seem to fall asleep quite yet," she said.

Lawrence went outside to get the horses ready to go. After a while, Daddy put his guitar back behind the chair and sat with his eyes closed for a few minutes. Mama sighed.

"I guess I should clean up the kitchen before turning in," she said.

"I'll help you, Mama," said Jessie.

"Will, if you and Charlie help, it will go that much faster," Mama said as she winked at us both.

Daddy went to help Lawrence, and we had just finished cleanin' up by the time they were ready to go home.

For as awful a night as it started out, I suppose it ended just fine. I couldn't wait to climb into bed, lay my head down, and think about Hannah. I already knew I loved her, but spendin' the evenin' around Maryanne just made me more certain than ever. So I guess if there was any good to come of havin' supper with the Stephensons, it was that. I'm sure Maryanne would be disappointed to know that she had helped in such a way, and the ornery part of me wanted to tell her. But Mama always says we have to fight against the ugly we all got within ourselves so that the good parts have more room to grow. And anyhow, Maryanne will know about me and Hannah soon enough. I reckon she'll have some hurt feelin's over the whole thing, but I'll try real hard not to lose any sleep over it.

August 26, 1905

This is the fourth time this week I've spent the evenin' with Hannah. We've been courtin' now for goin' on three weeks, and I just can't seem to keep myself away for too long. We usually end up sittin' on her porch or takin' long walks. I never get tired of holdin' that girl's hand either. It's been extra hot the past couple weeks, but no matter how sweaty our hands get when we're walkin', neither one of us lets go.

Pastor Brown has been real invitin', and I don't get nervous comin' over anymore like I did in the beginnin', and Mrs. Brown is pleasant but not overbearin'. She's different than Mama though. Mama is real warm, and you feel special when you're around her because she means for you to. It may be that I just don't know Hannah's Mama very well yet, so I'll give it some time and see if she warms up at all. And even if she doesn't, I like her just fine.

September 9, 1905

I learned this evenin' at supper that uncle Albert is comin' for a visit. He'll be here week after next and is plannin' to stay on five or six days this time. Mama told us while we were sittin' around the table, and me and Jessie looked at each other and then down at our plates at the same time. I hate when he comes to visit. It isn't very often, but never again might be one time too many for me. I can't figure how he and Mama came from the same stock. It would break Mama's heart if she knew what kinda man he really is. But she sees the good in other people. It's one of the best things about her, but it also keeps her blind to the truth sometimes. I suppose if you get rid of the bad, you also get rid of the good. And Mama just wouldn't be Mama without lookin' for the good when nobody else cares about findin' it.

Daddy never seemed to care much for him, but he tolerated Uncle Albert's visits since it made Mama so happy to see him. Mama gave up the fancy life she and Albert were used to once she married Daddy. But Uncle Albert hung onto it for all he was worth. Seems he took his portion of the inheritance after Grandpa Doyle passed and put it into the sheep shearin' business.

To be real clear, Albert doesn't shear a single sheep, he's just the money behind the outfit. I'm bettin' the only kind of dirt his hands ever see isn't the kind that comes from workin' hard. I'm not quite sure why he travels with the outfit come shearin' season. They go to Arizona, New Mexico, and Texas in February. Then it's up to Utah, Idaho, and Wyomin' in the summer. Shearin' season only lasts about two to three weeks in each place, and then the men go home the rest of the year.

Albert lives in Alabama, and he always goes back home by way of Arkansas so he can visit us a couple times a year. He used to live just ten miles or so away from us, but then he moved to Alabama after he got Grandpa Doyle's money. That's where he met his business partners and started up the shearin' company. He tried to get Daddy to go into business with him, but Daddy wouldn't have anything to do with it. It had nothin' to do with the money part of things. I reckon he just knew that toleratin' Uncle Albert was about the best he could do, and so signin' up for anything more than that was just a recipe for disaster. Mama didn't press the issue too much. She knows Daddy is happy enough here on our land, raisin' our sheep. And the idea of him bein' gone a few times a year didn't appeal to her either. I have my suspicions that Uncle Albert didn't care one bit about havin' Daddy as a business partner. I think he was lookin' for a way to get Mama's share of Grandpa Doyle's inheritance. If you were to ask Daddy, I'm guessin' he'd say the same.

I think one of the reasons Daddy doesn't like Albert very much is because he spends the first night he's in town at the tavern with Sherriff Coleman. First of all, Daddy doesn't like heavy drinkin', and he likes Sherriff Coleman even less. There was one time a few years back when Uncle Albert came back to our place after his night of drinkin', and he was drunk as a skunk. He made such a ruckus that it woke the whole house. Daddy was furious. Against Mama's pleadin's, he made Uncle Albert sleep it off on the porch. And when mornin' came, Daddy woke him up with a bucket of cold water! Mama didn't speak to Daddy for a good three days after that, but it was the last time Uncle Albert showed up at our house all boozed up. Only heaven knows where he sleeps it off now. Truth is, I don't care. It's just one less night he's with us, and I count that as a blessin'.

Folks around here think Uncle Albert is wonderful. Women are always tellin' Mama how charmin' and handsome he is, and what a shame it is that he moved away. Can't say I feel the same. The day he told Mama he was leavin' was the best day of my life. I grew real weary of havin' him over for supper on Sunday evenin's and tryin' to pretend for Mama's sake that we got on well. Anytime that snake is in our house, I don't let Jessie out of my sight. Me and Jessie are the only ones that know what he did, and so we stick together, at least when he's in town. I just try to tell myself when he's here that it's only a few days. Mama always says that you can do anything for a few days. She tells us that, when we have somethin' challengin' in front of us. Spendin' time around Uncle Albert definitely qualifies.

September 16, 1905

Mama let me out of my afternoon chores today so I could go get Charlie and head down to the swimmin' hole. I worked hard as I could all mornin' so that Mama would feel glad about lettin' me go. I also told her I'd do some extra lessons tomorrow to show my gratefulness. Mama wants me to think about goin' to college, but I keep tellin' her that I don't need college to work the sheep business. Why on earth would I spend all that money and waste all that time to then just come back home and do what I intended to do all along? Daddy needs my help anyhow, and I don't see how I can just leave him to do it all himself.

I appreciate Mama's intention. She says that someday I might consider doin' somethin' else, and she wants me to have the opportunity to do it if I see fit. I tell her that I have all the opportunity I'm gonna need right here, workin' alongside Daddy and Lawrence.

We talked it to death this mornin', and I thought it was done, but it's one of those subjects that keeps findin' its way back onto the table for discussion.

"Isn't there anything else you'd like to do, son?" Mama asked as I was on my way out the door to go get Charlie.

"Like what?" I said.

"I don't know. Something that interests you."

"I'm interested in stayin' put.

"Will, you know I'll be happy with whatever you choose to do as long as it makes you happy." Mama smoothed her apron. "I just want you to think it through and make sure you're making the right decision for yourself."

It was hard for me to understand why she pushed me so hard about this sometimes because she never cared that Daddy was in the sheep business. Why would she care that I wanted to do the same thing?

"Mama, we've talked about this lots of times," I said, "feelin' kinda bothered."

"I know we have," she said.

"I'm not fixin' to change my mind about it either. I like sheepin', I really do. And I want to be close to my family. I'll keep doin' my lessons, seein' as how it's important to you, but I have no interest in college."

"Studying a bit is good for you whether you decide on college or not," she said.

"And so I'll keep on with it, Mama. But I've already decided about college. Besides, how can I ask Hannah to marry me if I'm off at school somewhere?"

Mama didn't say anything. She just sat there real quiet.

"Don't let this upset you so much, Mama," I said.

"I just don't want it to cause you problems down the road," she said.

"What kind of problems would it cause?" I asked. "I have a workin' sheep business right in front of me, and I already know how to run things. You never gave Daddy frustration over goin' to college, did you?"

"That was different," Mama said.

"How?" I asked, tryin' as hard as I could to be patient with the conversation but feelin' the muscles at the base of my neck tense each time it was her turn to say somethin'.

"I agreed to it beforehand," she said. "I knew what I was getting into with your Pa and I chose this life over the one that I had for many reasons. We built this life together, the two of us."

"Ok. So if it's good enough for you and Daddy, why isn't it good enough for me?" I said.

"It isn't just about you, Will," said Mama, soundin' a might agitated.

Then I realized what all the fuss was about. We had been goin' around and around in circles without ever really talkin' about the issue at hand. Mama was worried about Hannah.

"Mama, are you sayin' that this life isn't good enough for Hannah?"

"I guess what I'm saying is that I don't know," she said.

I felt like I had the wind knocked right out of me. It never even crossed my mind that Hannah wouldn't want me on account of my not goin' to college, or that she'd turn me down if marryin' me meant we'd live the life my folks have.

"I reckon it never occurred to me," I said, feelin' discouraged.

"Son, it wouldn't occur to you. You've never known anything else. But Hannah has. She may feel just the way I did when your Pa asked me to marry him and be perfectly happy to live here and do what we do. But she might not. If you were sweet on one of the local girls here, I wouldn't give it a second thought, but Hannah isn't like those girls.

"She's not a snob, Mama."

"That's not at all what I'm saying, Will. It's just that Hannah has had different experiences than those other girls have had. Take Maryanne, for example..."

"Hannah is nothin' like Maryanne!" I snapped, feelin' like I had to come to Hannah's defense.

"No, no. I'm very aware of how different they are, but the truth of it is that they come from similar backgrounds. There are some families who feel it's beneath them to cook and clean for themselves."

"Hannah isn't like that," I said, not really knowin' for sure if she was or wasn't.

"It isn't a criticism, son. I'm simply pointing out the differences. This is a very different life than the one those girls are used to. It's a lot of work and it requires a girl with very strong character."

"I want to believe that Hannah is that kind of girl." I looked up at Mama, hopin' for some reassurance.

"She may very well be, honey. But don't you think you should find out first?" Mama's voice softened just a bit.

"I could be wrong, but I'm fairly certain that Hannah loves me as much as I love her," I said, tryin' to sound confident.

"I'm sure she does. But getting married is about much more than love, Will. It's hard to understand that when you're young and you feel the way you do about each other, but it's not long after you're married that you realize how much more is required. Do you remember when you were nine years old and your Pa gave you the only colt that was born to us that summer?"

"I remember," I said.

"You loved that little horse as much as its own mother did." Mama smiled, rememberin' back to that time. "But as it got bigger, there was some training that had to be done. And when we took that horse away from its mother, he spent all day, every day, whinnying and pacing the fence line. You were frustrated because he fought against you and your pa for quite a while. Do you remember what you told your pa after about the third day?"

I sighed. "I told him that I didn't want the colt anymore. But Mama, you can't compare that to gettin' married," I said.

"The point I'm trying to make is that you were too young and inexperienced to understand what needed to happen and how to do it. You had your pa with you to show you that with some commitment and patience, that horse would come around."

"So what you're sayin' is that Hannah is like a horse?" I said, real exasperated.

Mama started laughin', but I think it was more out of frustration than anything. She put both hands up to her forehead and took a deep breath.

"No, Will," she said. "Are you listening to me, son? What I'm sayin' is that a lot of times, people your age go into marriage with that same feeling you had when your pa gave you the colt. It's new and exciting, and you think it's the greatest thing that could happen. But then you'll have some hard times, and it's better to know that before jumping into it, is all. You need to be sure that the girl you marry is the kind of girl who would stick with that colt through all of the aggravation it causes until it is broken in. Because that is the girl who will be a good wife to you and one that can make it here, doing what we do. I just think that you might want to talk with Hannah about it, when the time is right of course, so that you know where she stands on things.

I stood there in the doorway, lookin' at the ground, and I felt my irritation slowly drain away. What Mama said made sense. I suppose a conversation with Hannah wouldn't do any harm, and it might even be a good idea.

"I hear you, Mama. I really hear you. OK?"

"I'm glad," she said, sighing long and hard.

"Now can I go swimmin' before the sun goes down?"

"Is Jessie going with you?"

"Yep, She rode out with Daddy to the east pasture this mornin'. I'll stop out that way and get her before headin' over to Charlie's."

I jumped off the porch, eager to get to the swimmin' hole..

"You'll be home in time for supper, won't you?"

"Yes, ma'am."

When me and Jessie got to Charlie's house, he came out to meet us by the front gate before we could even climb down off of our horses. He looked different. Charlie was usually pretty happy, but today he seemed real serious.

"You ready to go?" I asked.

"You'll have to get on without me today," said Charilie.

"What do you mean?" I said. "It's the perfect day, and I got out of my afternoon chores so we could go!"

"There's a rally in town, Will."

"A rally? What kind of rally?" I said.

"Deputy Jenkins is gonna let folks talk about some issues that concern the town," said Charlie.

"Issues about what?" asked Jessie.

"Things that have to do with colored folks," said Charlie.

Just then, two boys came out of Charlie's house and over to us.

"Will, Jessie, this is Nathan and Terry."

I leaned down to shake their hands. I'd never seen Terry before, but Nathan looked familiar. Charlie could tell that I recognized him.

"Nathan is my cousin. He used to live here in Arkansas when we were kids, but his daddy moved them to Alabama a long time ago," said Charlie.

"I thought I knew you," I said to Nathan.

"We used to jump off the shed at your place," said Nathan.

"Your mama wanted to tan our hides a few times!"

"That's right!" I said, rememberin'. "Didn't you break your arm or somethin' once?"

"My wrist," he said.

"Terry is a friend of Nathan's," said Charlie. "He's from Alabama too."

"So you fellas are just here visitin'?" I asked.

"They're here to go to the rally with me," Charlie said.

I sat there wonderin' why Charlie never mentioned anything to me about goin' to this rally. I would have gone with him.

"Should we go along with you?" I asked.

"Will, it's alright if you come, but you should check with your daddy first. We're hopin' for some peaceful resolutions today, but things could get ugly, I'm afraid. And the truth of it is, you might not want to come with us."

"Why on earth not?"

"You know as well as I do that the townspeople won't take kindly to you takin' the wrong side on things."

I sat there feelin' more than offended. Since when did I ever give two hoots about what them townspeople thought about me?

"I want you there," said Charlie. "Ain't nobody I ever want with me more than you, Will, but I just don't want to put you in harm's way. And you got Jessie with you."

I believed him. Charlie was the kind to think about other people before himself. I think he learned that from Lawrence. And he'd seen me do my time in a cell on account of sidin' with him before. So I put my bein' offended aside and tried to come up with the best way to handle things.

"You said it's a town discussion, right?" I asked.

"It's supposed to be," said Charlie.

"Then me and Jessie will go on ahead of you. I'd like to hear what's bein' discussed," I said.

"You sure about this?" Charlie asked.

"I'm sure. I won't even say anything. I'm just goin' to listen. I'm a part of this town too, ya know?"

Charlie laughed. "You? Just gonna listen?" he said.

"It's possible," I said, soundin' a bit defensive. "I'll set my mind to it ahead of time so I don't get roped in."

"If you say so," said Charlie.

On the way over to the meetin', I was real quiet. Jessie was goin' on about somethin', but I just nodded and acted like I was listenin'. All I could think about was this rally. I was fairly certain that our town wasn't ready for a meetin' like this one. There are some good folks in this town, mind you, but the truth is that there are lots who are ignorant... and mean and nasty because of it. Most of the people here have been livin' here all their lives. They like things the way they've always been and aren't fixin' to do much changin', especially when it involves northern ideas of colored and white folks bein' equal. We have some folks that won't change until the law tells them they have to, and the rest won't even change then.

I told Daddy once that I felt we were born in the wrong part of the country since our ideas didn't seem to go along with the ideas of our own townspeople. He said that if all the people with common sense ended up in one place, we wouldn't be able to do much good where it was truly needed. He said there has to be balance. I suppose he's right, but I find myself growin' awful tired of a fight that I just can't seem to understand.

I felt my stomach turn a bit when thinkin' about how bad this could go. I like to think the best of people and hope that all the Christian teachin' we get every Sunday will help us in doin' right by each other, but some folks won't do the right thing until they've had a good, honest, come-to-Jesus experience.

By the time we got to the town meetin' house, Deputy Jenkins had already started the discussion.

Lloyd Jenkins came to our town about a year ago from somewhere up North—Pennsylvania, I think. He's done a real fine job in his position, and I can't imagine anyone harder to work for than Sheriff Coleman. The townspeople seem to like him, and he's friendly enough without gettin' in your business.

It's hard to know where Deputy Jenkins stands on some things because he sorta keeps to himself, but I've never had the sense that he and Sheriff Coleman are anything alike. He seems like a decent fella and one that does right by the town he serves. The only problem I can see him havin' is because of his ideas about coloreds and whites. They're real different from the ideas of most of the folks down here in the South. I don't believe Sheriff Coleman had much say in Deputy Jenkins bein' assigned here either. I'm not sure how all that happened, but I get the impression that Jenkins is here to address the complaints by the colored folks. Heaven knows that if it was left up to Sheriff Coleman to do it, nothin' would get done.

Charlie, Nathan, and Terry came in shortly after us and sat on the colored side of the room. It struck me funny that there was a colored side, a white side, and then a group up in the balcony that didn't take one side or the other. The neutral group was there to just watch, but not participate. Now, can you tell me how, in all that's good and right, was there to be a discussion that would accomplish anything when the people involved were divided by color and already set up for a competition?

It surprised me that Deputy Jenkins arranged it that way, and I told Jessie that I had thought different of him. Then, Mrs. Jones, who was sittin' next to Jessie and obviously listenin' to our conversation, said that Deputy Jenkins had nothin' to do with it; it was all Sheriff Coleman. She said that Jenkins had it worked out so that you could sit wherever you wanted and that there were no sides, just like any other town meetin'. We don't show up to our normal town meetings with the sheep ranchers on one side of the room and the dairy farmers on the other, or the Christians on one side and the Jews on the other. But apparently, about half an hour before the meetin' was to start, Sheriff Coleman told Deputy

Jenkins that he had to separate the groups. He said it was for the safety of the townspeople in case things got fired up.

The ridiculous thing about it is that Sheriff Coleman was the match that lit the fire before a single issue was even brought up, on account of how he set up the room. Mrs. Jones, oblivious to the fact that I could smell what she had for lunch as she forcefully whispered to me and Jessie, said that she got here real early and was sittin' up top, watchin' the whole thing. She said that Deputy Jenkins pointed out to the Sheriff that dividin' the groups based on color was creatin' an atmosphere of contention. Sheriff Coleman wouldn't hear it. I reckon Deputy Jenkins had no choice but to oblige since he works for the Sheriff and all.

Sheriff Coleman sat in the front of the room, leanin' back in his chair with his arms crossed over his chest, seemin' indifferent to the sweat stains under his armpits that were growin' bigger every time I looked over at him. The windows were open, but the chance of a cool breeze blowin' through seemed about as likely as the peaceful resolution Charlie was hopin' for. Both the men and the women were fannin' themselves with whatever they could get their hands on.

The issue that was bein' discussed was the very one that got me a week in jail back in March after helpin' Eli Carver to see the error of his ways. And wouldn't you know that Mr. Carver was sittin' on the front row of the white side? I could have come in with my eyes closed and told you that that's exactly where you'd find him. One thing I've learned in my eighteen years is that cowards and bounders rarely surprise you. They're about as predictable as a fox in a hen house. I would say that Eli Carver fits the description.

After a brief greetin' to open the rally, and a reminder of why we were here, Deputy Jenkins said, "It would be most beneficial for us to hear from the store owners on the issue. Tom Martin, have you got anything to say about this?"

"Deputy, everyone here knows that I've got no problems havin' coloreds and whites alike in my store," said Tom.

"And Indians too!" Called an angry soundin' voice from the back of the white side.

Tom turned and looked behind to see that it was Charles Harris who had said that.

"That's right, Charles," Tom responded defiantly. "And Indians too. It don't matter one lick to me one way or the other, and I don't mind sayin' so, neither."

"Mr. Harris," said Deputy Jenkins, "do you have a counter argument that you'd like to share?"

"Darn right I do!" said Charles.

"The floor is yours," Deputy Jenkins said.

"The way we have things is working just fine!" Charles yelled. "We shop at our stores, and they shop at theirs."

Mr. Harris actually pointed his old bony finger over at the colored side and shook it like he was givin' them a good scoldin'... for what, I don't know.

"Well, sir, to be fair," said Deputy Jenkins, "the reason it's an issue on the table is because the current system is not benefitting everyone as you might think. There have been some legitimate complaints."

"From who?" roared Charles. "Raise your hand if you've got problems with the way we've been doin' things, and let me get a good look at you!"

"Mr. Harris, with all due respect, I'm conducting this meeting, and we'd like to keep things calm," said Deputy Jenkins. "There's no reason to get so excited."

"No reason?" Charles yelled.

"I won't warn you again," Deputy Jenkins said, takin' a step forward and standin' up just a might taller. "If you need to take a minute to step outside, then do so. Otherwise, settle on down and let's get on with things."

Mr. Harris sat down hard in his chair. He looked like a bully who'd been told what for. He was angry alright, but he shut his mouth.

The Deputy turned his attention to the colored side of the room. There was only one store owner in the bunch—if you could call him that. James Bailey runs an old run-down shack of a store. He started runnin' that store a good while back to serve the colored folks since most of the white store owners were makin' it difficult for the colored folks to get what they needed. I remember Lawrence sayin' that whenever he went to get supplies, they always seemed to be out of what he was askin' for. Then there were other stores that just plain wouldn't serve him. Most coloreds work the cotton farms around here, but there are a few men who have a little schoolin' and do other things besides farmin'. Mr. James Bailey is one of those men, and it seemed only fair that he be asked to comment on this issue as well.

"James Bailey, what are your thoughts?" asked Deputy Jenkins.

"Well," he said, "I've tried for almost ten years now to provide folks with the supplies they need, but I haven't been able to get some of the things you all get in your stores. I can't afford to. We don't have lots of colored folks in these parts, and so it's hard to keep my store open year after year when hardly anybody shops in it."

"Do you only serve coloreds?" asked Deputy Jenkins.

"I reckon I'd serve whoever needed somethin' from me," said Mr. Bailey. "But the white folks have no reason to come into my store. They've got their own stores with better supplies."

"Is there anything that you sell, Mr. Bailey, that is hard to find in any of the other stores?" Deputy Jenkins said.

"Hard to find in the white stores, you mean?" said Mr. Bailey.

"Yes, sir. Unfortunately that's what I mean."

Sheriff Coleman didn't like that at all. He sat up in his chair and shot a look at Deputy Jenkins, who wouldn't make eye contact with him. I guess it was the Deputy's way of makin' his opinion known without bein' too aggressive about it.

"Well, it's been said that I have the best honey in all of Arkansas," said Mr. Bailey real sure of himself.

"That's good. That's very good," said Deputy Jenkins, noddin' his head like he'd just solved the problem. "Now who in this room uses honey?"

Almost every hand went up, some much slower than others.

"I'm proposing that James Bailey become our town's honey distributor," said Deputy Jenkins. "There's no reason why he can't sell directly to individual stores. This way he can make the profit he needs, and all the stores will be supplied with the honey they need."

The room erupted with talkin' from every direction while Deputy Jenkins tried to shush the crowd. He turned around to Sheriff Coleman for support, but the Sheriff just sat there like the bump on a log that he is. Charles Harris stood up, shakin' his fist at Deputy Jenkins, then turned his attention to the Sheriff.

"Are you going to stand for this, Hank?" Mr. Harris asked with outrage in his voice.

Sheriff Coleman stood up real slow and calm-like.

"This is why everyone has been invited to this meetin', Charles," said the Sheriff. You all get your say, and then we'll make some decisions. So if you've got an opinion, make sure you let it be heard."

It felt like Sheriff Coleman was stokin' the fire. I could see the irritation on Deputy Jenkins's face. This meetin' wasn't just to let folks show up and complain about matters, it was to try and work together to make some things better around here... for everybody.

"Mr. Harris, why are you opposed to buying honey from Mr. Bailey?" asked Deputy Jenkins.

"I'm not buyin' honey from no baboon! And I'll be the first to take all my business elsewhere if the store owners here in town see fit to sell that honey!" barked Harris. "Don't think for one second that I'm alone in this either!"

Several people on the white side of the room started clappin' and cheerin' while others just nodded their heads in agreement. I felt sick. Even the decent men like Tom Martin and Rex Smith didn't say a word after that. It was real clear that they'd be run right out of business if they tried to go head to head against the likes of Charles Harris.

I looked around the room and found Charlie. His shoulders were slumped over, his head hung down, and his face registered a look of defeat. It was obvious that our town just wasn't ready for such change. I respected Deputy Jenkins for tryin', but I was hopin' that he would shut the meetin' down before things got out of hand.

Deputy Jenkins put his head down and shook it back and forth, knowin' that he hadn't accomplished anything. He glanced disgustedly at Sheriff Coleman, but it was so sly that you had to be watchin' to have seen it, which I was. We need more folks like Lloyd Jenkins so he doesn't have to try and make things right by himself. We need more people who will be better than they have been willin' to be in the past. It seems to me that we have two kinds of people in this town: the kind who are filled with hate and the kind who are filled with fear. I'm not sure which is worse.

September 17, 1905

If I hadn't heard the discussion led by Deputy Jenkins yesterday with my own ears, then I might not be inclined to believe that the news I got today about Charles Harris passin' away in the night was a sign from heaven above—like Mr. Harris was bein' punished for his evil heart. I might be persuaded to think that it was just his time, if it wasn't for the fact that he went belly up not twenty-four hours after stirrin' the pot and gettin' everyone all excited.

Charles Harris was the worst of them in that town meetin'. He displayed both ignorance and hatred before it was all over. That ornery old cuss was one of the main reasons that nothin' got accomplished. I'm not convinced it would have turned out much better without him, but he sure didn't help things any.

Charles Harris was the kind of man who spent his whole life makin' others feel small. He wouldn't think twice about gettin' what he needed from you and then movin' right on to the next sucker. He had no morals when it came to cheatin' and stealin,' either—and didn't care who he hurt in the process. He was mean, nasty, and awful... God rest his soul.

I was watchin' Daddy this mornin' over breakfast to see what his reaction to the news would be. Daddy has spent so much energy makin' sure that Mr. Harris didn't weasel one more inch of Grandpa's land than he already had, that I'm not sure what he'll do with all that energy now that the old buzzard is dead. I reckon he'll have to fight it out now with John Harris, who is sure to inherit his Daddy's pecan orchards. We don't know much about John Harris, but if he's anything like his Daddy, he's not worth knowin'.

Even though John and Kathryn Harris have lived on that property with old man Charles for several years now, it's like they're ghosts. They only have one child, Jacob. Nobody is sure why they didn't have more children. Maybe all they wanted was a son to carry on the family name, and once they got one, there was no need to have any more. That's all speculation, of course, seein' as how I know nothin' about them people, except that they come from the likes of Charles Harris. Can't rightly think of a less desirable family tree to be a branch on.

"So what did they have to say about Charles Harris's passin'?" I asked Daddy, who was finishin' up his biscuits and coffee.

"Said his heart gave out on him in his sleep," he mumbled with a full mouth.

"Did he suffer much?"

"I reckon not," replied Daddy.

I'll be the first to admit that I'm not a perfect man, and my disappointment when Daddy said that is proof of it.

"That's good," I said, tryin' to sound convincing.

"What do you suppose will happen to his land and such?" I asked.

"Oh, I'm sure John will manage things from here on out," he said casually.

"I understand what you're sayin', Mama, but it's hard to feel it."

"I know. It takes practice."

"It just seems to me that a man like Charles Harris doesn't really deserve kindness."

"We don't always know the reasons why people behave the way they do. Maybe some people are hateful because they've never been shown any other way to be, and it's possible that if someone is kind to them, it gives them a chance to see and feel something other than the ugliness they've grown accustomed to."

"That's pretty hopeful, Mama. You give people like Charles Harris and his kind more credit than I'm comfortable givin'," I said.

"Whether or not a person chooses to accept the gift of love and make a change is not the ultimate reason we do it," she said. "We do it so that our own hearts are pure. It's selfish in a way, I guess. It's as much for us as it is for them."

I put my elbows up on the table and rested my head in my hands. It's hard to argue with Mama. It's hard because everything she does is purposeful. I'm sure she had to work on it at some point, but now it's just who she is.

"What do you think about the whole thing, Daddy?" I asked.

"I don't have to," he said as he winked at her. "Your Mama does it for me."

"Oh, Benjamin!" Mama scolded.

"I mean that in the best way possible," he said. "I know your Mama is always gonna try to do right. So when I don't feel much like sortin' through somethin' on my own, I look to her."

"Don't let him fool you, Will," said Mama. "You know your Pa better than that. He couldn't sooner do something that he didn't feel in his whole heart and soul was right than he could milk a bull."

I shuddered at the image of that in my mind. Mama went over to Daddy, still sittin' at the table drinkin' coffee, and slid her hands down the front of his shoulders and crisscrossed them across his chest. Then she kissed his cheek and rested her face against his a minute. Daddy put his hand over the top of Mama's and leaned into her. Then she went on back about the business of makin' those scones, while Daddy drank what was left in his cup and then headed out to the pasture before it was time for church.

Me and Jessie always give Mama and Daddy a hard time about bein' lovey-dovey in front of us, but the truth is, I wouldn't have it any other way; makes me real happy for both of them that they found each other.

Later that mornin', all four of us made our way over to the Harris place to deliver Mama's scones. She made me and Daddy put on our best Sunday shirts, and I couldn't, for the life of me, figure how me wearin' a white dress shirt made any difference at all when it comes to givin' someone food. I've accepted the fact that we dress up to go to church. Mama says it's a sign of respect to God. And while I personally don't believe that God cares one lick about the clothes I've got on, it's an easy enough thing to do to make Mama happy. But I wasn't so interested in how I came across to the Harris family. If I'd had my way, I would have worn my old blue shirt with the torn pocket and the stains on the collar.

"Jessie, stop fussing with your dress," said Mama as we walked up the long driveway to their house.

"But it's all twisted in back."

"Will, help your sister tie her bow in back," said Mama.

"Since when do I know how to tie the bow on a dress?" I asked Mama, laughin' at the fact that she asked me to do it.

"Oh for heaven's sake," she said as she handed me the plate of scones and tied Jessie's bow for her. "It's just like tying anything else."

Daddy looked at me and shrugged, like he was sayin' that he wouldn't know how to tie that bow any better than I could.

"Do you suppose they're even acceptin' visitors?" Jessie asked.

"I don't know," said Mama, "but we won't stay. We'll just drop off the food and offer our condolences."

We stood in front of the door, waitin' for someone to answer it. I couldn't believe the size of the house. It was a good three times bigger than ours. I guess that's what a life of swindelin' and stealin' gets you—a big house and food for your loved ones, made by people who, in all honesty, aren't too disappointed to see you go.

A couple of minutes later, Jacob Harris came to the door. He looked as surprised to see us standin' on the other side of it as I felt when Mama said we were goin' over.

"Hello, Jacob," said Mama pleasantly.

"Hello, Mrs. Wright," he said, tryin' hard not to look in Jessie's direction, but failin' miserably.

"We don't mean to intrude. We just wanted to—"

John Harris, now standin' behind his son, opened the door further.

"Good morning," he said cheerfully as he stepped out to greet us. "Come in, come in, won't you?"

"Oh no," said Mama politely. "We simply wanted to bring some scones and express our sorrow for your loss. We won't keep you."

"Oh, I wish you would," he said. "It's a gloomy place around here this morning. Nice to see some friendly faces! It will give us a chance to get to know each other better. We are neighbors, after all!"

None of us knew quite what to do. John Harris had taken us by such surprise. I can't speak for anyone else, but I was imaginin' him to be the spittin' image of his Daddy, Charles. But from the minute and a half we'd spent with him so far, I wouldn't have guessed for anything in the world that those two were related. I could see that Daddy was just as shocked as I was. While he isn't a man of many words, Daddy has fine social skills. He's cordial and polite, but it was almost like he didn't know how to behave with Mr. Harris. Mama even nudged him at one point to get him to say somethin' so that she wasn't the only one talkin'.

"Well I suppose we can come in for a few minutes," said Mama as she looked at Daddy, hopin' he'd contribute to the exchange with Mr. Harris.

"Sure we can," Daddy said. "That's mighty nice of you, Mr. Harris."

"Oh, not at all – and it's John. Benjamin, isn't it?"

"It's only Benjamin when my wife is sore or wants my attention. Otherwise, I go by Ben."

"My wife calls me Jonathan for the same reasons, so say no more," said Mr. Harris as he chuckled and shook Daddy's hand.

"Jacob, take the Wrights into the parlor, would you please, son? I'll go and fetch your Mama so she can join us," Mr. Harris said.

We sat in the parlor, awkwardly smilin' at Jacob while he did the same right back to us until his folks finally came in.

"Mr. and Mrs. Wright, how nice of you to stop by this morning," said Mrs. Harris as Daddy stood up and then waited for her to sit before he did. "And these must be your children?"

"Yes. This is Will and Jessie," said Mama. "I'm Lily, and this is my husband, Ben. It's so nice to finally meet you. I'm sorry it's under these sad circumstances."

"Well, you're very kind to say so," said Mr. Harris.

"How are you all doing?" Mama asked. "I'm sorry... that's a terrible question at a time like this."

"We're really doing just fine," said Mrs. Harris, smilin' politely.

"It was peaceful, we hope," said Daddy.

"We assume so," she said, lookin' over at her husband.

"We weren't with him when he went," said Mr. Harris. "It wasn't until very early this morning that I found him. I couldn't sleep very well last night and was up before the sun. I figured I might as well go for a walk; enjoy the fall air. When I passed by Daddy's room, I noticed a lamp burning, so I figured he was already up. The doctor said he probably had been gone for quite some time when I found him."

"My goodness," said Mama. "Had he been sick?"

"No, no. Nothing like that," said Mrs. Harris. "It looks like he suffered a heart attack."

"I see," Mama said kindly. "Well we're just so sorry for you."

I sat there waitin' for some kind of sadness to make its way into the conversation, but there just wasn't any. All the right words were there, but none of the emotion you'd expect to go with it. John, Kathryn, and Jacob all seemed perfectly happy. Charles Harris hadn't been dead for eight hours, and yet there wasn't a single tear shed between all three of them. I suppose it wasn't just the fact that nobody was cryin'—I mean, some folks just keep composed better than others—it was that the air wasn't heavy, and their eyes didn't have that glassed over look like you see on most people when they're grievin'. I don't claim to know the Harris family very well, but I would have bet my right leg that they weren't sad at all about Charles passin'.

We sat there a few minutes longer, makin' pleasant conversation. But I was surprised when Daddy jumped in and started askin' questions.

"John, he said, I reckon you plan to take over for your Daddy... with respect to his business and such."

Mama's cheeks colored slightly at Daddy's statement, and she said, "Honey, I don't really think this is the right time for that discussion."

"That's alright," Mr. Harris said. "It's as good a time as any; not much we can do about funeral preparations until the pastor gets here anyhow.

"Pardon my bein' insensitive," said Daddy. "That wasn't my intention."

"Nonsense, Ben. It's a fair question. You know, Kathryn and I haven't had much time to discuss it, as you could imagine, but I'm fairly certain we'll stay on here and manage the property. Haven't yet come up with a reason not to."

"It's nice that you have that option," said Mama. "Your father has a fine orchard here."

Mr. and Mrs. Harris looked at each other. Everyone in the room knew the history with Charles Harris and Grandpa Wright, but it didn't seem proper to mention it, not now anyway.

"Ben, I'd like to apologize to you," said Mr. Harris.

"Apologize?" said Daddy. "I'm not sure I understand."

"I can't tell you how surprised I was to see you standing on my front porch this morning," Mr. Harris said. "Your family hasn't been dealt with properly by my father, and for you to come here with all that ugly history, to offer your sympathies to us... well that's just about as good as it gets in my opinion."

Daddy was noticeably stunned. It took him a good minute or two to get his mouth and his brain to cooperate with one another so he could respond to Mr. Harris.

"In all fairness," said Daddy, "the conflict was between my daddy and your daddy. I, myself, ain't had much contact with the man since my daddy passed."

"That may be true, but I'm betting you've been looking over your shoulder ever since to protect what was rightfully his," he said.

"You'll have to pardon me for sayin' so, but that's exactly what I've been doin'," Daddy said.

"Ben, I know who my father was," said Mr. Harris. "He was mean and selfish and dishonest. There may have been some good things about him, but I don't know what they were. I've watched him cheat and use people for years, but I didn't feel like I could do anything about it. I knew that, as awful a thing as it is to say, I wouldn't be able to try to undo what he'd done until he was gone."

Mr. Harris's face seemed to flush a bit—with embarrassment I expect—as he said this. Then he continued. "My mother asked me long ago, not to interfere. She knew as well as I did that to challenge my father would have been the thing to tear our family apart. I hope you understand that I didn't step in, because I had to protect my family."

"I... I really don't know what to say," said Daddy. "I had no idea."

"There were so many times that I wanted to come over to your place and sit down with you," said Mr. Harris. "I guess I just wanted you to know that someday we'd be able to fix things... make them right."

"There's really nothin' to fix at this point," said Daddy. "It's just real nice to know that we won't have to be nervous about you the way we were about your daddy."

"You're a good man, Ben Wright. I'm not sure I would be as forgiving."

"It's not you that needs forgivin'," Daddy said.

"Well, you never would have gotten it from my father. I never heard the man apologize for a single thing in his whole life."

Daddy was silent for a moment, then he said, "While it would have been proper for him to do, I, personally, never needed his apology. We all have to face up to our choices at some point. Some of us are lucky enough to see the error of our ways and get things sorted out with folks while we're still livin'. Those that don't, . . . well, they get to do their sortin' with God himself. I reckon your daddy is doin' that right about now."

"Knowing my father, I can't imagine it's going very smoothly," Mr. Harris said as he sighed.

"Well, thank you all the same," said Daddy. "I think a lot of a man who can say what you said."

"Rest assured." said Mr. Harris. "You'll get your daddy's land back as soon as I can figure the best way to go about doing it."

"That's good of you, John," Daddy said.

"And I'll make sure you see the money he had coming to him."

"There's no need for all that..."

"I won't have it any other way," said Mr. Harris.

"John, I appreciate what you're doin' here. I really do. But as far as I'm concerned, as long as we have honest business dealin's from this point on, that's all I need. We're not lookin' to dig up old dirt. Let's just let it lie and start fresh."

"How would you handle things, if the tables were turned?"

"I'm not quite sure," said Daddy.

"Could you do what you're asking me to do and feel good about it?"

Daddy thought long and hard. The struggle he was havin' with the question was all over his face. Havin' long discussions like this wasn't Daddy's strong suit. He likes to make a decision and have it be done. But Mr. Harris was makin' that difficult to do. He felt strongly about doin' right by Daddy and wasn't takin' "no" for an answer.

"I suppose I would want to go about it the same way you're doin'," said Daddy.

"Please understand," said Mr. Harris. "I can't feel good about running this place unless I feel honest."

"I do understand that," Daddy said in a way that let us all know it finally clicked for him.

"Thank you," Mr. Harris said. "Now, if you'll be kind enough to just give me some time to think things through, I'll get them worked out."

"That's more than fair," said Daddy.

We left the Harris place feelin' mighty different than we did on our way there. Daddy had a look on his face I didn't recognize. The burden he'd been carryin' for so long was gone. There's nothin' that Daddy respects more than a decent man, and it was clear to see that John Harris was just that.

Daddy took hold of Mama's hand as we walked home. His step was lighter than I ever remember it bein'. The air was cool, the sun was shinin', and wasn't nothin' else to do but smile.

September 18, 1905

I stood in front of the judge, right next to Charlie. I was tryin' as best as I knew how to explain to him that Charlie and I were like brothers, but he just kept bangin' his mallet on the table in front of him, or whatever you call that thing, and sayin' that we couldn't be friends anymore. Then one man took me by the shoulders, and another man took Charlie by the shoulders, and they pulled us apart until we couldn't see each other anymore. And all the while, that judge just kept poundin' that mallet!—over and over again until I thought my ears would explode!

I sat straight up in bed and found myself covered in sweat. Then I heard Mama . . . and realized I'd been dreamin'.

"Who's knockin' on the door this early?" I heard Mama ask Daddy from their bedroom.

"I can't imagine," Daddy said.

"Ben, it's plenty light outside," said Mama with surprise in her voice.

"What in the world...?" said Daddy. "Maybe it's Lawrence. He's probably been here a good hour, waitin' on me."

We usually get up with the rooster, but we stayed up real late last night, sittin' around visitin' and playin' games with Hannah and her folks; so it seems that every last one of us slept right through Big Red's crowin' this mornin'.

I could hear Daddy puttin' on his trousers and hurryin' to the door, his joints poppin' and crackin' as he went. As soon as he opened it, I recognized the voice on the other side . . . and I cringed when I heard it.

"Well aren't you going to let me in, brother?" There stood Uncle Albert, grinin', big as life.

Caught by surprise, Daddy stammered, "We...uh...weren't expectin' you for another week."

"Oh I know," he said, "but we wrapped up early, so there was no sense in my killing time for another week, just waiting to come here. You don't mind, do you?"

That was a loaded question. Daddy didn't like havin' Uncle Albert there to begin with, but havin' him show up a week early was even more disagreeable. I stood in the doorway of my room, watchin'.

"Of course we don't mind," said Mama, cinchin' up her robe as she made her way into the front room.

"Glad to see you, Lily!" bellowed Uncle Albert, huggin' Mama with one hand and pattin' Daddy on the shoulder with the other. "It's a good thing you're here, or I'm not sure this old bear would let me in the house!"

He was pokin' fun at Daddy, but the truth is, if Mama wasn't home, Uncle Albert would be lucky to make it past the front steps.

"Come on and sit down here at the table," said Mama. "Are you hungry?"

"Am I ever!"

"Well let me get my clothes on, and I'll get started on some breakfast."

Mama went to get dressed, and I saw Jessie peek out her door to see what all the commotion was about. As soon as she saw that it was Uncle Albert, she shot me a look of disappointment from across the hall and went back in her room. I decided to get dressed myself and head out to say hello. I'd have to do it sooner or later, and I figured I might as well get it over with now.

"Now Ben," said Uncle Albert, "I've never known you or my sister to sleep past five o'clock,"

"We had company last evenin', and the time got away from us," said Daddy.

"Well that's what I like to hear... you and Lily havin' a good time. You're not hung over are ya?" He laughed, knowin' that the only alcohol that ever touches Daddy's lips is the wine at Christmas, and that's only a sip, just to be social.

Daddy didn't even respond. If you didn't know any better, you'd think Uncle Albert was just makin' conversation, but he's not. He throws jabs at Daddy like he's got nothin' better to do, and he does it knowin' that Daddy cares more about Mama's feelin's than he does his own. So Daddy puts up with it for her sake. Mama doesn't even seem to notice, which is strange for her on account of her bein' so aware of others all the time. She tends to have a blind spot when it comes to her only brother. And it's not all her fault if we're bein' fair. Uncle Albert plays it real careful around her and then saves his worst for when she's in the other room or outside. It makes me stir inside. I think I hate that more than anything else; bein' a coward, that is. I believe I'd have more respect for a man who was a bully all the time, than a man who only bullied when he knew his target wouldn't fight back. But then again, I think of

Charles Harris, and I realize that's probably not true. I couldn't muster up an ounce of anything that even feels like respect for him. So I'll just leave it alone at sayin' that neither one of them deserves my respect, and if you got them in a ring together, I'd have a devil of a time knowin' who to cheer for.

I took a deep breath and made my way out to the kitchen, makin' sure to stand directly behind Daddy's chair so that Uncle Albert wouldn't even have the option of tryin' to hug me.

"Well, if it isn't my favorite nephew," boomed Uncle Albert.

"I'm your only nephew," I said, hopin' it didn't sound as irritable as I was feelin'.

"That's what keeps me from feeling bad about saying it," Uncle Albert said as he laughed at his own little joke. "Sit down, boy. Don't be afraid to talk with the men."

I sat down next to Daddy and found a spot on Uncle Albert's forehead that I could look at while we were talkin' so that I wouldn't have to look at him in the eyes. There was somethin' about his eyes that made me real nervous inside. They were just these two black marbles that had no life about them. It's almost like you'd forget there was even a livin', breathin' person behind them.

"You didn't happen to see Lawrence on your way in, did you," asked Daddy?

"Can't say that I did," answered Uncle Albert.

"That's strange," mumbled Daddy.

"Maybe he had company last night too," Uncle Albert joked.

"He's probably just runnin' behind," said Mama as she tied on her apron and got out the big fryin' pan.

"That man hasn't been late for work in all the years he's worked with me," said Daddy.

"Could already be out in the pasture," I said.

"I reckon so," agreed Daddy.

"So, I assume there is a girl," said Uncle Albert, turnin' his attention to me.

His question caught me a little off guard, but I thought it best to just answer him direct.

"There is."

"Are you going to tell me her name or do I have to guess?"

"Her name is Hannah."

"Hannah... Who is her Pa?"

"You wouldn't know them. They just moved here not too long ago. Her Daddy is the new pastor."

"Oh, a pastor's daughter," he said in a way that made me uncomfortable. "Well they're the worst ones!"

"You've got the wrong idea about Han—"

"Come on, Will! I'm just giving you a hard time. That's my job as your uncle. I'm sure she's a very nice girl."

Uncle Albert had a way of makin' even the most regular conversations awkward. I don't know why he can't just ask and answer questions like regular folks.

"Who's a nice girl?" said Mama as she made her way back into the kitchen.

"Will was just telling me about Hannah," said Uncle Albert.

"Oh she's just lovely," said Mama.

Not a full second later we heard a faint yell from outside, along with the sound of hoofbeats from a horse gallopin' like lightnin'. Mama went over to the kitchen window that overlooks the front yard and looked out for a minute, tryin' to make out who was comin'; then she threw both hands up to her mouth, and a look of somethin' awful covered her whole face.

"It's Charlie!" she yelled. "So something is wrong!"

Me and Daddy jumped up from the table and ran outside to see what was goin' on. When we got to the edge of our property that meets the dirt road, we saw Charlie ridin' like hell toward us. As he got closer, I could see that his face was bleedin' and he was holdin' his left side. Daddy ran up to meet him and help slow his horse.

"What is it Charlie? What's happened?" Daddy asked as the horse came to a halt.

"It's Daddy," said Charlie, out of breath. "He's hurt real bad."

"What happened?" I asked.

Charlie struggled to compose himself and, with some effort, was finally able to blurt out the story. "Five men rode by while we were doin' our mornin' chores," he said, "and without warnin', they jumped us and beat us both somethin' awful. Daddy got the worst of it. He wasn't in no shape to ride, so I did my best to make him comfortable and told him I'd come find you and get some help."

"Who was it?" Daddy asked. "Who did this?"

"I can't say." Charlie winced with pain. "It was still nearly dark, and they had their faces all covered up."

"Where's Lawrence now?" Daddy asked Charlie.

"He's at home, Mr. Wright."

"Did you leave him alone?"

"Didn't know what else to do." His voice started to crack.

"Of course, son," said Daddy. "I'm sorry, Charlie. I'm just concerned is all."

"I am too, sir," Charlie said.

"You're not fit to ride, either," said Daddy. "Let's get you inside and have Lily fix you up. Will and I will go get your daddy and bring him back here."

Mama and Jessie were already on their way out to see what needed to be done. I gave Mama the fast version of what happened. Then Daddy and I helped Charlie down from his horse, which was still breathin' hard. Mama got on one side of Charlie and Jessie on the other so they could do his walkin' for him. I was surprised that Uncle Albert hadn't come out to help. Then my surprise turned to disgust when I saw him just standin' there on the porch, watchin' Mama and Jessie struggle to get Charlie inside.

"Will you be alright?" I asked Mama.

"We're fine," Mama said. "Hurry now and go get Lawrence."

"Lily," said Daddy, "send Jessie for the doctor."

"You want her to go by herself?"

"Jessie," Daddy asked, "can you do this? Can you go alone and fetch Doc Wilson?"

"I can, Daddy," she said. "I'll ride as fast as I know how." Daddy knew that Lawrence wouldn't be able to ride, so he hitched up the buggy and we headed out. I was real proud of Jessie. I knew she was scared, but was willin' all the same. And from the way Charlie looked, I imagined Lawrence was in terrible shape. It would be best if we could have the doc there when we got back home.

As we got close to the Dixon's house, we could see much of the harm that had been done. Those devils didn't just hurt Lawrence and Charlie, they did some pretty serious damage to their property too. It looked like someone took a pickaxe to the garden; almost everything had been uprooted and was lyin' wiltin' in the hot sun. And there were several windows that had been smashed out in the front of the house. On seein' all that damage fueled by such mindless hatred, I was suddenly afraid of what we would find inside the house.

We both jumped out of the buggy as soon as we were stopped and ran inside to find Lawrence. He was lyin' on the floor, just inside the front door. I felt my stomach flip when I saw him. His face was beat pretty bad, and both eyes were swollen shut. I couldn't tell if he was still alive.

Then I heard his faint voice. "Who's there?" Lawrence choked out.

"Don't worry, old friend," Daddy said. "It's Ben and Will."

"Oh, praise heaven," said Lawrence, whose hands were tremblin' somethin' terrible.

"Is Charlie alright? He was scared to leave me behind in case... in case they came back. But I knew he'd make it to you."

"Lily is seein' to him now, and Jessie went to fetch Doc Wilson."

"I can't see a thing," Lawrence said.

Your eyes are real swollen," said Daddy calmly. "You just hang on, now. We're gonna figure the best way to get you out of here."

"I can't ride," said Lawrence. "Pretty sure my arm is broken."

I glanced down at his arm. It didn't look right; looked like it was goin' the wrong direction. I looked at Daddy, and he nodded to let me know he'd seen it too.

"You won't need to ride. We brought the buggy," said Daddy. "If we can get you in, can you sit?"

"I believe so." Lawrence winced with pain as he spoke.

"I thought about havin' the doc come out here, but I ain't sure it's safe," Daddy said.

"I reckon you decided right," said Lawrence.

"Now, Will and I are gonna lift you up and carry you to the buggy. I'm guessin' it's gonna hurt like crazy."

"I spect," Lawrence said.

"I can't think of another way," said Daddy.

"Then we'll do like you said," agreed Lawrence.

We had Lawrence cross his good arm over his chest, and then we tied the broken one down in place with a bed sheet so it wouldn't move. Even that made him yelp. The whole time we were helpin' Lawrence, I had an uneasy feelin' and kept glancin' outside, worried that those men might come back. They weren't men who fought fair, and I knew we'd be in trouble if we were forced to go up against them. I just wanted to get home as quick as we could.

Just as we were gettin' Lawrence settled in the buggy, we saw dust up the road, and I felt a sudden shiver run through my whole body. But as the dust settled and the sound of hoof beats got closer, we could see that it was Pastor Brown.

"I just heard what happened," he said, bringin' his horse to a halt about a foot shy of the buggy."

"How in the world did you find out so fast?" I asked him.

"I passed Jessie and Doc Wilson on their way to your place about fifteen minutes ago and rode as hard as I could to get here."

Daddy looked relieved. I wasn't sure if it was because Pastor Brown was there to help or because he knew that Jessie made it safe. I'm guessin' it was both.

"What can I do?" asked Pastor Brown.

"Ride alongside us," said Daddy. "We won't be able to go very fast on account of Lawrence's injuries."

While Daddy was talkin' to the pastor, I saw that car of Roger Stephenson's headin' in our direction. He stopped when he came upon us, to see what all the excitement was about. Maryanne was in the car with him, and would you believe that, that girl was flirtin' with me at a time like this?

"Now what in the world are you boys doin' out here?" said Maryanne teasin'ly, her voice just drippin' honey. "I've been hopin' I'd run into you, Will. Heaven knows I've been thinkin' about you since our dinner date last month."

Daddy looked at me with irritation on his face. I imagine mine looked about the same as his.

"This isn't a good time for socializin', Maryanne," I said shortly.

"Will Wright, are you tryin' to hurt my feelin's?" she pouted.

Mr. Stephenson chimed in, "it wouldn't kill you to be polite."

I looked at Daddy and then up at Pastor Brown to see if they were as shocked as I was at the fact that both Maryanne and her daddy were actually tryin' to make small talk without even noticin' that Lawrence's badly bruised face was bleedin' and his eyes were swollen shut! I mean, they didn't look at the man once, or they would have felt like complete fools. And there was Roger Stephenson lecturin' me on bein' polite when he hadn't even noticed that the man sittin' three inches away from me had been beaten within an inch of his life!

"Mr. Stephenson," I said as respectfully as I could in the moment, "Mr. Dixon here has been hurt awful bad, and we're needin' to get him some help. So if it's all the same to you, we'll exchange pleasantries another time."

"Oh my!" gasped Maryanne as she finally looked at Lawrence.

"What's happened here?" asked Mr. Stephenson, suddenly soundin' concerned.

"Some men from town came early this morning and attacked Mr. Dixon and his boy," said Pastor Brown.

"Well this looks like business for the sheriff," Mr. Stephenson replied in a rather blustery and self-important manner.

"Ain't no need for the sheriff right now," said Daddy. "We got it managed."

"Roger," said pastor Brown, "it would sure be helpful if you go on ahead and make sure the doctor made it safe to the Wright place."

"Oh... I don't think I should get involved in this." He squirmed uncomfortably in his seat and looked down at his steerin' wheel.

"It's just that your car will go much faster than the buggy, and–"

"I...uh... I'm afraid we've got somewhere to be," Mr. Stephenson stammered. "Otherwise, we'd be more than happy to help."

Pastor Brown looked stunned. It took him a good ten seconds or so to respond, and by then, Daddy had lost the last bit of what little patience he had left. He slapped the reins across the horse's back, and we started out for home, leavin' Roger and Maryanne Stephenson sittin' there in their car. Daddy wasn't about to involve himself in a fool's discussion about what on earth could be so important that it trumped gettin' help to an injured man.

"I was mistaken to have asked," Pastor Brown said to Mr. Stephenson. "You'd better go now so you don't miss that engagement."

"It's just terrible timin' is all," said Mr. Stephenson.

"Of course," said Pastor Brown, tippin' his hat and givin' his horse a kick to catch up to us.

I shook my head in disbelief as I watched Maryanne and her daddy drive off.

"I'm sorry about that back there, Lawrence."

"Roger Stephenson ain't my concern," he said.

"I know, but it doesn't make it right."

"No, it doesn't."

The ride home was about as bad as you could imagine. Lawrence was miserable. Each bump in the road made him wince, and me and Daddy knew that he was in bad shape. The sight of our house never looked so welcomin'.

As we neared the house, we could see Charlie and Doc Wilson out on the porch waitin' for us. Even from this distance, the concern on Charlie's face was plain to see. As soon as they saw us, they both ran out to help.

"Daddy, I'm sorry I left you alone," said Charlie, tears formin' in his eyes as soon as he saw Lawrence.

"You did right, son," Lawrence said. "Don't you think about that for one more second, you hear me?"

"Yes sir," Charlie whispered, unable to raise his voice any louder due to his sobbin'.

Between the five of us, includin' Pastor Brown, we finally managed to get Lawrence inside without too much discomfort. Either that, or he's tougher than I imagined, because he hardly made a peep. I noticed right away that Uncle Albert was nowhere in sight. It struck me as strange, but I was glad he wasn't here.

Doc had us put Lawrence on the kitchen table so he could get a good look at what he was dealin' with. Mama had laid some blankets on the table to soften it a bit, and an old bed sheet on top of that to take the worst of the blood. Knowin' Lawrence, I'm guessin' he was mighty uncomfortable with all the attention. He likes to take care of things himself. But I'm sure he knew it had to be this way, and he was probably grateful for the help, never-the-less you can be grateful and still not like somethin' at the same time.

"Lawrence, your face is pretty beat up," said Doc. "Can you see anything at all?"

"No sir."

"Well, I'm going to have to pull your eyelids apart to know if your not seein' is on account of the swelling or if your eyes have been damaged. I apologize ahead of time if you feel some discomfort."

Lawrence nodded. Doc gently pulled at those eyelids, but it was dang-near impossible to get them apart, seein' as how everything around them was swollen too. Lawrence just kept takin' deep breaths while Doc tried over and over again, and I closed my eyes after a bit so I wouldn't have to watch anymore.

"There!" exclaimed Lawrence. "I saw some light... and something red."

Doc looked around and noticed that Mama was standin' right where Lawrence was lookin'. Her apron had a good amount of Charlie's blood on it. But Doc didn't tell Lawrence what it was he was seein', just encouraged him that he was seein' at all. Then he took to doin' the same thing to the other eye. That one was worse because it had two big cuts on it, along with the brusin' and swellin'. Each time Doc would try to get that eye open, the cut on his top eyelid would split a little bit more, and Lawrence would suck air in through his teeth and then let it out real hard and fast. Lawrence took the Doc's pullin' for as long as he could and then told him to stop. Charlie never left Lawrence's side for a second. As awful as it was to watch, Charlie did just that.

"We'll try that eye again in a while," Doc said. "Maybe restin' it some will help with the swellin' enough to do what needs to be done. Right now I need to get your shirt off you so I can get to your arm. Lily, bring me a knife, please. If I try to maneuver this shirt off instead of cuttin' it off, it'll be too much to bear, I'm sure of it."

When Doc Wilson got the shirt off, I had to keep from gaspin'. Mama, however, wasn't able to avoid it, and Charlie just laid his forehead down on Lawrence's good shoulder and cried.

"Ben," said Doc, "I'm gonna need your help with this, and it won't be easy. Have you got any liquor in the house?"

"We don't drink it, I'm afraid."

"Doc turned to me. "Will, there is a bottle in my bag with the word 'Amylocaine' on it. Bring that to me, along with a needle and syringe. I haven't used it but one other time. So I'm fairly certain there should be enough left to help some."

What needs to be done, asked Lawrence?

"Your shoulder is out of its socket, and one of the bones in your arm is broken. I've got to re-break that bone to make it fit how it should. I'll do my best to keep you from feelin' as much of it as possible. I'll give you all the medicine I've got, but even so, I'd be lyin' if I told you that it won't hurt. And aside from the pain, you won't like the way it feels when it breaks. It can be real off-puttin'."

"Alright then," Lawrence said. "Let's get it done."

"Lily," Daddy said, "maybe it'd be best to take Jessie outside."

Mama put her arm around Jessie and started out to the back porch.

"I'm not a baby, Mama," objected Jessie on the way out. "I'll be alright to stay inside."

"Lawrence might not want you to see him like this," said Mama, tryin' to make it sound like Jessie was doin' right by Lawrence to leave him be with Doc and the men. "He'll need us afterward to tend to him. Would you be willing to help me with that?"

"Of course I would," said Jessie.

Doc Wilson gave Lawrence a whole lot of shots all over his arm to numb it as best he could. I felt my stomach churnin' with anxiety as we got ready to hold Lawrence down.

"Son," said Lawrence, sensin' Charlie's nerves, "I know this is real hard to see, but I'm gonna be alright. You just stand close so I know you're there, and Doc will fix me up good as new."

"Yes sir," replied Charlie as he stood up and wiped his eyes with the sleeve of his shirt.

"You trust me now, don't you, son?"

"You know I trust you, Daddy."

"Good. Then you remember what I said. It'll be awful for a few minutes, but then I'm gonna be alright."

Right then Doc spoke up. "I need a strap or a stick."

"Would my belt work?" asked Pastor Brown, who had been standin' over by the front door.

"I believe it will," said Doc. "Put that between his teeth. Yea, that's right. . . Now, Jeremiah, you come and help Will hold his legs down," said Doc.

I had to stop for a second and remember that Pastor Brown's name was Jeremiah. We never called him by his first name, so it took me a minute to put it together, but he quickly came around and took the left leg, and I took the right.

"Put one hand on his thigh and the other just under his knee," Doc said.

"Where do you need me?" asked Daddy.

"Right up here on his good side," said Doc. "You're going to need to put all your weight on his chest and his good shoulder, and no matter how hard he fights, hold him. I'll do it as fast as I can."

We were all doin' as Doc said, but he just stood there starin' at Lawrence with a real serious look on his face.

"What's the matter?" Asked Charlie.

"I don't know which to do first," said Doc. "I want to cause as little pain as possible..."

"Do the arm first," said Lawrence.

"That'll be the worst of the two," Doc said.

"I know. Just get it over with."

"Alright then. Everybody ready?"

We all nodded, and Lawrence took a deep breath.

"Lord, God of Heaven and Earth, be with me now in my time of need... in my hour of affliction," whispered Lawrence, like he was recitin' some prayer I'd never heard before.

"On the count of three, men," said Doc, who was positionin' himself around Lawrence's arm. "One... two... three!"

Lawrence's arm snapped, and it sounded like someone steppin' on an old tree branch. He screamed through his teeth as loud as he was able with the belt in his mouth, and I thought he'd bite a hole right through that thing. His whole body tensed and shook, and I had to use every ounce of strength I had in me to hold his leg down. Charlie stood by Lawrence holdin' his head stable with both hands, just swayin' from side to side, tears streamin' down his cheeks, waitin' for it to be over. Then, without so much as a moment to breathe or even a warnin', Doc looked at Daddy square in the eye and then pushed Lawrence's shoulder right back in its socket where it was supposed to be.

Daddy seemed to know what was about to happen without Doc havin' to say it. But me and Pastor Brown weren't expectin' it and had relaxed our hold on Lawrence's legs by then. Pastor Brown was startled by Lawrence's sudden and violent movement as the shoulder snapped back in place, and he wound up gettin' kicked right in the gut by Lawrence's unrestrained leg. Then Lawrence turned a shade of grey and threw up all over himself. Charlie did what he could to turn his daddy's head some to keep him from chokin' on his own vomit. It seemed cruel of Doc, at first, to put that shoulder in without givin' Lawrence a rest from what had just happened with his arm, but I could see after a minute or so that it was best to just get it done. I can't say if Lawrence saw it that way or not, but he never said any different.

After it was all over, and we had him cleaned up, I just stood back and watched poor Lawrence lyin' there on the table, his eyes still swollen shut, tryin' to recover from the events of that mornin'. Doc was patchin' up some of Lawrence's cuts while he was waitin' for Daddy to get back with the materials he'd sent him out for so he could make a cast for that broken arm. Charlie was sittin' in a chair next to Lawrence's head and talkin' quietly to him about somethin'... I couldn't hear what; don't believe it was intended for me to. It was a moment for the two of them, so I sat over by the fireplace in the other room to give them some privacy.

Mama and Jessie had come back inside and were tendin' to Lawrence and Doc Wilson best they could. As I watched, I felt like I was in a different world... like I was seein' it from somewhere outside myself. The room was still, except for the quiet stirrin's of Lawrence tryin' to get comfortable on that hard kitchen table while Doc patched him up. I felt tears rollin' down my cheeks before I even knew I was gonna cry. It was so hard to get my mind around the kind of meanness that would drive somebody to do what was done to Lawrence and Charlie. They had always dealt with nasty comments or bein' snubbed on account of them bein' colored, but this was a whole new kind of awful. This was men out lookin' for it

– lookin' for an opportunity to be hateful. I don't suppose I'll ever understand that, and the truth of it is, I won't ever try. My biggest struggle is tryin' to keep my own heart from turnin' to hate toward those who make life so difficult for people like Lawrence and Charlie. Mama says we shouldn't hate people; we should hate the things they do. I'm not sure I know how to separate the two, and after witnessin' what I did today, I'm thinkin' it would be better for me to never know who did this to Lawrence and Charlie. I'm mighty certain I'd give up my Christian upbringin' if it meant I could have a solid wood bat and ten minutes alone with one of them. The Lord knows my weaknesses, and so I'm hopin' he doesn't tempt me with such an opportunity. But if He does, may He be merciful on my soul when I fail.

December 23, 1905

It's been three whole months since I even thought about writin'. After what happened to the Dixons, I ended up in a state of somethin' I never experienced before. I spent a fair amount of time tryin' to learn who hurt Charlie and Lawrence, which was strange since I knew from the beginnin' it would be better for me not to know. Lawrence talked to me one evenin' and told me to let it be. I was upset with him for givin' up so easy, but I reckon I can't judge the man about somethin' I just can't relate to. He convinced me that there was no good to come of it. He's probably right, but that makes me feel like we're caged in with nowhere to go and nobody to help do what's right. That's a terrible sad feelin'– and a lonely one too.

The only good thing that has come of it is that I got to see Hannah in a way I never seen her before. She was almost madder than I was, at first, and wanted to bring justice to those men who hurt Lawrence and Charlie, but I'm guessin' it's her respectable raisin' that helped her come around to a place of forgiveness and charity. She was better at seein' what Lawrence needed than I was, too. I suppose part of that is because she's a woman, and they just do better at that sort of thing than men folk. But she could tell that Lawrence was ready to put it behind him and that she needed to help him convince me to do the same.

Lawrence is doin' much better now. He didn't stay down for very long before he was right alongside Daddy in the pasture again. Doc told him to rest that arm a good two weeks before even thinkin' about work, so what does Lawrence do? He shows up to work not three full days later and works one-handed all day long. The swellin' had gone down some in his face, but the man could barely see, and we all knew it. He's as stubborn as they come, and I can't think of another man I respect more... aside from Daddy, that is. He said he couldn't leave Daddy with work enough for two men. And call me crazy, but I dare say he did just about as well with the one hand as any other man could do with two.

Lawrence and Charlie stayed with us for two or three nights, but then they decided to go on home and get back to livin'. I'd like to say they did it with ease, but I imagine they were scared most of the time. The night the Dixons went home, Daddy held a meetin' in our livin' room with several decent men from around here. He invited pastor Brown, Doc Wilson, John Harris, and Tom Martin. They worked out a system where one of them would be on Lawrence's property as soon as the sun went down, and wouldn't leave until it was up again the next mornin'. They did that for a couple months until Deputy Jenkins said he'd keep an eye on the place so those men could get back to sleepin' in their own beds. If it was Sherriff Coleman who had volunteered to look out for Lawrence and Charlie, you can bet Daddy would have never agreed to that. Lloyd Jenkins, however, is a trustworthy fella, and since the rally where he tried to do right by the colored folks in our town, we know he's good people. Better to have the law lookin' out for Charlie and Lawrence anyhow. And it's comfortin' to know that we've got a man like that on our side.

December 25, 1905

I woke up this mornin' to the smell of pure heaven. I always look forward to Christmas time, seein' as how Mama makes Christmas about as wonderful a time as it's possible to have. Our house is decorated from head to toe, and there are sweet smells of breads and cakes that drift through the house for days. My joyful mood might also have to do with the fact that Uncle Albert sent word a few days back that he wouldn't be able to make it this year for Christmas, and so we spent it without him. Mama seemed disappointed, but me and Jessie had to fight to hide our relief. Daddy didn't even try to hide his. But his relief doesn't come from the same place ours does, so he doesn't have to. There is somethin' else that has Daddy worked up about Uncle Albert... somethin' other than the usual nonsense.

It happened a day or two after Lawrence and Charlie went back home—after the incident with Lawrence, that is. Charlie was outside cleanin' up broken glass and tendin' to their property when he came across a gold pocket watch that was sort of buried in the dirt by the front gate. He'd never seen it before, but it looked like a real fine watch... real expensive too. When he opened it up, there was some writin' on the inside, but it had been scratched enough that he couldn't make out what it said. Charlie took it to Lawrence, who, after studyin' that thing for a while, was able to read part of it and knew exactly who it belonged to. He couldn't make out the first two initials, but the first four letters of the last name were D-O-Y-L. The only letter missin' was the E. Now Lawrence didn't want to jump to any conclusions, and so he took the watch to Daddy instead of Mama until they could sort through it. Only reason I know all of this is because Charlie told me what happened.

Daddy told Lawrence that Mama had a watch just like that and that he would go through her cedar chest, where she kept it, to see if it was still there. I remember Mama tellin' me once that Grandpa Doyle gave one to each of his kids when he passed as part of their inheritance. After goin' through Mama's things, Daddy found the watch right where he thought he would. The only explanation, then, was that the watch Charlie found belonged to Uncle Albert. And wasn't it curious that Uncle Albert's watch showed up on Lawrence's property almost exactly at the same time Lawrence and Charlie were attacked?

After thinkin' long and hard about it, Daddy decided to talk with Mama, seein' as how Uncle Albert was still at our house for another week or so. Daddy decided that he and Lawrence would do it together. I'm not proud to admit it, but I stayed real close to the window so I could hear the conversation, even though Daddy had sent me to the pasture to get an idea of our sheerin' potential this year.

It wasn't pleasant, and I almost wish I hadn't heard it. Mama was sure there was some explanation. She wouldn't even consider that Uncle Albert took part in such a horrible thing. Daddy pointed out Uncle Albert's indifference to both Lawrence and Charlie and his unwillingness to help at all after they'd been brought here with their injuries. He practically disappeared the entire time the Dixons stayed with us, Daddy reminded her – not to mention him showin' up at the house just minutes before Charlie came ridin' up to get help. But Mama wouldn't hear it. She insisted they talk to Uncle Albert and let him explain. So they did. He acted real casual about the whole thing. Said he had been drinkin' in town the night before, and the watch must have been stolen without him knowin' it.

"And you didn't notice it missin' when you put on your night clothes the next evenin'?" Daddy asked him.

"I guess I didn't," Uncle Albert said.

"And in the three days after it goin' missin, you never thought to check the time once? Daddy pushed."

"I must not have," said Uncle Albert, just as cool as could be. "I really don't use the thing for telling time so much. It's more for fashion than anything else. I am known for looking charming, after all."

Mama thought that made sense, and I reckon Daddy knew that there was no way around it. It was possible that it happened like Uncle Albert said. But it was possible that it didn't, too. After Mama had gone out to the hen house, Daddy made it real clear to Uncle Albert that if he ever found out that Albert had had a hand in what happened to Lawrence and Charlie, he'd make sure Mama knew, and they'd never have anything to do with him again. Uncle

Albert laughed about it like it was some kind of misunderstandin' and assured Daddy that the watch really had been stolen. So even though things got smoothed over, Mama was the only one who wanted him here. Havin' him in our house kills the Christmas spirit faster than a Blue Tick hound trees a 'coon.

We like our Christmases quiet. There are a lot of folks around here who make a big production out of the whole thing. There are about six parties that go on every year that are considered part of the town's traditions. We pick one or two and make an appearance, but we always leave early because of too much drinkin' goin' on and Daddy feelin' uneasy. I've tried to figure out what it is about drinkin' that Daddy takes such a dislikin' to. I suppose it could have somethin' to do with it gettin' in the way of folks makin' sound choices. Daddy is real level headed, and he doesn't abide nonsense. I'm guessin' that he doesn't see much point to it either.

But even without the drinkin' at those parties, Daddy isn't much for big social events like that. There's a whole lot of talkin' about nothin' important, and that just isn't his way. There was one year that Uncle Albert talked Mama into throwin' a party at our place on Christmas Eve, much to Daddy's protestin'. We spent the whole time havin' awkward conversations with folks we barely knew or didn't like and then had to spend Christmas Day cleanin' up after them. The holiday came and went without us feelin' like we even had it. So even though Uncle Albert, still to this day, talks about what a great Christmas that was, Mama decided before the party was even over that we wouldn't be doin' that again. This year we went to the Smith's and the Thomas's. There's no rhyme or reason to which parties we choose. Mama just keeps track of the ones we went to last year and then chooses different ones. Me and

Jessie like goin' more than Mama and Daddy do, but we're always glad when they're over so we can get on with our family traditions.

Christmas Eve has been my favorite part of the season for as long as I can remember. We start early in the afternoon and finish up when none of us can keep our eyes open any longer. Mama and Jessie get the goodies baked in the mornin'. Then when everything has cooled, they wrap them up real pretty, and we head out in the cold to make our deliveries. The last delivery we make is to the Dixons because they always spend Christmas with us. So we just pick them up on the way back home.

Lawrence isn't much of a cook, if I'm bein' honest, but there is one thing he likes to make at Christmas time on account of it bein' a tradition he and Adelaide had before she passed. Him and Charlie always make the most delicious salt-water taffy you ever sunk your teeth into. Daddy told him years ago that he'd always have a place at our house for Christmas as long as he brought that taffy along with him. We all knew that as fine a taffy as Lawrence makes, it's got nothin' to do with his and Charlie's standin' invitation to celebrate the holidays with us.

Once we get home from makin' our deliveries, our tradition is to get a fire goin' and decorate the tree. Mama gets out her best ornaments, and we string cranberries and popcorn until our fingers are numb. Then while the men finish up with that, Mama and Jessie put our Christmas dinner together. It's a meal they start preparin' two days earlier, and it's about as delicious as the Good Book's forbidden fruit itself... or so I would imagine. Daddy always gets a pig from Roger Smith, and that poor creature ends up on our table covered in brown sugar and butter. Along with the ham, our feast includes sweet potatoes, homemade bread with Mama's apricot preserves, corn cakes, and pecan pie to top it off. Except for Mama, we all eat until our stomachs won't hold another bite. Then after restin' some, we start in on Lawrence's taffy. It's one of the only times of the year that Mama lets us give in to pure gluttony without a comment or even a chastisin' look. That kind of eatin' usually leads to a catnap in the livin' room, and then we eventually end up sittin' by the fire, singin' Christmas songs while Daddy plays his guitar.

About three years ago, Daddy turned the tradition of readin' the story of baby Jesus from the Bible over to Lawrence, and so he does that after we've had our fill of singin'. I was real surprised when Daddy did that, so I asked Mama about it after the Dixons had gone the next day, and she told me that Daddy thought it'd be the right thing to do for two reasons.

First of all, it occurred to Daddy that since Lawrence and Charlie are always with us on Christmas, Lawrence never gets to be the man of the house... never gets to read that story to his son, or carve up the ham, or carry on his traditions the way he might if his wife was still livin' and they had Christmas together as a family. And while Lawrence and Charlie are as much a part of our family as any of the rest of us, Lawrence still respects Daddy as the head of the house and wouldn't do anything that might say he thought otherwise. Daddy also wondered if Lawrence might like the opportunity to read some, since he'd put all that work into learnin' how. That made sense to me. So Lawrence reads us the story every year, and it does my heart good to hear him do it. I mean, I like the Bible story plenty all on its own, but there's somethin' extra nice about Lawrence readin' it to us.

We wrap up our evenin' by exchangin' presents and drinkin' some of Mama's red eye cider. Then we blow out the candles on the tree and go to bed with the intention of sleepin' just as late as we feel. It's a nice idea, anyway, but not one of us can make it past sunrise. Mama is always the first up, makin' a Christmas breakfast with everybody's favorites, includin' that cinnamon cake that Charlie loves so much. It just doesn't get any better than Christmas at our place. I can't wait for it every year, and I'm always sad to see it go. This year was especially nice because, after the past few months, we all sort of needed the things that Christmas brings... like peace and joy and such.

Mama understands me better than just about anyone, and she invited the Browns over for supper tonight without me even knowin' about it until last evenin'. She knew I wanted to spend Christmas with Hannah, but it didn't seem proper since we aren't engaged. So I'll soak up every last minute of today and hold off bein' sad until tomorrow, because I know that tomorrow I won't have any choice on the matter.

December 29, 1905

I laid in bed, lookin' out the window at the fresh snow on the ground, thinkin' about my life and my plans for me and Hannah. If I had a way to give her a good life right now, I would march right over to her house and ask her daddy for her hand. But Mama and Daddy encouraged me not to be too hasty. Last night before bed, I asked Mama what it was like for her and Daddy when she was my age.

"Didn't you want to be with Daddy every second?" I asked her. "It's like I got a herd of butterflies in my stomach all the time."

"I could be mistaken," chuckled Mama, "but I don't believe butterflies come in herds."

"That's not the point, Mama," I said frustrated. "You know what I mean."

"I do," she said while she and Daddy tried to put on straight faces since they knew how serious I was about the whole thing.

"Was it like that for you... you know, before marryin' Daddy?" I asked.

"My experience was different, son," said Mama.

"Different how?"

"I didn't marry your Pa because of butterflies," Mama said. "I married him because of who he was, with or without me. I never wanted the responsibility of making my husband a good man. And so I found one who was already good. That way, I knew I could trust him to be who he was before he met me, instead of hoping he'd be better than he really was because of me.

"Oh, I said," thinkin' about what she said. "But you loved him, right?"

"Of course," said Mama. "Love comes in lots of forms, Will, and your love for Hannah will take different forms at different times as you experience life together. And as far as marriage goes, you can't make a decision before it's ready to be made just because of a belly full of butterflies."

Like he's told me a million times before, Daddy says I gotta use my head and take some time to sort things out before doin' a thing like that. "Don't be a fool", he tells me. He says that that girl ain't got half a brain if she accepts an offer from a man who ain't thought any farther down the road than sayin' "I do." I don't like him talkin' about Hannah like that, but I know he's right, confound it. I've been savin' almost every penny I earn so that I won't have to wait too much longer before Hannah will have me. But until then, my daydreamin' about it will have to do.

I was especially tired this mornin', which accounts for why I was layin' around, and why I was thinkin' about Hannah. I needed somethin' sweet to think on so I could get the nightmare I had last night out of my head. It was another bad dream about Charlie. It was different than the first one, but it was just as bothersome, and I woke up sweatin' and shakin' again. This time Uncle Albert was part of the dream. I'm sure it's because of the situation with Charlie findin' his watch at their place. I never could find peace with that. I had plenty of reason to dislike Uncle Albert before that happened, which made it that much harder to give him the benefit of the doubt and trust him when he said he had nothin' to do with hurtin' Lawrence.

The dream took place in some strange field, and there were lots of clouds overhead like it was fixin' to rain. I was standin' there alone when I saw Uncle Albert ridin' in my direction. He looked like he was ten feet tall, and I felt like I was six years old again. I remember feelin' real scared, but there was no one around. Then as Uncle Albert got closer to me, I could see that he had Charlie with him, ridin' on the back of Uncle Albert's horse. I felt relieved at first, but as I took a good look at Charlie, I could see that he'd been cryin'. The horse stopped right in front of me, and I called out to Charlie, but he acted like he couldn't hear me. So I tried to pull him off the horse, but my hands went through him like he was a ghost, which scared me somethin' awful. I tried and tried, but I couldn't get to him. Then Uncle Albert kicked that horse, and off they rode. When I woke up, I realized I'd wet myself. [I may scratch that part out before passin' this diary on to my kin.]

I'm not sure if I'm supposed to find meanin' in that dream beyond what's already clear as day to see. It's no mystery that I feel helpless when it comes to Charlie sometimes, seein' as how we live where we do and have to deal with the hateful stuff that frequently comes with it. As for Uncle Albert, well, I couldn't like the man less if he were a disease ridden mosquito, which is how I sort of think of him anyhow. Other than that, I think it was just all the chaos swirlin' around in my head, findin' a way to be heard. It seems the best way to clear my mind is to think about a beautiful girl who just happens to like me as much as I like her. Almost makes me glad I had the bad dream... makes the clearin' my head part that much sweeter.

December 31, 1905

"Will! Oh, Will!" called Maryanne as she followed me out of the church buildin'.

"Hey, Maryanne," I said, tryin' to sound somewhat friendly.

"Didn't you hear me callin' you back there?" she asked.

"I reckon not."

"Well, I just wanted to make sure you were comin' to my New Year's Eve party tonight. You got my invitation, didn't you?"

"Maryanne, I already have plans for this evenin'," I said in a way that hopefully didn't hurt her feelin's.

"The whole evenin'?" she asked as she lowered her chin and looked up at me, battin' her eyelashes like she was tryin' to fly away.

"Yep, the whole evenin'."

"I can't imagine what's so engagin' that you couldn't just stop by for a short while," she said.

I knew that what I had to say was gonna make Maryanne awful upset. I played it out in my mind before sayin' it, but it didn't help none.

"The Browns have invited us and the Dixons over to spend New Year's with them," I said.

"Oh... I see," she said, but she couldn't quite conceal the pout playin' across her face. "You sure have been spendin' an awful lot of time with the Browns lately."

I didn't know what to say, so I just smiled. Maryanne was fishin'. It's like she wanted me to tell her what she didn't want to hear. I swear, as long as I live, I'll never understand that girl.

We stood there awkwardly for a few seconds, with Maryanne waitin' for me to say somethin'. Finally, when it was clear that I wasn't goin' to offer anything more, she pushed harder.

"So tell me, Will, what's so special about the Brown's that would keep you away from me on New Year's Eve?"

"Maryanne, don't you know that I'm courtin' Hannah?" I asked; "Have been for over four months now."

"Well I knew that she was sweet on you, but I guess I didn't realize you felt the same way about her," she said as she took to fannin' herself, even though it was downright freezin' out.

"Well, I do feel the same about her," I said plainly.

Maryanne stood there, shiftin' her weight back and forth from one foot to the other. She'd look at the ground and then up at me, and then back at the ground. She seemed awful agitated, but I didn't know what to do about it.

"Well just how serious is this, Will?" She suddenly looked a might angry.

"Maryanne, I'm fixin' to marry Hannah someday. Now, I don't say that to upset you none; just want to be honest since you're askin' questions about it."

"I suppose I'm just surprised, seein' as how everyone knows that you and I have always fancied one another."

"What!" I blurted out.

"Well now you're just insultin' me," she said.

"Gosh, Maryanne," I stuttered, I... I've got no mind to insult you, I just didn't realize you thought—"

"So I'm just makin' it all up?" she snapped. "What you're tryin' to tell me is that all these years you've never thought of me romantically?"

"Maryanne,... I'm really sorry to say this, but no – I haven't."

I wasn't sure if Maryanne was about to cry or slug me. Her face was real hard to read. It changed from sad to confused to furious, and not necessarily in that order. I was havin' trouble keepin' up, so I just stood there and waited for her to make up her mind about how she was feelin', and then I figured I'd know best how to respond once she did.

Suddenly, it was like all the emotions Maryanne had goin' on inside her just disappeared. She stopped shiftin', straightened her stance a bit, and looked right at me with a smile on her face as wide as the sky.

"Well isn't this just the silliest thing?" she said.

Now I was plum baffled. I felt like things could go sour real fast, dependin' on how I answered. Trouble was, I didn't have the foggiest idea of how I was supposed to.

"I'm not sure I get what you're meanin'," I said cautiously.

"Oh Will," she giggled, "we've just had our first real spat."

"Yes... I guess we have," I said, not knowin' if that was a good or a bad thing.

"Now," she said, "what would you say to you and Hannah stoppin' by my party for a few minutes tonight? Just a few little ol' minutes is all. I'd like the chance to wish you both a Happy New Year."

"Really?" I asked. "Are you sure about this?"

"Of course I'm sure!" she said. "You'd do that for me, wouldn't you?"

"Well, I suppose we can come for a spell before we join the others," I said, hesitatin' just a bit.

"That's wonderful!" said Maryanne. "I look forward to seein' you two this evenin'."

Then she tossed her hair and kissed me on the cheek before headin' back inside. I stood outside in the cold December air and tried to talk myself into believin' that Maryanne Stephenson was alright with the idea of me marryin' another girl. She sure seemed alright, I told myself. Maybe she's grown up a bit, I thought. But the naggin' pit in my gut told me otherwise. My experience has been that, that feelin' is usually right. So I crossed my fingers and spit on the ground two times. Charlie says you do that for good luck. I reckon it's just hogwash, but I was willin' to give it a try if it meant there was the slightest possibility of everything goin' smoothly with Maryanne and Hannah. And while I'm not a superstitious man, I might as well say that I went ahead and did it four more times throughout the day... just to increase the chances that one of them might take.

When I fetched Hannah that evenin', I swear she looked prettier than she had earlier that day when I saw her at church. Don't know how she manages to do that, but it's not the first time it's happened, and I'm bettin' it won't be the last.

"Are you sure you don't mind goin' to the Stephenson's for a while?" I asked Hannah as I helped her on with her coat.

"I don't mind at all," she said cheerfully. "I think it will be fun!"

"Well, I wouldn't go that far," I mumbled. I felt my nerves start to stir, and I held back the urge to spit on the floor two times.

"What did you say?" asked Hannah.

"Oh nothin'—just happy to be spendin' New Year's with you."

"That's a sweet thing to say, Will. I guess it is our first New Year's together, isn't it?" she said.

"Hopefully the first of many," I answered.

Hannah blushed some and gave my arm a little squeeze. Then we went into the main part of the house to say our goodbyes.

"We're leaving now," Hannah said to her mother.

"Alright, sweetheart. You two have a nice time, and we'll see you back here after you've had your fun."

I couldn't help thinkin' to myself that they'll be waitin' an awful long time if that's the case.

"Bundle up now. It's a cold evening," said pastor Brown.

"My folks should be along shortly, sir," I said as I buttoned the final button on my coat.

"Now, will Lawrence and Charlie be with them, or will they be coming separately?" he asked.

"I believe they'll all come together. That was the plan—last I heard anyhow.

"Well that sounds just fine," the pastor said.

Hannah said her goodbyes, and we walked out to the buggy. I held Hannah's arm so she wouldn't slip on the ice, happy to have any excuse to hold any part of her. Maryanne only lived about two miles from the Browns, and normally we'd walk, but there was a chill in the air that smarted somethin' terrible when the wind picked up, so we took the buggy. I figured it'd get us back to the Browns that much quicker when we were done at the Stephenson's.

I was lookin' forward to an evenin' with all of my favorite people. I was real pleased that the Browns had taken to Lawrence and Charlie like they had. We don't have many friends, outside of just a few, who want much to do with us because we're what they call, "colored friendly". I don't give two hoots about associatin' with them kinds of people anyhow.

When Hannah and I first started spendin' time with one another, I wondered if she'd end up seein' things the way so many around here do. As hard as it is to say, or even think about, if I was put in a position to choose between Hannah and the Dixons, I'd have to say goodbye to Hannah. I'm not sayin' I wouldn't wrestle with that decision some, but I know I could never be with a girl who had that kind of ugliness in her heart. So you can imagine what a relief it was for me that the Browns don't involve themselves in that sort of thing.

We hadn't been at Maryanne's for more than thirty seconds before she came bouncin' in to greet us. I know it was a party and all, but she seemed a bit too happy for my comfort. It felt real awkward, like she was forcin' it. Either that or she'd gotten an early start on the punch.

"Will! Hannah!" called Maryanne. "Let me find someone to take your coats."

"Find someone?" I mumbled.

"She means one of the help," said Hannah.

"Seems a waste of time to go lookin' for someone to do what you could have done in the time it took you to find them," I said.

Hannah laughed even though I wasn't tryin' to be funny. I was serious. I was at first, anyway, but then saw the opportunity to play along with Hannah. I loved to watch her laugh, and so I kept on.

"The whole business of havin' a person to take off my coat, and another one to hang it up, and another one to wipe off the snow... well it's just ridiculous," I said.

"That's not how it works and you know it," said Hannah, still laughin'. "It's not that bad."

"Now let's see," I teased, "have you seen the one who's supposed to help me move my legs back and forth so I can walk around tonight? I'm afraid I can't go anywhere without him. It sure will be a lonesome party if I'm stuck out here in the entryway on account of the 'walkin' help' not doin' his job."

"Oh, Will!" Hannah laughed as she held her stomach.

"What's so funny?" asked Maryanne as she pushed her way through the handful of people huddled together in the front room.

"Will was just being silly," Hannah said, tryin' not to look guilty.

"Oh," said Maryanne who obviously didn't care for the fact that there was somethin' humorous takin' place between me and Hannah. "Well it seems the person tendin' to the guests at the front door has taken ill, so I'll just take those coats myself."

We handed Maryanne our coats, and Hannah gave me a look as if she was tryin' not to start laughin' again. She put her hand up to her mouth like she was hopin' to hold it in and ended up chokin' and coughin' a bit in the process.

"You alright?" asked Maryanne.

"Yes... I'm... I'm just fine," said Hannah, finally collectin' herself.

Maryanne, without so much as lookin' at Hannah, squeezed in between us and wrapped one arm inside mine and the other inside Hannah's as she escorted us into the center of the festivities.

"How about somethin' to drink," she said.

"That sounds lovely," responded Hannah.

"Will, be a sweetheart and get us girls some punch, would you?" Maryanne flashed a big, innocent smile in my direction.

"Sure," I grumbled and headed over to the table where there was food enough for the whole town, and two more just like it. I decided to make a plate for me and Hannah to share while I was there. As I was loadin' up, I kept my eye on Hannah and Maryanne sittin' off by themselves. There was a lot of smilin' and such goin' on, but I was too far away to hear what was bein' said—that and the music bein' so loud you practically had to shout right into a person's ear for them to hear you. I was grateful when the band the Stephenson's had hired for the evenin' took to restin' their instruments a while so they could get some food. My eardrums were even more grateful than I was. I figured our cue to leave would be when them band members got together again and started to blow. By the time I got back to the girls, Hannah did not look pleased. She was noddin' politely while Maryanne finished what she was sayin', but I could tell that somethin' had changed.

"Well," said Maryanne, "I better go mingle with the other guests. Will you two be alright without me?"

"Oh I think we'll manage," I said.

"OK then. Now just give me a holler if you need any little thing."

I smiled and waited until Maryanne was out of sight before turnin' to Hannah.

"Everything OK?" I asked.

"Yes. Everything's fine, she said, a bit awkwardly I thought. And she looked everywhere else but at me.

"You sure?" I asked carefully.

"I said I'm fine."

Without smilin' she smoothed her dress and folded her hands in her lap. Now I haven't had much experience with women, but I could tell that what Hannah was sayin' with her words was different than what her face was tellin' me. I'm used to goin' by what you say, and I wasn't quite sure what to do in a situation like this. We sat in silence for a while before I just couldn't take it anymore. Not ten minutes ago, me and Hannah were laughin' and lovin' bein' together. Somethin' happened with Maryanne, I just knew it.

"Hannah," I said.

"Uh huh," said Hannah quietly, still not lookin' at me.

"You say you're fine, but this is not fine. Now what's goin' on?" I asked more insistently.

She took a deep breath, and tears started to pool in her eyes.

"Hannah, what is it?" I pleaded.

"Why didn't you tell me, Will?" she said.

"Why didn't I tell you what?" I asked, feelin' downright puzzled.

"About you and Maryanne."

"What about me and Maryanne?"

"Will, Maryanne told me," said Hannah. "She told me about your engagement last year."

"What!" I blurted out.

"Is it my fault you two broke things off?" she asked with an awful sad look on her sweet face.

I sat there stunned, tryin' to get my head around what she had just told me. Finally my head and my mouth started to cooperate.

"Hannah, me and Maryanne were never engaged."

Hannah looked confused.

"But she told me—"

"I don't know what she told you," I interrupted, "but there has never been anything between the two of us."

"Is that really true?" asked Hannah, lookin' somewhat relieved.

"I swear it is true," I said. "She's just upset that I'm courtin' you and is tryin' to cause trouble. Knowin' Maryanne, I should have guessed this would happen!"

"So that's why she said you'd be upset if you found out she told me," said Hannah. "She told me not to tell you that I knew."

"That little weasel," I said under my breath, clenchin' my teeth to keep from sayin' more. I knew there was more to her invitation than just wantin' to wish us a Happy New Year.

"Is that why she invited us tonight?" said Hannah.

"I'm not puttin' it past her," I said, real exasperated.

"We should just leave," Hannah said.

"Not before I say my piece to Maryanne."

I looked quickly around the crowded room, tryin' to locate her.

"Oh Will, please don't cause a scene," said Hannah. "It's not worth all that, is it?"

"You bet it is!" I replied.

I scanned the room again until I spotted that little liar. My blood boiled as I watched her laughin' and carryin' on with everybody, not a care in the world about the venom she had just spread. I had tried to put my feelin's about her aside on account of it bein' New Year's – to be friendly even though I could barely stand her. But I had had it! This was one of those moments that Daddy always warns me about... reactin' instead of thinkin' it through ahead of time. But I didn't care. She needed to hear what I had to say, and I was fixin' to tell her.

"Stay here," I told Hannah. "I'll be back in a minute."

"Come on, Will. Let's just go," Hannah held onto my arm, gently tryin' to calm me down, but I wasn't of a mind to be calmed down just then.

"As soon as I have a little chat with Maryanne."

Hannah sighed. She could tell there was no talkin' me out of it. Maybe I should have been more thoughtful about her feelin' uncomfortable, but I wasn't; can't do much about that now. I'm hopin' she'll weigh it against my better qualities. If she'd do that, I believe I'd come out ahead.

I took her hand from my arm and kissed it. I think she probably understood that it was time to confront Maryanne. She wasn't protestin' that, really; she just didn't like the way it was happenin'. I just couldn't, for the life of me, think of a better way... not that I put too much effort into findin' one, if it existed.

"I won't be long," I said.

"I'll get our coats and meet you by the front door," said Hannah. "Don't be mean about it, okay?"

"I've got no intention of bein' mean," I said, "but the truth isn't pleasant, and I can't make it be somethin' it isn't."

Hannah turned and left, and I made my way over to Maryanne. She was surrounded by several of the boys from town, just gigglin' and flirtin' with every last one of them. It was shameful. But what was worse than that was the way the gigglin' and flirtin' got worse when she noticed me comin' toward her.

"Maryanne," I said with every ounce of patience I could muster, "can I talk to you in private?"

"Why, Will, I'm entertainin' these fine boys right now," she said. "Can it wait?"

"No," I said coldly.

'Well, alright then," said Maryanne. "Excuse me, won't you?" she said as she looked at nobody in particular and followed me out to the back porch.

"What's this all about?" she asked innocently.

"Maryanne, you know exactly what this is about."

"Whatever do you mean, Will?" She was obviously just toyin' with me and doin' a mighty fine job of it too.

"Why did you go and tell Hannah a fool's lie about us bein' engaged?" I said, my voice gettin' louder than what I meant for it to.

"Is that what she told you?" said Maryanne, lettin' that all-too-familiar pout begin to play around her features.

"Stop playin' games, Maryanne!" I shouted.

Maryanne startled, and she got a real serious look on her face. A few people inside must have heard me yell, and watched us through the window for a minute or two.

"So you called me out here to yell at me?" Maryanne said with a face as pouty as an old dried up raisin. "I never took you for such a bully, Will!"

"You are unbelievable!" I shouted. "You trick me into bringin' Hannah here by tellin' me that you've got good intentions—then you send me away so you can tell her lies about me. And for what? What did you think was gonna happen, Maryanne?—that Hannah would leave me because of it, and I'd come runnin' to you? Well let me tell you that you are—"

"I'm what?" yelled Maryanne.

I paused and took a deep breath. I played out the conversation in my mind the way my anger was wantin' it to go, and I... I decided against it. I remembered Hannah tellin' me not to be mean. 'Don't be mean,' I told myself. Just say what needs to be said and don't be mean. So I held my tongue; didn't know I had that in me.

Finally gettin' myself under control, I said calmly, "you know what, Maryanne? Hannah's right. It isn't worth it."

Maryanne took to cryin', and I think I actually saw real tears for once. I turned and started to leave.

"Will, I love you," she said imploringly.

I stopped and looked at her with a new kind of sadness... maybe even pity.

"You don't love me, Maryanne," I said. "You just want me because I'm the only one who doesn't want you."

"That's a horrible thing to say!" she said through her tears.

"That may be, but you know I'm right," I said. "You could have any one of those boys in there."

"None of them is you," she sobbed.

"And if I said yes, you'd no sooner have me than you would one of them."

"That isn't true!" she whimpered. But she knew it was.

"It is true," I said plainly. "Goodbye, Maryanne."

I listened to her snifflin' as I walked away. Part of me felt bad, but not a big enough part to make me do anything about it. Maryanne had some things to figure out, and the gosh-awful truth is that I wanted nothin' to do with it. So I closed the door behind me and made my way to Hannah, who was obviously anxious and ready to leave. I didn't even have both arms inside my coat before she was pullin' me out the front door.

Me and Hannah rode slowly home so we could talk about what happened. And even as underhanded as Maryanne had been, Hannah still felt bad for her. I suppose that's one of the things that I love about her. She's like Mama in that way.

We decided not to bring it up to anyone at Hannah's house, at least not at the beginnin' of the evenin'. We didn't want to spoil the mood-just wanted to enjoy our time together which is exactly what we did. It was gonna be the last time I'd see Charlie and Lawrence for a good while too, and spendin' that time talkin' about Maryanne was not appealin'. The Dixons were on their way to Alabama come sunup tomorrow. It wasn't their usual time to travel, but after the happenin's of the past few months, Daddy suggested that they get away for a bit. Aunt Lena is always happy to have them, and I know of a certain young lady who will be mighty pleased to have an unexpected visit from Charlie... Charlie bein' equally excited, of course. He might not admit to that if you asked him, so take my word for it. He can't wait to see Anita again!

January 7, 1906

It was a powerful strong sermon today. Pastor Brown sure knows how to stir up a congregation, and today it wasn't the kind of stirrin' that comes from the Holy Spirit. There's been talk goin' around about some secret meetin' bein' held by a handful of men in our town who are known for their hostility toward coloreds. Now it could just be rumor, but the pastor wanted folks to know what God himself would have to say on the matter, if it were true. Pastor Brown gave some scripture and talked about charity, love, and acceptance. He saved the chastisin' for the end, I'm guessin' because he knew he might lose a few people before it was over, probably to guilt or maybe even just plain old anger. Then there are some folks who don't like bein' told what to do, so they resist out of sheer defiance, even if they don't disagree with what they're bein' told! But Pastor Brown kept on anyhow.

"Raise your hands, brothers and sisters, if you think that Jesus preached hate," said Pastor Brown.

There was a loud gasp from Mrs. Jones on the front row, and then she started fannin' herself with her Women's League newsletter. She was fannin' that thing so fast that Mrs. Smith, who was sittin' next to her, had to keep brushin' her hair out of her eyes on account of the strong wind she was catchin'.

"And raise your hands if you believe that Jesus said, 'Love thy neighbor... unless he's different than you, that is. Because if he's different than you, well then, by all means, hate him!'"

Everyone sat absolutely still. There were a few folks lookin' around at one another to see if anyone was actually dumb enough to raise their hands. Mrs. Jones looked real disturbed. She even

covered her ears at one point but couldn't take the suspense and eventually started listenin' again. The pastor wasn't blasphemin'; he was tryin' to make a point—call folks out on the carpet for bein' hypocrites. We've never had a pastor do that before. Some didn't care for his approach, but I thought it was just perfect.

"It's good to see so many true Christians in the congregation today," continued Pastor Brown, "because it's been brought to my attention that there are some folks in our town who have turned their backs on what's right and are involved in hateful practices."

You could tell right away who the good pastor was talkin' about because they took to fidgetin' and fussin'. I've always had a feelin' about some of them men, guessin' that if the Klan came knockin' on their doors, they'd abandon their wives and families if it meant they could be a part of it. I never much understood the Klan. I mean, I don't quite get the attraction. You ride around with other awful men, wearin' bed sheets and scarin' folks. I suppose if you want to be a coward and a bully, there's no better way to do it.

At this point I started to feel a little worried for Pastor Brown. He got some frowns and angry stares while he was talkin'. But he's the kind of man who says what needs to be said, no apologies. And he believes he's got a duty to do it, seein' as how he's the pastor and all. The thing is, there's no Klan here, no true Klan anyway. That's been gone for a long time now. But every now and again we get these idiotic groups that form and try to call themselves Klan. Nothin' much ever comes of it, not in these parts. But a few weeks after Lawrence and Charlie were attacked, there was another colored family who got it just as bad as they did. So it seems we've got a real situation. In the past, it's just been a fire started somewhere to try and scare someone, or a commotion that had to be handled by the sheriff. But it's different now. Now we're talkin' about people bein' injured.

I forgot to mention that Daddy filed a complaint against Sheriff Coleman. He had Mama write it out for him since he can't read or write very well himself, and it was real official lookin'. After the incident with the Dixons, we just all felt so helpless. Mama, Daddy, and Lawrence all went down to talk with Sheriff Coleman and Deputy Jenkins. The deputy was real helpful-provided watch care over their house, like I mentioned before. He wanted to look further into it, do some investigatin' and such, Mama told me. But Sheriff Coleman shut it down fast as you can say "bigot". He went on about some nonsense... there's nothin' we can do... probably some men out drinkin' who didn't mean any real harm... no proof, blah, blah, blah.

Mama said that Daddy didn't argue one bit. He knew goin' in there that he wasn't gettin' any help from that horse's behind. But he needed to have good reason to file a complaint against him, and he was hopin' to get Deputy Jenkins on board. Well, Deputy Jenkins's hands were tied, as you could imagine. How was he gonna get that past the sheriff? And even if he did, it would go right to Mayer Harper, who is probably the only person worse than Sheriff Coleman, in my opinion.

It looked like our side was beat alright. But then wouldn't you know it?...just a couple of weeks after Daddy met with the sheriff, Mayer Harper was out huntin' rabbit and got shot two times by another hunter who took him for a bear. Can you believe that! So Mayor Harper was told that he'd be in the hospital for a good while, which relieved him of his duties for the time bein'. His replacement happened to be a friendly acquaintance of Deputy Jenkins from up north, and bless my soul, he shares the same opinions as the deputy about coloreds bein' treated poorly in the south. That's not to say that there aren't a good number of bigots in the North as well, but lucky for us, Jenkins and Mayor Harper's replacement seem to have been brought up on the right side of the matter. So Deputy Jenkins got Daddy's complaint to the actin' mayor, Mayor Roberts, along with a few personal complaints of his own, I reckon.

If there was ever a good time for change to happen, this seemed like it. Mama said they haven't heard much back yet, but these things take time. That's what Deputy Jenkins told her, anyway. So we're bein' patient. Now, I'll probably be repentin' for this later, but I feel the need to say that I'm real disappointed that the hunter who shot Mayer Harper stopped at two shots. I say that, understandin' that it's a sin, but in situations like these, you have two choices; you can choose the sin of lyin' and just say that you're glad Mayer Harper will be alright, or you can choose the sin of wishin' someone ill. I'm choosin' the second one and hopin' that my honesty about it will sort of balance things out.

January 12, 1906

Lawrence and Charlie got home from Alabama today. We picked them up at the station and brought them back to our place for some supper before takin' them home. Lawrence said it was real nice to get away for a while and enjoy some time with their family. Aunt Lena has a heart about as big as it's possible to have. I've only met her once and she was nothin' but hugs and cheek pinches. Normally, I imagine I wouldn't like that sort of thing, but I don't think the woman could get under my skin if she tried her darnndest. I think one of the reasons I like her so much is because of the way she loves Charlie and Lawrence. Charlie lights up around her, and Lawrence seems more content than I believe I've ever seen him without her bein' around. Maybe she reminds him of Adelaide. I reckon after twenty-one years of not seein' your wife, any little reminder of her would feel like comin' home. It's a shame they live so far apart. I'd like to see that look on Lawrence's face more often.

Charlie was awful distracted at dinner. He wasn't offerin' too much information about it though... probably because Mama and Jessie were in the room. So it was nice to finally talk with him after dinner was over, to hear about his trip.

"She's so beautiful, Will," Charlie said, lookin' like a lovesick puppy dog.

"You've always fancied Anita, but I've never heard you talk about her like that before," I said.

"I know. Somethin' was different this time. It's like... like she's all grown up."

"Well that's a good thing. So why is it that you seem so down?"

"There's a problem."

"What's that?"

"Her folks don't much care for me."

"Oh, I don't believe that" I said. "What's not to like? You're a nice fella, you take a shower on a pretty regular basis, and I would say you're decent enough lookin'."

Charlie punched me hard in the shoulder. He laughed a bit but went back to lookin' kind of torn up about the whole thing.

"I'm serious, Will," he said. "Her Mama even told me so."

"No she didn't," I said, thinkin' Charlie was puttin' me on.

"I was surprised as you are now."

"What did she say?" I asked, realizin' that he was tellin' the truth.

"She said, 'Aint no way a boy raised without his Mama can turn out quite right. I'm fixin' to raise these here kids proper if it kills me, and sometimes I reckon it just might. Now, how you gonna tell me you know what's what when you ain't had someone to show you?'"

"What did you say to her?" I said as I found myself sittin' on the edge of my seat to hear what Charlie would say.

"I told her that Daddy taught me everything I needed to know, and some extra stuff too. But she just told me, 'ain't a man alive who can teach you what a woman can.'"

"I can't believe it," I said, lookin' at the ground and shakin' my head in surprise.

"What am I supposed to do about that?" asked Charlie. "Me not havin' a Mama isn't my fault."

"And besides that," I said, "your daddy did a better job with you than most men and women put together. You turned out real good, Charlie."

"Thanks, Will, but Anita's mama won't see it that way. She's got it in her head that I'm not good enough for her daughter."

I listened to Charlie talk about how much he cared for Anita. He was serious about this girl, and I felt sympathy for him because I know what it's like to love a girl the way he does. And if someone told me I couldn't be with Hannah because of somethin' I had no control over, well..., I'd be spittin' mad. Then suddenly somethin' occurred to me.

"Charlie!" I said, loud enough that everybody looked over at us from the other room.

I smiled and waved my hand to let them know to go on about their business.

"Sorry," I said, "but I thought of somethin'."

"Thought of what?" said Charlie.

"Well, I know you don't have your own Mama around, but you've always had Mama."

Charlie sat there for a minute and thought.

"But she's white," Charlie said.

"What?" I said, feelin' real caught off-guard.

"She's white," he said again, like it was nothin'.

"So what," I said, soundin' irritated.

"Don't take offense, Will," said Charlie. "You know I don't care that your Mama is white, but we're not talkin' about me. We're talkin' about Mrs. Davis."

I suppose I hadn't thought about that before. We're surrounded by all this nonsense where colored folks are hated by white folks, but it didn't occur to me that things could go the other way. I found myself feelin' almost ashamed at my stupidity... or at least at my not bein' very aware.

"Does she hate white people?" I asked Charlie.

"She doesn't hate anybody," laughed Charlie.

"I'm confused," I said, feelin' even dumber than before.

"Will," said Charlie, "black folks are treated real bad in Alabama too, and Mrs. Davis has a hard time trustin' white folks for that reason. Does that make sense?"

"I guess so," I said.

"Just think on it for a minute," said Charlie. "White folks hate me because I'm black. I don't hate white folks, but I hate bein' hated by them. Some people can't keep those two separate."

That just made me sad. I wanted to understand what it was like for Charlie, but I didn't want to insult him by sayin' that I could. He knows I get it best I can, and I try even harder than that, but like Daddy always says, 'ain't no sense tryin' to walk in a man's shoes when your feet just ain't the same size'.

"Well," I said, "maybe a white mama is better than no mama... at least to Mrs. Davis, that is."

Charlie started laughin', which made me laugh too.

"Maybe so," he said.

"It's worth a try, right?" I said. "I mean, if it means gettin' a shot with Anita."

"I'd try just about anything."

Charlie sat there thinkin' for a minute, then he sighed long and hard as though he'd made up his mind.

"How does Anita feel about all this?" I asked him.

"She says that she'll handle things with her mama. I'm not sure what that means, but it sounded good. I just don't want any trouble. I want Anita's parents to give their blessin', ya know?"

"Yeah, I know.

"Aunt Lena and Anita have a plan," Charlie said.

"What kind of plan?"

"Beats me, but maybe between the three of them, Aunt Lena, Anita, and Miss Lily, them women will figure a way to talk some sense into Mrs. Davis."

"And Mr. Davis?" I asked.

"I get the sense that his opinions are decided by his wife," said Charlie. "So if we can get her, we won't have to worry about him."

Me and Charlie talked for a while more and then joined the others in the next room for dessert and coffee. I hadn't realized how much I miss Lawrence and Charlie when they're away and how much I prefer it when they're back home with us. It was nice to catch up and hear about the trip. After a while, the conversation turned to Hannah, and I told them I was workin' on my patience and plannin'. Lawrence got a good laugh out of that, and he and Daddy exchanged a look that a man might not be blamed for takin' offense to. But we all know that I'm not patient or good at plannin'. My history proves it. So I let them have their laugh and didn't give it a second thought. They'll see that I'm serious about doin' what needs to be done to be with Hannah. There isn't a thing I can think of that can motivate me the way she does. Yeah, this is different. They'll see alright.

February 1, 1906

"Will!" called Mama, "can you come inside for a minute, son? Your pa and I have something we want to talk to you about."

I'd been out in the barn, cleanin' the grime off the horse's shoes. They collect an awful lot of filth durin' wintertime, what with the snow meltin' and mud all over the place.

"I'll be right there!" I yelled.

I was glad to be called inside for a spell. It was a cold mornin', and truth is, I think the horses were as happy to see me go as I was to be goin'.

"What is it Mama?" I asked as I sat down at the kitchen table, rubbin' my frozen hands together and then blowin' on my fingertips to try and warm them up.

Mama brought me a cup of hot coffee and sat down next to Daddy, who was sittin' across from me.

"Will," began Daddy, "me and your mama have been talkin', and we're real pleased with how hard you've been workin' and savin'."

"You've shown a lot of restraint and discipline when it comes to your spending, honey," added Mama.

"Thanks," I said. "You know how much I want to marry Hannah, so if this is what it takes, then this is what I'll keep doin'."

"I've been lookin' into property nearby," said Daddy, "and I just don't see a way for you to afford anything for a long while."

"How long?" I asked, startin' to feel sort of panicked.

"Too long," said Mama.

"But I'm savin' every single cent!" I said.

"We know, son," Mama said. "Now settle down and hear your Pa out."

I sat back in my chair and took a deep breath.

Daddy stretched his legs under the table, gave Mama a quick smile, and said, "I think we should build a room off the west side of the house for you and Hannah. You two can live here with us." And then he sat and waited for my reaction.

"Are you serious?" I asked.

"Of course I'm serious," said Daddy.

"I... I don't know what to say."

"Well, what do you think, Will?" asked Mama. "We just thought that you'll be able to get married sooner this way."

"And you wouldn't mind havin' us here?" I said.

"Well, we already live with you," said Daddy, "and we like Hannah just fine, so I reckon it won't be too much imposition."

I looked at Mama who was tryin' not to smile, and I realized that Daddy was teasin' with me. It doesn't happen very often, so it's hard to recognize it when it does.

"Mama?" I said, wantin' her input.

"Oh we'd just love it!" she said.

I felt a warm rush come over my whole body. It was a combination of feelin' happy and excited and grateful all at once.

"Thank you!" I yelled as I stood up and hugged Mama.

"We'll get started right away," said Daddy, "so I suppose you better start thinkin' of a mighty fine proposal."

"Yes, sir. I will," I said.

"Alright then," Daddy answered. With that, he got up from the table and went outside to meet Lawrence and Charlie, who were bringin' some equipment to the shed in need of repair. Mama could barely contain her happiness, and it made me feel real good to know that she wanted us here. And although Daddy doesn't go about showin' it the same way as Mama, I think it'd be fair to say that he was happy about it too.

After one more quick Hug for Mama, I dashed out of the door, flew off the porch steps, and ran to where Lawrence and Charlie were working. Barely pausin' for breath, I asked Lawrence if it'd be alright for Charlie to help me with the horses for a while. The way Lawrence agreed to it so quick made me think he already knew why I wanted to talk to Charlie so bad.

The whole rest of the day, all I could think about was askin' Hannah to marry me. When was I gonna do it? How was I gonna do it? I thought about makin' it big and excitin', but every time I tried to come up with a big and excitin' idea, I just couldn't. I guess I'll have to give it some thought, and I'll have to stay away from Hannah until I'm ready to do it. Trust me when I tell you, even though I'm workin' on my self-restraint, it still needs some perfectin', and this is definitely not the thing to practice it on! So I'll keep my distance for now and hope I come up with somethin' real good, real soon!

February 4, 1906

Well, I made it a whole four days. I plan on proposin' this evenin' while I'm over at Hannah's place. I just have to figure out how to keep away from her durin' church services today; that'll be tricky. Charlie helped me come up with the way I'm gonna propose. Since it's cold outside and nothin' is bloomin' yet, I'm fixin' to use some of the art supplies Jessie got for Christmas and paint some flowers on paperboard. Then when they're dry, I'll cut them out and tie a ribbon around the stems to make them look like a real bouquet.

I was in the middle of paintin' when I realized somethin' I hadn't thought of before.

"Mama!" I yelled.

Mama came runnin' into the kitchen from her bedroom.

"What is it?" she asked in a panic. "Is everything alright?"

"I forgot about the ring!" I said.

"What ring, son? What are you goin' on about?" Mama was still holdin' her hairbrush and lookin' exasperated once she saw that I wasn't bleedin'.

"Mama! I don't have a ring for Hannah," I said.

"Is t hat all?"

"Is that all!" I said in a way that told Mama she was not seein' the seriousness of the situation.

"Mama, how am I supposed to propose to a girl without a ring?"

"First of all, that's utter nonsense," Mama said, shakin' that hairbrush at me.

"Well, what will she think of me if I don't give her a ring?" I asked.

"Hopefully she'll be thinking on whether or not she wants to spend her life with you, not whether or not she can be persuaded with jewelry," said Mama.

"But isn't that the proper sort of thing to do?" I said.

"I suppose it is," she said. "But I just want you to remember that a girl who would be disappointed without a ring isn't the one you want to marry."

"You wear a ring," I said.

"It came later. Your Pa saved for three years after we were married."

"Were you disappointed it didn't come when Daddy asked you to marry him? Be honest now, Mama."

"Sometimes it's like you don't know me at all," said Mama as she walked back into her room.

I sat there feelin' bad for two reasons now. I had offended Mama, and still didn't have a ring for Hannah.

"What was second of all?" I called to Mama.

"What?" she called back.

"You told me the first of all, but what was the second part?"

Mama came back in the kitchen holdin' a small, purple, silk bag. She put in on the table in front of me.

"What's this?" I asked.

"Open it," she said.

I carefully opened the little bag to find a pretty gold band.

"Is this yours? How come I've never seen it before," I said.

"It was your grandma's. Grandpa Doyle gave it to me after she... well, after she passed."

"Why don't you wear it?"

"I suppose it reminds me of her," she said.

Of course Mama wouldn't want to remember her own Mama and the terrible way she left this world. Even before killin' herself, she wasn't much of a Mama to begin with—at least from the stories I've been told anyhow.

Mama stared at the ring for a minute, took a quick deep breath, and then shook her head a bit like she'd been lost somewhere for a second.

"It's yours now," she said.

"You mean it?"

"I thought about getting rid of it years ago, but then it occurred to me that you might like to have it someday for this very reason."

"This is perfect!" I yelled. "I was so worried... and... I understand what you were sayin' about not needin' a ring, but—"

"Just as long as you get the point," Mama said.

"Oh, thank you, Mama!"

"You better hurry up, now." We need to be leavin' for Sunday service soon, and I don't want to be late. I laid out a clean shirt for you. It's on your bed."

"I'm just about finished with these flowers, and then I'll get changed," I said, feelin' an excitement come over me and tryin' not to act a fool in front of Mama.

Mama started to leave the room and then stopped, turned back for a minute, and smiled at me. "You've done a lovely job on those flowers. Hannah is going to love them."

"You think so," I asked eagerly.

"I do," she said, and she blew me a kiss and went back into her room to finish gettin' ready.

I finished paintin' those flowers and then stood back to take a good look. Most of them turned out nice, but there were a few that looked like they'd been stuck in the sun on a hot day for too long. Maybe that was a good thing, I told myself. It makes it more realistic. Whether it did or didn't, I can't say, but it's what I'm tellin' myself, and it will just have to do.

Mama is right about Hannah needin' to decide if she wants to marry me for me; and some fake, wilted flowers shouldn't change her mind. And boy am I glad to have that ring!

Avoidin' Hannah at church today proved to be just as hard as I thought it would be. There were two different times when I saw her comin' my way, and I had to turn in a hurry and go the other direction. One time she almost caught up to me, and I practically sent Mrs. Jones to the hospital on account of me climbin' right over her. I can't be sure, but I think I even held onto her ear for leverage while doin' it. I can't be held responsible for that. It was a desperate situation, and I'm certain if Mrs. Jones knew the nature of my assaultin' her, she would have gladly obliged, injuries and all. I finally just had Jessie go and tell Hannah that I'd see her that night at her place.

"What's wrong with him?" Hannah asked Jessie. "It's like he doesn't want to see me today."

"No, he does," Jessie said, "but he just... well, he just... has bad breath since he forgot to brush his teeth this mornin'.

"You said what!" I yelled at Jessie as she climbed into the buggy.

"I panicked!" Jessie yelled back. "I was just supposed to tell her you'd see her tonight, but then she started askin' questions! I wasn't expectin' that!"

"And you couldn't come up with anything else?" I was hoppin' mad, and I had to clench my fists and count to ten to keep from shakin' Jessie's teeth loose.

"I'm sorry, OK!" Jessie said.

Daddy sat in the buggy laughin' out loud. Even though we don't see him do that very often, I didn't care for the timin' of it. Daddy could tell I wasn't seein' the humor that he was seein'.

"It could have been worse, son," he said.

"How exactly could it have been worse?" I said, bein' careful that my irritation didn't turn to disrespect.

"Well," said Daddy, "she could have told Hannah that...um..."

"Yes?" I said, still waitin' for him to come up with somethin'.

"Nope, can't do it," Daddy laughed. "That's about as bad as it gets, I reckon."

Dang Jessie. And of all the days to do that. I'm fixin' to kiss Hannah for the first time tonight, and now how am I gonna try that when she thinks I've got poor hygiene? I sat in the buggy and stewed. Jessie apologized a few more times, and I just ignored her. Finally Mama said it was time to move on.

"Your sister said she was sorry, Will," said Mama. "Now let it go."

"But Mama!"

"Will Wright!" she said, "Jessie didn't mean to embarrass you. So accept her apology or not, but be done with it either way."

"You're makin' too much of it," said Daddy. "That girl ain't thought twice about what Jessie said."

"I hope you're right," I said.

"What time are you headed over there tonight?" asked Mama.

"Right after supper," I said.

"We'll be anxious to hear how things go," Mama said.

"I'm sort of anxious to get it done. I hope she says yes," I said as I felt my nerves start to act up.

"You got any doubt?" asked Daddy.

"I suppose I do. It never occurred to me before today, but when I picture sittin' there with her, I play it out both ways in my mind. I assume she'll say yes, but there's a chance she could say no."

"You know what I think?" said Daddy.

"What?"

"I think there ain't no way you'd ask her to marry you if you thought she was gonna say no."

I thought on that a minute. I guess he's right. I know Hannah loves me.

"Well," I said, "it's now or never."

"Good for you, son," said Mama.

"Things go well for you tonight," said Daddy, "and we'll start that work on the house in the mornin'."

"Yes sir," I said, tryin' to keep my smile from growin' too big.

My stomach was churnin' some, not in a bad way, just in a feelin'-the-excitement-of-life kinda way. Charlie said I should sit by myself for a while after supper before goin' over to Hannah's. He said I should clear my head and approach the situation with purpose. Of course I got a purpose, I told him. My purpose is gettin' Hannah to marry me! Charlie just shook his head and wished me luck. I'm hopin' he and Lawrence will still be at the house tonight when I get home. Wouldn't feel quite right sharin' the good news with everybody and them not bein' here. I'll make sure to write about it in the mornin'.

February 5, 1906

I could see several lamps burnin' as I walked up the steps after gettin' home from Hannah's last night. It was pretty late, so I was real surprised. As soon as I came in the front door, everyone in the room stopped talkin' all at once and looked at me, waitin' to hear how things went. Lawrence and Charlie were still there, and although Daddy was fightin' sleep, he was sittin' up with them. I felt grateful in that moment, standin' in the doorway, feelin' the way they all want to share in life's experiences with me.

"So how did it go?" asked Charlie, who sat up on the edge of the sofa when I came in the front door.

"Well," I said, "you know that question I had for Hannah tonight?"

"Of course we know!" said Mama. "What did she say?"

"Now let's see... I'm tryin' to remember," I teased.

"Spit it out, son!" said Daddy in a way that surprised everyone.

"Miss Hannah Brown has happily agreed to be my wife!" I said.

"Will! That's wonderful," said Mama.

"Congratulations!" said Lawrence.

The whole family started clappin' and causin' a commotion. I probably wouldn't tell any of them, but the truth is, I loved every second of it. Jessie ran over and hugged me tight, followed by

Mama. Charlie was smilin' from ear to ear, and when my eyes finally caught his, he gave me one solid nod. I knew that meant he was happy for me.

"Come sit down," said Mama. "Tell us how it went."

"Well, when I got there, I asked her to come out on the porch with me. At first, she just looked at me and said, 'are you crazy? It's freezing out there!'"

"I know," I said. "We won't be long. I just want to talk to you about something."

"Can't we talk inside?" she asked.

"Hannah, please," I insisted.

"Well, if you say so," she said, "but if I catch my death of cold, you'll be sorry!"

"Don't even joke like that," I said. "That's just awful." But I could see that with her shiverin' with the cold and all, she might not be able to concentrate on what I had to say, so I quit protestin' and let her go to get her coat and scarf while I walked out to the porch to wait for her.

A few minutes later Hannah came out and joined me on the swing. We sat there for a minute while I worked up my nerve to ask what needed askin'. Finally I turned to face her and took her hands in mine. Even though she was wearin' gloves, her fingers felt like icicles, and I sort of felt bad for havin' asked her to come outside with me. But I just felt I had to ask her in the same place we were when I first really knew that I was gonna marry her.

"Hannah," I started.

"What is it, Will?" she said, shiverin'.

"I've been happy all my life," I said. "I've had some ups and downs for sure, but my life is blessed, and I'm a lucky man."

"I'm so glad about that," said Hannah, lookin' a bit confused, but stickin' with me on account of my talkin' so serious like.

"I guess what I'm tryin' to say is that, with all the happiness I've had in my life, none of it compares to the happiness I've felt since I met you. I guess I just never knew what it was like before."

"Knew what what was like?"

"Lovin' somebody," I said."—the kind when you're in love with somebody, that is."

"You love me?" asked Hannah.

"Does that surprise you?"

Hannah's face turned red, and she looked down at our hands a moment before answerin'.

"I guess it doesn't. It just makes me so happy, is all."

"Really, Hannah?"

"Really," she said. "You know that I love you too, don't you?"

"Well," I said, tryin' to hide the enormous grin I felt startin' to take shape on my face, "I imagined you did. Wouldn't make much sense for you to spend the kind of time with me that you do if you didn't care for me at least a little bit."

"You're right about that," she said.

I felt real pleased with the way things were goin' so far. I'd learned that Hannah loves me and that me lovin' her makes her happy. That seemed like a pretty fair start. Then I remembered the flowers.

"I almost forgot," I said. "I have somethin' for you."

I leaned over and grabbed the knapsack I'd brought with me and had put underneath the swing when I first got there. I pulled out the paperboard flowers I'd made for her, and as I was handin' them to her, I realized how awful they looked. I guess I bundled them before all the paint had dried. Some of them were stuck together, and the paint had dripped all the way down the stems. I wanted to take the last ten seconds back and pretend I never brought the flowers to begin with.

"I thought they'd turn out nicer, I said, feelin' a little embarrassed.

"Well that just wouldn't be possible," said Hannah.

"You don't have to be so polite. I'm lookin' at them with my own two eyes, and they're a mess. It's just that nothin' is bloomin' this time of year, and I wanted you to have some flowers tonight."

"I think it's the sweetest thing anyone has ever done for me," said Hannah. "You really are so wonderful, Will."

"Well I'm much obliged that you'd say so. It seems I haven't had the best of luck with givin' you flowers," I said, rememberin' the time I knocked her over in front of the post office, threw a daisy at her, and ran away.

"That reminds me," said Hannah. "I'll be right back. I have something I want you to see."

Hannah hurried inside, and when she came back she was carryin' a copy of the book, The Hound of the Baskervilles.

"Is that what you wanted me to see?" I asked curiously.

"No, silly," said Hannah. Then she opened the book to the middle and pulled something out from between the pages. It was a daisy.

"Do you remember this flower?" Hannah asked me.

"Is that... the daisy?"

"The very one," she said. "As soon as I got home that day and cleaned up all my cuts and bruises from being knocked down," she teased, "I put it in my book to press it, and it's been there ever since."

"Hannah... I can't believe you kept it. I was so embarrassed that day! I was shocked you were willin' to have anything to do with me after that."

Right then a soft, sweet look came into her eyes as she said, "Will, when did you realize that you loved me?"

"Um...," I said, feelin' sort of caught off guard, "it was the first night I came over here and sat on this porch with you. Why?"

"Well I knew the moment you gave me that daisy," she said.

"You did?"

"Yep," said Hannah matter-of-factly. "I felt that you were brave and romantic and chivalrous and sweet, and my heart decided for me before my head even had a chance to think about it."

I was speechless. All this time I had been thinkin' that I made a total fool of myself that day. And here I was, eight months

later, sittin' on the porch with that very girl and havin' her tell me that she loves me.

I let go of Hannah's hand for a second and reached into my front coat pocket. I pulled out the silk pouch with the ring in it.

"Hannah?" I said as I took the ring out, "I get the feelin' that we're supposed to be together. And I want you to know that it would make me so happy to spend the rest of my days with you-if you'll have me."

"Oh Will!" she said. "Do you mean it?"

"With all my heart," I said, at the same time pullin' the glove off her hand and slippin' the ring onto her cold finger. She was smilin' that beautiful smile of hers as she sat there a minute and stared at her finger. Then she looked up at me, tears fillin' up her eyes, and threw her arms around my neck.

"Yes!" she shouted. "I can't think of anything I want more than to marry you, Will Wright. I'm just glad you finally asked me," she said, and we both started laughin'.

I pulled my head back away from Hannah a bit so that our faces were real close to one another's.

"I'd like to kiss you if that's alright," I said, "seein' as how we're engaged now."

Hannah didn't even answer; she just leaned forward and gave me the sweetest kiss I thought it was possible to get. Even though it was freezin' outside, and my flowers hadn't turned out like I'd wanted them to, I felt total happiness.

After we kissed, I put my arms around her and pulled her into me.

"I was meanin' to get down on my knee to ask you, but I guess with all the excitement, I forgot," I said.

"It wouldn't have made me any happier than I am right now if you had," said Hannah.

I sat there holdin' her as long as I could, but the cold finally forced us to go inside and share the good news with her family, who had all gathered together in the parlor, kinda anticipatin' what my visit was all about. They were all smilin' and excited and talkin' at once, and Pastor Brown said he had a feelin' I was fixin' to propose, which was the only reason he allowed Hannah to sit out in the cold with me for so long. Hannah's sisters all swarmed around, huggin' and kissin' her until she couldn't breathe. We talked and laughed and enjoyed some hot chocolate together before I finally set out for home.

I barely slept a wink last night. I couldn't manage to calm myself down enough to fall asleep. And the funny thing is, I don't even feel tired this mornin'. I almost feel more energetic than I remember feelin' in a long time. I'm eager to get to buildin' this room so that Hannah and I have a place to come to once we're married. – Mr. and Mrs. Will Wright – Sure does have a nice ring to it—if I do say so myself.

February 13, 1906

Me and Charlie were walkin' through town, tryin' to come up with somethin' to get our girls for Valentine's Day. Charlie got a letter from Anita just a few weeks after he got home from Alabama. It was real sweet. She was askin' him not to give up on her even though her folks make things so difficult. Charlie was so excited he could hardly stand it. Not much has changed with Anita's mama, but at least Charlie knows that Anita is still thinkin' about him as much as he's been thinkin' about her.

"I want to get her somethin' special," said Charlie.

"Me too," I said, "but what?"

"They had some chocolate hearts at Carver's last week."

"I wouldn't set foot in that store," I said. "I'm surprised you'd even mention that place."

"Yea, but where else can we get chocolates?" Charlie asked.

"If that's the only place, then we'll just have Mama help us make some caramel nuts instead. The girls will like that better anyway."

"By the time my package gets to Anita, it's gonna be way past Valentine's Day, and the caramels will probably be old and stale," said Charlie.

"That won't matter," I said. "She'll be gettin' exactly what she wants, which is to know that you still fancy her after all the nonsense that happened when you were there last."

"Gosh," said Charlie, "I sure hope you're right."

"I am."

"I thought about gettin' her a nice hair scarf for Sunday services. You think she'd like that?" asked Charlie.

"I imagine so. Maybe I'll do the same for Hannah. Girls like that sort of thing... I think."

"Well, like it or not," Charlie said, "I'll be danged to come up with somethin' else. Been thinkin' on it for a whole week now, and the scarf is all I come up with."

"Scarves it is," I said.

We made our way into Martin's and headed for the back of the store where he keeps lady's scarves and hats and such. When I saw who was standin' there I almost turned to leave, but Charlie grabbed hold of my arm and said I had to face her eventually. And besides, we needed hair scarves, and I wasn't gonna let Maryanne Stephenson keep us from gettin' them. I just didn't know how she was gonna behave around me since our last interaction at her New Year's Eve party went so bad. I've seen her at church every

Sunday, but she acts like we're nothin' but strangers. She's not rude. She's not polite. She just doesn't say a word to me, and that's plenty fine by me, If I'm bein' honest. It makes it easier that way so I don't have to keep bein' nice for the sake of bein' nice when what I really want to do is ring her aggravatin' neck!

Charlie went over to the scarves, and I followed close behind. I felt a little bit like a coward, but one thing I've learned about Maryanne is that she's about as predictable as our summer monsoons. Sometimes there's a nice warm rain followed by sunshine; other times it comes down so hard you think the roof's gonna cave. I never know if I'm just gonna need an umbrella or a safe place to wait it out. It's kind of the same thing with Maryanne.

I don't think Charlie was payin' close attention. There was a scarf that caught his eye, and he went right over to it without even realizin' that Maryanne was standin' just a few feet away, lookin' at hats.

"Charlie Dixon," flirted Maryanne, "how have you been?"

"I've been just fine," said Charlie, realizin' what he'd just gotten himself into.

"I haven't seen you around in a long while," Maryanne said. "Where have you been hidin'?"

"Not hidin'," said Charlie, "I suppose we just spend our time in different places, is all."

"Well that's a shame, isn't it?"

Charlie just smiled and kept on lookin' at the scarves.

Right then Maryanne turned in my direction. "Oh, Will. I didn't see you there," she said coldly.

"How are you, Maryanne?"

"Wonderful," she said. "I don't think I could be better if my life depended on it."

She smiled at me, but it was real insincere. Then she turned her back to me and started in on Charlie again. She kept on with makin' him feel uncomfortable, like she always does. I can't figure why she does that. She knows he doesn't care for it, but it seems like a game to her. Then again, maybe she just thinks she's flirtin'. It's hard to say with Maryanne.

"Now why would you boys be back in the lady's section of the store?" she asked Charlie as she poked him in the arm.

"We're buyin' scarves for Valentine's Day," said Charlie plainly.

"Oh, I see."

"I'm fixin' to send my girl one, and Will is lookin' for one for Hannah. Don't know if you heard, but they're engaged," Charlie said, soundin' almost proud of himself for bringin' it up.

"I heard," she said. "It would be impossible for me not to know since Hannah won't stop talkin' about it. I'm sure everyone in the town knows by now."

I know Maryanne was tryin' to upset me, but it did just the opposite. To know that Hannah was so excited that she was already tellin' folks about our engagement—well, that just filled my heart right up.

"Well don't you want to congratulate him?" asked Charlie.

I could have socked Charlie for that. The last thing I need is phony congratulations from Maryanne, but Charlie seemed to be enjoyin' himself. I don't think he meant to be mean, he just wanted to give Maryanne a taste of the discomfort she's always givin' to everybody else. I just wish he'd considered that I was on the other end of that discomfort before decidin' to play that game with her.

"Yes, of course congratulations are in order," Maryanne said. "I wouldn't dream of havin' you leave here without hearin' that from me."

And the monsoons had started. It was still too early to tell which way things would go, so I stood firm and braced myself for whatever type of weather Maryanne might be sendin' my direction.

"Well, that's real kind of you to say, Maryanne," I said cautiously.

"Why wouldn't I say it?" she said. "What kind of person do you think I am not to congratulate a friend who's found happiness?"

I wasn't in the mood to play Maryanne's games. I could have brought up the New Year's party, but all that would do was turn this mildly uncomfortable storm into a full-blown hurricane. I just wasn't interested in that.

"I believe you'll be needin' to congratulate me soon as well," said Maryanne.

"Oh really?" I asked, tryin' to sound interested. "Why's that?"

"Well, James Carver has been courtin' me for a while now, and things sure are gettin' mighty serious between us."

"Eli Carver's boy?" asked Charlie.

"Uh huh," Maryanne said proudly and raised her nose a little bit in the air.

"Rumor has it you've been seein' the Harper boy... what's his name?" asked Charlie.

"Melvin? That's ridiculous! Who would say such a thing?"

"Sorry," Charlie said with both hands raised like he was surrenderin'. "If it ain't true, don't fret over it."

Maryanne seemed frazzled. If you were just overhearin' the conversation, you'd think it was because she didn't care for Melvin and was embarrassed at the idea that she'd allow herself to be courted by him. But that wasn't the reason. She was doin' her best to make a big deal about seein' James Carver and wanted us to play into it, or be shocked... or somethin' along those lines. So when Charlie changed the subject from James to Melvin, it was obvious that she wanted to stick to the original subject of her serious relationship with James.

"I certainly won't fret," said Maryanne. "It's not me I'm worried about anyway. Poor James would be so upset to hear such a rumor.

He's so in love with me, I'm afraid it would break his heart to think of me with someone else."

"I'm sure it would," I agreed – but only because I thought it would get us out of there quicker.

"Will, take a look at this one," said Charlie as he turned away from Maryanne, hopin' she would move along.

"That's real nice," I said. "Is that the one you're gettin' for Anita?"

Maryanne was still hoverin'.

"I believe so. Green is her favorite color so this one seems perfect," Charlie said.

"I can't say I even know Hannah's favorite color," I said, thinkin' about it.

"Well she always wears that simple yellow dress to church," said Maryanne, "so she'll probably want a yellow one to match it. Some girls just aren't much for fashion, but that's probably not what you like about her anyway, so what does it matter?"

Charlie could see that I had reached my limit with Maryanne. She can give me a hard time all day long, but as soon as she started throwin' shots at Hannah, well, I was about to lose it.

"Nice to see you again, Maryanne," said Charlie. "And good luck with James now."

Then Charlie grabbed a green and a yellow scarf and nudged me in the other direction.

"No luck needed when you've got what James and I have," she called after us.

Maryanne mumbled on about true love as we walked away, smilin' and noddin' and such. This was the first time I really noticed how messed up Maryanne is. I always just thought she was a spoiled brat and a tease, but it goes deeper than that, I think; not sure why, but she's just not thinkin' straight about a lot of things. If what she said about James is true, I pity that poor boy. He's in for a whole lot of somethin', and he's gonna need a real sturdy raincoat.

February 19, 1906

Daddy woke us all extra early this mornin' and said we had to get out to the south pasture quick as we could. He couldn't sleep last night after hearin' the Smith's talk about the sheep scab that came through two neighborin' towns lately. They said that the sheerin' company that worked those towns last fall knew the sheep were infected and kept usin' the same equipment anyway, spreadin' it from farm to farm. Rex Smith says his son raises sheep in one of them towns and has lost half his stock so far. It's been about four years now since Uncle Albert's sheerin' company got into some trouble for doin' the same thing. He lost a handful of farms on account of them not wantin' to do business with him after that. I remember him talkin' with Mama about it.

After he left, Mama and Daddy decided to build a cement pit in the ground where they could quarantine infected sheep if that ever happened on our farm. That way, the infection wouldn't spread and they could use that pit for washin' and treatin' the sick sheep. Uncle Albert had told Mama that some of the other farmers were doin' just that. Then last year, Tom Martin and Eli Carver started sellin' sheep dip in their stores. We'd heard of it before, but nobody around here ever sold it before that. Farmers fill up those pits with dip and water, makin' a mixture that treats the infection. It's mighty powerful stuff that kills the mites that cause sheep scab to begin with. But they learned that you had to dip all the sheep because chances are that if one of your sheep has it, some of the others do too. You can't always see the signs right away so you treat them all.

Daddy took a lamp and went out to check on our sheep to see if any of them showed signs of it. Sure enough, there were at least a dozen sheep with lesions on their shoulders and flanks. As soon as he saw that, he rode to Tom Martin's house in the middle of the night and asked him for enough dip to treat our entire flock. Tom, bein' the good natured man that he is, obliged and went on down to open up the store for Daddy.

We spent the whole day, preparin' the dip mixture, herdin' sheep, and treatin' them all for infection. We also had to wash and disinfect all the sheerin' equipment, just to be safe. Lawrence noticed that one of the breedin' rams seemed to be the worst of the bunch. It would make sense that he's had it the longest. Uncle Albert gave that ram to us last year as a gift, and you might know that that particular sheep would be the cause of our troubles. Uncle Albert probably didn't know it was sick, but it just seems fittin' that he would give us somethin' that spreads infection around. Daddy said we'll have to keep that ram, along with the other sick animals, under quarantine for about two weeks before they can join the rest of the bunch.

By the time sunset came, we were finished. I sat on the ground, restin' my back against the fence post, and Charlie plopped down next to me and found a post of his own to lean on. We were so glad to have that done with. Then Lawrence reminded us that we had to dip the animals twice.

"Twice?" I said, exhausted.

"About eight or nine days from the first time," said Lawrence.

"The thought of doin' all that again makes me—"

"No sense in doin' it at all if you ain't gonna do it proper," he said before I could finish complainin'. "If we don't do it two times, it makes all the work we did today a waste of time."

I sighed and accepted the fact that we'd be here again next week, doin' the same thing.

"Are you still pleased with the idea of sheep ranching after today?" asked Mama.

"Should I get ready for another discussion about college?" I said.

"Maybe if I wasn't so tired," said Mama, and we both laughed.

The evenin' had a chill to it, but it actually felt nice. Mama and Jessie brought out some bread and cheese for a little supper to tide us over until we all made it back to the house for a real meal.

"Why don't we head on into town tonight for a proper supper," Daddy told Mama.

"That's unlike you, Ben," she said.

"Doesn't seem right for you to break your back out here with us all day and then have to go fix a meal for everybody," said Daddy. "Will and I will get the buggy hitched and we'll head out."

"I reckon we'll head on home," said Lawrence.

"Nonsense," Daddy said. "You'll join us for supper."

"That's good of you, Ben, but there ain't nowhere in town that's gonna let me and Charlie in."

"Then you tell us where there is a place that will, and we'll go there."

Lawrence looked at Charlie, then back at Daddy.

"There is a place we could go... serves the best chicken and dumplin's you ever sunk your teeth into, no offense, Lily," Lawrence said.

"Just as long as they can't beat my cinnamon cake," said Mama.

"Will they serve white folks?" Daddy asked.

"Can't say I ever seen a white person in there, but I'd be surprised if they wouldn't serve ya'll," said Charlie.

"It's worth a try," said Daddy.

"Alright then," Lawrence said, and he worked his tired self off the ground to help get the horses hitched.

We all followed suit and got the buggy ready to go in no time. It took a bit longer to go to the west side of town, but the ride was real nice. I suppose the extra time was good for my appetite because by the time we got there, my mouth was waterin' for some of them chicken and dumplin's Lawrence mentioned.

The restaurant was small, but clean. There was a band in the back of the place and a handful of people dancin'. It looked real cozy. We sat down at a table toward the front, and I'd be lyin' if I said that we didn't get lots of stares. I wondered if we were gonna have a problem, seein' as how we were the only white folks in the place. Almost immediately a short, round lady came over to our table to find out what we wanted to eat. She and Lawrence knew each other and they took to chattin' and laughin' about somethin'.

"That's Loretta Jackson, the owner's wife," whispered Charlie. "She knew my mama better than just about anybody around here."

"She looks nice," I said.

"Now who you got with you here?" asked Mrs. Jackson.

"These are our friends, the Wrights," Lawrence said.

"Well I'll be!" she laughed. "We ain't never had no white folks want to eat in our neck of the woods."

"It's alright then?" asked Lawrence. "Charlie told them about the dumplin's, and I reckon it'd be nigh on to impossible to get them to leave at this point."

"I knew it'd just be a matter of time before the word about my dumplin's spread to the other side of town" she said. "I can't help it if they're irresistible! Now don't you mind the stares none. Colored folks in these parts ain't used to havin' dinner with white folks."

"I imagine it's worth it, for a plate of those dumplin's, that is," I said.

And it was. Those dumplin's were better than Mama's—though I'd never tell her that. And we didn't seem to cause too much disruption. We got a few looks of disapproval, and one couple had even left when they saw us come in, but overall, nobody really seemed to mind. It was a nice way to unwind from the day's work.

After supper, we dropped Lawrence and Charlie off and then made our way home. When we got there, we were surprised to see Deputy Jenkins sittin' on the front porch.

"Can you manage the buggy, son, while me and your mama talk with the deputy?" said Daddy.

"Sure," I said. "Jessie can help."

"Do I have a choice?" Jessie sassed.

"Jessica Wright!" scolded Mama.

"Sorry, Mama," said Jessie. "I just wish Will would ask me instead of tell me."

"I didn't ask for a reason," I said. "If I'd asked, you would have thought you had a say in the matter."

"Stop bickerin' and get it done," snapped Daddy as he climbed down and started toward the front porch.

"Why do you have to do that?" asked Jessie after Daddy and Mama were out of hearin' distance.

"Do what?" I said.

"Treat me like I'm a little kid," she said.

"Come on, Jessie, you're makin' too much of it."

"Maybe so, but I deserve a little respect. I'm seventeen years old, you know... almost eighteen, if we're bein' specific."

"OK, OK, I said," tryin' not to laugh.

"This is a perfect example!" Jessie said. "You don't take me seriously!"

"Jess," I said, "this conversation is wearin' on my nerves."

"Fine," said Jessie, and she stomped her way out of the buggy and started with the unhitchen'.

"I get it, Jess, OK? I'm just done talkin' about it is all."

Jessie ignored me. That girl is so moody. It's only been gettin' worse the past couple of years. I know I should probably try harder to hear her out and such, but I was just too dang tired.

It was startin' to get mighty cold, so we finished quick and went inside. When we walked in the front door, there was Deputy

Jenkins, sittin' in the chair by the fireplace and talkin' with Mama and Daddy.

"I can't believe it!" said Daddy with a big old smile on his face.

"I couldn't believe it at first either," said the deputy.

"If that's not the best luck, I don't know what is," Daddy said as he slapped his knee and shook his head.

"What's goin' on?" I asked, undoin' my coat and hangin' it on the hook by the door.

"Yeah," said Jessie, "what are you guys talkin' about?"

"Deputy Jenkins here," started Mama, "came by to tell us that Mayor Harper won't be returnin' to his duties as Mayor after all."

"Why not?" asked Jessie.

"Seems he got an infection from the gunshot wound to his leg. They had to take it off."

"And we're happy about that?" said Jessie, soundin' disgusted.

"No, no, of course not," said Mama. "That's the sad part. But unfortunately, sometimes good things can come from sad things."

"The good part is that actin' mayor, Mayer Roberts, will be the new Mayor, and he'll be good for our town, I'm certain of it," Deputy Jenkins said.

"What about Sheriff Coleman?" I asked.

"What about him?" said the deputy.

"Well," I said, "it might not be my place, but I feel I've got to say that our town won't see a lick of real change as long as he's the sheriff."

Everyone was quiet, and I wondered if I'd spoken out of turn. Deputy Jenkins looked at the ground for a minute, and then he slowly raised his head and looked right at me.

"One thing at a time," he said.

As simple a thing as that was to say, it was enough. I could see that Deputy Jenkins already knew what kinda trouble we're in with Sheriff Coleman bein' in charge. It was dumb of me to think I had to point it out to him, but it wasn't bein' said, and so that's why I said it.

"Would you like to stay for some coffee?" asked Mama.

"No thank you, Mrs. Wright. That's a kind offer, but I should be heading home. Mrs. Jenkins will start to worry soon."

Daddy walked Deputy Jenkins out to his horse. They talked a minute or two longer, and then Daddy came back in the house and closed the door behind him. Then he just stood there, leanin' against it.

"Everything alright?" asked Mama.

"Couldn't be better," said Daddy. "The good Lord sure works in mysterious ways."

I didn't know how it would all turn out, but it was nice to see the relief on Daddy's face, especially after such a long, hard day. And now that those dang sheep have all been dipped, we can get back to buildin' that room for me and Hannah tomorrow.

March 31, 1906

I find myself unable to write much lately. We work like animals durin' the day, and I can't help but just fall into bed at night, without writin' down so much as a single sentence about anything. I suppose it wouldn't much matter if I did though... it would all be about Hannah and how excited I am to marry her. Can't seem to think about much else these days. The weddin' is less than four weeks away, and I'd say we have a good six weeks of work left on that room. I'll work from sunup to sundown, and then into the night with a lamp if I have to so we can get it done in time.

Love seems to be in the air, seein' as how it's springtime, and it's not just me that gets to enjoy the feelin'. Charlie and Anita are doin' real well. Anita's family came through about a week ago Friday on their way to Arizona. Mama offered to put them up here for the evenin' so they could get a break from their travels. They had train tickets for the followin' mornin', and Mrs. Davis reluctantly agreed to stay with us. We ended up havin' a real hoot of a time. It was awful uncomfortable at first, what with Mrs. Davis keepin' her nose in the air, Mr. Davis actin' like a mute, and everyone else usin' every trick they had to try and get them to loosen up. It felt like a circus for a while on account of everyone's nerves. The only thing missin' was a clown with his head in a lion's mouth.

You know what finally did it? It wasn't Mama or Anita. It was Jessie. Jessie took to Mrs. Davis like they'd been long lost friends that had finally found their way back to one another, and Mrs. Davis took to Jessie in the same way. I can't think of a single thing they have in common, but they must be kindred souls. There's no other way to explain it. Maybe the reason Mrs. Davis liked Jessie so much is because Jessie was the only one of us not tryin' to get Mrs. Davis to like her. I don't believe Jessie even knew the situation with the Davis' not likin' Charlie. She just figured they were friends of the Dixons and treated them proper. It was probably the first time I took time to sit back and notice how much Jessie has really grown up. She's not a little kid anymore and I'm the worst when it comes to seein' that.

By the end of the evenin', everyone was talkin' and laughin' and really gettin' to know one another. Daddy even took out his guitar and played for a while, the rest of us singin' old spirituals together. Seems that churchgoers know most of the same songs, even if we sing them different from each other. I imagine our versions bored the Davis' a bit, but they sang along anyhow.

When the evenin' was over and we were fixin' to get to bed, I heard Mrs. Davis pull Charlie aside and tell him that any mama who raised a girl like Jessie was alright, and if that same mama had somethin' to do with raisin' Charlie, then she'd give him her blessin' to court Anita. However, courtin' for them was gonna be sorta difficult since they could only see each other three or four times a year, but Charlie says that doesn't matter one bit. He knows Anita is the girl for him and will make the most of those three of four times. Charlie told me that he might see if he can go stay with Aunt Lena for a while, once things really get goin' with Anita. As much as I would hate him bein' gone, I don't blame him at all for wantin' to be with the girl he loves. I'm not sure how Lawrence would do without him though. I reckon he'd be mighty lonely without Charlie around. But nothin' is decided yet. We'll see in time.

I found out from Mama yesterday that Jessie and Jacob Harris still fancy one another.

"How do you know?" I asked Mama.

"John Harris came over to talk with your pa on Tuesday," Mama said, "and after they discussed their business, we had some scones and talked."

"You asked him about Jacob?" I said real surprised.

"No!" said Mama. "He asked me about Jessie!"

Sometimes when me and Mama talk, I end up feelin' like one of them old biddies at church, caught up in the gossip of the day. She can rope me in somethin' terrible.

"What did he say?" I asked.

"He said that Jacob would have his hide if he knew that John was talking to me about Jessie, so don't you say a thing about it."

"Mama, I won't think about this five seconds after you tell me, so you don't have to worry about that. Now what did Mr. Harris say?"

"He said that Jacob has been sweet on Jessie since they were in grade school together."

"Is that when they started kissin' behind the school house?" I said as I laughed to myself.

Mama hit me with the dishtowel.

"That only happened once," said Mama, "and we talked with Jessie long and hard about that."

As we talked about Jessie and Jacob, I remembered that Mama had said John Harris came to discuss business with Daddy.

"What business did Daddy and Mr. Harris have to discuss?" I asked.

"Oh, John Harris had some legal papers drawn up to say that Daddy gets the money from the pecans sold from the trees that grow on the land Grandpa gave to Charles Harris all those years ago."

"Are you kiddin'?"

"Isn't that something?" she said.

"That's good money, Mama!"

"Well, we won't know how good until the harvest, but it should help out quite a bit. And after having to dip all the sheep and losing a handful of them to the scab, it comes at a good time."

"How did John Harris come from a man like Charles?" I said.

"Strange how that works sometimes," said Mama.

"Let's just hope that Jacob takes after his daddy and not his granddaddy, huh?"

"Yes," said Mama, soundin' concerned, like she hadn't thought of that before, "let's hope so."

"What will Daddy do with that money?" I asked.

"The first thing he'll do is raise Lawrence's and Charlie's wages. After that, I'm not sure. It's something we still have to talk about."

It was so nice to know that after all this time, Mama and Daddy were finally gonna get what Grandpa Wright should have gotten all along. They've been sweatin' and savin' – and never a word of complaint from either one of them. Charles Harris must be turnin' in his grave over this. But I suppose that's fittin' for a man like him to spend eternity fumin' over somethin' that wasn't rightfully his to begin with. I hear weird noises outside sometimes, and it has occurred to me that Charles Harris haunts those orchards. That's a ridiculous thing to say, I know, but I thought I should at least mention it in case somethin' unexplainable ever happens to me. Mama would put me over her knee and whoop me for talkin' like this, about ghosts and such. So it's fair to say that I'm lookin' out for her feelin's, and my behind, by not discussin' it with her.

April 26, 1906

We finished the room today! We never could have done it without Lawrence and Charlie. There were even a few days when Jacob Harris came to lend a hand. Now I know that he didn't do it out of the plain goodness of his heart; and even knowin' that he did it on account of wantin' to look good in front of Jessie is just fine by me.

I stood there, lookin' at that room and thinkin' about the fact that I'm marryin' Hannah in two days! I've been countin' down from eighty three days, and I can't believe it's almost here. Mama and Jessie have been workin' real close with Hannah's mama and sisters. Maybe I should be more involved in all that, but the truth is, we could get married in the middle of a field, no flowers, no food afterward, just me and Hannah, and I'd be the happiest man alive. Havin' said that, it will be nice to share this day with the folks who are closest to us. Now I would write more, but I've got two more days of countin' down to do, and I best get to it!

"Your mama wants me to talk with you man to man before you get married tomorrow," Daddy said.

I was leanin' up against the split rail fence that Daddy and Lawrence built together, writin' a letter to Hannah. I was plannin' on givin' it to her right before the ceremony, sort of as a weddin' present.

"Alright," I said as I folded the piece of paper and sat up straight.

He sat down next to me on the old wood choppin' stump and spit out the long blade of grass he'd been chewin' on. It was the first time I really noticed that he was startin' to look old. He couldn't bend down as easy as he could before, and his knees made an awful grindin' noise when he did. His brown skin was dry and leathery from spendin' so much time outside. I'm not sure why I never noticed before. Could be because we don't spend much time sittin' and talkin' like this where I can get a good look at him. He took his hat off and set it on the ground next to him.

"Men and women are different, Will," he said.

"I knowthat," I said.

"Now don't interrupt me, son!" he said, his voice rather abrupt and a bit on the nervous side. "Just let me say what I got to say."

"Sorry," I said, feelin' startled.

Daddy scratched the back of his head and started again.

"Men and women are different," he said.

We've already covered that, I thought to myself but didn't dare share that with him.

"And when they come together as husband and wife for the first time, it's real important for the man to be sensitive to the woman so she feels comfortable... because the woman might feel uncomfortable if the man ain't sensitive," he said.

I just sat and listened, not sure where he was goin' with it. He didn't seem to be goin' anywhere except around in circles. All I could seem to grasp was that I'm supposed to be sensitive—about what... I had no clue. And Hannah is gonna end up feelin' comfortable or uncomfortable – I'm not sure which. And speakin' of bein' uncomfortable, Daddy looked like a lone rabbit in a coyote's den. I don't believe he looked at me the whole time he was talkin', just fidgeted and looked at the ground.

"You understand?" he asked.

I couldn't bring myself to tell him I had no idea what in tarnation he was talkin' about. So I just nodded instead.

"Uh huh," I said.

"Good," said Daddy as he put his hat back on and stood up to leave.

"Thank you, sir," I said. "This was real helpful."

Daddy stood there for a minute, not sure what to do next. He nervously shifted his weight from one foot to the other, and at one point, I thought he might shake my hand, but then he just said, "Alright then", and went back in the house.

While he isn't good with words, and I came away more confused than before we started, I was glad he took the time to talk to me about somethin' he thought I needed to know. And even if it wasn't him, but Mama that wanted me to know it, I'm still grateful he'd suffer through it the way he did on account of it bein' important to her.

Letter to Hannah
April 28, 1906

Dear Hannah,

Today is our weddin' day and there are some things I feel I should say to you. Might have said them before, but this way you get to have them on paper so you can look at this letter from time to time and remember this day. I plan on tellin' you every day for the rest of eternity just how I feel about you, but maybe this way, when you're sore at me and don't feel like hearin' the sound of my voice, you can still read my words and know how much I care for you.

I knew from the time I was young that I had to marry a decent woman because I'd been raised by Mama, and it just wouldn't be possible to find happiness with someone who didn't have the qualities that she has. I got lucky, I suppose, to have been brought up by such a fine woman. Lots of folks out there don't have that kind of luck. You see all kinds of women who are afraid to work, sweat, and sacrifice. And then there are women like you and Mama. You were brought up fancy, but your souls are humble. You see life for what it really is; you want to love and be loved; you see the value and worth of every person, and you understand that sufferin' is just part of life you can't hide from. I know where Mama gets all that. She's been around lots of years, experienced more heartache than any woman should, and had time to figure some things out. But you're a mystery to me. You're wiser than you should be for someone so young, and your heart is more carin' than you know what to do with sometimes. You are a special kind of person that I believe God put on the earth to make the rest of us want to be better.

I look at you, and it takes the breath right out of my chest sometimes. Part of it is because you're so beautiful, but the other reason is because I'm amazed by you. You're just not built for bein' unkind, and I love that about you most. I know that when sadness comes, we'll fight through it together until we find happiness again. I know that you are meant to be the mother to my children... I've already seen it *happen in my mind. And I know that I'll spend every day I have on this earth, lovin' you and bein' grateful that you love me back.*

　　　　　　　　　—*Your lovin' husband, Will*

April 28, 1906

I'm marryin' Hannah today. Three hours, forty-six minutes, and twelve seconds... eleven... ten... nine...

April 30, 1906

I told Hannah that I was gonna sit outside for a spell and write about our weddin' day. She said that since I'm a man, she was sure I wasn't gonna include the important stuff, so she made me promise to mention a few things. I'm hopin' it will be obvious which stuff she had me put down so whoever ends up readin' this won't think I'm the sort of fella who fancies all this feminine stuff.

The apple blossoms were in full bloom, and it felt like it was rainin' pink and white flowers as we walked out of the church after the ceremony. Hannah's colors were light yellow and bright purple. I can't say that I even knew that, but she insisted there were purple and yellow flowers and ribbons on the dinner tables. Kathryn Harris made enough pecan pies to feed three times the number of guests we had at the reception, and I'm sorta glad about it because she sent some home with us afterward. Let's see... oh yeah, and I'm supposed to mention that Hannah wore her great grandmother's weddin' gown. She also said to mention that the letter I had Jessie give her right before the ceremony made her cry. Now onto my own thoughts...

The day was just as it should be. I found myself feelin' awful nervous, which surprised me. I couldn't stop pacin' the floor, waitin' for everyone to get ready. I put my suit on a good two hours before I needed to and regretted it for about an hour and forty-five minutes. Mama and Jessie took some extra time to paint their faces and pin up their hair, and Daddy also wore a suit. It would embarrass him if I asked, but I'm pretty sure that Mama made him scrub underneath his nails and put some cream on too. I've never seen Daddy's hands so clean. I didn't notice it until he shook my hand after the service, and thought to myself, 'It's amazin' the things Mama can get that man to do.'

When we finally got into the church, I was pleased to feel the cool breeze blowin' through the open windows. It was evenin' time and the lamps were all ready to burn in case we ran out of sunlight, which we did. Someone had even made a path lit by torches that led from the church house to the tents where the celebration was bein' held. I don't remember much about the music or the decorations, but I'll never forget two things as long as I live: the first one bein' the comfort I felt from Charlie standin' by my side until the ceremony started and pattin' me on the back before he sat down; and the second one was when I saw my Hannah for the first time in that weddin' gown. She looked like an angel come from Heaven.

I've been to a few weddin's in our town before, and some of the dresses the girls wear are downright silly. They're covered in lace and bows and nonsense. A man would have a devil of a time even gettin' to his woman in a dress like that. And they have so much paint on their faces that you can't even recognize who they are half the time. I reckon there's been a time or two when a man has held his breath, waitin' for all that makeup to come off after the weddin' is over, hopin' he married the right girl! But none of that was Hannah. No silly dress, no war paint, no hundreds of curls takin' over her head. She looked like Hannah, and she was beautiful.

I'd by lyin' if I said I heard a word Pastor Brown actually said. I tried to listen at first, but I just couldn't. I had melted into the experience, and it was all I could do to just keep my feet on the ground. Actually, there is one part of that ceremony I will never forget – it was when the pastor asked Hannah if she would take me as her lawful, wedded husband, and she looked deeply into my eyes for a moment and then answered, "I do." Right then I felt that everything in the world – in the universe – was as it should be. All I could do was look at this amazin' woman and think, "she is mine, and I am hers, and we are now one."

After the ceremony was over, we made our way down the church aisle, with folks clappin' and cheerin'. I stopped along the way to hug Mama, who was blubberin' somethin' terrible. Then Hannah and I walked hand in hand down that lighted path, with all our friends and family members followin' along behind us, to the tents that Daddy, Lawrence, Charlie, and Pastor Brown had pitched that mornin'. We danced and ate. We laughed and rejoiced. We soaked up every moment of that celebration, and I was a fool to think that it would have been as special without our loved ones around to share in it with us. All those people there to celebrate me and Hannah lovin' each other...I've never had such a wonderful time in all my life.

After things settled down a bit and folks were startin' to head for home, I felt a nervousness take hold in my belly. Tonight would be the first time that me and Hannah would be together as husband and wife. I thought back on that talk with Daddy the day before, and I imagined he was tryin' to give me some guidance. The only thing I could remember him sayin' was to be sensitive. "Well," I thought, "that's all I got, so I hope it's all I need."

Hannah hadn't seen the room that we built yet. It was a surprise, and I was real excited for her to see it. After it was built, Mama helped me decorate it up nice. We only had a day to do it in, and Mama had scurried around, doin' her very best to make sure things looked just right. Me and Daddy made a solid bed frame, and Mama restuffed an old, down quilt that she had put away in her closet a while back to go on the bed. There were lamps hung on either side of the bed and a nice lookin' dresser against the wall underneath the window, that Lawrence had sanded and polished for us.

Hannah's mama had gotten together with Mama and some of their friends and tied a handsome rug that dang near covered the entire floor. It was mostly brown and blue with a little bit of green in it to match the quilt. Our humble place was modest and simple, but it was home, and I just knew Hannah was gonna love it. When I first told her that Mama and Daddy had offered to let us live there with them, she laughed with pleasure and said she was so grateful for their kindness. She didn't turn her nose up or complain about not havin' a place of our own. She was real pleased and made of point of expressin' her thankfulness to them the very next time she saw them.

As the evenin' was drawin' to a close, I went over and whispered to Mama that we were tired and would probably head on home. Jessie and some of the other girls from church had decorated the buggy and even tied a big purple bow around Daddy's mare. Mama said that she and Daddy would stay behind and see to things until everyone had gone.

"Go on home, now," said Mama. "We'll be along in a while."

"You don't have to stay away on our account," I said, "feelin' a little awkward."

"Don't you worry about us, son. We're having a lovely time."

I knew Mama was tryin' to give us some privacy, and I was grateful. Even though our room was off the side of the house, we'd be more comfortable knowin' that we were alone.

The band played a lively song for us as we rode away, and the folks who were still there gathered around and cheered goodbye and congratulations.

When we got home, I unhitched the horses and helped Hannah out of the buggy.

"I just brought one suitcase for now," said Hannah. "I figured we could ride over tomorrow after church or on Monday to get the rest of my things."

"Of course," I said, as I took the suitcase and led her inside the house.

"I can't wait to see it!" she said excitedly.

"Close your eyes," I told her.

"Don't let me bump into anything." She squeezed my hand.

"I won't. We're almost there," I said. "Just a few more steps... and... OK, you can open them."

Hannah opened her eyes and threw her hands up to her face as soon as she saw the room.

"This is beautiful, Will!"

"Do you really like it?"

"I love it!" she said. "It's even better than how I imagined it."

Hannah started walkin' slowly around and lookin' at every little thing. She looked so pleased, which made me happy – and a little relieved. She eventually walked over to me, put both arms around me, and buried her head against my chest. I just held onto her and felt her heart beatin' against me.

"You can change it however you like once we're settled," I said

"I don't want to change it," she replied.

"Well, . . . you know, add your girly touches and such," I said.

"Oh, well—I do want to do some of that," she teased.

The room got quiet, and we just stood there huggin' one another.

"Will?" she said.

"Yes, Hannah."

"Are you nervous?"

"Why do you ask?" I said, feelin' like she could read my mind.

"Because you're shaking," she said.

"Are you nervous?" I asked.

"Yes." Her voice was soft and sweet and couldn't conceal the shyness she felt.

"Me too," I said.

I stood there holdin' her and tryin' to figure how to go about this. Even though we were finally married and had the proper privacy, it seemed that we were both feelin' hesitant. Maybe we weren't quite ready for what was supposed to happen next in this new relationship. The funny thing is, Daddy's "sensitive" and "comfortable" kept ringin' in my ears. I don't know if I was takin' it how he meant for me to, but it ended up bein' helpful after all.

"Hannah," I said as I gently pulled away from her and held her face in my hands. "Would it be alright with you if we changed into our night clothes and just talked for a while?"

"That sounds just wonderful," she said, and she turned her cheek into my hand and kissed it.

"Are you sure that's OK with you?"

"Well, I know you can't wait to get your hands on me," I said, "but I guess I'm old fashioned."

"Oh, Will," Hannah said as she blushed and tried to keep from smilin'.

"I'll change in the other room," I said. "You just let me know when you're ready."

A few minutes later, I heard Hannah call for me. When I went in, I found her snuggled up in our bed. I put out the lamps and opened the curtains to let the moonlight into the room. Then I climbed in bed next to her and pulled her into me. She lay there on my chest, and I stroked her long hair as we talked about the day.

"It was perfect in every way," said Hannah.

"Even when Mrs. Jones drank too much wine and tried to cut in on our first' dance?" I said.

"Even that part," she said as we both took to laughin'.

"I never imagined I'd be starin' at Harriet Jones' face durin' my weddin' dance. Boy was I glad to see you again after poor Mr. Jones politely pried her away from me!"

Hannah couldn't stop laughin' about that, and the more I thought about it, the harder I laughed too.

After a while, we finally managed to settle down, and I couldn't help but notice the warmth of Hannah's body next to mine. It was unlike anything I'd ever felt before, and I didn't ever want to let her go.

"I can't believe we're married," Hannah said.

"How do you feel about bein' Mrs. Will Wright?"

"It's even better than I dreamed it would be."

"Did I tell you how beautiful you looked tonight?"

"You may have mentioned it a once or twice... or nine or ten times," Hannah said, and I could tell she was smilin' when she said it – even without lookin' at her face.

"Well, you did... look so beautiful, I mean. From the moment I saw you walkin' down that aisle toward me, I thought, 'how did I get so darn lucky?'"

Then I leaned down and kissed her forehead. She raised her face to meet mine and kissed me in a way that let me know she was just as in love with me as I was with her. Then she laid her head back on my chest and snuggled into me even tighter.

"I love you, Will," she whispered.

"And I love you, Hannah," I said.

Then sleep took hold of both of us, and I'd never slept better in my whole life. I only woke once when Mama, Daddy, and Jessie came home, then I pulled Hannah into me again and went right back to sleep. Turns out there's plenty of time for the other stuff, when we're both ready. I'm not sayin' I don't want to, because Heaven knows I do, but when I think back on my first night with her, I wouldn't change a single thing about it, and I'm fairly certain she feels the same.

June 9, 1906

"You ain't gonna believe what happened last night!" said Daddy as he rode around the side of the house where me and Hannah were helpin' Mama with some gardenin'.

"Oh, Ben!" Mama gasped, holdin' onto her chest. "You scared the life out of me!"

"I'm sorry, honey, but I got to tell you what I just heard!"

"What is it, Daddy?" I asked.

"I just ran into Deputy Jenkins, and he said that Sheriff Coleman was arrested last night. He's actually sittin' in a jail cell right this very minute!"

"What on earth for?" Mama asked as she stood up and took off her gardenin' gloves.

"Well, he couldn't give me all the details, of course, but he said that someone is accusin' the Sheriff of havin' a hand in a fire." Daddy jumped down off his horse and walked over to Mama.

"A fire? What kind of fire?" said Mama.

"Well, James Bailey's store was blazed somethin' terrible last night; and there was a handful of men seen leavin' the tavern right before it happened."

"And the Sheriff was one of them?" I asked.

"He was."

"For a man who's not supposed to give you all the details, you sure did get plenty from Deputy Jenkins," Mama said.

"I only got the part of the Sheriff bein' accused from Deputy Jenkins. The rest of it was told to me by Tom Martin when I went in for supplies this mornin'. He said that Sheriff Coleman was the drunkest he's ever seen a man be when he left."

"Why was Tom Martin at the tavern?" asked Mama. "That seems unlike him."

"He was just makin' a delivery, is all."

"I can't believe it," said Mama. "Poor Mr. Bailey. Is he alright? He wasn't hurt was he?"

"Nobody was there when it went up in flames. I reckon he'd already gone home for the night."

"What will he do about his shop?" Hannah asked, real concerned.

"I couldn't say," said Daddy. "It's an awful shame."

"What's gonna happen to the Sheriff, do you suppose?" I asked.

"Deputy Jenkins said he'd be appointed Sheriff until things get sorted."

"Until things get sorted? What's that supposed to mean?" I said, startin' to feel myself get agitated.

"Well," said Daddy, "someone's got to prove he did it."

"So who's doin' the accusin'? That person can just tell the judge what he saw," I said.

"It's not that simple," son," said Daddy. "And even if it was that easy, you know that Sheriff Coleman and Judge Moore are longtime friends. That trial ain't never gonna happen."

"Doesn't that break some law!" I shouted.

"Of course it does," said Daddy. "But they'll get to the witness before he even gets two seconds to think on whether or not he wants to testify. They'll threaten his family or somethin' awful like that."

"How can that be true?" said Hannah. "There has to be something we can do."

"I'm afraid the things we can do to fight this are just as ugly as the things we're talkin' about right now," Daddy replied.

"What about Deputy Jenkins?" I asked. "He's got some power."

"He's fixin' to do all he can," said Daddy. "We just have to hope it's enough."

"None of this is right," I said.

"No it isn't," said Mama sadly. "And no matter what happens, you remember that."

"Anyone seen Lawrence and Charlie this mornin'?" asked Daddy.

"They haven't been in yet," said Mama.

"Lawrence and James are friends. I'm guessin' he's offerin' what help he can," Daddy said." I'll head on that way to see about it."

"Find out if there's something we can do, Ben," said Mama.

Daddy rode off, and me, Mama, and Hannah finished our work in silence. Knowin' somethin' is wrong but feelin' like you got no power to fix it is one of those things in life that can tear you up inside. You wanna believe that there are more people who see things the way you do than the ones who disagree with you. That might even be true in our town, but even the ones who see things the right way, . . . well, most of them just keep their eyes closed to it all. They want no part in it. They won't take a side, and it leaves those of us who will to be eaten alive if we try to do anything about it. And it may just come to that someday.

August 4, 1906

I'm not sure if it's my anger that keeps me from writin', or if it's because life got lots busier after marryin' Hannah. The anger part comes from seein' Sheriff Coleman get away with what he did to James Bailey. We all knew it was gonna end up that way, but the sickness I feel over it sometimes is enough to make me want to get my gun and teach Sheriff Coleman and that crooked judge a lesson. I know that's an evil thing to say, which is the reason I write it down instead of sayin' it out loud for someone to hear. It took us weeks to get that burned-out mess cleaned up, and we all donated what supplies we could spare to help Mr. Bailey rebuild, but I'm not sure he'll be able to feed himself until the new store is up and bringin' in money. The first day me and Daddy showed up to help, Mr. Bailey turned us away. I didn't understand that until

Lawrence explained that Mr. Bailey was just lookin' out for us. It probably wasn't the safest place for us to be right then. The colored folks in that area weren't feelin' real Christian-like toward white folks after what had happened, so he sent us home. Within a few days, things had calmed enough that we were able to help some, and Mr. Bailey was real grateful.

The only good thing that came of that situation was that Sheriff Coleman was asked to step down from his position. I'm not sure how they did it, but I'm bettin' the Sheriff's drinkin' played a part. He's drunk more than he's sober these days. It's been that way for a while now. The sad part is, there are a handful of people over Sheriff Coleman, and they didn't get rid of him because of the crime he committed against James Bailey; they got rid of him because he was startin' to be an embarrassment to them. He couldn't do his job on account of him bein' a drunkard and was makin' the folks in charge look bad. Now whether they offered him somethin' to step down quietly, or threatened him if he didn't, I just don't care. The only thing I care about is that he's not runnin' this town anymore.

As far as bein' married goes, it's about as nice as I could have hoped for it to be. Hannah has fixed up our room real pretty, and she seems to feel comfortable livin' with us. Mama, Daddy, and Jessie are about as welcomin' as can be, and I've been real grateful to them for doin' all they can to make it a nice situation for Hannah. There has been one thing that's a little hard for me. Almost as soon as me and Hannah got married, I felt Mama pull away a bit. Don't get me wrong, she's still the same mama – lovin' and kind, thoughtful and funny, but somethin' is different. Her affection toward me changed, and I'm not sure I can even explain how. I wouldn't even know what to say to her about it if I decided to bring it up. I suppose it's her way of encouragin' me to rely on her less and Hannah more. I love Hannah, but I've only had her for a short while. I've had Mama my whole life. And as much as I love Hannah, she doesn't take the place of Mama. So it's hard for me to figure it all out... who I'm supposed to turn to and for what. I'm sure that livin' in the same house makes that figurin' out harder to come by.

Both Hannah and Mama haven't been feelin' well. I thought they'd both caught the same bug, but Mama thought different.

"You've been sick for several days now, Hannah dear," said Mama one mornin' after breakfast.

"I know," said Hannah. "Sometimes I think I'm starting to feel better, and then I end up feeling terrible again."

"You sure have been sleeping a lot lately, too," Mama said.

"I know, Lily. I hope you don't mistake my being ill for laziness."

Mama laughed and stroked Hannah's arm as she walked past her while clearin' the dishes from the table.

"Hannah," said Mama. "Have you missed anything in the last week or so?"

"Missed anything?" said Hannah, soundin' confused. "Like what?"

Mama went over to Hannah and whispered somethin' in her ear. I didn't know why she couldn't just say what needed to be said in front of me, but once I knew what it was, I was mighty grateful that Mama had kept me out of it.

"Oh, Lily, do you really think that's the reason?" asked Hannah excitedly.

Well, why don't we take a ride down to see Doc Wilson today and make sure," said Mama. "I need to see him anyhow."

I just couldn't stand bein' left out of this conversation any longer.

"Would somebody mind tellin' me what we're talkin' about?" I said.

Mama excused herself from the room and went out back to fetch the clothes off the line. Hannah looked like she was about to burst. Her shoulders were shrugged up so far that her neck just about disappeared, and she covered her mouth with her hands like she was fightin' to keep in whatever secret Mama had shared with her.

"What in the world is wrong with you?" I asked her.

"Your mama thinks ... ," she started..."Well... your mama thinks I'm going to have a baby!"

"A baby?" I said, feelin' the blood drain from my face until I thought I might pass out.

"Will, are you OK?" Hannah asked as she came behind my chair and put her hands on my shoulders.

"A baby," I said, feelin' kinda stunned.

"Yes, love," said Hannah. "A baby."

"Do we want a baby?" I asked without thinkin'.

Hannah threw her head back and laughed my favorite laugh – then she sat down next to me and put her arm around me best she could.

"Well if we didn't want a baby," said Hannah, "then we probably shouldn't have been doing what it takes to get one. You do know how this happened, don't you, Will?"

"Of course I know how it happened," I said, startin' to feel the color come back into my face and realizin' that Hannah was givin' me a hard time.

"And the answer to your question is, yes! We do want a baby," Hannah said.

"I believe you're right," I said as I felt the excitement for the first time. "We do want a baby. It's just that I'm barely gettin' used to havin' you around, and now we're gonna have a baby too?"

"Very romantic, Will."

"I didn't mean it like that."

"So you're happy?"

"I think so. I might need a few minutes before I can answer properly, but I think so."

"Well, I'll see the doctor today and find out for sure."

"Yeah, you should do that. That's a good idea. Doc Wilson is the right person to talk to about this sort of thing."

"Yes," said Hannah." She laughed and shook her head with amusement as she left the room.

It took me a few minutes of sittin' there tryin' to get my head around this new development, before I could move my legs out from under me and stand up. Everything was just happenin' so fast, but the more I thought on it, the happier I felt.

Mama came back in the house to get her purse so she and Hannah could head on down to see Doc Wilson.

"So?" asked Mama. 'How do you feel about that possibility?'

"I think I feel good," I said plainly.

"Well, don't think about it too much yet. We'll see the doctor, and then you'll know for sure."

I saw Hannah and Mama off and then got started on my chores. I know Mama told me not to think too much about the idea of a baby until I knew for sure, but the more I tried not to think about it, the worse it was. Baby thoughts took over my mind and made it awful hard to focus on my work. I found myself watchin' the dirt road that leads to our place for signs of Mama and Hannah returnin', and I realized while doin' it, that I was hopin' it was true. I imagined Hannah climbin' out of the buggy with a smile on her face, and that's what I wanted. It took me some time to figure it out, but there it was.

I'd been out to the west pasture with Daddy for most of the mornin', reparin' some of the fence posts that had fallen durin' our last rainstorm.

"Why do you keep lookin' toward the house?" asked Daddy, soundin' bothered.

"I'm just waitin' on Hannah to get back from the doctor."

"Is she sick?"

I thought about tellin' Daddy, but decided to wait until I knew for sure what to tell him.

"She hasn't been feelin' well," I said, somewhat distracted.

"Neither has your mama," said Daddy. "They're probably sharin' somethin'."

"Well, Mama went with Hannah, so I reckon we'll find out soon enough," I said.

Just then Daddy missed the nail he was swingin' for and hit his thumb with the hammer. He drew his hand back and took to shakin' it hard as he could.

"You alright, Daddy?" I asked.

"Oh, I'm fine," he said real exasperated. "I just can't wait for Lawrence and Charlie to get back. I'm more careful when they're here on account of me not feelin' like I got to rush everything to get it done."

"They're expected back tomorrow, aren't they?"

"Believe so," said Daddy.

Lawrence and Charlie were down in Alabama again. I know it's been inconvenient for Lawrence, but he's been doin' all he can to make it possible for Charlie to see Anita. I'm sure he doesn't mind passin' the time at Aunt Lena's either. They get treated somethin' special there, and they usually come home havin' to let out their belts some for a couple of weeks due to Aunt Lena's southern cookin'.

"Looks like the girls are back," said Daddy, motionin' toward the dirt road.

"You mind if I ride in to see how things went?" I asked.

"I'll ride with you," Daddy said. "It's about time for lunch anyhow."

I felt a little thrill as we were ridin' to the house. As soon as I saw Hannah's face, I would know, I thought to myself.

Mama got out of the buggy first, but I couldn't read her. Then Hannah climbed out right after Mama, but her back was to me. As I got closer to them, they both looked real serious, so I figured we weren't havin' a baby after all.

A moment later I reached their buggy and climbed off my horse. Unable to hide the concern in my voice, I asked, "what did the doctor say?" I had a fear that I already knew what she was goin' to answer.

"It's good news!" said Hannah. "The baby will be here sometime in the late spring."

The relief I felt was so overwhelmin' that all I could say was, "really?"

"Well, I'll be," said Daddy. "Congratulations, you two!"

But somethin' wasn't right. Hannah was so excited this mornin', but now that she knew for sure, it almost seemed like she was forcin' happiness about it. Mama too.

"Isn't this what you wanted?" I asked.

"Yes, of course it is," she said quietly. But I could detect a certain sadness in her eyes as she spoke.

"Then why don't you seem happy?"

"We're all so happy!" said Mama as she gave me a big hug. "Why don't I make some lunch and we'll talk all about it."

"Lily," said Hannah. "I think it's best if we just tell them."

"Oh, Hannah, let's enjoy this wonderful news for a while, shall we," said Mama, her eyes startin' to fill with tears.

"Tell us what?" asked Daddy, soundin' real concerned.

Mama's chin fell to her chest, and she suddenly looked sad and somewhat far away — as though she were tryin' to understand somethin' that was just beyond her ability to grasp.

"Let's go inside and sit down," she said. "Does anyone know where Jessie is? She should be here for this too."

"She's out by the crick doin' her studies," I said. "At least she was when I left to meet up with Daddy."

"Run and check, will you, son?" said Mama.

I found Jessie just where I thought she'd be, and after a hurried explanation, we rushed back to the house as fast as we could to hear what Mama had to say. I felt a terrible knot in my stomach, and I wasn't sure if it'd be best to warn Jessie that it might not be good news we were about to hear, or just let it be until we knew what it was. I decided to let it be.

Arrivin' almost breathless back at the house, we hurried inside, and I found my place next to Hannah on the sofa, where we waited anxiously for Mama. She and Daddy had gone into their room and said they'd be out in a minute. I knew that if she had to tell Daddy the news first, and in private, it wasn't gonna be good.

A short while later, the bedroom door opened, and the two of them walked slowly back in to where we were all waitin', hardly darin' to move. Daddy looked real somber, and Mama had a forced smile on her face, just like she did when me and Jessie were little and one of our animals had died. Mama would try to make it seem better than it was so we weren't so sad.

"Well," Mama started, "it seems that I've got a growth in my belly, and Doc Wilson thinks that I need to do some testing to find out exactly what's going on."

"What kind of testin'," asked Jessie.

"He says the kinds of tests I need done, he can't do. So he's sending me to Jonesboro to see a specialist there."

"Why can't he do it here?" asked Jessie.

"It's a small town, honey, and Doc Wilson's clinic just has the basic equipment."

"Mama," I said, "I feel like you're keepin' part of it from us."

"It's better to wait until we have all the information before we start guessing about what it could be," she said. "That will just make everybody crazy."

"But did Doc say what he thought?" I asked, tryin' to get her to spit out what she was chewin' on.

"Will, please," said Mama.

Daddy stood behind her and put his hand on her back "Tell them what Doc said, Lily. Waitin' to know for sure ain't gonna make anyone feel any better."

Mama switched her weight from one foot to the other and took a deep breath. The smile she had on her face earlier was gone.

"Doc Wilson said that it could be cancer," said Mama. "But they won't know for sure until I have those tests."

"Cancer, Mama?" I said, feelin' a hot sickness rush over my whole body.

"This is why I didn't want to say anything just yet."

"Well if it's not cancer, what else could it be?" asked Jessie, the panic showin' in her voice.

"Doc doesn't know," Mama said.

"When will you go to see the specialist?" I asked.

"Your Pa and I will leave first thing Monday morning. We'll take the eight o'clock train."

"How long will you be gone?" asked Jessie.

"I'm not sure. We'll get word to you as soon as we know."

"Oh, Mama," I said as I reached out and held onto her hand, which was shakin' somethin' terrible.

I felt a miserable mix of emotions: sadness, anger, and numbness all at once. There was a voice in my head that just kept screamin', "NO, NO, NO!" I could see how uncomfortable Mama was with all that talk about her. And I know how she always tries to comfort everybody else, even when it's her who needs the comfortin'. So I did my best to put my own heartache and worry aside for a moment so I could take some of it from her and change the mood of the room.

"Alright, Mama," I said as I went over and hugged her. "We'll wait to hear from the specialist, and we'll try not to get worked up until we know more."

"Thank you, son," said Mama. "Now who wants some lunch?"

"I sure do!" said Hannah. "I'm eating for two now, remember?"

"How could we forget such exciting news?" said Mama.

I sat down again next to Hannah, doin' my best to swallow my concern for Mama and hopin' that nobody could see how upset I really was. "Tell me about your doctor's appointment. Does everything seem to be goin' OK so far?"

"Well," said Hannah, "it's a little early to tell, but Doc told me what to expect and that I should go see him again in a few months."

"How are you feelin'?" I said. "Do you need anything?"

Hannah chuckled and patted my hand.

"I feel like I have the flu," she said. "According to Doc, and your mother, I'll feel like that for a few months. But now that I know I'm not sick, I'll just have to tough it out, I suppose."

"Lying around doesn't make you feel any better," said Mama, "so you might as well get some things done."

We talked about the baby for a spell, tryin' all the while to make it seem like we'd forgotten the news Mama had brought home from the doctor. But not a one of us had forgotten. Daddy was real quiet all through lunch. He responded if someone asked him a question, but other than that, he kept to himself. I can't say I blame him. I can't imagine what's goin' through his mind.

After lunch, Daddy excused himself to get back out to the pasture to finish those fence posts, and I decided I'd join him. As we rode out together, I broke the painful silence by tellin' Daddy not to worry about things here.

"We'll manage all that needs to get done while you're gone, Daddy," I said. "You won't have to worry about a thing."

"There's a lot of things need tendin' to," said Daddy.

"Lawrence and Charlie will be back tomorrow. We'll handle it. I promise."

"Thank you, son."

We didn't say another word to each other the rest of the day until it started gettin' dark and Daddy said we should call it good. Then we rode home in silence again.

I try to say my prayers every night before climbin' into bed. Sometimes I forget; sometimes I'm just too tuckered; but most of the time I at least make contact. Tonight I've got two things to discuss with the Lord. He needs to know I'm grateful for the baby Hannah has inside her, and He needs to know I'm scared to death for Mama.

August 18, 1906

We've been waitin' nearly two weeks without a word from Mama and Daddy. Some days I feel I might lose my mind, but Jessie and Hannah are in an awful state as well, so I've gotta keep it together for their sakes. Daddy asked John Harris if he'd be willin' to take a phone call or two and pass on the information seein' as how we don't have a telephone in our house. He said he'd be more than happy to oblige and offered any other help that might be needed. He even told Daddy to have me call on him and Jacob should we need any help with the chores around here while Mama and Daddy are gone.

Hannah has been real sick. I think the stress and worry about Mama is makin' her already unsettled stomach even worse. Every time she throws up, I want to go fetch Doc, but she tells me it's normal and it will pass soon. Some days she throws up six or seven times. It's all I can do to just let her be, but she assures me she doesn't want me around for it. Jessie has been helpful to her, which is nice. I'm glad they get on so well. Speakin' of gettin' on well, I forgot to mention that Charlie proposed to Anita! When he and Lawrence got back from Alabama a few weeks ago, they jumped right into work here, and Charlie didn't say a thing about it. Finally after a few days had gone by and we had some time together cleanin' some old hay out of the barn that had gone and mildewed, Charlie told me.

"Will, I've been meanin' to tell you somethin'," said Charlie.

"What is it?" I asked as I kept on shovelin'.

"I'm not sure this is the right time, but I can't seem to find one lately, so this will have to do."

"This is a fine time," I said.

"I was fixin' to tell you when me and Daddy got back from Aunt Lena's, but everybody was worried about Miss Lily, and then there's Hannah, what with her bein' pregnant and so sick..."

I stopped shovelin', stood up straight, and wiped the sweat from my forehead.

"Go ahead then," I said, lookin' at Charlie. "I'm all ears."

"Well," said Charlie, still hesitatin' some, "I asked Anita to marry me, and she said she would."

"Charlie Dixon, you old dog! That's great news! I couldn't be happier for you."

I rushed over to Charlie and lifted him right off the ground. I don't think Charlie expected a bear hug like that from me, but he hugged me back all the same and laughed while doin' it.

"How could you think I wouldn't want to know about that?" I said.

"It just didn't seem proper at the time, I suppose. It's hard to bring up happy things when there's so much worry floatin' about."

"I understand," I said. "But I hope you know that no amount of worry would keep me from bein' happy for you. So what did her mama say?"

"She said she was real pleased.

"And her daddy?"

"He didn't say much of anything ... just shook my hand and said he expected me to take good care of his daughter."

"I'm bettin' Aunt Lena was about as excited as it's possible to be," I said.

"She couldn't hardly contain herself," said Charlie. First she was all over me, then she was all over Anita, huggin' and yellin' and such. I about lost the hearin' in my left ear on account of her excitement!"

"That sounds about right," I said, and we both broke out laughin' at the thought of Aunt Lena carryin' on. "I imagine your mama would have done the same thing."

"I imagine so," said Charlie.

"Is your daddy pleased?" I asked.

"He's been sorta quiet about it, but he hugged me tight when I told him and gave me his blessin'."

"Where are you two fixin' to live?"

"I reckon we'll live with daddy," said Charlie, like it was the first time he had thought about it.

"It's worked out well for me and Hannah."

"Yeah. And besides, even if me and Anita got our own place, we'd have Daddy come live with us. It ain't right for me to leave him alone."

"You know your daddy would never leave that house."

"You're right about that. Which is why it just makes sense for us to live there with him."

We talked for a while more and then got back to work. Charlie was all smiles the rest of the day, and I remembered the feelin' I had like it was yesterday when I asked Hannah to marry me. I was real happy for Charlie. He needed a good woman in his life, and I think he and Anita will do real well together.

August 25, 1906

Jacob Harris came barrelin' down the path that connects our properties. He looked like he was either runnin' from somethin' or tryin' to catch up to somebody, I wasn't sure which.

"Will! Jessie!" he yelled as he slowed his horse in a hurry once he saw us on the porch.

We hadn't finished our chores but twenty minutes ago and were enjoyin' some relaxation and the warm breeze of the August evenin' air. Hannah had made some sweet tea for everybody except Charlie, who doesn't happen to care for the taste, so she made him lemonade instead.

"Evenin' ya'll," Jacob said, out of breath and tippin' his hat.

"What are you runnin' from?" I asked him.

"Your daddy is on the line at our place. He wants to talk to you, Will."

I jumped to my feet and ran to get the mare.

"Don't take time to saddle her," said Lawrence. "Just ride bareback and go!"

When we got to the Harris place, I followed Jacob inside. I was real anxious to get to the phone but still wanted to be polite to Mrs. Harris, who was sittin' in the front room sewin'.

"Evenin', ma'am," I said.

"Oh, Will. You made it," she said. "The phone is on the desk right around that corner there. Hurry now. Your father has been waiting."

I nodded, went around the corner and grabbed the phone.

"Daddy? You still there?"

"I'm still here," son.

"Daddy, what's goin' on? We've been waitin' to hear about Mama. How is she?"

"She's restin' right now," said Daddy.

"Well, what did the specialist say?" I asked.

"Now listen, son. Let me tell you what I know and then you can ask your questions."

"Yes, sir," I said.

"The doctor here gave your mama an operation a few days ago; took out that growth."

"An operation!..."

"Let me finish, Will. He took out that growth, and he says it's cancer."

"Why didn't you call us sooner?" I asked, almost feelin' furious.

"I tried and tried," said Daddy, "but the lines wouldn't connect for some reason."

"How is she, Daddy? Is she in pain?"

"She doesn't seem to be," Daddy said. "The doctor said the operation went real well but that she needs to rest a spell."

"So if he took the growth out, will she be fine?" I asked.

"He says she's gotta take some medicine for a while and we'll see. I don't think they know much more about it than Doc Wilson does, if you're askin' my opinion. It looks fancy enough here in this big hospital, but they all can't seem to make up their minds about how she got it and what to do about it. Some say it's her cells causin' the problem, others say it's her lifestyle. The whole thing has been exasperatin'."

My head was reelin'. Daddy sounded downright exhausted, and I felt bad for both him and Mama.

"When can you bring her home?"

"Another week or so, we think."

"I'll tell the others," I said. "And, Daddy ... things are goin' just fine here."

"You sure you're managin' alright?"

"Yes, sir, we are. And you? Are you managin' alright?"

The phone was silent for a minute, and I thought we'd lost the line. Then I heard Daddy clear his throat.

"We're fine here," he finally said. "Now get on back to the house, and thank Mrs. Harris before you leave."

"Will you kiss Mama for me?" I said. "Just let her know we're all thinkin' about her."

"I will," replied Daddy.

I hung up the phone and slowly walked toward the front door. Mr. Harris had come in while I was talkin' to Daddy, and all three of the Harrises were sittin' in the front room, tryin' to act like they hadn't heard our conversation.

"How's your mother, Will?" asked Mrs. Harris.

"I'm not sure," I said.

"What did your pa have to say about it?" asked Mr. Harris.

"Well, I said... seems she's got cancer."

"My goodness!" said Mrs. Harris. "Are they treating her up there in Jonesboro?"

"She had an operation, and she'll be comin' home in a week or so," I said, tryin' not to sound as heavyhearted as I was feelin'.

"What can we do to help?"

"That's awful kind of you," I said absently, "but we'll be alright until they get home. And thank you so much for lettin' us use your telephone. Don't know what we'd do without that."

"You're welcome to it anytime," she said.

"Well, I better be gettin' back."

"Will, can you remind Jessie that I'll be by to pick her up for supper after Sunday service? I meant to tell her today, but forgot with all the commotion."

"I'd be glad to," I said. "Goodnight now."

When I got home, everybody was still out on the front porch waitin' anxiously to hear the news. I told them what Daddy had told me. Nobody knew what to say. It wasn't long after that when Lawrence finally told Charlie it was time to head on home.

"You sure you don't want to stay?" I asked.

"I'm about as tired as I've ever been," said Lawrence; but I suspected it was more than that on account of the way he got real quiet after learnin' of Mama.

"We'll expect you for supper tomorrow then?" said Hannah. "I'll make sure and have those biscuits you love so much."

"We'll be here," said Charlie. "Right, Daddy?"

"I couldn't turn down those biscuits for anything," he said as they started to leave.

I followed them outside and saw them to their horses and watched for a minute as they rode away. Everything about me was tired. My body was tired, my mind was tired, my heart was tired. I just wanted to climb in bed next to Hannah and go to sleep, even though our sleep hadn't been so peaceful lately, what with Hannah gettin' up three or four times a night to use the outhouse. And her gettin' up means me gettin' up.

Hannah is still nervous about goin' outside by herself at night, so I get up with her and wait for her on the porch. A few nights ago, I was so tired that I told her to just use a pitcher or a bowl and we could dump it off to the side of the house in the mornin'. I think she was real embarrassed that I proposed that idea. She said she'd just be brave and go outside by herself so it wouldn't disturb me, but how can I keep sleepin' if I know she's outside feelin' scared? So the way I get through it is, when Hannah wakes me to go outside with her, I sit out on the porch and remind myself of how good it will feel to get back into bed. I can't say it's helpin' all that much, but it's the best I've got.

September 3, 1906

"It's them!" cried Hannah from the front yard.

I came runnin' out to see what was goin' on. There was John Harris, drivin' Mama and Daddy up the dirt road to our house. Jessie ran out of the barn and over to the car.

"Take it easy, now," said Daddy, as Jessie reached in to hug Mama. "She's still healin'."

"Mama," Jessie said, kissin' and huggin' her, "are you really ok? We missed you so much! How do you feel? Can I help you out of the car?"

"Hi honey," laughed Mama. "Let's see, which question shall I answer first?"

"Sorry, Mama. I'm just so glad to see you!"

"I'm so glad to see you too, Jessie."

Hannah and I had been standin' behind Jessie, waitin' for Mama to get out of the car. Daddy came around to our side of the car, and I shook his hand and asked him how their trip went.

"It wasn't too bad," said Daddy.

"I bet you sure are glad to be home," I said.

"More than you know, son."

Jessie helped Mama out of the car, and it was then I noticed that she didn't look quite like herself, and it took me by surprise. I guess I hadn't expected her to look any different, but she was thinner, and her face didn't hold as much color as before. I think Mama could see that I had noticed.

"I'm sure I just look a mess," she said as she smoothed her hair back away from her face, repinnin' loose pieces back into her bun.

"Are you kiddin'?" I said. "You look wonderful," and I gave her a gentle hug so I wouldn't aggravate her incision.

Mama turned her attention to Hannah and said, "how are you feeling, dear?"

"Oh, Lily, I'm just fine," Hannah replied, blushin' just a bit with discomfort at bein' the focus of everyone's attention right then.

"How's the sickness?"

"Some days are better than others. You remember what that's like, don't you?"

"Fortunately, not very well anymore!" said Mama, givin' Hannah a faint smile.

Daddy walked around the side of car and held his hand out to Mr. Harris.

"I'm real grateful to you for fetchin' us from the train station," said Daddy.

"Not at all, Ben," Mr. Harris said.

"Would you like to come in for a while?" asked Mama.

"Thank you kindly," he answered, "but Kathryn and I have an engagement to attend this evening. She's probably pacing the floor as we speak!"

"Well, that's just fine," said Mama. "We won't keep you then. Thank you for your trouble, Mr. Harris."

"It was no trouble at all, Mrs. Wright." I hope you get to feeling better," he said, smilin' real friendly-like and tippin' his hat as he got in his car and drove away.

Jessie turned to Mama and said, "let's get you inside," as she and Hannah got on either side of Mama to help her in, while me and Daddy carried the bags they'd taken on their trip. Mama asked to lie down on the sofa, which was somethin' I'd never seen her do before. That was always Daddy's spot. Once Mama was on the sofa, Daddy went into their room and brought out a pillow and a thin blanket to make Mama more comfortable. Then the rest of us found a spot close so we could visit with her.

"I know that your pa has told you what we're facing," said Mama. "Does anybody have any questions about it?"

We all sat quietly, thinkin' about Mama's question. I felt like I had a hundred questions, but couldn't come up with a single one.

Jessie broke the silence. "Are you gonna get better, Mama?"

"I think so, my dear. I'm going to be taking some medicine to help, and I'll be seeing much more of Doc Wilson than I ever thought I would."

"Are you hungry?" Hannah asked.

"Not right now, but thank you," said Mama.

"You look real tired," I said.

"That's probably because I feel tired," Mama said as she chuckled. "Let me just close my eyes for a few minutes, and then we'll visit some more."

Mama feel asleep just minutes later. We all stayed and talked with Daddy some, but he was real tired too. After about an hour or so, Daddy woke Mama and helped her to bed. She apologized for not bein' better company, which, under the circumstances, we all thought was silly.

I took to my knees that night and prayed some more. I prayed that Mama would sleep comfortable, and I prayed that she would get better, and I prayed that we'd be what she needed through this. I can't say which of those things I want most, so I'm hopin' the good Lord feels even more generous than usual and gives us all three.

November 5, 1906

Tonight, while Hannah and I were lyin' in bed together, I told her about Uncle Albert. I had thought about tellin' her so many times before, but always stopped myself. Part of me felt ashamed. Another part of me thought it might make Hannah think different of me. But mostly I just don't like thinkin' of or talkin' about that weasel. Hannah was kind as could be about it. She was real understandin' and told me she loved me just the same. I asked her to keep it between the two of us, and she agreed. She knows how much it would hurt Mama to know such a thing. As awful a thing as it is to tell, I sure am glad to have that off my chest. And bless my sweet Hannah for havin' such a good heart and for her lovin' ways.

December 29, 1906

Our holidays weren't quite what we'd hoped for this year. I was excited that it was my and Hannah's first Christmas together, and that Mama has been feelin' much better the past few months. I was also pleased that Hannah isn't sick anymore and that her belly is really startin' to stick out. Everything was goin' on as it usually does around Christmas, what with the goodies and the tree and the singin'. But the night before Christmas Eve, there were seven men arrested for burnin' crosses in the colored part of town. There were plenty more than seven men who were part of the whole thing, but only seven were caught. Eli Carver and Joe Simmons were two of them. The other names were men I didn't know. They say three of them were associates of Mr. Carver, and the other two, . . .well, nobody quite knows where they came from. We tried to continue on with our traditions, but there was no way to do it and feel alright about it. Even though there was nothin' we could do to help, it still didn't feel good actin' like we didn't know what was happenin'. It was also the first Christmas I remember havin' without Lawrence and Charlie. They were in Alabama this year with Aunt Lena, and it turned out to be a good thing they were. One of them crosses was put in their front yard.

We know that Deputy Jenkins is doin' his best around here, but it almost seems like things have gotten worse since he became the sheriff. It makes sense though, that folks would try to rebel against the things he's tryin' to do in this town. They're the same folks that were causin' trouble before, they just didn't have to worry about the law, seein' as how Hank Coleman was the sheriff, and he never did a thing to help the coloreds.

So Christmas has come and gone, and we spent most of it feelin' both sad and angry. But as disappointin' as it was this year, it'd be hard to find somethin' that could dampen my spirits entirely. There was happiness to be found in the fact that Hannah is carryin' the first grandchild in our immediate family, and also that Mama has been back to all her regular chores for over a month now. And that's what we tried to focus on this year. We were grateful for the good, even though there was bad goin' on all around us.

April 10, 1907

Jack William Wright was born today. He may be the handsomest boy that was ever born. He has all his right parts, and nothin' extra. He weighs more than eight pounds and he's already partial to his daddy. I was real proud of Hannah. She suffered for a good long while before our boy was ready to meet the world. I'm not even sure he was actually ready yet, but Hannah was, and I believe she insisted. I've never seen her so determined about anything. I think it was nice for her to have her mama there with her. I reckon a woman needs another woman about her in a time like that. It'd be mighty hard to only have men folk around, tellin' you that what you're feelin' is normal and that you can do it. How do we know? We've never done it. So I was real happy that Grace was there and Hannah could hear it from her instead of me.

I've never seen Mama and Daddy so pleased with anything before. I knew how Mama would be – cryin' and lovin' on that baby, but I wasn't sure about Daddy. I was real surprised when I came in the room to find Daddy holdin' little Jack. He made it seem like he was just doin' it because somebody needed to while Hannah was restin', but Mama told me later that while she was holdin' Jack, Daddy took him right out of her arms. Jessie, too, was as thrilled as could be. She went on about havin' a baby in the house and how she was gonna be the best auntie to Jack. Lawrence and Charlie came a few hours after he was born, and they both gave me hugs, which was unusual for Lawrence, in particular. Then they found Mama and Daddy and took turns holdin' the baby.

It's a mighty strange feelin'... bein' a father. As soon as Jack was born, I felt a change take hold in me. I was holdin' this little person, feelin' the most overwhelmin' joy I've ever known and the weight of the world all at the same time. I wasn't sure about how to go about carin' for him and makin' sure he has everything he needs, but I was sure that I'd die tryin' to figure it out, if it came to that. I also felt a different connection to Hannah. I've loved her from the very beginning, but I looked at her now and saw somethin' more than the girl I love, I saw the mama to my son. She would be the one to help me figure out how to do this. And I knew she would love that boy the same way Mama loves me. I had no doubt about that. I've been on the receivin' end of Hannah's love, and it's the kind of love that warms your heart and gives you hope. So of all the decisions I've made in my life, as I sat there lookin' at Hannah and Jack, I knew that marryin' her was the best one I ever made.

July 6, 1907

"I'm shakin' like a leaf," said Charlie as he fumbled around, tryin' to tie his tie.

"Hold still," I said. "Let me help you."

"I can't believe you all came for this," Charlie said.

"You can't?", I asked in surprise. "Charlie, we wouldn't miss this day for anythin'. It's a shame you'd think otherwise."

"It's just such a far way to go," he said, "and with Miss Lily not feelin' completely herself lately. Well, ... I'm just grateful is all. How is your mama feelin' today?"

"Oh she's doin' real well," I lied.

Truth is, Mama hasn't been feelin' her best the past few weeks. She doesn't know if it's because of the medicine Doc has her takin' or if somethin' else is goin' on. But she wasn't about to miss Charlie's weddin', not for anything in the world. She loves that boy like she bore him herself, and while she's never tried to step in as his mama, I don't believe she could feel any stronger for him if he was her own. I'm certain that Charlie feels the same, so havin' Mama miss this would be devastatin' to them both.

Charlie was just about ready when there was a knock on the door. It was Lawrence.

"Anita's mama asked me to tell you that they're fixin' to start the ceremony," he said.

I thought it would be right for Charlie to have a few minutes alone with his daddy, so I patted Lawrence on the shoulder as I pushed past him in the doorway and went to find Hannah and the others. When I got to our seats, I noticed Mama didn't look so good.

"Are you ok, Mama," I whispered.

"I'm just fine, son," she said.

"You sure?"

"Stop fussing now," said Mama. "Let's enjoy this beautiful wedding."

I looked at Daddy who obviously felt the same way I did. But we respected Mama's decision to be there and would stay for the ceremony.

As we sat there, waitin' for things to get started, Hannah leaned over and whispered in my ear.

"Have you noticed that we're the only white people here?"

I looked behind me to the right, then to the left.

"I guess I hadn't," I said as I chuckled. "Does it make you feel uncomfortable?"

"Maybe a little," she said.

"How come?" I asked.

"I'm not sure. Could be that I'm just not used to it."

"Yeah," I agreed. "It feels a little different."

"Hush you two," said Mama. "They're starting."

We stopped talkin', and the music for Anita to walk down the aisle started. It was a real nice weddin'. It brought back memories of when me and Hannah got married, and now there we were, not more than a year later with a baby. Jesse would be gettin' married soon herself, and I thought of the way our whole family was changin'. I remember hatin' Jacob Harris and bein' real disappointed in Jessie for even considerin' him, but now that we know him better, I'm pleased that he'll be joinin' our family in a couple of months. Jacob asked Jesse to marry him just a few weeks after Charlie and Anita got engaged.

Between Charlie and Jessie, it feels like we've been doin' nothin' but plannin' weddin's lately. Even though it's stressful on Mama, I do believe she's lovin' every minute of it. And it couldn't work out any better that the Harrises live right next door. Jacob and Jesse may be movin' to a small place of their own just up the way from his folks, which is still fine because they'll be so close. I think it would be hard on Mama to have her only daughter far away. As a matter of fact, I do believe that if it were up to her, she'd have the whole dang family livin' in the same house, Lawrence and Charlie included!

Most everybody was friendly to us at the reception afterward, and we ended up havin' a real nice time. The food was probably the best I've ever eaten. Them Alabama women sure know how to cook. There was dancin' and laughin' and carryin' on for hours. Daddy took Mama back to Aunt Lena's about half way through the party so she could rest. She gets tired pretty easy these days, and there was so much goin' on today, I'm surprised she made it as long as she did. I'm guessin' she'll pay for it tomorrow, but at least she enjoyed herself plenty tonight.

Charlie looked happy, and so did Lawrence. I don't know Anita very well yet, but what I do know of her, she's real pleasant. I imagine she'll find it difficult bein' apart from her family once she moves to Arkansas with us, but we'll do all we can to make her feel welcome. It will be nice now that Charlie's married. Me and Charlie haven't had as much time together since me and Hannah got married, and even less time since Jack was born. I'm hopin' that Hannah and Anita get along so that it makes things easier for me and Charlie.

After the reception was over, we went on back to Aunt Lena's. It's a good thing we all like one another because we were squished together in that house like sugar peas in a pod. Hannah was worried about Jack keepin' folks awake, but Aunt Lena told her to quit that kinda talk. She'd "done raised plenty of babies and wasn't worried none about a little cryin'".

We finally got settled, and soon after, I drifted off to sleep. It wasn't long into it before I had another one of my nightmares. This time I was in the middle of some town. I suppose it was our town, but it looked different in the dream. There was a buildin' on fire, a supply store. Standin' on top of the buildin' was Charlie, and he was holdin' Jack, tryin' to keep him away from the flames. I couldn't find a soul around and had no idea how to get the two of them down from there. Finally, Eli Carver and Hank Coleman appeared, but they wouldn't help me. They just stood there laughin'. Charlie said the only way out was to throw little Jack to me and then jump himself. I was so afraid I would drop Jack and that Charlie wouldn't make it. But there was no time to think of anything else. The flames kept risin' and Jack was cryin' somethin' terrible. Charlie screamed at me to get ready and then threw Jack—

"Will! Wake up!" said Hannah, who was shakin' me hard as she could.

"Where's Jack?" I asked in a panic.

"He wouldn't settle, so Aunt Lena asked if she could take him out and rock him for a while. Are you ok?"

"It was just a bad dream," I said. But my heart was still poundin', and I could feel the coolness of the sweat on my face.

"Will, you were screaming and crying," said Hannah. "What happened?"

"I keep havin' these nightmares about Charlie."

"What kind of nightmares?"

"They're different every time. This time there was a fire, and Jack was there."

"Oh my," Hannah said, her voice registerin' some concern. "That's just awful."

"I'm alright now," I said, wipin' the sweat from my forehead. "I'm gonna go get Jack and sit outside for a while."

"Do you want me to come with you?"

"No, honey. You get some rest. We'll be in soon."

I sat out on the porch with my boy and watched him while he slept until I could shake the feelin' of bein scared. Then we went back inside and laid down next to Hannah. Jack doesn't usually sleep in our bed, but that night, I wanted him close by me. We all slept fine after that, and I apologized to everybody in the mornin' for causin' such a disturbance.

"I wondered what in the world was goin' on in that room," said Aunt Lena over breakfast.

"It was just a bad dream," I said. "I'm sorry if I woke anyone."

"Oh, I was awake half the night anyhow," Aunt Lena said, "thinkin' about that weddin' and how my nephew isn't a little boy no more."

"It was a beautiful wedding," agreed Mama.

Our ride home was fine. We were all glad to get home, even though it meant gettin' right back to chores and work. I don't mind the work. It makes me feel like I'm livin' a purposeful life. Can't think of a better feelin' than gettin' to the end of a day with dirty hands and sore muscles, and knowin' that all I did that day means my family will have food on the table and a place to sleep that night. Any man tells you there's a better feelin' than that, you can bet he's either (one of two things;) a fool or a liar.

September 27, 1907

Jessie and Jacob got married yesterday, and it was about as nice a weddin' as you could imagine, even though Uncle Albert showed up day before yesterday to attend the event. When Mama sent out the invitations, Jessie didn't have the heart to tell Mama that she didn't want him there. So she just let it be. Mama had made an invitation for Uncle Albert when me and Hannah got married. I never told anybody, but I tore it up and burned it without Mama knowin'. When Mama talked to him about whether or not he was comin', it was too late to make plans. He said he never got the invitation, and Mama never thought anything other than the mail service must have made a mistake. I felt bad about not tellin' Mama, but I knew I couldn't have Uncle Albert there on that day. The experience with marryin' Hannah was so filled with light, I just couldn't bring myself to invite in the darkness I always felt around him.

It was pretty much the same routine as it's always been—he and Daddy keepin' their distance from one another, with Mama just doin' all she can to make him comfortable. Mama believes in family, and Albert is what she's got left of hers.

Anyway, regardin' the weddin', Kathryn Harris went all out for her only son. Maybe it was because she knew this would be the only weddin' she'd get to plan. Everything was fancy and expensive, and Jessie just ate it all up. I think she's alright with the fact that we live a humble life, but there is a part of her that is drawn to nicer things, always has been. I think that's part of the reason she wanted to be friends with Maryanne Stephenson so bad. I'm guessin' it was probably more about Maryanne's things than it was about Maryanne. That sounds awful to say about Jessie, but she was young at the time, and we all know how manipulative Maryanne can be to get what she wants. So it worked out well for Jessie to marry someone like Jacob Harris because he's a decent fella and just happens to have nice things. He's even takin' Jessie on a fancy honeymoon to New York day after tomorrow. She's beside herself about it.

Seein' as how it was Sunday evenin', Hannah and I decided to walk over to her folks's place for a visit. We'd normally take Jack with us, but since we were walkin' instead of ridin', we figured it'd be best to leave him home with Mama.

We didn't end up stayin' very long. Kathryn wasn't feelin' well and wanted to turn in early, so we made pleasant conversation for a bit, said goodnight, and headed home.

As Hannah and I got to the end of the road and turned down the path to the house, I saw Mama and Daddy walkin' in our direction alongside Jessie and Jacob. My heart started poundin', and I pulled Hannah along as I hurried toward them.

"What are you doing? Where's Jack?" I asked in a panic.

"Don't worry, son, he's with your uncle," Mama said.

Hannah let go of my hand and started runnin' toward the house even before Mama finished her sentence, and I took off right after her.

"Oh Mama!" I said without lookin' back.

"Will, what's the matter?" Mama called as they all tried to catch up to me. "I'm sure they're just fine!"

Hannah got to the house before I did and raced inside, leavin' the door wide open. When I reached the front steps, I could see her holdin' Jack and exchangin' words with Uncle Albert. I hurried into the front room in time to hear him tell Hannah that she must be mistaken. I went to Hannah and put my arm around her. Within seconds, Mama, Daddy, Jessie, and Jacob all filed in. I wasn't sure if Jessie had told Jacob about Uncle Albert, but the look of confusion on his face told me that she probably hadn't.

"Will," Mama said, out of breath, "we just walked down the lane to invite Jessie and Jacob over for dessert, but we didn't want to wake the baby. So Uncle Albert said to go on ahead and he'd keep an eye on him until we got back. We didn't think you'd mind, son."

"I know, Mama," I said.

"Then why the race back to the house like it was on fire?" asked Daddy as he rubbed his knees.

I was in the middle of a moment I couldn't get my head around. I wasn't sure if anything had happened to my boy. I didn't know what to say that would explain me and Hannah racin' off like that, and I didn't know who it was I was protectin' anymore with all this secrecy. I used to think it was Mama, but right then, it didn't feel that way.

Uncle Albert took to nervous laughin' and said it was all a big misunderstandin'.

"Everyone is fine now, so let's get on with supper and enjoy the evenin'," he said.

Hannah turned to me, and I knew what was comin'. I couldn't stop it, and I couldn't blame her for it, either.

"Will, as your wife, I've held my tongue out of respect for something you've wanted to keep hidden. But as Jack's mother, I will not abide this secret for one more second."

She turned to face Mama. "Lily, I'm painfully sorry to have to tell you this, but your brother is not to be trusted around children," Hannah said.

Out of the corner of my eye, I could see Uncle Albert squirmin' in his own skin, like the snake he was. Daddy stood up tall and looked at Uncle Albert.

"Hannah, that's an awful thing to say," whispered Mama, like she couldn't get the breath to say it out loud.

"Will hasn't told you about what Albert did to him and Jessie when they were little because he knew how much it would burden you," said Hannah.

Mama put her hands up to her face, shakin' her head in disbelief. Jacob looked at Jessie, who confirmed that it was true without havin' to say a word. I felt real bad for both of them in that moment. That's a hard thing to learn just a day after bein' married.

"What is she talkin' about, Will?" Daddy said real forcefully.

"She's absolutely crazy!" Interrupted Uncle Albert. "I would've never hurt those kids, Ben! She's confused."

Daddy didn't even look at Uncle Albert. He kept fixed on me, waitin' for me to answer.

"Will, I'm askin' you again, son. What is Hannah talkin' about?"

I wanted to tell him because it had been such an awful thing to keep private all these years, but I couldn't swallow the lump in my throat, and it was keepin' me from bein' able to get the words out.

"Will?" said Mama softly.

I've never seen the look on Mama's face that she had right then. It was a mix of sadness and hurt and confusion. I hated Uncle Albert more than ever in that moment for causin' her to feel like that. I swallowed as hard as I could and hoped I'd be able to say what needed to be said. I looked at Jessie, who was curled up into Jacob, sobbin'.

"Mama," I said, Uncle Albert put his hands on me and Jessie when we were too young to know what was happenin'. It went on for some time. Jessie and I decided not to tell you because we didn't want to hurt you... the way you're hurtin' now. So when you told me that he was with Jack, I panicked.

"You don't believe this nonsense, do you, Lily?" asked Uncle Albert angrily.

Daddy took a step toward him. Mama turned and put her hand on Daddy's chest to stop him. Then she turned back to face Uncle Albert herself.

"I want you to turn around and walk out of this house, and don't you ever think about coming back here," said Mama in a low, firm voice I'd never heard her use before.

"Lily, you don't mean that," said Uncle Albert mortified.

He was still smilin' like he was tryin' to charm his way out of it. I couldn't believe the nerve. It made my skin crawl, and I felt so sad for Mama.

"If you aren't gone in five seconds, Ben has my blessing to get his shotgun," she said calmly, without so much as a single blink.

"Lily!" said Uncle Albert, "I'm your brother!"

"You are not my brother!" shouted Mama in a way that startled everyone in the room, her eyes wellin' up until they couldn't help but spill over.

"How can you say such a hateful thing to me?" he said, lookin' wounded.

"I don't know when the devil took hold of you, but when he did, my brother disappeared," she said.

"Lily, if you would just listen to—"

"So help me, Albert Doyle! I'll shoot you myself!" Mama said with tears streamin' down her face. "Now get out of my house!"

Uncle Albert looked defeated. None of us has ever seen Mama like that. Her whole body was shakin', and I just wanted to hold onto her until she was alright again. I couldn't imagine learnin' such a filthy thing about someone I cared for. I stood there, watchin' her and thinkin' how remarkable it was that she didn't even question me on it. There was no hearin' sides, no discussion of any kind. I don't know if it's because she knows me well enough to know that I'd never lie to her, especially in a way that would cause her such pain, or if she could just feel that it was the truth. I'm not a perfect son, but Mama knows that I'd sooner put a knife into my own heart than I would break hers in two. Maybe a part of her always knew... knew that somethin' wasn't right with Uncle Albert, and so when it was finally out in the open, she didn't have to question herself about it.

There have been a few signs along the way that Uncle Albert wasn't quite the man Mama had hoped he was. We all knew she wasn't fond of his boozin' or the company he kept while doin' it.

And when she learned that he possibly had a hand in what happened to Charlie and Lawrence a couple of years ago—that he had the same venom in his heart as those jackals who harassed and beat them—her clouded vision of who he really was cleared up a bit. She seemed to have put it behind her at the time, but I know that there was a part of her that always wondered if Uncle Albert lied when he said that his watch had gone missin' without him knowin' it. Mama has always practiced love. She's believed that love can heal all wounds and fix all kinds of brokenness. Today she learned different. Heaven knows that Uncle Albert got more chances than any man ought to, but at least this way, sometime down the road from all this, Mama might know that she did all she could for him.

I used to think that if a man was surrounded by goodness long enough, he wouldn't want anything else... like the good would rub off and change his desires for evil. But there are folks who are surrounded by all kinds of goodness, and they don't want it. It's like somethin' inside them is broke. That's the only explanation I can think of when a person craves darkness over light. Can't make sense of it any other way.

Uncle Albert moved toward the door, and Jessie and Jacob turned their backs to him as he did, Jessie still sobbin'. After the door closed, Daddy started after him.

"Benjamin," Mama whispered, shakin' her head like she was pleadin' with Daddy not to.

"I won't kill him," said Daddy, hard and firm. "That's the best you'll get from me, Lily."

Daddy slammed the door shut behind him, and a moment later we heard the sounds of Uncle Albert gettin' just exactly what he deserved from the man who had every right to give it to him. Mama put both hands over her ears and closed her eyes while we waited for things to quiet down outside. Hannah handed Jack to me and went over and held Mama until it was over.

A few minutes later, Daddy stormed back into the house, leavin' the front door wide open. He went right into the room where Uncle Albert had been sleepin' and then came back through the main room with his arms full of Uncle Albert's personal belongings. He went outside again and threw everything off the front porch. I could see Uncle Albert doubled over on the ground, barely movin' at all. Then Daddy came back in and closed the door. He was breathin' hard and carried a look of anger I don't believe I'll ever forget.

"I'll say my peace, and then we won't ever talk about this again, he said. Is that understood?"

I nodded in agreement and waited to hear what Daddy had to say.

"What your uncle did to you and your sister is the worst kind of evil. I will never forgive myself for not knowin' what was happenin'. I didn't realize..."

Daddy's voice caught a bit, and he cleared his throat before it could take hold of him.

"Lily, I let him live, but only because I can't stand the idea of breakin' your heart more than it already is today. But you should know that if he ever comes back here again, he won't make it a foot on this land before I put a bullet through his filthy chest. This ain't your fault, Lily. I should have done better to protect our family. I felt somethin' was wrong for years... felt it in my gut. I just thought it was on account of me and Albert always bein' like oil and water. Now I know different."

"The only one to blame is Albert," Mama said as she sat on the arm of the couch, tears still streamin' down her cheeks.

Hannah had an uncomfortable look on her face. She was starin' at Daddy's hands. I hadn't even noticed that they were covered in blood. I wasn't sure if more of it was his own or Uncle Albert's.

"Do you want me to take a look at your hands?" Hannah asked Daddy.

Mama wiped the tears from her face, and looked over at Daddy.

"I'll tend to them," she said. Daddy went in and sat down at the kitchen table. Mama joined him a minute later, carryin' the alcohol and a clean towel. Nobody knew what to say to each other.

"We're going to head on home," said Jacob as he and Jessie stood in the doorway together.

"Jessie," Mama said, her eyes fillin' with tears again.

"I'll come over tomorrow, Mama. Alright?" said Jessie.

Jessie had had her fill. She was done with it... at least for tonight. Mama nodded and tried to blink the tears away as she continued cleanin' Daddy's wounds. Hannah and I went over and sat on the couch near the fireplace while Jack rolled around the floor lookin' for things to chew on. Every few seconds we'd hear Daddy take a quick breath in through his teeth as Mama dabbed his cuts with alcohol. Daddy was just about as tough as they come, but you'd have to be made of stone not to wince at alcohol in an open cut.

Aside from that, we all sat there in silence... except for Jack who was jabberin' on in his own language. Havin' him go on like that made it feel less awkward, so I was glad he was in a good mood and had lots to say.

I knew it wouldn't be right for me to check, but it was all I could do not to look out the front window to see if Uncle Albert was still lyin' in the dirt or if he'd finally dragged himself off our land. As much as I dislike the man, I hoped he was gone. I believed Daddy when he said that he'd kill Uncle Albert if he ever came back. Even with the things he did, can't say that I ever wanted him dead. I just didn't want him around here.

"Ben, this knuckle might be broken," Mama said with concern in her voice, while she studied Daddy's fingers real close.

"I'm sure it ain't broken," he said. "Just swollen, is all."

"I'll have Will go fetch the doctor," said Mama.

"Never mind all that. Just clean me up and I'll be fine by mornin'."

Mama would normally insist on somethin' like that until Daddy would get so tired of goin' back and forth that he'd just agree to whatever it was Mama was tryin' to get him to do. But Mama didn't insist this time. She just finished up and then went into her room and closed the door. Daddy got up from the table and went out back.

"Are you angry with me?" Hannah asked.

"No, honey. I'm not angry." I put my arm around her and pulled her into me.

"It's just that when I thought about somethin' happenin' to Jack... I just..."

"I know." I said. "You did the right thing.

"Is your mother going to be ok?" she asked.

"She'll struggle with it, I imagine. But knowin' Mama, she'll find her way."

Hannah leaned into me and kissed my neck. Then she rested her head on my shoulder. I sat there thinkin' about Mama in the other room. She's had to deal with some real hard things in life, and the hardest things have probably been the ones that involved someone dyin'. Her mama killed herself, and then later Mama had had to bury her own twin babies. Even though uncle Albert isn't dead, I reckon it feels about the same to Mama. And for her to learn it at a time like this, when she's strugglin' with her own health, is nothin' short of a cryin' shame.

Mama didn't come out of her room the rest of the evenin'. She was gonna need some time to think on things, and maybe just to grieve some. And after what she'd been through, we were gonna have to be real patient and give her all the time she needed.

October 1, 1907

Today, when I got home from fetchin' supplies in town, Mama, Hannah, and Jessie were sittin' out on the front porch together. I was surprised to see Mama talkin' to anyone since she'd been keepin' real quiet the past few days. She didn't even come out of her room until yesterday. Daddy said she was alright – just needed to be left alone for a spell.

"Come on over here, would you, son?" said Mama.

I slid off my horse and unloaded the supplies onto the ground. Then I went up on the porch and sat down next to Jessie on the swing.

"I need to talk with you and Jessie," Mama said, "and I'm sorry it's taken me so long to be able to do it."

"I'm going to go inside and tend to Jack," said Hannah.

"You can stay if you like," Mama said.

"Thank you, but I'll leave the three of you alone to talk."

After Hannah had gone in, Mama started talkin' again.

"I have spent the past few days trying to figure out how something like this could have happened and I not even know about it. I continued to bring a man into our home who hurt both of you. My knees are about as tired as they can be from all the time I've spent praying for answers... and forgiveness."

"Mama," I said—

"Please let me finish, Will."

I sat back and closed my mouth, but it was torture listenin' to Mama blame herself for somethin' Uncle Albert had done.

"I think it's going to take me a long while to sort through all of this. One minute I want to hurt your uncle, the next minute I want to just hug you both and tell you how sorry I am; and then there are times when I just want to go to sleep and pretend none of it happened. So what I want you to know is that I'm working on it. It will be a part of everything I do until I can put it in its proper place and let it go. But for the pain that you two have endured all these years . . ." she paused, took a deep, agonizing breath, and struggled real hard to keep from cryin'..."my heart will forever be broken."

"Oh, Mama," said Jessie as she went over and held her. "You aren't to blame."

"It was my job to keep you safe," Mama said, "and I failed you."

"No," I said strongly. "You have never failed us, Mama. Not ever. Uncle Albert is to blame, and he's the only one. So in the time you'll be taken to sort it all out, please remember that."

Mama and Jessie separated, and Mama wiped her eyes with her handkerchief.

"Is there anything you want to talk about?... anything you want to tell me about... about what happened."

"There's no good that will come of that," I said. "Jessie can make up her own mind about what she wants to do, but now that Uncle Albert won't be comin' around anymore, it's over for me."

"Me too," said Jessie, wipin' her eyes with her hanky.

"And Mama," I said, "I'm real sorry that you lost your brother."

Mama came over to me, and I stood up to meet her. She put her arms around my middle and buried her head in my chest. Then she cried for a bit. I came close to cryin' myself as I felt the hurt she was goin' through. I figured it wouldn't help her none if I took to cryin' too, so I just held on tight until she was done.

I couldn't really get my head around all that she was feelin'. She felt guilty and angry and heartbroken all at once. If I didn't know her better than I do, I might wonder if she'd make it through alright. These are the kinds of things that can make people ugly if they let it, by allowin' the pain turn their hearts to hate. That would never be Mama. And knowin' that brought me all the comfort I needed.

January 5, 1908

It's all I can do to find a few rushed minutes here and there to write down what's been happenin'. I try, I honestly do, but every time I think I'll take some time to do it, somethin' comes up. I used to answer only to Daddy and Mama for my time, but now I answer to Hannah and Jack too. When I'm done answerin' to everybody else, there's usually nothin' left. So I'm hidin' out in the barn this mornin', and I'm fixin' to write until I'm done writin'!

Me and Hannah keep thinkin' she's gonna turn up pregnant again, but she doesn't. We didn't think too much about it at first, but then after several months went by, we both started to wonder why it wasn't happenin'. I think Hannah is more worried about it than I am. I just keep tellin' her that when the Lord has a baby for us, he'll send it. She nods and says "OK", but I know she wants another baby real bad. She was actually doin' alright with it, and then Anita and Charlie announced at Christmas Eve dinner that they were pregnant. I saw Hannah's eyes fill with tears even though the smile on her face was as wide as the day is long. Later that night when we were climbin' into bed, I asked her about it.

"That's some pretty great news about Charlie and Anita, huh?" I said.

"It's so wonderful for them," she replied.

I leaned up on my elbow and put my other hand on her cheek, gently pullin' her face toward me.

"I know it hurts you," I said.

"Anita being pregnant doesn't hurt me, Will. I couldn't be happier for them, and I sincerely mean that."

"Then why did you look sad when she told us?"

"Will," said Hannah, sittin' up and facin' me head on, "it's always there. The desire I have for another baby is always there, and I stuff it down inside of me so that life can go on. But when someone mentions anything about babies and pregnancy, it pulls a piece of that hurt up, and there's nothing I can do about it. I'm happy for Anita and Charlie, but I'm sad for me at the same time. Their news doesn't cause my sadness, it's just a reminder of the sadness that I already feel. Can you understand that?"

I thought about what she said, and I did my best to try and understand.

"I think so," I said.

"Please don't ever confuse the two," said Hannah.

"I'm sorry, sweetheart," I said.

"You don't need to be." She settled comfortably back down next to me. "I just want you to understand."

I blew out the lamp and waited for Hannah to fall asleep. Then I lit a candle, sat on the floor at the side of the bed, and wrote her a letter.

> *Honey,*
>
> *I can't sleep. My mind keeps runnin' around what we talked about tonight, and I find myself feelin' real sad about it. I guess of all the things I want you to know, the most important one is that I think the world of you. When we got married, I thought I couldn't love you more than I did then. But after havin' the experience of seein' you as a mother to our Jack, I can't even begin to tell you how much that love has grown. There have been a handful of times when I come into a room without you knowin' I'm there, and I just watch you with our boy. The feelin' that puts in my chest – well, there just aren't words for somethin' like that. You are the love of my life and a better mama to Jack than I could have wished for. Now, we'll keep tryin' for more, but if he is the only child we ever have, then we'll thank God every day for givin' us the opportunity to raise such a wonderful boy.*
> *--Will*

May 26, 1908

Mama and Daddy are on their way back to Jonesboro. Mama's been seein' a whole lot of Doc Wilson lately, and he says he can feel that the growth in her belly is back. I think Mama has known that for some time, what with her poor health lately, but Doc finally confirmed it. So Daddy is takin' her back to that specialist to get it taken out again.

"I don't understand all this," I said to Mama before they left.

"I'm not sure I do either," said Mama.

"You have another tumor?"

"I guess so."

"What does that mean?" I asked, feelin' a terrible frustration over the whole thing.

"We'll let you know what the specialist says, son," Mama said. "I just don't know what else to tell you right now. I wish I did."

I could tell that my questions weren't helpin' things, and I didn't want Mama feelin' agitated and worried on her trip, so I told my mind to stop my mouth from sayin' anythin' else.

"Alright, Mama. Now, just like before, we'll manage things fine here. That's not to say we won't miss you... and your famous pancakes, but we'll manage," I said, tryin' to make her smile.

"We'll be home before you know it," Mama said. "And keep an eye on Anita for me. Tell her she can't have those babies until I get back!"

"I'll tell her, Mama," I laughed, "but from what I remember about watchin' Hannah, when it's time, it's time!"

"Won't it be so exciting to have twins running around here?" said Mama excitedly.

"It sure will," I replied, grabbin' onto Hannah's hand and squeezin' it some.

"We're fixin' to miss our train, Lily," said Daddy, standin' by the front door.

"Ok, dear. I'm coming. Give Grandma a kiss," Mama said as she picked Jack up and loved on him for a minute.

Then they left. It was a strange feelin' sendin' them off like that again. It sorta felt like this was becomin' a normal part of our lives. I remembered what it was like last time, waitin' and worryin'. We'd have to keep real busy this time around to help with all that.

After they were gone, we got Jack and headed over to see how Anita was feelin'. When Hannah was pregnant, she threw up for about four months or so, but Anita is six months along and she's still real sick. It could be because she's carryin' twins, but I can't really speak on the matter.

When we got to their house, Lawrence, Anita, and Charlie were all sittin' outside under a fine shade tree, havin' some lunch.

"So what are we havin'?" I asked, after we tied the horses and made our way over to join them.

Anita started to fuss like she was gonna go inside and get more food. Charlie had to tell her that I was only jokin'.

"It hasn't been an hour since we had our lunch," said Hannah as she sat down next to Anita, shakin' her head at me.

"What are you trouble makers up to?" asked Charlie.

"We just thought we'd come by to see how things are goin' around here," I said.

"Your folks gone?" Lawrence asked.

"They left a little while ago."

"I'm sure this time will go just as smooth as last time," said Lawrence reassuringly.

"I sure hope you're right, sir," I said.

"How are the babies?" asked Hannah as she patted Anita's belly.

"Aside from kickin' their mama twenty three out of twenty four hours a day? Well, they're doin' just fine," said Anita.

"I remember when Jack used to kick me in my ribs," Hannah said, "but I can't imagine two of them doing it at the same time!"

We stayed and talked for a good long while since it was real pleasant, sittin' out there, enjoyin' the sunshine. And there was plenty of it. Then when we were done enjoyin' the sunshine, we stayed and enjoyed the evenin' too. We were surprised to see Tom Martin ride by, and that late into the evenin' too. You don't see many white folks out that way, but he was tryin' to head off a delivery of some kind because he'd forgotten to order more cannin' jars. He only stopped for a few minutes when we waved him over and then was on his way again.

We eventually said our goodbyes, agreein' to meet in the south pasture tomorrow mornin' a little earlier than usual so we could get a good start to the day. We all knew the kind of work load we had to look forward to, what with Daddy bein' gone again, so we figured it was best to get goin' on it soon as we could. I don't know what I'd do without Lawrence and Charlie. There's no way I could do all that work myself. I think it's been real nice for them to have an increase in their wages too. Daddy held true to his word, and as soon as he started seein' some of that money John Harris had promised, he gave Lawrence and Charlie what he's been wantin' to give them for a long time now. It's good timin' too, since Anita will be havin' them babies before too long.

Me, Hannah, and Jack rode home real slow. We just wanted to spend the rest of what was left of the evenin' with one another, doin' close to nothin' important, and lovin' every minute of it. We didn't even attend Bible study today, which I'm sure we'll hear about from Hannah's folks at some point. Work would be there first thing in the mornin', so we did our very best at soakin' up our time together, and agreed not to worry about it one bit.

June 20, 1908

Mama's health is up and down. Just when she starts to feel a bit better from one of her surgeries, it isn't long before she takes sick again. She does her best to be pleasant, but I know she's real tired of feelin' bad. And truth is, I'm tired for her.

Charlie and Anita welcomed their babies into the world today. The doctor said he was surprised she carried them as long as she did. Thank goodness they are real healthy and strong. I've never seen Charlie like this before. I'm not quite sure how to describe it. I guess it's the boy in him that I've known so long givin' way a bit to the man he's become. It's really somethin' to see a man become a father for the first time. As soon as I looked at Charlie, it reminded me of how I felt after Jack was born, and I knew how overwhelmed he was feelin'. It's a good kind of overwhelmed though... the kind that gives you purpose and focus.

Charlie said they named the boy Charles Junior Dixon, and they'd call him Junior. They named the girl after his mama, Adelaide, but she'd go by Addie. Lawrence looked real proud, and he didn't even try to hide it. He was braggin' on them babies to Mama and Daddy like he'd given birth to them himself. I was so glad Mama was up to seein' them. Her last surgery took a little bit more out of her than the first one did. She's doin' fine now, but it's taken her longer to recover and get back to normal this time.

Two babies. Just the thought of it made my head spin. We didn't stay long on account of Anita bein' so tired. And besides, she had her family comin', along with Aunt Lena, so we decided to give her some peace and quiet before they got there. It might not be polite to say, but we all knew that peace and quiet weren't things Aunt Lena and Anita's mama would be bringin' with them!

Before we left I gave Charlie a big hug. We didn't do that very often, but I couldn't help myself. The idea that our kids would get to grow up together, same as me and Charlie, just put a warmth in my heart somethin' terrible, and so I grabbed him and let him know it. Today was a real good day.

November 15, 1908

Maryanne Stephenson was seen throwin' up in the grass outside the church house just as the service was gettin' started. She made a big, dramatic scene about the whole thing and announced to everybody within hearin' distance that she had a touch of stomach upset on account of the help not washin' their hands before preparin' her food. But rumor has it she's carryin' a baby. Her cheeks are fuller than they used to be, and her dresses pull across the waist. That's the same thing that happened to Hannah a few months after learnin' she was pregnant with our Jack. She spent the better part of four months throwin' up more than she was keepin' down. But even with all that throwin' up, she still had to let out her dresses to make room for her growin' belly.

If Maryanne is pregnant, a scandal like that would be too much for her folks, seein' as how she isn't married. I might even suspect they move away when it's all said and done.

I suppose it never occurred to me that Maryanne wouldn't get married. She's already twenty-two, and with her history, marriage just may never happen for Maryanne. I mean, even though I can't stand her myself, I guess I thought someone would end up wantin' her. Well, if I'm bein' honest, there have been many men who have wanted her, but none that have ever loved her. She's even been engaged a couple of times, but somethin' always went wrong, and accordin' to Maryanne, it was the man's fault. Men have an initial attraction to her because she's easy to look at and, forgive me for sayin', because she's willin'. But as far as I see it, there's just no way you can start with such disregard for another person's body and heart and soul, and then end up with love when it's all said and done. That's like wantin' to open the oven door and find molasses cookies when you started out usin' the recipe for liver and onions.

Well, anyway, after leavin' Hannah up in the front of the chapel with the other choir members, me and Jack made our way to our usual row toward the back of the church house where Mama, Daddy, Jessie, and Jacob were already sittin'. Mama took little Jack like she always does, and I squeezed my way past Jessie so that I could sit by the window. The air had finally cooled down from what had been a terrible hot summer, and there was a nice breeze blowin' through. I sat there on that hard bench without a care in the world. I don't think it'd be possible to love a day more than I love Sundays. Sundays are usually spent attendin' services followed by supper with Mama, Daddy, Jessie, and Jacob, and then off to the Brown's to spend the evenin' with Hannah's family.

Just as the pastor got started, I heard some chatter comin' from outside. I sat up straight as I could and peeked out the window to see who it was. Right underneath my window stood Maryanne Stephenson and Harriet Jones. They were talkin' awful loud and I thought about hushin' them, but the less interaction I have with Maryanne, the better.

At first, I tried to focus on the sermon, but after a few minutes, I couldn't help but listen in on their conversation.

"Maryanne, dear," it's better to be forthcoming with these kinds of things," said Mrs. Jones.

"There's nothin' to be forthcomin' about," snapped Maryanne. "Like I told you, I just have a sour stomach."

"There's a vicious rumor that you are... with child," whispered Mrs. Jones, like she wasn't the one that started that rumor.

"At first I didn't believe it, but I've seen you three times this month, and each time you've filled out a bit more than the last."

I was lookin' around the room to see if anyone else was hearin' what I was hearin', but nobody let on that they were eavesdroppin' like me.

Maryanne sounded downright angry, and her voice was shakin' when she responded to Mrs. Jones.

"Well it's nothin' more than a rumor!" she barked. "I don't know why everyone has to be so unkind and treat me so unfairly."

Even though I couldn't see her, I knew that Maryanne probably had one hand coverin' her face, which tended to have a permanent pout on it lately, while the other hand would be claspin' her chest. About ninety-five percent of the time, she looks like she's auditionin' for the lead in the town play. I've never known anyone with such emotion over every little thing. It's a tragedy if the fabric she ordered is the wrong shade of blue because it won't match her eyes just right, or if the market is out of sugar, or if folks are talkin' too loud on a day she's got a headache. If you spend too much time around her, pretty soon you start to feel the life bein' sucked right out of you!

"Now, now," said Mrs. Jones. "I understand this is an issue of extreme sensitivity, but you won't be able to hide it much longer. Grace Carver happened to notice you picking up some ginger root last week, and Nancy Smith was curious why you bought a yard more of fabric than you usually buy. People are simply starting to put the pieces together, dear."

Maryanne was silent for a good minute and a half. I found myself anxious to hear what she would say. Finally, I couldn't take the suspense, and I had to peek out the window to catch sight of the whole thing. Maryanne was just standin' there, lookin' every which way but in Harriet Jones's direction. She was fiddlin' with her hands and shiftin' from side to side. All of a sudden, Maryanne burst into tears! A handful of people in the rows in front of us turned around and scowled at me like I was the one causin' the ruckus! Mrs. Harper, who had a nasty look on her face, shushed me with a very stiff finger, for extra emphasis, I'm sure.

As I watched, I saw Maryanne break into tears and fall into Mrs. Jones's arms.

"I just don't know what I'm gonna do," wailed Maryanne, whose sobs were bein' muffled by Mrs. Jones's very large bosoms.

"There, there," said Mrs. Jones as she rocked Maryanne back and forth pretty aggressively. "Now what does your mother have to say on the situation?"

"My mother?" said Maryanne, who paused for a moment when asked that question, then took to hollerin' even louder than before. "She doesn't know a thing about it!"

"Oh my," said Mrs. Jones. "Well this just won't do! We've got to tell her before she finds out by way of these awful rumors flyin' about."

Maryanne stopped cryin' and pulled away from Mrs. Jones. "I can't tell her!" said Maryanne like she was horrified by such a suggestion.

"Well then, what on earth do you plan to do, dear?" asked Mrs. Jones, soundin' real sweet, even though you could tell she was just as worried as Maryanne.

I sat there smashed up against the end of the pew as close as I could get to the window, still peekin' out, waitin' for Maryanne's response.

"It's... it's just too hard!" cried Maryanne. "She'll be devastated!"

"Well of course she will," said Mrs. Jones. "But she's your mother, and she has got to know."

"I never wanted this," said Maryanne.

"What do you mean, dear?" asked Mrs. Jones, lookin' kinda surprised. "Are you sayin' that you... that you were taken advantage of?"

I didn't, for one second, think that's what Maryanne was sayin', but Mrs. Jones doesn't seem content with just the usual amount of drama. She prefers to take an already tragic situation and then add a pinch of exaggeration or a dash of scandal, dependin' on which one would work best with the current story.

Like last summer when her husband cut his hand while sharpenin' the kitchen knives; by the time she got through tellin' the story, you would have thought the man cut his whole arm clean off! I was surprised to see him at the post office two days later with nothin' but four stitches on his thumb. I told him that he looked pretty good for a man who soaked a blanket and three towels with his own blood only two days ago. He smiled, patted me on the shoulder, and said that I'd be lucky to find five or six drops on the very shirt he was wearin' at the time. He knows how his wife is, and he seems to love her all the same. He's a better man than me. A woman like that would make me want to change my name and move out of state.

From my window, I watched Maryanne to see what she would say. As soon as Mrs. Jones asked her that question, Maryanne's whole face changed. She just stood there like a statue starin' at Mrs. Jones and didn't actually answer her question, one way or the other.

"Well this is much worse than I thought!" said Mrs. Jones as she paced back and forth in the dirt, both hands on her cheeks.

For a minute or two, I wondered if what Mrs. Jones was implyin' really happened. Had someone taken advantage of Maryanne? As much as I dislike her, I'd never wish that on her, or anyone else for that matter. I'm ashamed to say it, but I couldn't imagine a man ever needin' to persuade Maryanne... on account of her... of her willingness.

I was watchin' Maryanne's face real careful while Mrs. Jones continued mumblin' to herself. There was no emotion on it. She had gone from blubberin' somethin' terrible to a blank stare in a matter of seconds. I didn't know what to make of it all.

"Harriet," Maryanne said, "what I was tryin' to say was—"

"Oh I know perfectly well what you were trying to say, poor thing," said Mrs. Jones. "You don't have to go through the agony of giving me details. It's none of my business. I can see why you've been nervous to tell your parents, but you've got nothing to be ashamed of. They'll understand that this wasn't your fault."

"They will?" asked Maryanne, like that was just occurrin' to her for the first time.

"Well of course, dear. No man has the right to demand that of you, especially by force!"

They both stood there lookin' at each other for what seemed like forever.

"Was it just awful?" pried Mrs. Jones.

Maryanne paused. She nodded her head yes and then started the cryin' routine all over again, but this time there were no tears. Her face was doin' what it should for someone cryin', but her eyes were as dry as a hot summer's day. She took to rubbin' them with her handkerchief at one point, but I couldn't figure why since there was nothin' to wipe away. I realized in that moment that Mrs. Jones had just given Maryanne a way out of her public shame and her parents' disappointment.

I felt my stomach turn at the thought of that. I was disgusted in a whole new way by Maryanne. I couldn't imagine accusin' someone of such a thing... that kind of talk would ruin a man. I'm guessin' that Maryanne doesn't even know who the father of that baby is. From what I've heard, it could be any number of men, and not all of them are single. There have been a handful of snakes around here that have rolled around with Maryanne and then headed on home to their unsuspectin' wives. Jessie came over to Mama's and Daddy's one evenin', sick and upset from havin' seen an improper exchange between Maryanne and Eli Carver in the alley out back of his store. She wouldn't say exactly what she saw— well not in front of me and Daddy anyhow—but I could tell by the look on her face that it was as bad as I was guessin' it was.

Now, in the scene takin' place outside the church, Mrs. Jones put both hands on Maryanne's shoulders and looked her square in the eye.

"You just tell me what scoundrel did this to you!" she demanded.

Maryanne startled, and her face looked almost panicked.

"Um... I uh...," stumbled Maryanne, fidgetin' with her handkerchief.

"Don't be afraid, dear," said Mrs. Jones. "Your secret is safe with me."

I almost laughed out loud at that.

"I shouldn't say," said Maryanne nervously.

"Of course you should!" said Mrs. Jones. "We've got to bring this man to justice for what he's done to you!"

"It's just that... well..., you don't know him," said Maryanne.

"Don't know him?" Mrs. Jones said, surprised. "Child, I've lived in this town for forty-six years and there isn't a soul I don't know."

Everybody knows that Harriet Jones is in her fifties. I'm not sure why she goes through the song and dance of it bein' somethin' different than it is. Each year she throws herself a birthday party and invites half the town. Mama said that she turned forty-two, three years in a row. I wouldn't be surprised if she has her headstone made up ahead of time so that nobody will ever know her real age.

"Now go on and tell me who it is," pushed Mrs. Jones.

"He's... he's colored," blurted out Maryanne.

Mrs. Jones' face turned a shade of ghostly white. She threw both her hands up to cover her mouth as she gasped. Maryanne was watchin' Mrs. Jones, like she was waitin' to see her reaction.

"What's his name?" whispered Mrs. Jones.

Maryanne looked behind her, then down at the ground, and then up at Mrs. Jones.

"Charlie Dixon," said Maryanne.

When she said Charlie's name, I was absolutely astounded. I sat there on the church bench in complete shock, unaware of whatever else was goin' on around me in the room. I felt my face get red, and it was like my whole body was on fire. Seconds later, the rage I felt pushed me to my feet, and I shoved my way past everyone in the pew in order to get outside and confront that contemptible liar.

"What's wrong, Will? Where are you going?" Mama whispered.

I couldn't answer. I moved to the rear of the chapel and pushed open the back door to the church house, makin' no effort to close it quietly behind me, and I heard it slam shut as I reached the bottom step. I raced around the side of the buildin' to where Maryanne and Mrs. Jones were talkin'. Maryanne saw me comin' first. Her eyes got real wide, and she actually took a step behind Mrs. Jones.

"Maryanne Stephenson!" I yelled.

Mrs. Jones spun around with a look of panic on her old, gossipy face.

"I heard you, Maryanne! I heard what you said, and we both know it's a lie!" I said.

"Will," said Maryanne, "this doesn't concern you!"

"Maryanne Stephenson, you better fix this right here and now, before it's too late," I said, tryin' hard to control my anger. "You make this right!"

I looked up to see several people starin' out the windows, includin' pastor Brown. Before long, folks were filin' out of the church house and gatherin' around.

"What on earth is goin' on out here?" asked Daddy.

"Your son just came out of nowhere, threatening an already fragile young woman!" interrupted Mrs. Jones. "That's what's going on here Mr. Wright!"

"Will?" said Daddy sternly. "Tell me what's wrong, son.

"Maryanne seems to be strugglin' to find the truth," I said, glarin' at her.

"The truth about what?" asked Mama, still holdin' little Jack.

The air was still, and it was silent. Everyone was lookin' at me, then at Maryanne, waitin' for an answer. I saw Hannah out of the corner of my eye, runnin' up behind Mama. I stared hard at Maryanne who was starin' back at me.

"You know that what you're doin' is evil," I said. "You go through with it and there's no goin' back. This is the only chance you're gonna have to fix it."

"How dare you!" shouted Mrs. Jones.

I ignored Mrs. Jones and kept my gaze on Maryanne, waitin' for her to take back what she'd said about Charlie. A moment later Roger and Lucy Stephenson pushed their way through the crowd tryin' to get to Maryanne. Mrs. Stephenson went right over to her and put her arms around Maryanne's shoulders. Mr. Stephenson squared off against me.

"Now what's the meaning of this, Mr. Wright," he asked me.

"Your daughter has somethin' she needs to tell you," I said, still lookin' at Maryanne. "And I'm here to make sure she tells you the true version."

Mr. Stephenson looked over at his wife and daughter.

"Maryanne," he said, "what is Will talking about?"

Maryanne looked embarrassed and clearly didn't want to talk about it with all the people standin' around.

"We can discuss it at home," she said. "It's a private matter."

"Yes, of course," said Mrs. Stephenson. "We'll discuss it in private."

"Maryanne?," I said with a warnin' tone in my voice.

"Will!" she yelled. "Why can't you just leave me be? This is none of your business!"

"You know perfectly well why it's my business," I said firm as I know how. "Either you tell the truth, right here in front of everybody, or I will."

Mrs. Jones had taken a few steps back and was whisperin' somethin' to a group of women who had gathered near her.

"You shouldn't have forced my hand, Will," Maryanne said angrily.

She turned to face her parents. Then she waved Harriet Jones over to stand with her.

"What is it, darling?" asked Mrs. Stephenson.

Maryanne looked at me and then back at her parents. She put her handkerchief to her eyes and then started back up with her tearless cryin'.

"Harriet," she sniffled, "can you tell my parents what I shared with you? It's just too painful for me to say it out loud," said Maryanne.

"Of course I will, dear."

Mrs. Jones put her arm around Maryanne's waist and huddled the Stephensons around her. Then there was quiet talkin', followed by gasps and tears, which ended with Lucy Stephenson's legs turnin' to rubber, and Roger Stephenson catchin' her before she hit the ground.

"Is this true, Maryanne?" asked Mr. Stephenson, who sounded like he was out of breath.

"Yes, Pa," lied Maryanne. "I... I tried to stop it, but he was just too strong for—"

"That's a filthy lie!" I shouted.

I assume Sherriff Jenkins had heard all the commotion and came outside with the others to see what in the world was goin' on. He made his way over to us and stood in between me and Roger Stephenson.

"Everyone needs to settle down!" said the Sheriff. "Mr. Wright, what in the world is this all about?"

I felt my heart poundin' so hard I thought it would jump right out of my chest. I had never felt so much anger and hatred toward anyone as I did toward Maryanne in that moment. She was settin' Charlie up for an awful lashin' in order to cover up her own indiscretions, and all I could think about was clearin' his name.

"I'll tell you what it's about!" yelled Roger Stephenson. "My daughter has been violated by Charlie Dixon!"

"What?" said Sheriff Jenkins.

"It isn't true!" I shouted.

"How do you know?" asked the Sheriff.

"I heard Maryanne and Harriet Jones outside the window durin' the service talkin' about Maryanne bein' pregnant. Mrs. Jones jumped to conclusions and gave Maryanne a way out of havin' to tell her parents that she was havin' a baby out of wedlock."

"That's outrageous!" yelled Mrs. Jones.

"What's outrageous is tryin' to blame a man for somethin' he didn't have any part of!" I said.

Sheriff Jenkins was stunned. He turned to Maryanne.

"What do you have to say about this, Miss Stephenson?" he asked.

Maryanne looked around at everyone, who were waitin' onpins and needles to hear what she had to say. Then she looked at her parents.

"Charlie Dixon took advantage of my kindness toward him, and he violated me," she said.

"Why would Will lie about what he heard you and Mrs. Jones talkin' about?" asked the Sheriff.

"Will has been upset with me for years, said Maryanne. He has always fancied me, and I've never returned his feelings. After I turned down his marriage proposal when we were younger, he just hasn't ever been kind to me since.

My head was spinnin'. I had no idea which lie to try to fix first, and now I was not only tryin' to defend Charlie, but myself too!

"Sheriff, can't you see what she is tryin' to do?" I asked in desperation. "She got herself into trouble, then got caught, and now she's tryin' to blame anyone but herself. I have never had feelin's for Maryanne, and there was never a marriage proposal. I've spent the better part of ten years doin' everything I could to avoid that girl. You can ask anyone that knows me."

"Maryanne," said sheriff Jenkins, "what you're claiming Mr. Dixon did is a mighty serious accusation."

At this point, Mr. Stephenson, red-faced with a mixture of embarrassment and anger, tried to defend Maryanne's already lost honor, "if my little girl said that's what happened, then that's what happened! Now I want that coon brought in and dealt with!"

Sherriff Jenkins replied calmly, "Mr. and Mrs. Stephenson, I'll need you both to accompany Maryanne down to the jailhouse where we can sit and talk more thoroughly."

The Sheriff looked out at the crowd of folks lingerin' about. "You all get on about your business now," he said. This is in the law's hands, and I'll make sure it's seen to."

"Sheriff, please—," I started.

"Mr. Wright, that means you too. You trust me to do this the right way. You hear me, Will?" he said.

I took a deep breath and felt Daddy's hand on my shoulder. "Yes, sir. I hear you," I said.

"Let's head on home," Hannah said nervously as she took Jack from Mama and came over to me.

I looked over at Daddy, and I could tell that he was thinkin' the very same thing I was. He didn't say a word—just gave me one firm nod that let me know we were on the same page.

"Hannah," I said, "get everyone in the buggy. Daddy and I will see you home, and then we've got some business to attend to."

"Business?" Hannah asked. "What does that mean, Will?" Mama came up behind Hannah and put her mouth next to Hannah's ear.

"They just need to go and check in on Charlie," she whispered. "Some folks might think to take this situation into their own hands before the law has a chance to handle it."

"We'll try not to be late, honey," I said. You all can get supper started, and we'll be along as soon as we can."

"Hannah nodded, and she and Mama walked arm in arm to the buggy.

"You two coming to supper this evening?" Mama asked Jessie and Jacob.

"I'd never turn down your cookin'," Jacob said as he and Jessie followed along behind them, tryin' to sound casual.

I felt a rush of appreciation for Mama in that instant. She was always so good at bringin' peace and calm to any situation. She could see the need to help Hannah and Jack and Jessie feel like things would be alright, and she was extra good at it in the moments when I didn't think to do it first. I've never been very good at managin' my own emotions while still watchin' out for others at the same time. Daddy's always told me that I react to things before I take time to think them through. I suppose he's right. But sometimes, if you stop to think on things first, you realize that the time you wasted thinkin' was the only time you had for doin' somethin', and then it's too late. I know it doesn't always work that way, but this was one of those times when the doin' had to come first.

We rode home a bit quicker than usual, let everyone off, and rode fast to the Dixons. As we were pullin' up, we saw Lawrence out front fixin' the fence post that someone had taken an axe to a week before. It certainly wasn't the first time, and I reckon it won't be the last, either. Lawrence has dealt with all kinds of poor treatment by some of the folks in this town. If they're not damagin' some part of his property, they're harassin' him and his family. And from what I've observed, their hatred seems to come from the fact that they are uncomfortable with a colored man who can read and write, who owns his own land, and who works side by side with a white man. That appears to be awful threatenin' to some, I guess mostly because they have no self-respect and no basic sense of decency.

As we got to Lawrence's and Charlie's place, Daddy jumped down off his horse and did his best to say hello before gettin' right down to it.

"Everybody alright out here?" Daddy asked.

"Well sure we are," Lawrence said as he set his mallet down and chuckled. "We weren't expectin' you today."

Lawrence headed in our direction and shook Daddy's hand first, then mine, wipin' the sweat from his brow with the back of his forearm.

"How you doin', Will?"

"Just fine, sir," I answered, unable to look at him in the eyes.

"Charlie, Anita, and the young'un's will be along anytime now. They went on to church without me today. I've had a nasty cough goin' on a few days now, and I can't seem to shake it. Didn't want to keep folks from hearin' the Word due to my hackin'!"

"I need to talk to you, old friend," said Daddy abruptly. "I ain't here for a friendly visit, I'm afraid. It's mighty urgent too."

Lawrence took on a serious look. Then he led us inside where we gathered in the front room. It was a modest house, but well taken care of. Charlie told me once that Lawrence hasn't changed a thing about the house since Adelaide died. The same pictures hang on the walls, the chairs sit where she put them, and her shawl still hangs over the back of the rockin' chair Lawrence made for her when she was pregnant with Charlie. He even keeps her coffee mug in the back of the cupboard, but never uses it.

"The Stephenson girl is pregnant," Daddy started. "I'm not sure how much you know about that girl, but she ain't married and her people are real high society folk."

"Ok, said Lawrence. Don't see what that's got to do with me."

Daddy continued. "It all came out in the open today that she is pregnant, and she has confessed as much. Seems she got real nervous at the idea of folks knowin' she'd been improper, so she said she'd been forced."

Daddy hesitated before continuin' on.

"She said... it was Charlie."

Lawrence's face went blank – frozen like –, and he put both hands over his ears. He just sat there and stared at Daddy like he couldn't believe what he was sayin'.

'The Sheriff is talkin' to Maryanne and her parents now to get more information. Will confronted her right in front of the Sheriff, but I just don't know if that's gonna help any."

"Why would she do that?" Lawrence said, barely able to speak. "Doesn't she know what they'll do to my boy?"

"I don't think that even entered her mind," I said. "There's nothin' more dangerous than a selfish person in a desperate situation."

"It's not so much the Sheriff I'm worried about," Daddy said. "He's a reasonable man, and he knows as well as anyone that Maryanne is a loose young woman. So I think he's gonna do his job and do it right. You and I both know who we got to watch out for."

Lawrence nodded his understanding. His voice was low and discouraged as he replied, "Coleman and his boys. That man still acts like the Sheriff around here, and he's as hateful as they come when it concerns the colored folks."

Daddy reached over, put his hand on Lawrence's shoulder, and looked at him with concern. "Even if Sheriff Jenkins sees the truth of it and clears Charlie's name, those boys won't let it die without sendin' a message," he said . "This is the kind of thing they've been waitin' for. This gives them an excuse to act on their hate and paint it up to look like justice."

Just then, Charlie and Anita came in, each of them holdin' one of the twins. They came in happy, but it wasn't five seconds before they could tell somethin' was wrong.

"Hey, Will," said Charlie as he took off his hat and nodded. "What's goin' on? Why all the serious faces?"

"Charlie," Lawrence said, "sit down, son."

Anita laid the babies on a blanket on the floor and came over to sit next to Charlie.

"Ain't no way to do this but just say it," Lawrence said.

"Say what?" asked Charlie, puttin' his arm around Anita, knowin' he was bracin' her for whatever it was Lawrence would say.

"That Stephenson girl is pregnant, and she said that you raped her."

Charlie and Anita both just sat there, starin' at Lawrence like they couldn't process the information fast as he was givin' it. After takin' a minute to catch his breath, Charlie started stutterin' and ramblin'.

"There's gotta be some kind of mistake," he said, shakin' his head now and talkin' to himself.

"Why... why would she... what kind of girl says...," Anita mumbled.

"No," said Charlie, lookin' at each one of us, his fear and confusion clearly apparent. "It's a mistake. She made a mistake. We just have to talk to her and straighten it out."

"Charlie," I said, wantin' to calm and reassure him, "she wasn't raped. She got herself pregnant, and she needs a way out of bein' held responsible."

"But once she thinks it through," said Anita, "surely she'll see that what she's doin—"

"All she cares about is not lookin' bad," I said. "Thinkin' it through won't fix a thing. I'm sorry to be so forceful, Anita, but I know this girl, and she is trouble."

Now Charlie was gettin' real panicky, and I couldn't much blame him.

"My family," he said. "My babies. What... what am I gonna do?"

"We can't think like that," said Daddy firmly. "All we can do is handle right now. You all need to be somewhere safe. Get your things packed as quick as you can, enough for several days, and you'll come home with us."

"What about Sheriff Jenkins?" asked Lawrence.

"He has to sort things out with Maryanne before he'll come lookin' for Charlie. But the others won't wait."

"Won't folks know where we are?" Anita said.

"Maybe," said Daddy, "but it's the only thing to do. It's almost dark now. We've got to hurry."

"Daddy," I said, "would John Harris help?"

Daddy looked at me and thought on my question a minute. "I believe he would," he finally said. "Now, son, you need to ride faster than you've ever ridden, you hear me?"

"I hear you, sir," I said, feelin' my heart pound against my chest.

"Tell John what's goin' on and ask him to bring his car."

"Do we got that kind of time?" asked Lawrence, his growin' nervousness showin'.

"Ain't no way we can ride with them babies and have ya'll out in the open like that," Daddy said.

Lawrence knew Daddy was right. He took to rubbin' the top of his head back and forth and pacin' the floor.

"Go on, Will," said Daddy. "Don't stop for nothin'."

I raced outside, jumped on the back of that mare, and rode for my life. I'd never felt that kind of panic before. All I could think about was them men showin' up before I got back. And what if John Harris wasn't home? Those thoughts racin' through my mind made my stomach sick, and I couldn't help but throw up just minutes after leavin'. I did like Daddy said, though, and I didn't stop, even for that.

I rode hard for a while but still had a ways to go, when comin' toward me was John Harris' Buick. I couldn't believe my eyes, and I slowed my horse and started wavin' my hands like a fool to get his attention.

"Mr. Harris! Mr. Harris!" I yelled.

"Will!" he called as he pulled up next to me. "I know. Your mother sent me."

"She did?" I asked, real surprised.

"You ride back and tell them I'm on my way."

While I wished that car went faster than it did, I still felt a rush of relief come over me. I couldn't believe Mama had thought of callin' on Mr. Harris too. Her doin' that saved us some real valuable time.

When I got back to the Dixon's, they all looked surprised to see me back so quick. I explained that Mama had already sent Mr. Harris and that he wasn't far behind me. The babies were cryin', which I'm sure was on account of all the tension in the air. I did my best to calm Addie, while Anita got little Junior ready to go. I held the baby the same way I used to hold Jack when he was upset, and she quieted down for the most part.

Minutes later Mr. Harris showed up. We moved fast and got the Dixons in the car with their belongings. Then Daddy and I rode behind until we got home. The ride was long, and every minute that passed was more painful than the one before it. Mama and Hannah were waitin' out front for us when we finally got there. They helped Anita get the babies inside. But Lawrence went around the side of the car where John Harris was standin'.

"I don't rightly know how to thank you," said Lawrence.

"I'm just glad we got here safely," Mr. Harris said as he put his hand on Lawrence's shoulder.

"Riskin' yourself for my boy—"

"Now you all better get inside," interrupted Mr. Harris, who obviously isn't the kind of man who does what's right for the praise. "Ben, we can put people up as well if you need us to."

"That's awful kind of you," said Daddy. "We'll see how things go tonight."

Mr. Harris nodded his agreement and left, and the rest of us went inside. Daddy walked right up to Mama, who was layin' out blankets and things for people to sleep with, and hugged her right in front of everybody. We all knew, includin' Mama, that that was Daddy's way of thankin' her for thinkin' to send John Harris to help us.

"I ain't sure we would have had enough time without you doin' what you did," Daddy said quietly.

I don't think it was meant for the rest of us to hear, but you can't help what your ears pick up.

"I'm glad it turned out the way it did," Mama whispered back.

Then they both went about gettin' the Dixons settled while Hannah helped Anita with the twins. Everyone was exhausted and scared. Mama got some biscuits and buttermilk ready, and we all sat by the fire and tried to calm our nerves some before headin' off to bed.

"We'll talk with Sheriff Jenkins first thing tomorrow," Daddy said.

"You trust him? asked Lawrence.

"He's a good man," said Daddy.

I can't say any of us slept longer than thirty or forty minutes at a time that night, sometimes holdin' our breath anytime there was rustlin' of any kind outside. But mornin' finally came, and we were all grateful for it.

November 16, 1908

There was a knock on the door, first thing this mornin', and we knew it was Sheriff Jenkins before Daddy even opened it.

"Mornin', Sheriff," said Daddy.

"Good morning, Ben. I'm sorry to come here so early, but—"

"You need to talk with Charlie Dixon," Daddy interrupted.

"Yes I do."

"We ain't hidin' him from you, Sheriff. We just figured it'd be safer to have them here with us until you can sort through things."

"I know that," he said. "Is there someplace that he and I can talk in private?"

Daddy escorted Sheriff Jenkins into the front room and then went to fetch Charlie before headin' out to the barn. Lawrence and Anita insisted on bein' there too, and the good sheriff obliged. They talked for what felt like forever. I'm a little ashamed to admit it, but even though we could hear most of the conversation from the other room, we didn't do much in the way of tryin' not to. I suppose the fact that Mama and Hannah tried even less than I did made me feel a bit better about it. Mama was holdin' Addie, and she was sittin' in such a way that she could see right into the livin' room where they were talkin', so she could tell us just what was goin' on.

"Now Charlie," began the sheriff, "I need to know what your interactions with Miss Stephenson have been like."

"I barely even talk to the girl!" said Charlie, already soundin' fired up. "I see her in town sometimes, and she does all she can to flirt and make me feel mighty uncomfortable."

"Have you ever been alone with her?"

"Sheriff Jenkins, no disrespect, sir, but are you crazy? Ain't no white girl in this town gonna be alone with me, and ain't no way I'd be dumb enough to be alone with her!"

"Charlie, I know this is difficult, but I'm not askin' you these questions because I think you're guilty," Sheriff Jenkins said calmly. "I'm askin' you these questions so that I can be as thorough as possible. If there are holes in Maryanne's story, I need to find them. So just keep that in mind while we're talking."

Charlie took a deep breath while Anita rubbed his back with one hand and took a tissue to her eyes with the other one.

"Now can you tell me where you were on the evening of May twenty-sixth?"

"May twenty-sixth?" said Charlie in disbelief. "How can I even know that? That was five months ago!"

"I know," Sheriff said, "but I really need you to try and remember."

"Is that when she said it happened?" asked Anita.

"Yes."

May twenty-sixth, repeated Mama quietly, like she was thinkin' on somethin' important. Why does that day stand out to me?

Then it occurred to Mama. That was the day she and Daddy went to Jonesboro to see the specialist.

"What happened around here after we left?" Mama asked me.

"Nothin' really," I said.

"Will!" Hannah started to shout, and then she covered her mouth after hearin' how loud she said it. "We were with Charlie that day," she whispered.

"We were?" I said, tryin' to recall.

"Don't you remember?" she said in frustration. "We were feeling down after your parents left and decided to go see the Dixons."

"That's right!" I said. "And we were there until late that evenin'!"

"You were?" asked Mama, sittin' straight up in her chair and then wincin' from the pain in her belly.

"You alright, Mama?"

"I'm fine, I'm fine," she said as she held her side. "We've got to tell the Sheriff about this!"

But we couldn't just run right out there and tell Sheriff Jenkins what we knew on account of we weren't supposed to be listenin' in the first place; so I switched places with Mama. From where I was sittin', Sheriff Jenkins had his back to me, and I was lookin' straight at Lawrence. I waved my arms to get his attention and then motioned for him to keep quiet. Then Mama wrote on a piece of paper and handed it to me.

May 26 – Lily in Jonesboro – Will & Hannah at your house

I held up the paper for Lawrence to see. He squinted some, but read it carefully. All the while, Charlie was strugglin' to remember where he was on May twenty-sixth. Then I saw Lawrence's face light up.

"May I remind my son what happened on the day you're askin' about?" asked Lawrence.

"It would be better if he remembered on his own," said the Sheriff.

"If I could just give him a word or two to spark his memory, sir, he can tell you the rest."

"Alright then," Sheriff said.

Lawrence looked right at Charlie, hopin' he'd get the message he was about to send him.

"Lily's surgery in Jonesboro," he said, and then waited.

Charlie sat there thinkin' real hard.

"Does that mean anything to you, Charlie?" asked Sheriff Jenkins.

My hands were clenched as I watched his face. Then I knew. Charlie remembered.

"I got it!" said Charlie.

"Tell me what you remember," Sheriff said.

"Miss Lily went to Jonesboro that mornin' to have the specialist take out the tumor in her belly again."

"OK," said the Sheriff. "And where were you?"

"I was at home. We were havin' a picnic outside under the big shade tree."

"And who was with you?"

"Daddy and Anita," said Charlie.

"Anyone else?" asked the Sheriff.

"Yes!" Charlie said. "Will and Hannah came over for a spell."

"How long did they stay?"

"I can't say for sure, but it was dark when they left."

"You're positive it was dark?"

"Absolutely, Sheriff. I got up to light some lamps after havin' dessert.

"Was there anyone else there?"

"No, sir."

"Wait!" shouted Anita. "Who was that man who rode by and stopped for a minute?"

"Tom Martin," said Charlie. "I forgot about him."

"Why would Tom Martin stop to talk to you? Are you friends?"

"I wouldn't say we're friends, but he's always been kind to me. He knows the Wrights real well, so he stopped to talk to Will."

"That's very helpful," said the Sheriff as he took a deep breath and let it out slow. "I'll just need to talk with Mr. Martin."

"Does what I told you put any holes in Maryanne's story?" asked Charlie real serious-like.

"I hope so," said Sheriff Jenkins. "I truly hope so."

After wrappin' things up with Charlie, Sheriff Jenkins asked to talk with the rest of us to make sure our stories matched. Now I know that it wasn't completely honest since we had already heard Charlie's story, but we figured it's not dishonest to tell the truth, and that's exactly what we did.

While Sheriff was talkin' to Hannah, I thought it couldn't hurt to look through my journal to see if I'd written anything on that day, and sure enough, there it was!

"Pardon me, Sheriff Jenkins," I said. "I'd like you to see this."

He took the journal from me and read through the entry dated May 26. He looked up at me in astonishment.

"Of all the things to help your friend," he said, "this has got to be the best."

"I only started writin' a few years ago," I said, "but I try to keep it pretty regular. I just do it for my kin to read about me someday. Never thought I'd need it for somethin' like this."

"And you just happen to have written on that day," said the sheriff, shakin' his head in amazement.

"Pretty lucky, huh?" I grinned.

"I'd say so. Keep this in a safe place in case I need to see it again."

"Yes, sir."

Seems the Sheriff went right over to Tom Martin's after he was finished questionin' us because it wasn't long before he was back at our house. He said that Mr. Martin confirmed what we had told him, and after gettin' his story, he went to talk to the Stephensons again. He told them about the journal entry, the witness, and then he pointed out all the problems with Maryanne's version of what happened. He said she was speechless, but even after all that, she still wouldn't change her story. Pride, I suppose. Sheriff Jenkins said that there wasn't a lick of proof, and that he wouldn't look into it any further.

"What a relief," said Anita as she put her arms around Charlie's neck and rested her head on his shoulder while he hugged her back.

Daddy saw the Sheriff out, and then he and Lawrence exchanged some words at the front door, away from the women.

"It's only a relief as far as the law goes," said Daddy.

"We still ain't safe," Lawrence said, lookin' over at Charlie and Anita.

"I think it's best if you all stay on here until things settle down."

"You sure it ain't no trouble?" asked Lawrence.

"Not a bit," Daddy said.

That night we felt like we could relax some. Now that Sheriff Jenkins had handled things proper, we were hopin' it was just a matter of time before Lawrence and Charlie could take Anita and the babies back home. And even though we're real crowded, I like havin' everybody together like this. Bein' around them twins makes me realize that I really do want more babies with Hannah. But, I can't worry about that right now. I'm just gonna enjoy our time together with the Dixons while we have it, and after not sleepin' a wink last night, I'm fixin' to sleep like a rock tonight!

November 17, 1908

"Will, wake up, son!"

I startled somethin' awful when Daddy tried to wake me, and I swung my arm around the side of the bed for my rifle. Daddy grabbed my hand before I could reach it and waited until I came to my senses.

"What's the matter," I asked, breathin' hard.

Hannah sat up quick, all worried like.

"Ben, what's goin' on?" she asked.

"They've come for Charlie," Benjamin whispered. "Get dressed, Will, and bring your gun. Keep the lamps out. Hannah, take the kids and go with Lily and Anita to the back room, and be real quick about it."

I felt Hannah's cold hand on my arm. I put my hand over the top of it and told her to go. She raced across the room to get Jack who was already cryin' from all the commotion. I felt a pain in my chest as she ran out of the room with our boy, not knowin' how this would turn out for any of us.

Then I noticed a figure standin' in the doorway and had to squint hard to make it out. It was Lawrence. Even in the dark I could see him shakin'. Don't know if it was out of fear or anger. Lawrence is not a violent man. He's probably one of the most peaceful men I've ever known. But he loves his family just about as much as any good man should and would take on a mountain lion with his bare hands if it meant protectin' them.

I jumped to my feet and threw on my trousers and boots. I could hear Mama tryin' to calm Anita who was beside herself. I grabbed my rifle and met Daddy and Lawrence in the front room. Daddy was standin' next to the big window, peekin' out to see about how many men we were dealin' with.

"Looks like ten or so," he said.

Hard as he tried to hide it, I could hear the worry in his voice. I'm certain Lawrence could hear it too.

"Ten men," said Lawrence. "Don't know how we can handle ten men, but it's got to be done."

Just then, Charlie came out of the bedroom, gun in hand.

"Give me the gun and get back in that room!" Lawrence said real firm.

"Charlie, just as firmly, answered back, "can't let you all go out there, riskin' your lives on my account while I just hide in some dark room!".

I never heard Charlie talk so strong. He had a real calm way about him most of the time. Lawrence put his hands on Charlie's shoulders and looked at him square in the eye.

"This can't be your fight, son. This is a fight for me and Ben and Will. You go out there, and it's over before it's started. You stay in this house now – and keep out of sight. You hear me?"

Charlie was standin' tall and strong at first, but then his body kind of loosened up and his chin fell to his chest. He was torn up because he knew his Daddy was right, but wasn't sure how to make it fit in his mind. Then Daddy spoke up.

"Charlie, you get in that back room with the women like your daddy said, and if it sounds like them men made it into the house, you get everybody out the south door and run like hell to the Harris place. Go by way of the orchard to avoid bein' seen."

Charlie nodded and went to the back of the house where Mama and Hannah were tryin' to get Anita and the kids to calm down and keep quiet. Not even a full minute later we heard a voice outside.

"Ben Wright! We know you got that colored boy in there! Send him out so your family don't get hurt! Be smart about this, Ben!"

That voice sounded awful familiar. Didn't take long to realize that it was Hank Coleman. We couldn't swear to it in front of a judge, seein' as how those cowards cover up like a bunch of ghosts, but we all knew it was him.

"Get off my land! We don't want no trouble!" Daddy yelled.

"We'll deal later with the fact that you're protectin' a boy who preys on young white women, Ben! As for right now, we're here to settle things with Charlie Dixon! You send him out or we'll come in after him! I'm givin' you fair warnin', Ben!"

Daddy took a deep breath. He looked at me, and then turned and looked at Lawrence. Lawrence nodded like he knew what Daddy was thinkin' without him even sayin' anything.

"Will, go around the west side of the house," he whispered. "Lawrence, you take the east."

Then he broke out the bottom part of the front window so he could shoot at any man who tried to get inside. Lawrence and I went in opposite directions. I felt like I was on fire. My heart was poundin' and my hands were shakin'. I'd never been so scared in all my life. I didn't like bein' separated from Daddy and Lawrence, either.

The night was as black as I ever saw and I could hardly see a thing. Only light at all was comin' from a torch bein' held by the leader, which we'd already determined was that devil, Sheriff Coleman. I sat in the dark, shiverin' and waitin' for some kind of sign from Daddy. I could hear him and the Sheriff hollerin' back and forth but couldn't tell what they were sayin'. All of a sudden it was quiet. Only sound I heard was the snorts made by the horses tryin' to blow the cold out of their nostrils. Then the sound of a gunshot blasted through my ears, but I couldn't tell where it came from. I picked up my rifle and pointed toward the light of the torch. Shots started, one after another from every direction. I aimed as best I could and fired. I heard a man cry out and knew I'd hit him. I had never killed a man before, and I was filled with panic. My mind was spinnin', and I wanted to run to Hannah and the others and make sure they were all alright. Then I heard one of the ghosts shout "They're runnin' toward the orchard!"

My heart sank, and I ran faster than I thought possible toward the back of the house. I saw two shadows on horseback chasin' Charlie and the women. Daddy came runnin' like a tornado out the south door right in front of me and jumped off the back porch without takin' a single one of the four steps. He was still runnin' when he aimed his gun at one of the shadows and shot the man clean off his horse. Between all the gunshots, you could hear babies screamin' and cryin' in the distance. I was runnin' after Daddy when I heard another shot and saw him fall to the ground. I tried to call out to him but nothin' came out of my mouth. I knew I was runnin' toward him, but I felt like my legs were made of rubber, and I just couldn't get there quick enough.

As I rounded the corner of the house, I saw they'd taken Lawrence, and three men were holdin' him down. When I was just a few feet away from Daddy, I heard a loud noise and felt a blindin' pain in the back of my head. I tried to spin around to see where it came from, but it seemed like everything was happenin' in slow motion. I saw one of the ghosts hoverin' over me with the butt of his rifle pointed in my face. That was the last thing I remembered before everything went black.

When I came to, the first thing I noticed was my head felt like it was split in two, and my hands and feet were bound. I was propped up in front of the shed. Daddy was in the same predicament, sittin' next to me. The bullet had got him in the shoulder, and he was in all kinds a terrible pain. There was a fire burnin' to the left of us over by the willow tree east of the house. I was tryin' to put all the pieces together, but my head was spinnin' so fast.

"You alright, Daddy?" I whispered.

"I'll be okay, son," he grimaced. "Looks worse than it feels." I knew he was lyin' for my sake.

"Where's Lawrence?" I asked.

Daddy didn't say a word, just motioned with his head. I looked in that direction, and there was Lawrence, layin' face down in the dirt with his feet bound and his arms tied behind him at the wrist. I felt like I would be sick.

"Is he... is he dead?" I stuttered.

"No," Daddy said real quiet. "But part of me wishes he was."

I looked at Daddy, wonderin' how he could say such a thing.

"Will, if they find Charlie, they're gonna lynch him. Ain't no father ought to see his own son..."

Daddy stopped talkin'. We heard a bunch of whoopin' and hollerin', like there were Indian warriors comin' from the direction of the orchard.

"We got him!" someone shouted.

When we heard that, Lawrence started squirmin' around on the ground, tryin' to get himself loose. He turned and looked at me and Daddy with a look of panic I've never seen on the face of any man before. Daddy started breathin' heavy and was tryin' to get his arms free. He was moanin' from the pain in his shoulder, but he just kept on tryin'. It was no use. The knots were too tight, and there was no way to get free.

The hollerin' was gettin' closer, and we saw about a half dozen men ride up, draggin' Charlie behind one of the horses. His hands were bound with a rope, and his stomach was all bloody from bein' scraped along the ground. Lawrence was screamin' and wailin', the likes of which I pray to never hear again as long as I'm livin'.

Charlie was still alive but had all the fight dragged right out of him. They pulled him roughly to his feet and carried him, staggerin', over to the big old willow tree, all the time cursin' and eggin' each other on. One of them removed the ropes off his wrists, made a noose, and swung it over a big branch above them. I thought my heart would explode from my chest. I couldn't bear it. My mind was racin' from one thought to the next. I couldn't even imagine the kind of evil that would cause someone to do what they were bent on doin'. Charlie was my best friend in all the world. How can we stop this? What about Anita and the babies? And Lawrence... oh Lawrence! God in Heaven, stop this from happening! Then I was jerked back abruptly to the reality of the terrible scene around me by the sound of Daddy screaming.

"Sheriff Coleman! Don't you do this!" he hollered. "You go through with it, and there's no turnin' back."

That coward stopped and looked in Daddy's direction like he was surprised we knew it was him. He paused for a minute and then started shoutin'.

"Take a good look boys!" yelled Coleman. "This is what happens when you rape a white girl!"

"This ain't right, Coleman!" shouted Daddy. "This ain't the law!"

Coleman didn't even bother tryin' to defend their actions.

His answer was to utter a stream of curses, turn back around, place the noose over Charlie's head, and synch it up tight around his neck.

Charlie called out desperately to Lawrence with as much strength as he was able to muster. "Daddy!" came the sound of his terrified voice.

At that, Lawrence stopped fightin' his ropes and got real still. Then he looked agonizin'ly at Charlie. He just laid his cheek on the ground and looked at his boy. Charlie looked back at Lawrence, tears streamin' down his face. Their eyes were locked on each other—and nothin' else.

Coleman looked at the man holdin' the rope and nodded. At this signal, those cowards pulled Charlie's body a few feet off the ground and tied the end of the rope to the trunk of the tree. Charlie took to shakin' and chokin', and I closed my eyes as tight as I could, tryin' to shut out the sight of the horrible thing that was takin' place. But even if I couldn't bear to look at what was happenin', I couldn't stop from hearin' that awful sound: the sound of a man watchin' his son bein' hanged from a willow tree.

Then I heard hoofbeats in the distance and opened my eyes to see what looked like a dozen torch lights headed in our direction from the Harris place. It must have panicked the ghosts because, amid much cursin' and shoutin', they hurriedly mounted up and rode off, vanishin' into the darkness quick as lightnin'. A minute or so later, John Harris rode up and looked around, tryin' to make sense of what he saw.

"The willow tree!" Daddy choked out.

John raced over to the tree and quickly cut the rope, easin' Charlie's body to the ground. A few other men hurried over to help, but it was too late. Charlie was gone.

"Cut me free," Lawrence whispered. He struggled in awful agony as he repeated the words, "Cut me free. Cut me free. Cut me free."

One of the other men went over to Lawrence and started cuttin' the ropes off his hands and feet. But even before he was free of the ropes entirely, he started crawlin' in the dirt toward

Charlie's body. Same man came back for me and Daddy and cut us out of our ropes. By the time we got over to Lawrence, he was sittin' in the dirt, holdin' Charlie in his arms like a baby, just sobbin' and rockin' back and forth.

Nobody knew what to do. Daddy held his bleedin' arm as he sat down next to Lawrence on the ground. I found myself kneelin' in the dirt at Charlie's feet. The front of his pants were shredded, and his legs were all torn up. I knelt there in a daze. Couldn't do nothin' else. I just knelt there. I looked at my friend in disbelief – my closest friend who had always felt like my own brother. He was right in front of me, but he was gone. I thought of Anita and little Addie and Junior. I thought of Lawrence. I thought of Mama. I thought of Aunt Lena. But more than anythin', I felt my own heart. It hurt so bad I wanted to rip it from my chest.

John Harris had sent one of his men for the Sheriff, and it wasn't long before he and several deputies arrived. One of the deputies came over to Lawrence and tried to pry him away from Charlie, but Daddy grabbed hold of the man's arm so hard I thought he might break it. Then he said, in a voice so deep and intense that it startled even me, "you leave this man be."

The deputy quickly pulled his arm away from Daddy's grip and nursed it some. Then he slowly walked away without sayin' a word. A minute or so later, Sheriff Jenkins came over and knelt down beside Daddy.

"Who did this, Ben?"

"Coleman," spat out Daddy, not even tryin' to hide the hatred he felt at that moment.

The Sheriff hung his head with a look on his face like he thought somehow this was partly his fault. Then he looked up at me.

"Your Mama and the others made it safely to the Harris place," he said.

"Good," I said absently. "That's good."

"Should we send for them?" he asked.

"Send John Harris," Daddy said.

In the flickerin' torchlight, we were only vaguely aware of the other men who had come to help, until one of the Sheriff's men broke the awful silence that hung over us all by callin' out that Coleman and the others had been seen ridin' toward Dead Man's Ridge.

"We're goin' after them," the Sheriff said. "I'll leave two men behind here with you."

Daddy nodded, and Jenkins and the others rode off. A few minutes later, Lawrence stopped rockin' and stood up, still holdin' Charlie. Then he started toward the house.

"Where are you goin'," Daddy asked Lawrence.

"I'm takin' my boy inside," Lawrence said plainly.

Me and Daddy went in the front and opened the back door. When Lawrence came inside, he started to lay Charlie down on the floor, but Daddy covered the table with a blanket and told him to place Charlie there instead.

"I need some towels and water to clean him up," said Lawrence, chokin' on his own words... "and a knife."

I got what he needed and brought it back to him. Thinkin' to help him, I moved closer to the table, but Daddy motioned for me to stop and let Lawrence do it alone. So, we stood back and watched as Lawrence washed the blood from Charlie's broken body after cuttin' away the clothes that had been torn to shreds. He took such care each time he put the cloth to him, like Charlie was still alive and Lawrence didn't want to hurt him none. He slowly rubbed the cloth across Charlie's brow, then gently down each of his cheeks, makin' sure to get every bit of dirt.

He tended to his shoulders and arms and hands, and when he got to his chest and belly, he froze for a minute as he examined the deep wounds that had left his body almost unrecognizable.

Then Lawrence took to sobbin' again, only this time it was quiet. His expression stayed the same as tears poured down his face. He kept on like that as he cleaned the blood and dirt from his boy's legs and feet. When Lawrence was done, he covered Charlie up with a blanket and sat down in a chair by his side, holdin' his cold hand. He stared at nothin' for a good while.

"I need to bury him with his Mama," he finally said after some time.

"Alright," Daddy said. "We'll wait until his wife and babies see him and say their goodbyes. Then we'll go."

It was like Lawrence had gone away somewhere, the way he was talkin'. I reckon it's the place a man goes when he has to muster up what it takes to do somethin' so painful that it's beyond him to do it otherwise. We waited with him a good long while until John Harris and one of the Sheriff's men brought Mama and the others home. Me and Hannah tended the babies while Anita and Mama took their time with Charlie.

Anita couldn't contain her grief. I've never seen anyone cry so much or so hard. She hugged and kissed him, and then cried some more. It was torturesome watchin' her hurt that way. Mama was grievin' too, but was tryin' to be strong for everybody else at the same time. She shoulders her pain differently than most folks. Could be because she's seen more sufferin' than any woman should in a lifetime, so she's learned how to carry it instead of bein' swallowed up in it. But Anita... poor Anita. She is young and now has two babies to care for without her husband.

In the middle of all the heartache in the room, I noticed Daddy lookin' awful pale. With Charlie bein' killed, I'd forgotten that Daddy had also been shot. Although he had been in dreadful pain, he had put himself in a chair a few feet behind Lawrence, and I knew he wasn't about to leave his friend. So I asked one of the Sheriff's men to fetch Doc Wilson and bring him back.

Lawrence wanted to take Charlie and bury him after Anita and Mama had some time with him, but it wasn't safe to be out there, and Daddy's arm still needed carin' for. So I was greatly relieved when Doc finally arrived and was able to tend to Daddy. A short while later, he had the bullet out and then stitched him up and bandaged the arm , givin' Daddy a good measure of relief. After he had finished, he gave Daddy some pills to fight off infection – and somethin' for the pain too. Doc Wilson has seen our family through some mighty tryin' times, and I felt such appreciation for him as I watched him fix up Daddy's arm. He was willin' to come in the middle of the night into a dangerous situation, and all in the spirit of doin' what's right. He's a decent man, if there ever was one.

By the time everybody was ready to go, the blackness outside had turned to grey, and I knew the sunlight would find its way to us within a couple of hours. Sheriff Jenkins had sent four men back to make sure we were safe, and with the convincin' of Daddy and John Harris, those good men agreed to go with us to bury Charlie. We hitched the buggy, and Lawrence and Anita sat inside together, holdin' Charlie's body. It took us a good while to get to the mountainside where Adelaide had been buried some twenty- three years ago. Lawrence paused briefly at her gravesite, lookin' down with heartrendin' grief on his face and tears streamin' from his eyes. A few minutes later, the Sheriff's deputies started helpin' us dig a grave for Charlie, but Lawrence asked them not to. He only wanted me and Daddy to help. Daddy couldn't do much of anything with his bad arm, so he did what he could with the good one.

We dug a proper grave for Charlie a few feet away from his Mama. It took us quite a while since the earth was nearly frozen. Then Lawrence and Anita wrapped him up in a quilt Mama had made for me when I was little. We placed Charlie in the ground and stood over him. It took Lawrence a few minutes before he was able to put the first shovelful of dirt over Charlie's body. Then the second one came sooner, and third even sooner than that. When the hole had been filled, we each took a private moment to say our final goodbyes.

By the time it was my turn, the tears were pourin' from my eyes, and I couldn't stop my body from shakin'. I wasn't sure what to say. I told him how much I loved him... and how much I was gonna miss him. I told him I'd look out for Anita and the babies and make sure they were taken care of. Then I said goodbye to my best friend and joined the others. Lawrence went last. We had all gone over to the buggy and horses to wait. I stood there next to Daddy, watchin' Lawrence. He was down on the ground at the side of Charlie's grave on his knees. He talked to Charlie for a while, and then said nothin' at all. He stayed there so long I thought his old legs wouldn't let him up. But eventually he rose wearily and made his way back to the buggy – without a word – and we rode home in silence.

November 19, 1908

Sheriff Jenkins has been tireless the past couple of days. He has arrested seven of the ten men who murdered Charlie. Hank Coleman, Eli Carver, and Albert Doyle were the only names that I knew. I wasn't surprised to hear that Uncle Albert was part of it, but it made me sick all the same. Daddy asked the Sheriff to please not tell Mama. She was sufferin' somethin' terrible inside over what happened to Charlie, and was dealin' with her own illness along with all of that. Daddy thought that kind of news about her brother would be too much for her. So Sheriff agreed to keep it from her, and we hoped she wouldn't hear it from anyone else. Sheriff Jenkins assured us that those men would have to answer for themselves in a trial, and that Mayor Roberts would be sendin' a judge from the big city to preside.

Our own judges are all corrupt and everybody knows it. Wasn't no way those men would be held accountable by the judges we've got here, so I was pleased to know that at least there was a chance of justice. But there really isn't justice for what they did to Charlie. There's no way to make it right... no way to bring him back.

I'm not sure how to go on right now. None of us do. Jesse wants to talk about it all the time, but I just can't. I know it's her way of dealin' with things, but it gets to be too much for me. I can't sleep without playin' that night out in my mind over and over again. I close my eyes and I see Charlie, hangin' from that tree, and I hear Lawrence cryin' for his boy.

Lawrence hasn't said two words since it happened. He didn't even seem to hear the Sheriff when he told us about the men bein' arrested and the new judge comin'. He doesn't eat, doesn't work, doesn't talk. He just sits outside in the cold by himself. Mama tries to bring him blankets, and jackets, and hot coffee, but he won't have any of it. He's not rude to Mama, he's just disappeared. Daddy can't even reach him, but he doesn't try to do that. He just goes out and sits with Lawrence. They don't talk, they just sit, and then they sit some more. Lawrence may not know how to reach out, but with Daddy, he doesn't have to. He knows that Daddy will be there, and I reckon that's about as much comfort as he allows himself to feel right now.

November 27, 1908

Lawrence went home a week ago. He wanted to be in his own home, the home that reminded him of his son. He agreed to let Mama and Daddy come out every day to bring him food and see to anything he might need. It's been interestin' watchin' Daddy with this whole thing. I remember readin' in Mama's diary about the time she lost her babies, and the way Daddy helped her through it. I felt like I was seein' the very same thing with him and Lawrence.

Daddy isn't one to push himself on others. He's a private man and tries to respect the privacy of other folks too, and he doesn't like to talk about feelin's and such either. I used to think that made him cold, but I've learned somethin' about him through this experience; he is fiercely loyal, and he's aware of the sufferin' of others. He may not give lots of physical affection, or know how to talk away people's hurt, but he'll be by your side until he knows you can stand on your own again. Him and Mama make a good team. They have different strengths and gifts, and I'm just hopin' that one of them will be what Lawrence needs to get him through.

November 30, 1908

Anita has gone. Her Mama and Daddy came for her and the babies day before yesterday and took them back to Alabama. Aunt Lena came with them to check on Lawrence. I think it did him some good to see her. They've always been close. She tried to get him to go back with her and live with the only family he has left, but Lawrence said no for the same reason he said no before. He won't leave the home where he raised Charlie. I reckon he feels that's the only thing he has left to hold onto. He also told Aunt Lena that we are as much his family as anyone ever has been. We heard that from her, of course, but it did my heart good to know that he felt that way. So she went on without him. I think him sayin' goodbye to those babies would have broken his heart under normal circumstances, but he's in so much pain already that I don't think he can feel any more.

We also found out today that Hank Coleman was released from jail Saturday and taken to the hospital in Jonesboro. They say his kidneys don't work right on account of his drinkin', so they sent him to get fixed up so he doesn't keel over before his own trial. Well, it wasn't twenty-four hours of him bein' released before he had some people sneak him out of that hospital, and he's been on the run ever since. They should have known that that scoundrel has friends everywhere.

When Lawrence found that out, he didn't even blink. He didn't look surprised, he didn't look upset. It was like he didn't care. I try to imagine how he feels but I can't. I don't know what it's like to lose a son, and every time I try to imagine it bein' Jack, I can't stomach it long enough to get the feel of it. So I'll just keep up to date with Sheriff Jenkins, and when Lawrence is ready to hear what's goin' on, I'll have the information to pass on to him.

Hannah's callin'. I better see to it.

December 1, 1908

It was early evenin' when we got a visit from Sheriff Jenkins today. He told us that Hank Coleman had been seen in town late last night, tryin' to collect some of his belongin's before headin' out of town again.

"Did you catch him?" I asked anxiously.

"No," he said, "but somethin' strange happened. We got the man he was ridin' with, a real skittish fella. He said that Hank was taken at gunpoint when they were just outside of town."

"What? By who?" Daddy asked, soundin' real surprised.

"Don't know for certain," said the Sheriff, "but it was a colored man."

Me and Daddy sat there, not knowin' what to say.

"You haven't seen Lawrence around, have you?" The Sheriff asked.

"We saw him yesterday evenin'," said Daddy. "Took him some dinner and stayed for a spell. You can't honestly think—"

"Like I said," interrupted the sheriff, "I'm not sure what happened, but I'm asking you to send for me if you hear anything at all."

"Of course," Daddy said.

After Sheriff Jenkins left, I looked at Daddy.

"Could that have been Lawrence?"

"I can't imagine," he said.

"Should we go check on him?" I asked.

Daddy thought for a minute.

"Let me tell your Mama we'll be gone for a while. You go get the horses saddled."

I put on my coat and the warm pair of gloves Hannah knitted for me last Christmas. Then I headed out to the barn to get the horses ready. I was only halfway there when I saw what looked like blood in the snow. It was trailin' from the road all the way up to the barn. I felt my stomach flip, and I ran back inside to fetch Daddy. I could barely get the words out before Daddy ran right past me. I followed close behind. We ran to the barn and pulled open the doors. What we saw inside was enough to haunt my dreams for a long while.

Hank Coleman was tied up to an old milkin' stool. He was bound so tight his skin was cut from the ropes, and he was bleedin' all over himself. Lawrence was standin' over him with a rifle pointed at the side of his head. I've never seen Lawrence like that. It almost didn't look like him. His eyes were all wild and glazed over. He was just starin' hard at Hank but not sayin' a word. Hank was sweatin' and shakin', and from the smell of it, he'd gone and soiled himself. Daddy moved slowly a couple of steps into the barn and stopped. Very quietly and deliberately, like tryin' to calm a distressed child, Daddy began talkin' to Lawrence, tryin' to reason with him and draw his attention away from what he was fixin' to do. But Lawrence didn't budge, just stayed fixed on Hank Coleman like a hunter fixed on a buck.

"Lawrence, you don't mean to do this, old friend," Daddy said. "I've known you practically all my life, and you ain't this man."

I stood there feelin' my legs shake inside my boots, waitin' for Lawrence to say somethin'. Daddy kept on talkin' to Lawrence to try and keep him from goin' through with it.

"We both know this won't fix it," Daddy said.

Lawrence didn't say a word. I don't know how long we stood there in silence. It felt like half the night. Every time Daddy would take a step closer to Lawrence, he would get all twitchy, and Daddy worried that Lawrence would pull the trigger on account of his nerves. So we just stayed put and waited it out. Sheriff Coleman was breathin' fast and hard, and his face was all flushed and twisted up with pain. I thought he might end up havin' a heart attack before Lawrence could finally decide what he was gonna do with him. Daddy broke the silence one last time.

"I miss Charlie," Daddy said.

At that, Lawrence shifted his body weight and took a small step backward. He blinked his eyes real hard a few times like he had somethin' in them, but his eyes stayed locked on Hank.

"It makes me real sad to think of him," said Daddy, "and sometimes when I do, I'm sure my heart is breakin' in two. So if I feel like that, ain't no way to imagine what you're feelin'."

It was strange to hear Daddy talk like that. But then I noticed Lawrence's face begin to change. His eyes weren't wild anymore, and the corners of his mouth started to curl under. He took his right hand off the rifle and wiped the sweat from his wrinkled forehead onto his shoulder. He stared at Hank for a long time with a look on his face I never knew Lawrence could make. At first it looked like pure hatred, but the more I looked at him, it became real clear to see that it was overpowerin' pain... not physical pain, mind you, but the kind of almost unbearable agony a man carries inside when all he loved in the world has been ripped away from him.

After a minute or two, Lawrence looked over at Daddy and nodded slowly just once. It was almost as if seein' Daddy reminded him of the man he really was. Then he slowly lowered the gun to the ground, and his shoulders sank in resignation. Daddy walked over to him, and as soon as he got close, Lawrence's legs seemed to give out. Daddy caught him before he hit the ground and sat him back against the wall, at which point Lawrence broke down and wept with great sobs of grief. He sat on the ground with his head between his knees repeatin' Charlie's name over and over again. Daddy looked at me.

"Go fetch Sheriff Jenkins," he said real quiet.

There was no time to saddle up a horse, so I just jumped on and rode bareback as fast as I could manage. When I reached the Sheriff's office, he was lockin' up to head on home. I raced over to him and jumped off my horse before she could even plant her hoofs to stop. I believe I startled the Sheriff, and he swung around to face me with his left hand over his holster like he was fixin' to draw.

"Sheriff Jenkins!" I called out.

"Will Wright? Is that you, son?" he asked.

"Yes sir. I didn't mean to startle you, but I need you to come back to the house with me as fast as you can get there."

"What's the matter, Will?" he said as he hurried over to the side of the buildin' to get his horse.

"We found Sheriff Cole... I mean Hank Coleman," I sputtered.

It was hard gettin' used to not callin' him Sheriff on account of him bein' ours for so long.

"What do you mean you found him? Found him where?" Sheriff Jenkins asked, lookin' real confused.

"Lawrence Dixon's got him," I said. "He's got him tied up in our barn."

Sheriff Jenkins stopped dead in his tracks and looked at me in disbelief. Seemed he couldn't figure what to say next.

"Daddy got Lawrence calmed down, but Mr. Coleman is in pretty bad shape," I said.

Sheriff Jenkins shook his head like he was tryin' to make sense of the whole thing.

"We need to fetch Doc Wilson and have him ride out with us," I said.

"Yes, of course," said the Sheriff. "I saw him leave only a few minutes ago. We can catch up to him if we go now."

We mounted our horses and rode hard to head off Doc Wilson before he turned off the main road for home. I felt bad as we caught up to him. He looked exhausted, and I'm sure the man just wanted to go home to his family and get some rest. But without a word of complaint, he came with us to make sure Hank Coleman was alright.

When we got back to our barn, it was just as I'd left it. Hank was still tied up, and Lawrence was still on the ground with Daddy next to him. Mama and Hannah hadn't heard a thing and were still inside, probably assumin' we were at Lawrence's place. I was real grateful for that because I wouldn't want either one of them to have the image in her mind of what had taken place in the barn.

Sheriff and Doc saw to Hank first. They untied him and made sure his wounds weren't life threatenin'. When they realized that he was more scared than anythin', Sheriff handcuffed him and made him wait until he was through talkin' to Lawrence.

"Well, Mr. Dixon," Sheriff said, "seems you caught our escaped prisoner."

"Lloyd Jenkins," shrieked Hank, "that's a lie, and everybody here knows it! This lunatic almost killed me!"

I couldn't believe the nerve! I looked over at Lawrence to see if he'd react to that, but he didn't. I believe he was finished with Hank Coleman at that point.

"Looks like there are four men here who saw exactly what I did," said the sheriff, "and I'm sure they'd be willing to testify to that if need be. And if I hear that filthy mouth of yours mention anything about you being treated unfairly after what you've done, I'll make sure they're the last words you ever speak."

You could tell Hank was furious, but he stopped shoutin' and just sat in his own filth, stewin' and mutterin' under his breath. Sheriff told Daddy to keep Lawrence at the house that night and he'd check in on us in the mornin'. Then he sent Doc Wilson home and left shortly after him with Hank in tow. After they had all gone, Daddy helped Lawrence to his feet, and we all walked silently to the house. Mama and Hannah were startled to see Lawrence that way – so thin and lifeless. I'm sure his face hadn't seen a razor in days, and he smelled like he hadn't seen a bar of soap in that time either.

Mama drew Lawrence a hot bath while Hannah stoked the fire and put on some coffee. After Lawrence had been properly taken care of, they made him a bed on the sofa, and Daddy slept on the other one just to make sure Lawrence was alright. Mama stayed up late scrubbin' his clothes in the tub to try and get that stink out of them. Then she laid them out in front of the fire so they'd be dry by mornin'.

When mornin' came, Lawrence was gone, all of his clothes still laid out where Mama had left them the night before. Daddy said he hadn't heard a thing. He woke up with the sun, but it appeared Lawrence had already left. Daddy went out to the barn, but all the horses were still there, so he knew Lawrence was on foot. We decided that, given the condition he was in, Lawrence shouldn't be out there by himself, so me and Daddy mounted up and went out to look for him. We rode straight over to his house and noticed, when we got there, that the front door was wide open. We looked inside, but there was no sign of Lawrence. Daddy walked out and stood on the front porch for a good five minutes, just thinkin'. Then he got on his horse and started toward the mountains.

"Where are we goin'?" I asked.

"He's gone to be with Charlie and Adelaide," said Daddy matter-of-factly.

Almost a half hour later, when we got to where we'd buried Charlie, I could see somethin' blue and white in the snow. We got off our horses and slowly walked over. There was Lawrence, between Charlie and Adelaide, lyin' still. He was in his nightclothes, holdin' onto the shawl Adelaide had left on the back of the rockin' chair. And in his other hand was one of the animal figures Charlie had carved. Daddy bent over him like he wanted to wake him, but there was no use tryin'. Lawrence was dead. We figured he must have left in the middle of the night to make it all this way. His feet were bruised and bloody from the long walk, but somehow, he looked peaceful.

I've heard it said that a man can die from a broken heart, but I never thought that notion to be worth much, until now. I'd never seen a man so broken as Lawrence was after Charlie died. It seems that some burdens are just too heavy to bear. Lawrence bore his the best he knew how, until he couldn't anymore. And so in his moment of lookin' for comfort, he laid down between the two people he loved more than life itself, and surrendered his.

January 19, 1909

Things have been so shaken up around here that we've hardly focused at all on Mama and her declinin' health. She's as pleasant as she can muster in front of other people, but sometimes I watch her when she doesn't know I'm doin' it, and I can see that she's real worn down from it all. While she doesn't say so, I believe she's in constant discomfort. You can tell by the way she quietly winces every time she gets up from the table or the way she holds her belly when she coughs or sneezes. She moves a little slower than she used to and has a hard time gettin' things done. Mama's always been a worker, and so I know it's more than just the physical pain that is hard for her. She'll want to be doin' spring plantin' soon, and she'll want to be there to help Daddy durin' birthin' season like she's always done.

Last evenin', after everything had settled down and Hannah was bathin' Jack, I had a chance to sit with Mama by the fire, just the two of us. It was the first time I heard her admit to feelin' the challenge of what she's facin'. She said that she feels like she's at the bottom of an avalanche, and the snow just keeps on comin'. You fight real hard at first, but after a while you realize that if the snow won't stop, there's really nothin' you can do but pray that you develop a tolerance to the cold.

February 3, 1909

I know it's only been two months since Lawrence passed, but it feels like a year. Each day drags on longer than the last. I feel like I'm livin' with the ghosts of my family members since everybody is still grievin' in their own way. There are days that I climb into bed and realize I haven't said a word to anybody all day. Sometimes when Jack is pullin' on me, wantin' to play, all I can do is sit there and let him bring toys to me. He gets tired of that pretty quick and moves on to other things. I've been up to the place where Lawrence and Charlie and Adelaide are buried more often than I probably should. Sometimes I go up there when the hurt gets to be too much and I don't know where else to go. I sit up there and cry a while, then I shake it off and get back to my chores.

When I close my eyes at night, I think tomorrow will be better. Then I wake up in the mornin' with that stabbin' feelin' in my chest, same as the day before, and I know that I was foolish to think that I'd have any reprieve. I learned early on that I gotta stay real busy. So I get up before Hannah and Jack are awake, and I get started on my work before the sadness can take hold of me. Hannah or Mama usually brings me somethin' to eat in the middle of the day, and then I get right back to work. We all sit down together at night for supper, but there isn't much conversation. We eat fast and go to sleep early. There is more work to be done around here since we don't have Lawrence and Charlie to help, and that's about the only thing I feel grateful for lately.

February 19, 1909

Sheriff Jenkins came out to the house today to give us an update on the trial. Mama still doesn't know that Uncle Albert was involved, and we intend to keep it that way. It's a miracle that someone hasn't told her yet. I keep thinkin' that one of these days she'll run into Harriet Jones or some other gossip in town who will ask her somethin' about it, but with her health, she doesn't get to town much.

The sheriff said that Judge Nichols is a fair man. He's makin' sure that those murderers are gettin' the trial that they deserve. He said that Maryanne was called in to testify last week. He said she stuck with her story that Charlie had raped her, but that she never wanted for him to be killed over it. The judge told her that the trial was gonna be put on hold until she had her baby in a few weeks. When the baby's born, they'll know then if it had a colored father or not. Sheriff Jenkins said that Maryanne turned white as a ghost when he said that, like it was the first time it had occurred to her. I wouldn't be surprised if Maryanne's folks took her and ran as far as they could go to get away from this mess. They'd never recover from such a scandal, no matter how fancy a car Roger Stephenson drives.

Mama seems to be doin' more poorly than she ever has before. I've caught her more than once doubled over in pain. She keeps it to herself. I reckon it's because she doesn't want to burden anybody, what with all we've been through lately, but she's mistaken to think that we don't know she's sick.

Hannah is doin' the best she can with what she's got in front of her right now. You'd think she would get fed up with all the grief and loneliness, but she seems more concerned with the rest of us than she does for herself. She's such a good Mama to our Jack, and she does for him what I'm not doin' right now. I suppose she knows that this will take some time to sort through, and she continues on in patience until that time comes. I don't deserve her. And when I can pull myself out of this sadness, I'll tell her so.

March 11, 1909

Maryanne Stephenson gave birth to a blond haired, white skinned, baby girl four days ago. Sheriff Jenkins said that the Judge himself went to the hospital to see the baby. Apparently Maryanne took to cryin' and goin' on about how she was pressured into sayin' such a thing about Charlie, and that she finally admitted she wasn't raped. Her folks tried to act surprised, but you'd have to be an idiot to think that they didn't know all along. They just couldn't admit to it after Charlie had been murdered on account of Maryanne bein' a liar and a coward. Even with Charlie bein' killed and Lawrence dyin', Maryanne still plays like she's the victim in all of this.

Kathryn Harris came over to talk with Mama this mornin' and said that the Stephensons have been locked up in their house since Maryanne brought the baby home. There have been folks standin' outside on the front lawn yellin' obscenities and callin' Maryanne a murderer. The crazy thing is, Maryanne lied about Charlie so that she wouldn't be looked down on. She probably should have thought that through better. I've been surprised to see how many people hate her for it. The folks in this town have never taken a stance when it comes to the coloreds. But when that baby was born white as a snowflake, I believe folks felt tricked. All those people who stood by Maryanne, and she was lyin' to their faces all along—

well, they felt betrayed. So in the end, they aren't really standin' up for what's right, they aren't outraged that a young, innocent father was murdered for no reason. They're just embarrassed and angry that they were sucked into Maryanne's lies to begin with.

Me and Daddy already testified at the trial. We had to sit in that court room, lookin' at the men who killed Charlie, and tell the story all over again. You'd think that Uncle Albert would be ashamed, that he would try to hide his face, but he didn't. He looked us straight in the eye the whole time, almost like he was proud of what he'd done. He wasn't ashamed, he was just mad he got caught.

While we're glad that these men are havin' to own up to what they did, we're just ready for it to all be over with so we can go on about our lives. I'm not sayin' we know how to do that, move on, that is, but we'd sure like to try and figure it out.

March 23, 1909

The men that killed Charlie were all found guilty. Our town was in an uproar. We couldn't believe it. They are all goin' to hang. Findin' out didn't make me feel as good as I thought it would, but it was the right thing, and for that I'm satisfied.

April 5, 1909

Mama has decided against havin' any more surgeries. She says there's just no point to takin' the tumors out since they seem hell-bent on comin' back and bringin' more with them each time. She's tired of always recoverin' from surgery and wants to let things run their course. That was real hard to accept. To be honest, I'm not even sure I have. What I do know is that I'll support Mama in any way I can, and if that means holdin' my tongue about her treatment, then so be it. That doesn't mean that I don't go out into the woods and scream as loud as I can sometimes, hopin' to release some of the sadness and denial, but I've decided not to let Mama know about those times.

May 30, 1909

Hannah told me last night that she is pregnant. I tried to show some excitement about it, but she could tell it didn't mean to me what it meant to her, and she took to cryin' and left the room. We've been tryin' for so long, and I know it's a blessin', but I can't seem to find my way out of this dark hole I've been in for months. I find no joy in life. I miss my best friend. I am a shell of a man.

June 5, 1909

"I'm fine, Mama," I said as I headed out the door.

"I wasn't finished," Mama said.

"I've got work to do. We'll talk later."

Daddy came barrelin' from the other room and slammed the door shut in front of me before I had a chance to go out.

"Your Mama wasn't finished," said Daddy.

"Fine," I said. "What is it, Mama? I'm listenin'."

"I don't like your tone, boy," Daddy said.

"You don't like my tone? OK, well which tone would you prefer? Higher? Lower? You tell me which one you want and I'll go with it," I said angrily.

Daddy's fists clenched so tight that his fingers and knuckles turned white.

"You're not fine," Mama said.

"Of course I am!" I yelled. "I do my work every day, I stay out of your way, I fulfill my responsibilities, don't I?"

"You do all those things," son. "But you're disappearing little by little."

"I'm right here!" I yelled. "I wish I could disappear, but I'm right here!"

Daddy came toward me, and I saw my life flash before my eyes. I stood up straight, closed my eyes tight, and almost welcomed the lickin' I was about to get. Maybe if he pounded me hard enough, it would distract me from feelin' the constant pain in my chest. Then before I knew it, Daddy's arms were around me so tight I could barely breathe. I stood there, not knowin' what to do with it. After a minute, I tried to get free, but the harder I pulled, the harder he held on. After a while, I found myself tired of the fight, and there was nothin' left to do but give it up.

I felt a wave of sadness rush from the bottom part of my stomach to the top part of my chest. Then it made its way into my throat, and I couldn't hold it back any more. I broke down sobbin' like a child. Once I started cryin', I couldn't stop. I put my arms around Daddy and held on for all I was worth. I don't know how long I cried, but Daddy never said a word. He just stood there and held onto me while I did. After I was finished, Daddy let go of me. He looked at me a minute like he was tryin' to make sure I was alright. He said nothin', then just headed outside and went on about his business. I didn't realize at the time exactly what business that was.

Mama and I sat in the livin' room for a spell and talked about Charlie and Lawrence. It hurt so bad at first. It was painful just to mention their names, but I felt a relief I hadn't had before. Ever since they died, I felt a pressure in my chest that wouldn't go away, like I had a fifty pound boulder just sittin' on me, waitin' to crack my ribs. I also felt guilty for talkin' to Mama like that in her condition. I apologized to her as sincerely as I could, and after we finished talkin', that pressure was still there, but it felt like some of the weight had been taken off, and it was easier to carry. It freed me enough to use that energy for Hannah.

Mama left and I sat in the livin' room by myself for a while. I just sat there and thought about Charlie and Lawrence. I would have done anything to see them one more time. But I knew I couldn't think like that because it made the pressure in my chest feel worse. So I just sat there through the pain. Then I went outside to find Hannah.

As I walked past the house, there was Daddy, choppin' away at that Willow tree with all he had in him. I felt the sadness find its way back to me again as I watched the chips fly from his swingin' that ax over and over in a determined rhythm that seemed almost angry. He was so intent on his task that he was completely unaware of the world around him. You might think that those were tears on his face if you didn't know him any better. It was probably just sweat.

I hadn't been able to go near that tree since it happened, but seein' Daddy now, engaged in removin' the reminder of that awful day, I went to the shed and grabbed the other ax. Then I joined him over by the willow. I can't exactly say how long it took us to chop her down, but when it was done, I just stood over the old stump and felt a whole new kind of mournin'. I could see that Daddy felt it too. There were plenty of happy memories invovlin' that tree; from the times Mama would lay out a picnic for us in the summertime once the work was done and the heat of the sun had lost its fire for the day, to hidin' behind it in a game of "find the rabbit" with Jesse when we were kids, to just sittin' out underneath its shade with Charlie on Sunday evenin's, throwin' rocks at the fence to see who could hit it the most times in a row without missin'.

"There was a lot of happiness in that tree," I said to Daddy after a spell.

"Ain't no memory happy enough that it could calm the sick I felt in my stomach every time I walked past that willow and thought about Charlie," Daddy said as he put the ax over his shoulder and slowly walked to the shed, his head hangin' down about as low as I reckon it could.

He was right. What happened to Charlie sucked the happiness out of every good memory tied to that tree. I was glad it was gone, but it didn't make me feel better about things. I almost felt worse somehow. I needed Hannah more than ever in that moment, so I put my ax up alongside Daddy's in the shed and went to find her. She was playin' with Jack out by the crick. As soon as I could reach her, I put my arms around her and pulled her into me.

"I'm still here," I whispered. "And I'm so happy about our new baby."

Hannah sank into me and pulled me even closer. Then she cried, and so did I.

July 27, 1909

Mama went back to Jonesboro to have another operation last Thursday. I guess Daddy talked her into it. He doesn't ask for much, but it seems he wasn't as ready to let nature take over as Mama was, and so he pleaded with her to try one more time. It was a conversation I shouldn't have heard, but I was in the next room and couldn't help but hear it. Before all this happened, I wouldn't have believed that desperation could take hold of Daddy, but there I sat, listenin' to it happen.

Daddy called from Jonesboro right away with the bad news. Instead of one tumor, there were several... too many to count, in fact. The doctor said he couldn't get to all of them, and that it was just a matter of time now. I hung up the phone at the Harris's place and walked slowly back home. I decided to stop by Jessie's to tell her what was goin' on. It really wasn't much of a shock to any of us. Mama has been so sick for months. She can barely eat without throwin' up, she's in pain all the time, and she is so thin that I worry sometimes that I'm gonna break her when I hug her. I think we haven't been willin' to address it since we're just gettin' back on our feet from what happened to Charlie and Lawrence. But now there was no way around it. We'd have to face it and do whatever we could for Mama now.

When I got home and told Hannah, she seemed real concerned about me.

"I just don't want you to go away again," she said.

"I know."

"Are you ok?" she asked, takin' hold of my hand.

"I'm not sure how to feel. It's like I knew it was comin, but now that it's right in front of me, I almost feel like I can't breathe."

"I'm so sorry, Will. I'm just so sorry." She reached up and kissed me gently on the cheek.

"Don't worry, honey," I said. "I won't leave you."

"Whatever you need, I'm here," she said.

Daddy had said that they'd be home in a few days. There was no reason to keep Mama there if they couldn't do anything for her. So Hannah and I decided to work like dogs until Mama came home so we could have a little time to spend with her once she did. I don't know what I would do without Hannah.

September 2, 1909

Tonight after everyone had gone to bed, I saw a light out in the main part of the house. I crawled out of bed, thinkin' that maybe Daddy accidentally left it burnin'. I started to open my door, when through the crack I saw Mama and Daddy dancin'. There was no music. It was just the two of them, holdin' each other close, dancin'. I closed my door, climbed back into bed and cried myself to sleep.

October 29, 1909

Mama is goin' faster than we'd thought. Sometimes I help get her to bed, and then when I see her the next mornin', she looks worse than she did the eight hours before. We've been takin' turns tendin' to her and makin' sure she's as comfortable as possible. There are times she hurts so bad and there's nothin' we can do. Doc Wilson comes by at least once a day to check on her and do what he can. I have grown to love that man, and watchin' him care for Mama just makes that even stronger.

Daddy has a hard time leavin' her side, so I do most of the chores to try and relieve the pressure for him. The evenin's have become ours as a family. After supper, we sit around in the livin' room, tellin' stories and laughin'. Mama is sleepin' half the time, but she wants to be out there with us all the same, even if she can't really participate much. Sometimes we'll think she's asleep, but then someone will say somethin' funny, and Mama smiles. We decided as soon as she got back from Jonesboro that we would spend as much time with her as we could, and that we'd make it time worth spendin'.

I had my moment with Mama a few weeks ago. It was on one of her good days when she was awake more than usual. We sat and talked, just the two of us. She didn't tell me anything I didn't already know, but it was real special to me because I knew it would probably be the last time I'd hear it from her.

"You're going to be alright," whispered Mama softly.

"I'm not even sure what that means anymore, Mama," I said. "I'll go on. Not much choice in the matter, but the idea of doin' it without you is..."

I shook my head and cleared my throat, tryin' to contain my heartache so as not to upset her.

"Will, I've always known you would become this wonderful man that you are now. I just feel so blessed to have seen it."

She smiled, puttin' her thin hand on my cheek and lookin' at me with a look of love I will lock in my memory for as long as I'm alive. She was makin' it tough to stay composed.

"Mama...," I choked. I wanted to say so much, but I knew if I opened my mouth, I'd fall apart.

"This life brings sorrow, son," Mama continued weakly. "I'm afraid you've seen much more than I ever would have wanted you to. But there is beauty all around you if you can figure out where to look for it.

"I'm not sure I know how," I told her, givin' up the notion that I could any longer keep the tears from fallin'.

"I know, honey. I know. But you will."

"How can you be so sure, Mama?"

Musterin' her strength, she said more strongly, "because I know you, and everything about you is good. You are made of love and kindness, and you will find your way."

I carefully put my arms around Mama and buried my head in her neck and gave in to the sadness.

We stayed there for a good while, just talkin' quietly. She told me how she felt about me, and I told her how I felt about her. Then she gave me some counsel about livin' my life and bein' the kind of man my wife and children can depend on and look up to. It's an experience I'll never forget, and I'll be grateful for the rest of my days for it.

I know I should be writin' more than I am. It's hard for me to do it because every time I sit down to write, I feel like cryin'. I look back at when I started writin', and it reminds me of some of the happiest times in my life. It reminds me of Charlie and Hannah and Lawrence. It reminds me of the good memories I have of Mama and Daddy and the times Jessie made me crazy while we were growin' up. It reminds me of a time when life was simpler, and I didn't know what it meant to really suffer.

Now when I open this journal, I see the sadness that has found its way into my life, and I want to shut it and never open it again. But I know that sadness will still find me, and I want my kin to see it all. If they're gonna know me, they need to know what happened to Charlie and Lawrence. They need to know how that experience nearly put me in the ground too. They need to know about the love of my Daddy and the encouragement of my Mama that got me through. They need to know about my Hannah and the way she holds onto me, even when things are hard. They need to know that while I haven't been the best father, I'm tryin' to be better. If they don't know all of that, then the first part of the journal is just a fraction of the man I am. So as hard as it is sometimes to do it, I'll keep writin'.

November 8, 1909

Daddy sat by Mama's bed for hours in that hard wood rockin' chair in the corner. Every once in a while she started to stir, lookin' real uncomfortable. Daddy sat on the bed next to her, puttin' a cold cloth on her forehead and strokin' her hair until she settled again. We all wanted to be with her, sayin' our goodbyes and such, but it seemed proper to let the two of them be.

Hannah fell asleep in the big armchair by the fireplace, and I sat on the rug in front of her, leanin' back against the down blanket coverin' her legs. Mama made that blanket not two winters ago. I remember her out there in the chicken coop, collectin' all them feathers. She did that for probably three straight weeks because she wanted that blanket to be nice and warm when the cold came.

Then she'd bring the feathers inside and wash them real well to get the chicken stink off of them. After they were clean, they had to get dry, so Daddy made Mama a big net with lots of tiny holes in it. It let the air in, but the holes were too small to let the feathers out. She'd take it to the side of the house and swing that thing around and around in circles over her head to get rid of the water. Then she'd lay it out nice and flat on the porch where the sun could reach it. Feelin' the warmth of that blanket on my back put a lump in my throat somethin' awful.

I drifted off to sleep sometime after two. I was only asleep for a few minutes, but woke up to find Daddy kneelin' down next to the side of the bed. He was never a prayin' man, so I reckon he just needed to change positions for a spell. Around three, Daddy got up and slowly walked out of the room. His steps were heavy and his face looked tired. A minute later he came in with his guitar and sat at the foot of the bed so he could lean against the bed post.

Mama wrote in one of her diaries about that bed. She said that Daddy made it with his own two hands as a weddin' present for her. It was made of oak and had four thick posts in the corners. Mama said she'd never loved a thing so much in all her life. It's kind of funny, though, because I imagine the bed Mama had before knowin' Daddy was real fancy. Probably had a brass frame and a store-bought quilt. But the bed Daddy made for her meant somethin' – meant they were husband and wife. So it seems just right that the bed they started their life together in was the same one Mama was in when they said goodbye.

Daddy played real soft for what seemed like all night. Mama settled better than she had for two days. Just as the sun made its way over the east ridge and into the bedroom window, Mama started breathin' funny, like she couldn't get any air. Then she'd take a deep breath and be real still and calm for a time. Daddy got up from the foot of the bed and went over and sat right next to

Mama. He held her hand and put his face next to hers. He talked so quiet I could barely hear him.

"Lily Doyle Wright, in all my life I couldn't have dreamed a better woman than you. Ain't never deserved you, and we both know it. But I'll thank the good Lord 'til the end of my days that you was mine."

Just then Mama took a real deep breath, so deep it raised her chest up off the bed. Then she was still a minute or two. That happened a few more times, until it was done. Can't say I've ever seen my Daddy cry. I suppose he wanted it that way. So I took Hannah by the hand and led her into the other room. As I started to close the door to Mama's room, I saw Daddy reach underneath her back and pull her up into him. I shut the door quiet as I could. The sound of Daddy sobbin' on the other side of it put me on my knees. I stayed there, holdin' on to the doorknob until I was able to find my way back to my feet again.

An awful rush of sadness came over me, and I grabbed my chest with both hands to keep it from achin' so bad. We knew it was comin' for quite some time now, but the moment it finally happens is one that can't be explained. Although I knew she was gone, it somehow didn't make sense to me. I felt a swirl of emotion the likes of which I've never felt before. We'd watched Mama suffer with her sickness, and I didn't want that for her, none of us did. But as selfish as it sounds, even knowin' that she was sufferin' the way she was, I couldn't ever get myself to truly want her to go.

My mind raced over all the ways I needed her still, and I felt myself start to panic inside. How could I explain to my boy where his Grandma had gone? Then I thought about the baby in Hannah's belly. The thought of raisin' children without them knowin' Mama made me feel like I'd had the wind knocked right out of me, and I had to gasp for breath. Hannah came over and let me fall into her while I cried. I cried harder than I ever knew I could. And in the midst of all that cryin', I couldn't remember if I'd said what I needed to say to Mama... if I had told her what she meant to me. I said all kinds of things after she got sick, after it seemed she couldn't hear me any longer. Did I treat her proper as a son should? Did I show her enough love, enough respect, enough kindness? I think what I wanted more than anything was to know that Mama felt loved, loved in a way that was meant only for her. I wanted her to leave this earth without ever havin' doubted for one single second how we felt about her and how life without her would create a hole so big it'd be impossible to ever fill up again. And even though people say that you learn to go on again in time, I just knew that I'd never stop missin' her.

My first experience with death was when Charlie was killed. I didn't even have time for the sadness to settle before Lawrence was gone too. For some time afterward, I found myself tryin' to stay as busy as it was possible to be. I'd work hard as I could all day long so that when nighttime came, I could just fall into bed and be asleep before my mind had a chance to start thinkin'. There was always just a split second in the mornin' when I was wakin' up that I would forget about what had happened. But then I would open my eyes and remember. So I'd jump out of bed before the memory, and the pain that goes along with it, had time to settle. That worked for a while, I suppose. But then I started to feel like a bottle of ginger ale that had been shaken up with nowhere for all the bubbles to go.

It took me a while, and the help of Mama and Daddy, to realize that in order to find the calm and peace I needed, I had to sit still for a spell. The problem with sittin' still was that it allowed my mind to paint the pictures of Charlie's and Lawrence's deaths. Sittin' still meant there was nothin' to chase those images away. I couldn't imagine bein' able to get rid of a hurt that consumed me the way that it did. But at the same time, I knew I wouldn't be able to live like that. I wouldn't be able to bear it. I suppose the pain I was feelin' was like a fresh wound that, after a time and some healin', becomes a scar. The scar doesn't hurt, but it abides none the less as a reminder of the original wound, and becomes a part of you forever.

At first I could only sit still for a minute or two because the pain was so bad I thought it might take hold of me and not let go. But then each time I sat still, one or two minutes turned into three or four, and three or four turned into five or six. In time, I was able to be still and think on Charlie and Lawrence without the only images in my mind of them bein' the hauntin' ones. The painful images faded away, and I was left with the ones of me and Charlie down at our favorite swimmin' hole, and of Lawrence and Charlie stayin' over on the couches after a hard day's work, and of me and Charlie gettin' married and seein' each other become fathers for the first time. I wish I had realized at the time that I had been chasin' the good memories away with the bad ones. As long as I live, I don't believe it'll ever be possible to think on Lawrence and Charlie without some part of my heart breakin', but at least now I get the good stuff along with it.

So I'll think on Mama. And I'll hold onto Hannah and Jack while I do. And eventually, I know that the memories of her plantin' flowers in the garden off the side of the front porch, and of her quietly whistlin' along with Daddy's guitar playin', and of her huggin' me in a way that made me feel that everything was right in the world, will all come back to me in time.

My heart now bears three holes: one for Charlie, one for Lawrence, and one for Mama. I understand now why some folks try to fill their emptiness with other things, but people like me and Daddy choose to live with the holes left in us so that we never forget what it is that's missin'.

www.ingramcontent.com/pod-product-compliance
Lightning Source LLC
Chambersburg PA
CBHW030035180626
46810CB00001B/376